AF260812

THE UNLIKELY LIFE OF OLIVER ATKINSON

A Novel of
America's Founding

David Jones III

simply francis publishing company
North Carolina

Copyright © 2026 David Jones III. All Rights Reserved.

No part of this publication may be reproduced, stored in a retrieval system or transmitted, in any form or by any means-electronic, mechanical, photocopying, recording, or otherwise without the prior written permission from the publisher, except for the inclusions of brief quotations in a review.

This is a work of fiction. Any references to historical events, real people, or real places are used fictitiously. Other names, characters, places, and events are products of the author's imagination, and any resemblance to actual events or places or persons, living or dead, is entirely coincidental.

NO AI TRAINING: Without in any way limiting the author's [and publisher's] exclusive rights under copyright, any use of this publication to "train" generative artificial intelligence (AI) technologies to generate text is expressly prohibited. The author reserves all rights to license uses of this work for generative AI training and development of machine learning language models.

Publisher's Cataloging-in-Publication Data

Names: Jones, David, III, 1962- .
Title: The unlikely life of Oliver Atkinson : a novel of America's founding / David Jones III.
Description: Wrightsville Beach, NC : simply francis publishing, 2026. | Summary: Teenager Oliver Atkinson escapes from indentured servitude, stowing away on a Boston-bound ship. Discovered and thrown in the brig, he is freed during the Boston Tea Party. "Adopted" by Paul Revere, he joins the Sons of Liberty and becomes a staff member for General Washington, participating in many of the major events of the Revolution.
Identifiers: ISBN 9781630620912 (pbk.) | ISBN 9781630620929 (ebook)
Subjects: LCSH: Revere, Paul, 1735-1818 – Fiction. | Washington, George, 1732-1799 – Fiction. | Adams, Samuel, 1722-1803 – Fiction. | Adams, John, 1735-1826 – Fiction. | Hancock, John, 1737-1793 – Fiction. | Franklin, Benjamin, 1706-1790 – Fiction. | Boston Tea Party, 1773 – Fiction. | United States – History – Revolution, 1775-1783 – Fiction. | Boston (Mass.) – History – Fiction. | Philadelphia (Pa.) – History – Fiction. | BISAC: FICTION / Historical / Colonial America & Revolution. | FICTION / Places / United States. | FICTION / Action & Adventure.
Classification: LCC PS3610.O54 U55 2026 | DDC 813 J—dc23

Library of Congress Control Number: 2026904356
Printed in the United States of America
Interior Design: Christy King Meares
Cover Design: David Jones III

For information about this title or to order books and/or electronic media, contact the publisher:

simply francis publishing company
P.O. Box 329, Wrightsville Beach, NC 28480
www.simplyfrancispublishing.com
simplyfrancispublishing@gmail.com

DEDICATION

To the people who fought to establish this more perfect union, and to those who keep it going as the Founders intended.

And to Jesus Christ, in whom true freedom is found.

Website: www.davidjones3.com
YouTube Channel: @olivershistoryproject

CHAPTER 1

THE BEAVER–1773

The stowaway dry heaved again. He'd quit counting how many times hours before.

For many days, the constant, gentle, rhythmic washing of the ocean waves against the ship's oak hull assured him they were making headway towards Boston. Out of nowhere, the pleasant passage had been replaced with the pummeling of the ship by a storm so fierce that he regularly heard grown men weeping and calling out to God for His help, making promises they probably wouldn't keep once they returned to dry land. If they did return.

Hour after hour it was as if *The Beaver*, the merchant vessel thirteen-year-old Oliver Atkinson had illegally boarded in Bristol, England, was being picked up and tossed around like a child might an unwanted toy. The fierce battle for supremacy continued as water seeped through every possible gap in the ship's hull and deck, streaming cold ocean water upon the shivering young man.

The ship rose with each magnificent swell, determined to remain lord of the waves. Oliver braced himself by latching mightily onto Chinese tea crates as the ship reached the top of the swell, creating a sense of weightlessness. He knew the sea would let go, leaving his heart suspended, and hit the ocean with the booming sound of a cannon, leaving his lungs without air. He thought at any moment the hull would snap inwardly, and he'd be sucked out to sea to become fish food.

The explosion of the waves against the ribs of the ship combined with grating sounds of loose chains, creaking wood, and the tumbling of everything not tied down rushed his ears. His left elbow bled from smashing into a crate, as did his knees. The salt water stung for the first few hours, but his entire body was now numb.

This was not part of the plan.

During the four-week voyage to date, water had regularly seeped into the small four-by-four hidden berth he created between one hundred crates of Chinese tea and the hull, making it difficult for him to stay dry. Becoming fish food was not a part of the plan he devised at Baron Effringham's estate when he decided to run away. He fearfully kept an eye on the crates around him, thinking if the sea didn't get him he'd be crushed by their liberation from their constraints and crush him to death. Then once he was discovered, belonging to no one on board and not found on the ship's manifest, he figured his lifeless body would be tossed overboard to become fish food anyway.

"I shouldn't be on this ship. I should've never run away from the estate." Oliver then began confessing every sin he could remember from his earliest recollections to the present, particularly emphasizing his running away from the baron's estate. His admissions did not quell the storm as he had hoped.

The "estate" belonged to a noble shylock named Baron Effringham, who among many business activities, acted as an illegal bank to many of central England's poor. If they paid him back on time he would make a nice profit. If not, he would force them into indentured servitude to pay off their debt, then add a year. Thirteen-year-old Oliver Atkinson never borrowed a shilling from the baron. But his uncle had. When he was unable to pay– intentionally so as not to have to care for his deceased sister's boy– the baron's goons grabbed the boy for a seven-year stint on the estate. Orphaned. Indentured. Unskilled. Hopeless.

Now, as the ship wobbled like a drunk sailor, tending to the fifty horses in the baron's stable for seven years was suddenly not such a bad thing. However, unlike a pedestrian choosing a different route home, there was no turning back.

Oliver wondered if turning himself in to the captain might help relieve him of his current state, provide food, clothing, and a better sleeping arrangement. But then wails coming from other parts of the ship were ribboned between the gusts of angry winds and surf. He knew no one could help him.

The raging migraines wouldn't let up. No amount of palm pressure against his temples eased the dehydration-triggered pain. He drew from everything on freedom he had ever read or dreamed of, but his current situation was demanding an audience with reality. He was as far from freedom as he had ever been.

"Freedom," he asked himself, "what was it?" He had read the Magna Carta and an assortment of philosophers but only knew it conceptually. He saw measures of it in high society, in the flight of birds, in the ways of Gulliver as he traveled to strange new lands. He decided to die in his pursuit of it. He shook as he muttered, "I'm going to die anyway."

The young boy from Derby entered a catatonic state that opened his memories and relaxed his body slumping against the pulsating hull.

As if in a dream, he remembered a bald vicar giving him a Bible as he sullenly stood watching a gravedigger shovel dirt onto his mother's casket. He next saw himself hiding it behind a slat in the wall next to his bed, knowing his uncle would not approve of the book as he had heard him cursing God many times for their difficult lives. When his uncle, aunt, and two cousins of the same age—a boy and a girl, had gone to sleep, Oliver would remove the book and read the first few chapters by candlelight becoming transfixed by the story of creation. His voracious appetite for this wondrous story was exchanged for the reality of a debt that wasn't his.

In his altered state, he then recalled trading coal he scavenged to a retired professor at Cambridge for books. It seemed the professor was just as giddy as he was in their transactions. Often hungry, books were meals for his mind. They were his escape from the mundanity of life prior to becoming an orphan, and even more so after. The wonder of being transported to other worlds, experiencing other people's lives, considering new ideas and wrestling with a few more, all without having to move from whatever girded his rear to read on, consumed him, and was his refuge from the abuse he daily received in his new home. He could travel the world for less than a penny and a few hours of coal scavenging.

During his lightless, solitary hours on board *The Beaver,* ideas and stories were his faithful friend. They belonged to him and couldn't be unjustly orphaned or forcibly indentured. At that moment on the ship, he couldn't see the smile that had formed on his face.

A scene change occurred in his state of mind when seeing himself hauled off to Effringham's plantation by two grotesquely unkempt men he named Catscratch and Gums—Catscratch, because he had a long deep scar from his right brow across his nose to his left jaw, and Gums, because he had no teeth—his drunk uncle was unable to pay back a debt he owed to the baron.

"Why are you doing this?" he tearfully asked his family as he was dragged from the home like a criminal.

His cousins were emotionless. His aunt fled the space weeping while his uncle, taking huge slugs of whiskey from a jug, belched out, "You're blood but not that much blood!"

Remembering this so clearly, he could feel the impact of the front door being slammed shut by his uncle as he was hauled outside and tossed on the back of a cart by the brutes.

In his state, his mind found a wisp of power to transition to the rare moments when Baron Effringham allowed him into his massive library filled with what he guessed were five-thousand books to pick a book to read at a desk in his study due to his curiosity over the boy slave. Oliver remembered his mother saying he could read by age three and speak like an adult by age five. The baron recognized these qualities, which fascinated him, and would make him wash up after finishing his duties in the horse stable and have him put on a proper green velvet outfit before entering his library, and allow him to read anything he wanted.

Oliver revered the Magna Carta and consumed anything he could find on America, but mostly, he loved adventure books like *Robinson Crusoe* and *Gulliver's Travels*. It made sense to him why he loved these things. His fantasy was to escape to a new land where he had freedom, rights, and opportunity. One day he read a newspaper story on the port at Bristol that shipped cargo and people to the colonies, and it stuck with him.

As his mind drove the recollections, he reflected on a particular visit to the baron's library where he met a short, balding man with a smile that made him defenseless. Effringham grabbed the rotund visitor's elbow and pulled him into an adjacent drawing room, ending a conversation with Oliver before one began. Oliver recognized him from his attendance at more than a few of baron's renowned parties when he had been required to help the overburdened house staff.

Though the vessel he was on kept gyrating, he stopped noticing. Time jumped to another wild Effringham party many weeks later. This short, rotund man with thin grayish-brown hair to his shoulders, who always arrived wearing a strange animal fur on his head, cut off the boy's path as he removed a silver tray from the dining area and said, "My name is Benjamin Franklin, Oliver. I live in America. Very pleased to make your acquaintance!"

"An American!" Oliver excitedly thought. Oliver wanted to ask him a thousand questions about the colonies but was commanded not to speak to the guests. All Oliver could do was stare at the man as if he were looking at royalty. The jovial man eyed the young boy through the early part of the evening until the group began their usual retirement to a part of the mansion not even the staff were allowed. Motioning for the boy, Oliver nervously approached the American.

"Baron Effringham has boasted to me about your intellectual gifts. Frankly, he thinks you could do England harm and cause class upheaval someday. I shouldn't be telling you this, but, frankly, you and I desire the same thing: freedom. I understand he plans on shipping you to one of his plantations in India soon to rid your potential nuisance from British soil. He could have me banned from England for this, but I suggest you find a way to escape, and to do so soon. Perhaps America?" With a wink and smile, the quirky man from the colonies disappeared.

Oliver immediately remembered the story about Bristol being a gateway to the colonies through trade and began making plans for his escape while completing his duties for the night.

The dream sequence suddenly ended. Oliver emerged from his catatonic state, not because he'd been shaken by another blast from the wind and sea, but because all was suddenly tranquil. It was as if the ship was resting on its pre-launch perch on a sunny day.

* * *

Instantly, his nose turned up and face recoiled at the smells of his cramped space reminding him where he was. He sat waist deep in his apartment slurry of sea water and vomit.

Miraculously, he'd been able to restrain his bowels during the

Atlantic's twelve-hour thrashing. But now, with the ship floating still upon the water, he locked up his backside as there wasn't any place for his waste. Once his bladder became full the first time, he had to improvise by placing his waste in a crate of tea. It was now full and reeking. He had to get up to the head on deck, which he would occasionally do at night when most of the ship was asleep.

Potable water and fresh food were twenty-five feet away. The cycle of eating and discarding became the most important mission of his besides not getting caught. "How in the world am I going to pull this off?" He fought constant negativity, though decided to be honest with himself about every aspect of this experience. Overcome or be overcome. Weeping often came unannounced. He'd bite down on his damp, rancid coat to stifle the noise when the galley cooks came to prepare meals for the crew and officers.

With the ocean's prolonged tantrum over, Oliver heard people gathering on deck. The voices were celebratory. Someone began playing the fiddle. Then a flute and banjo were added to the revelry. While not musically gifted, his ears perked up as did his countenance—he had never heard a more beautiful sound. The wooden soles of their shoes gleefully pounded against the main deck in celebration. Unsure of how long the relieved passengers and crew would be distracted with song and rum, he knew he had to make his move before an accident occurred.

Bowing his head, he asked the Creator for invisibility. Like a cat, he moved stealthily up to the main deck and double-timed through the gathering crowd to the head without being noticed. The strange relief from the victory over internal self-control almost collapsed him on his seat. He filled his lungs with fresh sea air and his eyes with the peace of the clear blue sky. When he finished, he struggled to stand, as if being weighted down. He wondered how long he could sit there until he regained strength.

"You there!" a sailor called out to Oliver, "We'll be in Boston before you finish and others have to go!"

As if lifting a 100-pound boulder over his head, the stowaway rose, and briskly pushed through the mirthful passengers and crew, rappelling quickly down to his deck.

Oliver looked in horror at the dreadful condition of his rotted clothes. He fingered his horribly wrinkled skin that had been brown on the estate but was now pale white. The water-logged garments fostered blisters and open wounds. Most of his body, as best as he could tell, was like this. The stench was intolerable.

He dangled again the idea of turning himself in. "If I give up I might be saved from some disease I've created in this putrid space. But we have to be close to Boston. I've come too far." The journey would continue.

After stashing food and water in the driest part of his berth, he moved again with cat-like stealth to the area where personal trunks were stored. He had found one, elaborately decorated unlike a commoner's, who had clothes that nearly fit him perfectly. They were almost as dandy as the velvet suit the baron gave him and were a class or two steps above his standard colorless linen and wool clothing.

While admiring a garment, a sharp commanding voice came from behind asking, "Who goes there?" Oliver turned to see a man he learned later was Ensign Anderson approaching him carrying a lantern. He stopped two feet from the shocked boy. "Who are you? What's your name?"

Oliver's eyes darted about, his instinct to run. "Run to where?" He asked himself. He was cornered. Feeling his heart stop momentarily, Oliver gulped and responded between deep breaths, "My name is Oliver Atkinson."

Without ever taking his eye off the boy, the sixteen-year-old Anderson, who had an unusually large head and the roundest eyes, loudly demanded that someone named Culbertson join them. A moment later a man of about twenty-five in a seaman's outfit was at his side. The ensign said, "I think we've found the thief."

Young Atkinson's heart switched places with his stomach, which, if filled with anything, would've given up its substance at that moment.

Anderson was about Oliver's size, and it just so happens that the chest Oliver had broken into during the massive storm was his. "Mr. Atkinson, you are wearing my clothes. Would you mind explaining yourself?"

Oliver straightened his back and tried to force his mind into believing this was only another part of the adventure his destiny had led him to for a glorious escape to add to the tale he was living. His intense eyes and furrowed brow relaxed, surrendering to the reality that faced him.

Lifting his right hand as if to give a speech, he hung his head and raised it a second later in shame. "Dear sir, my clothes had become so damaged and rank that my skin was swelling, wrinkling, and sores were developing, as you can see." He showed them his arms and chest. "I needed dry clothes," he said while motioning over his shoulder in their direction, "and opened up a chest and found them."

"Didn't your parents bring you a change or two of clothes for the trip to the colonies?" he asked, knowing the answer.

His mouth quivered as he said, "I think you know the answer to that, sir." He began to take off the clothes.

Reaching out and grabbing Oliver's right arm, the ensign said, "That won't be necessary. You don't have parents on board. You must be a stowaway."

Years of unspoken grief poured from the unpaid passenger as he replied, "I don't have parents at all, sir. I'm an orphan. My father was in the British Army and died three years ago. My mum passed from a fever last year."

The ensign's shoulders sank. His face relaxed as he silently stared at the frightened boy. Culbertson broke the quiet space, gently asking, "Shall I get the captain, sir?"

Returning to the hardness of his profession, Anderson said, "Young man, you have committed crimes against the owners of *The Beaver* by being a stowaway, for eating the ship's food, and against me in particular for taking and ruining my clothing." Bending down to go nose-to-nose with the boy took little effort as the ensign was just a few inches taller than the stowaway. "Captain Coffin usually makes thieves suffer at the end of a cat-o-nine tails. Do you know what that is?"

With a quivering lower lip, Oliver nodded.

Anderson continued, "Stowaways are usually ushered off the plank into the sea."

"Fish food," Oliver muttered.

"What?" the ensign asked before standing up straight.

"Fish food. If you throw me into the ocean, I'll become fish food."

The two officers began laughing, alternately looking at themselves and the boy, until Culbertson noticed the lamp was getting dim. "Sir, the lamp's about out."

"Right. Atkinson, time to meet Captain Hezekiah Coffin to decide your fate." Anderson nodded to Culbertson to lead the way as the ensign grabbed the boy by the collar and pulled him along with them past the cook preparing fish that had ended up stranded on the deck after the storm.

In minutes they had moved past the full deck of revelers and were standing before the captain in his quarters, having awakened him from the first sleep he'd had in twenty-four hours. He lumbered out of his bed with displeasure and sat at his desk sideways with an empty pipe in his mouth. He didn't allow smoking on board after two incidents early on in his career. One ship burned in port, and another set off a keg of gunpowder that blew a hole in the ship. They barely made it to safety, but that was it for pipes as far as Coffin was concerned.

The weathered captain's penetrating blue eyes read every line, and Oliver thought his very soul, while Ensign Anderson explained the missing food, the strange sightings of a young boy many thought to be a ghost, how his chest had been broken into, and the fact that the very clothes young Atkinson was wearing belonged to him. He was a stowaway.

The boy had survived undetected for four weeks aboard his ship. His brief embarrassment at how a thirteen-year-old boy could have pulled this off turned to intrigue and curiosity. So, the captain invited the boy to sit down and tell him his story from the beginning.

Anderson and Culbertson stood there amazed. They understood the stowaway was still a boy, though nearly an adult, and within a year or two could also become an ensign on a ship just like them. Perhaps the usually swift-sentencing Quaker Coffin needed some amusement before rendering his verdict and punishment. Time at sea was monotonous, and they had just endured a storm they would all remember for the rest of their lives, so maybe the boy could provide some momentary relief before the whip came down or the plunge from the plank was commanded.

To Culbertson, "Prepare a meal for the two of us. Quickly!" Coffin ordered. To Anderson, he said, "Go back to your post. I'll call you soon with my decision regarding young Atkinson."

Both men saluted and hurried out of the captain's quarters.

Turning to face the boy, he said, "From the beginning."

For the next two hours Oliver told his story of growing up in Derby with a military father he almost never saw because he was somewhere other than England.

"What was his name?" the captain asked.

"Major William Atkinson," the boy replied.

Sitting up quickly, his brow raised, the captain let out an "Oh!"

"Yes?" The boy said, his mouth full of swordfish, barely chewing as he let the otherworldly taste brew in his mouth.

"How strange life can be, Mr. Atkinson." He paused for an instant, then continued. "I believe I knew your father."

Oliver's mouth flew open, "You knew my father?"

"He was transported on the last ship I commanded before I left the Navy for this merchant ship. The money is much better here, I can assure you!" he laughed.

"My father?" Oliver asked him to continue.

"Yes, yes. I first met your father," speaking as he stuffed a large piece of fish in his mouth, "during a battle with some pirates down near the Carolinas before his unit was given orders to be stationed in Massachusetts. What irony. I heard later that he had died in a tavern incident in Boston. I'm very sorry," he offered as his voice trailed off softly.

"Did he ever speak of me or my mum?" Oliver wondered.

"I didn't know him well, Oliver. I'm sorry."

Oliver was hopeful this would get him out of any punishment, but as he was thinking that the captain seemed to have read his mind.

Motioning with his right hand, Coffin said, "Please continue."

Oliver told of his relatives, his indentured servitude at Baron Effringham's estate and how he got to *The Beaver,* how he'd survived, ending with him sitting before the captain.

The captain's left arm was across his chest, his right elbow resting on it vertically while his hand rubbed his bearded jaw. His narrow blue eyes filtered through Oliver's words, bearing down into his soul. He leaned forward into the boy's space, who had just finished his meal, and said, "Without discipline and rules on a ship, mayhem, mutiny, and murder will occur. I've seen them all."

Oliver was frozen stiff, expecting his sentence to be gravely punitive.

"I have to do something, Mr. Atkinson, you understand that?"

Oliver courageously sat up straight. His lower lip quivered once again as he nodded.

"You are one brave young man. Life seems to have tossed you around like the storm we just survived." Coffin stood, and contemplatively uttered, "but I have to do something."

Oliver stood and began disrobing.

"What are you doing?" asked the captain.

"I won't need them in the ocean, sir."

"What?"

"My life is cursed, sir. I don't want to end up like Catscratch or Gums."

"Who?"

"If I can be honorable in any way, it is to accept my fate for dishonoring your command."

The captain sat back in his chair, slowly rocking, seemingly fighting back amusement.

"Oh?"

"I will walk the plank and take the responsibility away from you. It is a just punishment, and everyone will understand," the boy offered, crying without tears as his ducts had run dry.

The captain finally spoke, saying, "I'm neither going to whip you, as you deserve, or make you walk the plank, as you also deserve." He paused as Oliver's blood-shot eyes rose to meet his. The boy dared not interrupt. "As I've said, I must do something as I don't want to get a reputation for being soft on criminal behavior or no one will ever respect me, and I'd just be inviting mutiny at some point. No merchant ship owners would ever hire me. It does behoove me to add to my notoriety as a disciplinarian while adding a little mercy to the mix, wouldn't you agree?"

Oliver looked somewhat confused. The captain continued.

"I'm going to put you in the brig for the remainder of the voyage."

"The brig, captain?" Oliver asked.

"Like a jail. We have a tiny one here as there's not much room on board, and thankfully my ferocious reputation scares away the riff raff that might otherwise try and get hired onto my vessel. You'll be clothed and fed, and let out to use the head, but once we get to Boston, I will turn you over to the military governor, Thomas Hutchinson, I believe, and he will ship you back to England, then back to Effringham to finish out your service with him."

"But he sold me," Oliver countered.

"I can assure you that the sale was voided when you didn't show. Effringham will probably double or triple your service time for what you've cost him in terms of money and reputation. No one likes to be embarrassed, son. I hope you understand I'm doing this as the least severe punishment I can offer you. I'm doing it because of your father. Plus," the captain spoke gently, "you never know what opportunities life has in store. Stay ready. You have so far. I hope you appreciate what I'm doing."

"I think I do, Captain Coffin," he replied, knowing full well that hope was between the lines of the captain's words, insofar as he might never board a ship for England again. Rushing the captain, he hugged the uncomfortable man.

CHAPTER 2

Oliver's holding cell was about the same size as his cubbyhole by the Chinese tea, so he was used to the discomfort and contortions. He was fed and watered and allowed to use the head three times a day, a huge improvement on his bowels and belly.

Anderson let him keep the clothes. They were ruined, in the officer's estimation, having been on an infected boy, who quickly began healing once out of the infernal cesspool.

Having become a source of entertainment with the curious passengers and crew, he was frequently visited. He was a celebrity, and he enjoyed the continual stream of people during daylight hours. Some talked about England, but most spoke excitedly and expectantly about their moving to America and the hopes they had. Oliver pried everything he could out of these folks, who gladly obliged him.

For the first time in two years, the attention he received was warm and encouraging. A middle-aged woman with one eyebrow across her forehead was moving to the colonies to marry a man she'd never met, gave him some hard lemon candies one day, advising him to not tell anyone, not even to save them for later. The boy immediately popped them into his mouth, and it exploded with flavors and sensations he'd never experienced before. She made him think of his mother, not because of looks or personality, but because she was about the same age and because she was "sweet," he cleverly thought.

Suddenly, everyone disappeared except the cook that fed him, and Cartwright, who would escort him to the head. Oliver was told that there was a delay going into Boston's port because a bout of smallpox had broken out on the ship. They were required to quarantine until it passed. It took two weeks.

One day in mid-December, Captain Coffin came down to speak with him privately. He'd only been down once before, and it was the day after he was placed in the brig. The captain wanted to see if he was all right. Now was much of the same, except he reminded him of what he had to do—turn him over to the military governor for shipment back to England and Effringham's estate. The boy nodded, thanked the captain for his mercy as the grizzled and gracious ascended to the main deck. Oliver never saw him again.

* * *

On December 15, 1773, there was a hubbub on deck as the solitary boy heard footsteps and shouts of joy from both the crew and the passengers. They entered Boston harbor, then docked at Griffin's Wharf.

After a while the commotion dissipated. A man in a British military uniform bounded below deck to the cargo area with Ensign Anderson on his tail. The soldier was part of a team that had boarded *The Beaver* taking control of it, as they did every ship sailing into the harbor, bringing it under the jurisdiction of the British military. They passed Oliver without a look on their way to inspect the tea and count the crates. After ten minutes, on their way out, the British officer suddenly stopped at the small brig where Oliver stood, hands clutching the bars. Turning to Anderson he asked, "Anderson, you have a child locked away in a brig? Didn't he eat his porridge as he was told?" The officer laughed to himself as he scurried away.

Over the next few hours Oliver witnessed the personal property of the passengers being offloaded from the ship. No one stopped to talk with him. They were as eager to get on dry land as he was, he surmised. Yet, he wondered, why the crates of Chinese tea remained unmoved.

Oliver learned later that a band of colonists who called themselves "The Sons of Liberty" were preventing the offloading of the tea as shifts of twenty-five men surrounded the dock. They were protesting The Tea Act of 1773 that the British Parliament had passed, in part, to replenish the government's coffers after the long and expensive Seven Years' War, which was mostly fought against the French over borders and land rights in North America. The act gave the British East India Company a monopoly on tea sales to the colonies, allowing them to inflate prices. Many colonists saw this as an attack on their rights as British subjects as they didn't have any parliamentary representation to combat unfair penalties, which they considered the Act to be.

Oliver would soon hear and learn the phrase, "No taxation without representation!" Once he did, he was immediately drawn to these Sons of Liberty because he, too, felt like he hadn't any representation, and was a slave of the British system.

As the daylight hours bled into night, it became clear that he was abandoned on the ship. He didn't hear any voices or footsteps. He kept waiting for Anderson, the sweet lady, a galley cook, someone, to bring him food and allow him to use the head. But no one came. Soon the brig below deck was coal black, every sound augmented. Only rats ran free around him.

The next morning, Anderson appeared, quite apologetic about having forgotten him.

"Am I going to see the governor now?"

"I'm afraid not," he glumly replied. Opening the brig with a key, Oliver quickly stepped out but was immediately handcuffed by the ensign. "Sorry, young Atkinson, you aren't to be trusted."

As the boy came on deck, his senses were overloaded with

sights and sounds of humanity, of dry land, trees, buildings, colors, and unfamiliar sounds. He was back on land! Sort of. He kept filling his lungs to capacity with the fresh air. There were buildings and people milling about the port, working much like he had seen in Bristol and London, which was a significantly larger town than Boston. It was hard for him to believe he had survived a five-week sailing journey from England. He made it. His tear ducts replenished, two warm tears gathered volume enough to slip over his bottom lids to dance down his pale cheeks.

The untrusting ensign noticed, glaring at him as they walked and said, "There's no hope for you here, Atkinson."

"No hope." He'd heard that so many times in the last year. The phrase infuriated his normally docile mind. He would continue to be motivated by that phrase for the rest of his life. It was the lie of the oppressor, the threat of the doomed, the accepted will of the coward.

Looking at his captor, he smiled and said, "Ensign Anderson, hope is exactly what I have."

Quickly changing the subject, Oliver asked about the men stationed around the dock as if on guard.

"Rabblerousers. Sons of Liberty, they call themselves. Because of them, we can't get paid, and if we can't offload this tea, we will have to sit here. If Captain Coffin tries to leave the harbor with the tea, the British government will still make us pay customs on the merchandise, which we cannot afford until we get paid, which requires us offloading the tea." Anderson and the boy undid their pants and sat back on the head side-by-side. "Does that make sense?"

"Why won't these men allow the tea off of the ship?"

Anderson loosely explained what he thought the reason was, turning to the boy as if to tell him a secret and speaking under his breath he quickly explained the Stamp Act, the Townsend Act, and the Tea Act. "And I agree with them, a wee bit. I'm from Nantucket. I was born here. We're citizens of England, but we're not."

Contemplating this, Oliver then turned to him and said, "The English are fighting the English?"

"Are you through yet?" Anderson demanded.

"I had to hold it all night!" In truth, Oliver was also trying to buy as much time on the deck as he could to survey the area and gather as much information as he could. His mind photographed everything it saw and then placed each visual in an appropriate file.

"No, no, there's no war, there's no civil war. That's ridiculous! I said I agreed with them on principle, but these men are borderline insane thinking they can oppose the British Crown in any way for very long. The King, the Parliament, and the military have zero tolerance for any kind of opposition, non-violent or not. And blood has already been spilled."

Anderson went on to explain the Boston Massacre, and how some colonists were harassing a group of British soldiers, who responded in fear by firing into a harassing crowd, killing five men, including Crispus Attucks, a man of African and Indigenous descent, who became the first martyr to what would become the American Revolution.

A wide-eyed Oliver stood and buttoned himself up, feeling confident in the proper path to flee if the opportunity arose.

"Finally," an exasperated Anderson sighed.

"Tell me more," the boy inquired.

"I haven't time. I have an engagement to get to and your slowness here is going to make me tardy, embarrassing me in front of a lady of renown I am escorting to a ball tonight." He grabbed the boy's left elbow and marched him off without cuffing him. Oliver continued to absorb all he could before being escorted back to the brig. He knew every building and street exiting from the wharf, as well as where every man in street clothes was stationed.

CHAPTER 2

He caught one of the men following him across the deck with his eyes.

The boy was fed a huge meal and given a jug of water. Anderson promised to stop by that night, but he got drunk and forgot to return. It didn't matter as Oliver wouldn't be there anyway.

CHAPTER 3

THE SONS OF LIBERTY

Oliver was irked that Anderson had abandoned him. The visibility where he was trapped was as black as the coal he used to gather and the color of his anger from being abandoned.

The rats ran wild, when during the voyage they seemed more cautious. The prisoner started a conversation with a rather large rat, who sat right outside the brig staring at him, until Oliver realized it might be of early-onset insanity. Shooing it away, he alternated between despair or the hope depending on what creaky sound fluttered through the hull. No one had visited him since the ensign stopped by. At least he left him with some food and water. But he had to go to the bathroom again. It seemed to him that half of his trip on the ship was focused on getting food and drink, and the other half on how to get rid of it.

The weary boy slumped back in his cell and stared at nothing in particular, mostly because it was too dark to bring anything interesting or thoughtworthy into focus.

The weakest parts of his heart and soul began to crave the idea of hopelessness. Flaming arrows flew back and forth between the two, battling for supremacy, but self-pity was becoming more desirable. Was it time to quit dreaming, to stop running from the inevitability of the class he was born into, the mess he had made for himself, and finally surrender to the words first uttered by Gums as he carted him off to Baron Effringham's estate: "No hope?" His willpower all but depleted, he was unable to defend the foolish aspirations he had deluded himself into believing.

Finally, unable to resist, his head dropped to his chest as he closed his eyes, having lost will to fight against his despair. "No hope," he murmured, before entering through the threshold of another catatonic state.

The disobedience he'd read about in Genesis 3 made more sense to him. Humanity and the world were cursed. There was no other explanation for it. The wealthy were evil. The poor were evil. He saw so little good in the lives of most humans he had interacted with. It seemed like wickedness abounded everywhere, and the garden he dreamed of living in was utterly contaminated, despoiled with thorns, weeds, and rocks. Occasionally, a rose would rise above them and bloom, but in his life, the bloom was never lasting. One had to rally one's senses before the fragrance was no more and the color declined, its petals abandoning the sepals before falling to the ground to rot.

The catatonic state approached with vigor. Negative recollections burst forward, pushing aside all competitors. It was not a time for reason but review, just like before. Books, philosophers, human bondage, the will of man, personal responsibility, the welfare of the people, and the responsibility of the community one for another. His body thrashed against the iron bars of his cage, contorting to the emotions and ideas that drove his state.

Hopelessness he understood. Freedom was a conceptual mirage.

His thoughts began dissolving into nothingness when he was suddenly shaken to coherence as the whoops and hollers of men punched through the darkness, notifying his soul that he was no longer alone. Shouting and thundering footsteps came down the hatch. His eyes wide and mouth agape, Oliver was shocked by what he saw.

Ten oddly dressed men with what looked like feathers in their hair, and odd markings on their faces, wearing leather coverings, descended from the top deck and began dismantling the tea crate restraints. He could see little else even though a few carried lanterns. They kept "whooping" and shouting strange sounds as they teamed up to take the Chinese tea crates to the deck. No one looked at him. It was as if Oliver was invisible.

Standing to get a better glimpse of these men, he suddenly recalled a picture book he had read in Effringham's spacious library on the colonies about Indians in America. They were magnificent beings to him, and, as he watched them offload the tea, were certain that he was witnessing them in action. He was convinced that that's who these men were. "Indians! Magnificent!" If one of these men could see him, they'd probably have said he looked like a surprised boy on his birthday.

As his eyes adjusted to the dim light provided by one lantern-carrying man, he noticed that they really didn't have the same features as the Indians from the book. In fact, they started speaking English with a British accent. 'Were these the Sons of Liberty?' he wondered. "Hello?" he meekly said. The men raced back and forth without giving him a glance. "HELLO!"

One of the Indians kicked his toe and let out a word he'd heard only the sailors say. It would not have been approved by his mother. But as the Indian grabbed the end of a crate and turned toward the hatch, he noticed Oliver. His partner pushed him as he stopped, and he let down his end.

"Hold on," he motioned to his mate, and stopped in front of Oliver, and in an earthy British accent asked who he was and why he was there.

"Indians speak with British accents?" Oliver asked.

The two men burst out in laughter! "We are British," the first man said, "and we are here to liberate this ship of its tea. Looks like you could use a little liberating yourself."

"Please get me out, mister!" Oliver cried.

"Let's go, Revere!" commanded his partner. "Before the Tories and soldiers come and shoot us!"

The man called "Revere" looked at Oliver and said, "I'll be back."

The ten men took about two hours to unload all the tea and toss it into Boston Harbor as Oliver watched with fascination at the precision and speed at which these men offloaded the tea. Once on deck, he heard loud splashes, later learning that these men were not offloading as much as they were dumping tea. What also clearly came through the hull were the sounds of metal against wood, to later learn that a group of men were rowing to floating crates to demolish each so the tea would be ruined and not salvageable by scavengers.

As promised, the man called Revere was back and was able to break the lock with a hammer. "Well, are you going to just stand there?" Revere asked a shocked Oliver. A broad smile stretched the boy's face from ear to ear, bringing a smile to Revere, who then said, "Follow me."

Oliver's atrophied legs scampered as fast as possible up the hatch before missing the top step. Revere caught him, preventing a terrible tumble down to *The Beaver's* belly.

"Where are we going, sir?" The broad-shouldered, square-jawed Revere ignored him as they raced across the deck and ran down the gangway to meet up with a group of very serious men, some bending at their knees from exhaustion, who had gathered at the outer end of the wharf.

"Just listen," Revere admonished Oliver, who debated whether to run back to the ship, stay with the men, or flee into the Boston night. "You're not going anywhere," Revere firmly said, as if reading his thoughts.

One of the men, a plain man with a medium build, and the only one present not dressed like an Indian, who Oliver later learned was Samuel Adams, raised his hands and proclaimed with a strong, yet quivering voice, "Sons of Liberty, you have served the unrepresented people of the colonies well tonight. England will not tax us until we have a say so in Parliament!"

As one, the men shouted, "No taxation without representation!"

Adams' dark eyes surveyed the men then raised his hands to quiet them down, and as he did, he saw Oliver and did a double-take but continued. "Off you go out of Boston for the time being. Our band will convene again in a week at the Green Dragon Tavern." Amused, Adams said, "I think we just sent a very loud message to King George. He is not going to respond with kindness. Gird yourselves, Sons of Liberty, for the battle has just begun!"

With that, the men shouted before dispersing in different directions.

Revere grabbed Oliver by his shoulder and looked down upon him with curiosity, and asked as he pulled him along, "What did you do to get the brig?"

As the men disappeared into the cold night, Adams studiously approached Oliver, and asked, "Who are you? Who are your parents?" Revere and Atkinson stopped.

Swallowing hard, Oliver wanted to run again, but his legs wouldn't move. He looked back and forth at the two men trying to think of what to say. "Hurry now, boy, before the Regulars come and take us to our own jail!" Revere commanded.

"My name is Oliver Atkinson. I'm an orphan who was a stowaway on *The Beaver*, a runaway from indentured slavery to pay a debt that wasn't mine. I didn't know where the ship would take me, I just didn't want to be where I had no say in the matter."

The two patriots looked at each other curiously. "You can turn me over to the governor in the morning, sirs."

All three stood silent for a moment before Revere and Adams broke out in laughter. A surprised Oliver asked, "What? What did I say?"

The barrel-chested Adams turned to Revere and, in his quivering voice, matched only by a persistently shaking hand, said, "Don't you love it when Providence reminds us that our labor is righteous?" Revere nodded, quite pleased. Scanning the harbor, Adams motioned with his head for them to follow away from the wharf. "My name is Samuel Adams, and this is Paul Revere." The boy politely nodded.

Adams' smile gave way to gravity, stating, "Seems to me you could be a Son of Liberty." Cocking his head to the side, Oliver sought clarification. "A what?"

Adams went on to explain, "Of course. A Son of Liberty is one who fights for the rights of the citizens of the colonies. Like you, the King of England keeps trying to force us to pay a debt that's not ours, gives us no say in the matter, threatens us with military force if we don't comply, and tries to keep us from earning an honest wage, except for Revere here, of course."

Revere offered, "I have a few side businesses as an 'importer.'" The men chuckled.

"Yes, he does. Parliament and the King are strangling our ability to earn and be free. Sounds like in your young life you've had a little experience with something similar, yes?" Oliver nodded. "Paul," Adams continued, "see to this boy for a few nights, would you? Bring him with you when we convene in Lexington."

Adams didn't wait for Revere's agreement but turned and was into the shadows before they could blink.

The air was no longer tense on the wharf. Every Son of Liberty had vanished from the area except a few who were demolishing the last crates of tea in the harbor. A fog had settled over the area. However, hope reappeared, and Oliver knew he was resuming his adventure, though couldn't possibly assess its gravity.

"God pity the soul who spies on us, as we've had plants from the Crown in our midst," Revere said. "Miraculously, though, tonight's event was flawless. No one died." Revere put a finger to his lips to say, "Don't say anything!" Oliver saw the intensity in Revere's face, who motioned with his right hand to follow him.

The two moved up, down, and across the tangled Boston streets as if moving across a dangerous chess board. Revere led them away from any light, escaping the homes that lined the cobbled street, as well as rays of moonlight that shifted with the moving gray clouds.

Walking on the balls of their feet, Revere, the printer-goldsmith and part-time smuggler with broad shoulders and a square jaw, would calculatingly take a few steps, pause, his eyes and ears straining for sights and sounds to interpret as friendly or not. Oliver remained at arm's length behind him.

The rebel printer, goldsmith, was also a smuggler who worked against the Crown and their unjust taxes and monopolies so that unrepresented colonists could get goods they needed and longed for at prices that were affordable. Creating havoc for the local Crown administrators and Parliament was a sport to him, albeit a dangerous one. Smuggling required him to be a master spy, allowing him to provide intel to the Sons of Liberty, while sowing disinformation among their British overlords.

"Three unhindered hours—was our plan that good?" he asked himself as they meandered towards their destination. Their intelligence helped spread some lies to create distractions, diversions, and distance, but anyone who attended the earlier meeting of five hundred at the Old South Meeting House would've known what they were going to do. "What about this boy? Could he be a plant? He looked back at the undernourished boy who looked like he'd been through Hell and leaned towards believing his story.

A few blocks later, Revere paused, raising his hand to stop. A wide-eyed Oliver nodded. Approaching them was a furious crunching sound. "Redcoats," Revere whispered. As it got closer, Revere yanked the boy into the inlet of a door space as the quick, clopping noise got closer, then passed.

Oliver's adventure was now serious business.

Believing the area clear, the two left their hiding place and cautiously moved with more speed through the darkness, moving east for a few blocks before finally arriving at Revere's home. Oliver followed on Revere's heels to an awning of bare trees along a backstreet. Taking a left into Revere's backyard, the twosome entered through the back door.

Revere's wife Rachel met him just inside with a hug and kiss, before Paul stepped back to reveal the unknown boy. "He's here for a few nights. We found him caged on one of the ships."

Oliver was instantly overwhelmed by the smell of a mutton vegetable stew. The second thing that enveloped him was warmth. He hadn't smelled anything so delicious since before his mother passed, and he hadn't been warm in over two months.

"Oh, mercy!" Rachel said tenderly, as she bent down and brushed some hair from his face to look at him. "Let me get you some food and something clean to wear."

"Thank you, ma'am," Oliver answered.

Her round brown eyes took in his piteous state with motherly compassion, "What is your name?" Rachel asked as she rose and walked over to the stove to continue with the meal she anticipated would be needed by her husband upon his safe return. She always made more than enough as Paul frequently brought unexpected guests home at all hours. Tonight, however, there was a boy. This was a first.

"Oliver Atkinson, Mrs. Revere," he responded as he stared at the pot of food. She smiled sweetly at him as the "importer" sat down and motioned for Oliver to join him.

"Not until you remove that paint and feathers and get into clean clothes," his wife kindly demanded. Smiling at the boy, he rose as she called out, "and get this poor boy some clothes." Revere acknowledged her command as he disappeared into another part of the home. Oliver sat down in silence, looking around the comfortable home.

In the heavy candle light, everything seemed nicer than any home he had ever lived in, but it wasn't as elegant as the baron's palace. His adjusting eyes scanned the kitchen that opened up to a large family room and saw two stoves, cookware, embroidered handcrafted furniture, and a rocking chair by a huge burning fireplace with a few cords of wood stacked to its left side. Lit candles on tables were spaced every few feet apart on pewter holders on the plaster walls. A checkers board rested on a storage chest behind a couch. In addition to the stew, the home smelled like a mixture of whale oil, bayberry wax, and maple wood from the mature fire. And while he couldn't see detail from where he sat, he saw quilts everywhere, reminding him of his mother and one of her means of bringing in money after his father had died.

As Rachel readied some corn muffins for the meal, she seemed distracted by something lingering in the air. Turning to Oliver, she broke the silence with measured words, asking calmly, "Oliver, would you like a bath as well?"

"I and everyone else would probably appreciate that," he said with a smile.

She hugged him with a laugh as she cleared some hair from his face.

"Ma'am, my stink might get on your dress."

"It's time for a clean anyway," pausing to look into his eyes like a mother would a son returning home from a long trip. Her reassuring touch and warm smile helped him relax. Even in the semi-darkness he noticed she had the whitest teeth he'd ever seen.

Within twenty minutes, Paul and Oliver were cleaned up and ready to eat. Over the next two hours, Oliver told the Reveres, between multiple helpings of stew, who were joined by a few of their older children, including Paul junior who was a spitting image of his father and about the same age as Oliver, of his adventure, from his time as a boy in Derby, his parents passing, his time at his relatives home, being sold to the baron, his time at the baron's estate, his escape, capture, re-escape, then how he ended up on *The Beaver,* as well as what happened on the crossing. He ended his story with Mr. Revere liberating him from the brig.

Paul sat back in his chair. "I've never heard a story like this...never." His kids were awestruck, though Paul junior. seemed doubtful. "You had a long voyage to come up with that story."

"Junior!" Paul barked as everyone was shocked at the statement.

Oliver shook his head. "Actually, Paul junior is right." Everyone leaned forward towards him. "I did have a long time on the voyage to concoct a story to infiltrate the Sons of Liberty. Or, I could have been a plant from here. If you need proof, I can show you the damage the trip made on my body. Look at me. I can't appear healthy. There's no fiction, no falsehood, and no plans to do anyone harm. I can leave now if you'd be more comfortable." He pushed off his knees to stand when Paul Senior grabs him, preventing his rising.

"Nonsense!" said Rachel.

"I spent every waking hour trying not to get caught and be tossed into the sea to become fish food."

The tension was snuffed out as they howled in laughter as one. Including Paul junior.

Rachel stood and said emphatically, "I believe you, Oliver Atkinson. From a Derby orphan to our home. Know that you are welcome here as long as Providence wills."

"Aye," said Paul, as the children nodded excitedly.

"I am a gold and silver smith, but am also a printer," Revere said, "Your story should be in print."

"A book?" Oliver asked breathlessly.

Joining his wife, Paul stood and nodded, "Yes. But not now. People will be looking for you, and if we print this story now, or any time soon, it will undoubtedly stir the ire of the King himself," to which Oliver smiled, "providing extra motivation for Massachusetts Governor Hutchinson to find you and make you an example," Revere said dramatically. "He would quickly realize the value of your story of your pursuit of liberty for the colonies to exploit." Revere knelt to speak to the boy. "I'd advise you not to leave my side until safe arrangements have been made for you. Yes?"

Oliver straightened up in his chair and said, "Yes, Mr. Revere. I will do as you say. For liberty."

Standing, Paul chuckled and said, "For liberty!"

Then they all said, "For liberty!"

CHAPTER 4

The Revere girls prepared their guest room for Oliver while the Revere men sat around the fireplace talking about their lives.

"It's ready," Rachel said loudly from upstairs.

Senior saw Oliver's eyes fight to stay open. "I'm ready, too," he said to the boys, who said goodnight to each other and headed for bed. Oliver walked upstairs picking up each leg as if it weighed an extra ten pounds and entered a serene bedroom. There was very little to it except a dresser, a bedside table, and a bedpan. The ladies asked him if he needed anything else. Seeing a sleeping garment on the bed, he nodded and closed the door behind them.

After changing, he climbed into the nicest bed he'd ever slept in—no bedbugs, for one, and the pillow was as soft as he imagined a cloud to be. Still, he stared at the ceiling. It was the quietest few hours he could ever remember. The house was perfectly silent. He was exhausted to the point of pain. And yet he couldn't fall asleep.

His mind kept replaying everything that had happened to him these last few years. "What did I stumble into?" he said as he enjoyed the down-feathered bed and pillow, his tummy full and warm. "This is not the estate, not my uncle's home. It's not England. It's not a water-logged hole on *The Beaver.*"

Finally, his exhaustion extinguished every thought, his last words being, "No hope. Thank you, Creator," causing him to fall asleep with a tender smile on his face.

The Reveres let him sleep in. They had their own matters to discuss, some which concerned Oliver.

Though out for ten hours, it seemed like only an hour to Oliver. He was awakened by a heavy pounding sound. The urgent front door knocking blew his mind fog away. Quick shuffles of feet were heard downstairs. Rachel called out, "Children, go to your rooms!"

Oliver sat up in bed and listened intently as he tried moderating a suddenly pounding heart. His first thought was that he had been discovered and was going to be sent back to England. He soon learned this wasn't the case. The thirteen-year-old rose from his bed, put his slippers on and went to the window. Startled, he quickly stepped back from the window curtain after seeing about five men dressed in British military uniforms similar to what his father wore.

Overwhelmed for a moment at the sight of the bright red jackets, white pants, and triangular black hats, his mind transitioned from personal danger to his father. He'd been dead several years. He barely remembered his face, not because it was so long ago, but because he was always gone leaving his mother and him to fend for themselves. He recalled his generosity when he was home, and how he was always affectionate, and made sure they received his government salary. But he was always gone.

He confessed one day to Oliver that he had no other skills other than being a soldier. One night after his father had had too much liquor—a rarity for him as he didn't drink away the house money like his uncle did, he confessed to the boy as they sat before the flames of their stone fireplace while the mother slept, that he had a recurring dream that he would die someday on the battlefield fighting for the Crown. "It will be in the most glorious way. My death will be the catalyst that inspires men to victory." This frightened Oliver. He didn't understand the glory his father spoke of but only heard him speak of his death.

There was silence for a moment. Oliver glanced at his father's face and saw a distant smile emerge, as if he was seeing it unfold on the battlefield. Oliver's head swiveled to see what his father might be looking at, but there was nothing but a fire, a brown bellow, a long iron poker, and an ash scooper. His eyes darted back to his father's face to see the smile leave like a cloud changing in the sky. Now he looked sad. The glory was gone. "But I'll be gone, never to see you or your mum again." As if coming to, the soldier sat up and took the boy's wrists with his large hands and said, "I so love you and your mum."

Oliver leaned back against his chest, both sitting in silence until his father fell asleep. Oliver chose to remain tangled in his large arms instead of going to his bed.

Three days later his father left home for the last time.

The loud talking outside below became increasingly intense, drawing Oliver back to the present.

A knock at the door startled him. Paul Junior peeked his head in and assured him, "They're not here for you. Last night at the wharf stirred up a hornet's nest." Wringing his hands, Junior looked at his feet before asking, "Did all those things really happen to you?"

Oliver wiped some sleepies from his eyes, and said, "Every single word. I don't understand my path, but the Creator knows."

"You mean God, don't you?" Paul Junior asked, stepping inside the room and sitting on a bedside chair.

Oliver sat up confused. "I don't know much about God. I do love the creation story, though. Look, I can understand how my story might be difficult to believe."

"Actually, we all believe you. At least I do now. But it's my parents who needed to be convinced." Paul Junior gave Oliver an agreeable smile, causing Oliver's tense body to loosen up and smile back. "I imagine you are hungry? It's late. My father's expecting you. Get dressed. I'll see you in the kitchen."

He then left, the clomp of his shoes hitting each stair as he descended. The outside noise ended while he and junior were talking. Taking one last peek out the window, he didn't see any military men.

Dressed in new clothes, Oliver wanted to leap from the top step to the bottom but thought it might be impolite, but he was that hungry. On his way down he wondered where his adventure would take him next. Maybe he was already there.

Perhaps the Creator, he now decided to call God because that seemed more encompassing than just one part of His work, had ordained him to be with the Reveres, at least temporarily. His plan for him since he read the first three chapters of Genesis had been a series of temporaries. He imagined that all wanderings had an end point, a time in which the wanderer and adventurer found whatever they were looking for, were destined for, needed to learn, experience, or fulfill. On that last step, it seemed reasonable to Oliver to remain with them and foolish to abandon this home and family after such kindness. They would tell him when he was no longer welcome. He was eager to learn more from Mr. Revere about the Sons of Liberty and what their problem with King George III and Parliament was.

He pivoted left and walked down the short hallway and turned into the kitchen where Rachel stood. She greeted Oliver with her hands on her hips, and a warm smile.

"Good morning, Mr. Atkinson!" she exclaimed. "Sit your hungry-self down here," as she pulled out one of the benches from the dining table.

"Good morning, Ma'am," he gratefully replied, and sat. "Thank you."

Junior popped his head in from the backdoor and said, "Father is ready for Oliver when he's finished breakfast." He then disappeared back out the door.

"We must hurry, then," Mrs. Revere noted as she brought the

boy a plate of bacon, eggs, and bread, along with a jug of water she'd pulled from their backyard well that morning.

"Thank you, Mrs. Revere," as he scarfed down the food without looking up. Between one of his first bites, he asked, "What is Mr. Revere going to do with me?'

Laughing, she leaned back against her cutting table and said, "Do with you? I think he wants to get to know you better while taking you on an adventure."

"Adventure!" was all he needed to hear. At this, the boy shoveled food into his mouth. He swallowed his mouthful and offered, "He means to continue my adventure!"

Rachel emitted another burst of laughter and agreed. "You are so right, Oliver!" She became mother-serious for a moment. "How have you survived and endured all you have at such a young age confounds us." She approached and sat next to him, running her hand through his hair.

"I haven't a clue. God, I guess."

Paul walked in the room. "Are you ready, Oliver?"

Rachel stood and walked to her husband's side and said, "He was just telling me about God's sovereignty in his life, in his own way."

Revere smiled. "May we all be smack dab in the middle of it!"

Oliver pushed back his plate and chair and rose. "I'm ready, sir." Rachel gave the boy a hug as he passed, Paul winking at her as she did. Oliver didn't resist. The affection energized him. His being wanted to cleave to her. He starved for human warmth. It dawned on him that he was probably holding on for too long and released her and turned and marched out the back door.

CHAPTER 5

"You worked the stables, but do you know how to ride a horse?" Paul asked Oliver as they walked back to the Revere stable deep into the backyard.

"Yes, sir, I do." Oliver replied as the wonderful smell of horses filled his nostrils, then without missing a beat said, "Would you like to race me to find out?"

Paul let out a hearty laugh. "Humility by way of self-assurance is a noble thing. But we aren't nobility. Neither here in the colonies nor in England," a serious Revere said as they entered the stable. Paul Junior had two horses ready for them to ride on this brisk day. His father quickly mounted his mare, and assuming the other was for him, so did Oliver with precise deftness. The two Revere men looked at each other and then back at their guest and shrugged their shoulders.

"Are you sure I can't go, father?"

"I'm sorry, Junior. The Essex wedding invitations need to be finished today. Perhaps next time."

Junior looked disapprovingly at Oliver, who avoided eye contact with him.

"Hiya!" the elder Revere said and gave his horse a slight squeeze with his heels. The horse darted forward and out the door and turned left down the back lane they entered late the night before. Paul turned around to see if Oliver had even made it out of the stall yet and found he was right there at his heel smiling as he rode.

Paul kicked his horse into a gallop and Oliver kept up with him, flying down streets, across fields, over a stream and a stone fence, and through some thick woods, and still, Oliver was there. After about fifteen minutes of racing, Revere slowed his horse down to a trot and he motioned for Oliver to come alongside him.

As Revere was about to speak, Oliver offered, "I taught myself more than was needed for the work we did because I had planned to escape the entire time I was there."

"You stole a horse?" Paul asked?

"I can understand how it appears that way. Rather, I borrowed the splendid beast and left it with a man whom I knew to be a business associate of the baron's in Bristol who promised to return her."

"Are you concerned that the baron would send someone here to the colonies to look for you?"

"I don't know. He openly raged when bested, I recall."

"I see," was all Revere could reply.

After a momentary break in conversation, Oliver asked, "Why did you save me last night, and why am I riding with you today? Where are we going?"

Let me answer those questions in reverse order, if you don't mind?" as he led Oliver through Boston Neck.

"We are headed to a house in Lexington where the man you met last night—"

"Samuel Adams."

"Right, very good. Sam Adams is staying there for a few days as he observes from afar the fallout in Boston over the very impressive "tea party" the Sons of Liberty threw the royal government and the British East India company last night."

"Why did you do that?" Oliver asked.

"Let me continue answering your other questions first, and then I'll get to more of my details, as you have with your story."

Paul then continued. "I wanted you to come with me because, in part, Mr. Adams requested I bring you."

"So, he's the leader of the Sons of Liberty?" the young man asked.

"Yes, he and Mr. John Hancock," Paul explained. Continuing, "You are also with me so I could learn more about your story, some of which you have shared with me, get an idea of who you are, and tell you about the Sons of Liberty, why we exist, and what our aims are as English citizens. Unrepresented English citizens, that is."

"I love the word 'liberty,'" Oliver offered.

Paul gave a short history of the colonies, the French-Indian war, the depleted coffers of the Crown that led to the Stamp Act, and the tea party.

Oliver was mesmerized as he listened to a kindred spirit.

"How much of what I've shared makes sense to you?" Revere asked the boy as they continued their modest trot through a path cut in the woods.

"All of it. Many colonists are loyal to England; they just want an equal voice. But as Americans, you are subjects in the unkindest way and have resorted to acts of violence and destruction until the King and Parliament take you seriously. You aren't looking to create a new nation, just to be left alone if they continue to refuse your demands for representation. How did I do?"

With a satisfied smile, Paul Revere said, "I think you have a remarkable grasp of the matter."

"And the tea you and the Sons of Liberty threw overboard last night was done to reject hidden taxes and monopolies that would hurt the economies of the thirteen colonies. This was as strong a message as you could send back to the King and Parliament without resorting to human violence," Oliver continued.

"Yes, I would say you do get it," Paul stated. "Any thoughts?"

The syncopated clops of shoe-clad hooves against the ground

mimicked Oliver's racing mind as thoughts fought for dominance and words cut inline to be the first across his lips, but he wasn't ready to speak yet.

After a minute, Revere asked him again what he was thinking. But just as the young man's thoughts congealed so he could speak a coherent thought-out answer, Revere raised his hand and stopped his horse. "Shhh," he ordered. Revere's head swiveled before eyeing a spot, motioning for the boy to follow him off the dirt road and into some thick woods and brush thirty yards off the country thoroughfare.

Paul hopped off his horse, motioning Oliver to do so as well, and he followed him behind brush until stopping and kneeling in wet leaves with the reins still in his hand. Oliver followed. He looked through the undergrowth and stayed still, not saying a thing. Oliver started asking a question quietly, but Paul just raised his hand signaling him to be soundless as he peered through the dense vines and branches that dead leaves collected on. As the two kneeled, so did the horses, having been trained to do so. This fascinated Oliver, who wondered if Mr. Revere was doing this for his sake, or was there really something out there they needed to avoid at all costs? "Adventure!" The teenager felt a mixture of excitement and fear turning somersaults in his mind and stomach, and he loved the feeling.

On high alert, the two heard what sounded like large drops of steady rain on a tin roof approaching from the west. As the sound came nearer, it became more like a popping noise to Oliver. He'd never heard something quite like this before, but he knew there were horses involved. Oliver looked at Mr. Revere, who finally looked at him and said, "Redcoats. Stay quiet."

A troop of about five hundred British soldiers marched along the narrow road towards Boston shoulder-to-shoulder, four across. Their uniforms were glorious, majestic, and beautiful.

Oliver was impressed as they marched in time, disciplined, fearsome. That could've been his father, he thought for a moment, adding to the pounding of his chest. While most of the troops marched, there had to be at least fifty horses on which rode lieutenants, colonels, and other senior officers. Revere glanced at Oliver's wide eyes and noticed a bead of sweat developing on his brow.

"Remain still and slow down your breathing," Paul exhorted his companion.

One soldier broke away from the troop and wandered towards the two concealed travelers, stopping about ten feet away to relieve himself. Oliver held his breath and began feeling the initial returning stages of stupor he had experienced on the Atlantic crossing. He felt Revere's hand on his left foot, a touch that thwarted entrance to his unresponsive state.

"Adventure!" Oliver said to himself as he avoided darkness.

The smallest movement by the two, or their horses, would have alerted him to their presence, and then whatever Mr. Revere feared would have come to pass, he thought. Finished, the soldier ran back to his position in the march and carried on. Oliver peeked at Revere, who raised his hand for him to remain quiet.

Ten minutes later, the rest of the soldiers had marched on. Paul and Oliver stayed put for an extra five minutes before mounting their horses and continuing through the woods adjacent to the road just in case stragglers or other troops came through. Revere told Oliver this was unlikely, but he thought prudence dictated this considering the night before, especially since they were nearing their destination. His wide-eyed mate nodded like a child would at Saint Nick when being admonished to behave.

Oliver Atkinson absorbed everything he saw and heard from Paul Revere. He felt safe with him and believed him to be the most remarkable man he'd ever met. While he was still coming to grips with the Sons of Liberty, and only superficially understanding the political and economic tug-of-war between England and the Americas, everything he learned seemed to speak to all his life experiences after his parents' passing. He was a prisoner in his own country because of another's debt, a young man without rights and very little hope to control his own destiny in any conceivable way.

Running had been his only option. It meant he broke the law. An unfair one.

The Sons of Liberty had nowhere to run. America was their home. They had families, businesses, a heritage, and, at least for many decades, the opportunity to be something they never would have been in England. While a social hierarchy still existed in the colonies, not dissimilar to England, it had still been a land of opportunity, of hope and freedom, where the fruits of personal responsibility born from effort, wisdom, and ingenuity were available to all.

Suddenly, his adventure took a new turn and matured into a purpose.

Oliver peppered his riding partner with questions for the next twenty minutes until they came into a clearing that had a stone home plunked right down in the middle of a field. Its chimney smoke gave away that it was occupied. As they approached at a trot, the same man who spoke to them at the wharf appeared at the front door and yelled, "So good of you to make it," while looking down at his pocket watch, then lifting it to his ear to shake it as if to see if it were working.

"I had some visitors this morning I had to get rid of. Plus, our new friend and I had to dodge about five hundred redcoats headed towards Boston." Revere and Atkinson hopped off their horses as a man emerged from around the right side of the house to take the reins of each and lead them to a stable Oliver could see a part of in the back.

Politely, Oliver greeted the leader of the tea party. "How do you do, Mr. Adams."

Smiling first at the boy and then at Revere, then back to Oliver, Adams, 51, said, "Mr. Atkinson, I am quite well. So good of you to join us. I hope you had a pleasant sleep last night." He turned and entered the home, whose walls were covered in colorful tapestries, two sitting chairs, a wooden bench, a dining table, and a door that Oliver assumed led to a bedroom. The two visitors followed.

Inside sat a man Oliver didn't see the night before.

John Hancock, 36, a charismatic businessman dressed in clothes equal to Baron Effringham's, arose and shook Revere's hand. "We had quite a night, Paul," he said.

"We did, didn't we!"

Hancock rotated his right arm while massaging it with his left. "My right arm feels as if it were to fall off at any moment. But there are some things you can't hire others to do."

"Your pain is not in vain, John. What I'd give to be in Parliament in a few weeks when word gets back!" Revere exclaimed.

Oliver stood with his hands behind his back, and thought through his uneasy smile, "What am I doing here?"

Revere motioned to him while looking at Hancock, a tall, handsome man, "John Hancock, I'd like to introduce the latest prospective recruit to the Sons of Liberty, Mr. Oliver Atkinson of Derby, England, and the good ship *Beaver*!"

As the men roared, Oliver took a step forward to shake the stately man's hand, saying, "Pleased to meet you, Mr. Hancock."

John took the young man's hand and studied his face for a moment without letting go, then said in his usual dignified demeanor, "I'm sure I'd enjoy hearing your whole story, Mr. Atkinson, but would you mind condensing a highlighted version as we have much to do here today."

The four men sat down on a bench at a scarred wooden table and drank coffee, the first Oliver had ever had. It energized him immediately, though he hated its bitterness. "May I have a little more sugar, please?" And in went a heaping spoonful. After a slight taste, Oliver looked at each man, all watching him with amused interest, and spooned another scoop into his coffee. The boy smiled as he nodded, approving the taste. He rotated his tongue to make sure each sugar granular found a taste bud to attach to. He rarely had candy, and now these adults were allowing him to use as much sugar as he wanted in this new drink.

As the stone fireplace roared and crackled, Oliver spent the next ten minutes telling his story as quickly as he could, occasionally pausing to shuffle a story to the side or exclude details. Revere listened intently in case details changed or the story became bigger. He needed to trust the boy, and so did the Sons of Liberty. There was too much at stake, and it wasn't beyond England and Hutchinson to plant spies among the "American troublemakers," though it seemed hardly reasonable that a boy placed in a brig on a night when over three hundred crates of tea would be destroyed could've been planned. It wasn't possible, Revere thought, but he had to make sure.

Hancock and Adams were also counting on him to do this. They read the boy while they listened. They each asked a few questions and even tried tripping him up in his story a couple of times. Oliver noticed but didn't care. He respected this tactic of theirs.

When finished, Adams asked Oliver if he wouldn't mind checking to see if the horses had been watered and fed. He understood that they needed to discuss him, and other matters, apart from his ears, because he knew the horses were being properly taken care of as they spoke.

"Before you step outside, Oliver," Hancock paused, "How do you feel about England, it's King?"

Oliver wasn't sure what he was really asking and thought for a moment how he should respond but decided to be forthright. "Mr. Hancock, sir, I am a subject of the Crown. I know no other nation or way of life." The boy looked down for a moment, then lifted his head and continued. "But if there is any other political, legal, or social system that exists that wouldn't require me to serve out the debt of another and keep me in chains, whether visible or not, I would very much like to go there and live."

Oliver then left by the back door.

Once the door had been shut, the men looked at each other in awe of the young man's response. Hancock was the first to speak. "He's a patriot. He just doesn't know it yet. What a story. Providence has kept him for such a time as this."

"He was born to be one of us," Adams added. "What do you think, Paul?"

Pensively, Paul stood up and walked to the fireplace and stirred the logs with an iron poker, then walked over to the window that looked across to the stable and said, "He has no home or family. I can provide that for him. He has no employable skills, other than being a stable boy, but I can teach him goldsmithing, printing, and my other side business. However," he quickly turned to face his fellows, "He's as good a rider as I've seen on a horse, as good as me, and I have a feeling that skill will be of great value to us all in the coming months and years."

Adams stood. "Paul, if you wouldn't mind, teach Mr. Atkinson how to get from Boston to New York and New England. He could be a courier for us. At his age, he still falls under the category of 'least likely' to be suspected by the Crown and its representatives here."

"Already a part of my plan," Revere said.

Hancock raised his hand and wondered, "Two things: aren't we moving a little too hastily? And, shouldn't we ask him what he wants to do? Frankly, I can't believe he understands our cause to the degree he'll need to be an effective agent of ours. Frankly, we might frighten him off or might reveal too much too soon. I suggest we move slowly with him."

"You just mentioned the incredibleness of his story, John," Samuel said, "and invoked providence in it. I agree that he needs to learn more, and much of it will come by way of being around us and experiencing first-hand the tyranny we endure every day."

Revere sat back down, "This is not something to argue about. I can provide a home and work. He can come to our meetings, listen, learn, and if what we say really does resonate with him, would you not agree that this young man would be better in our service than the Crown's when he grows up?"

"Good, then we'll not force feed him, but see how quickly he takes to water." Adams cleared some space on the table for a blank parchment and placed it next to a quill pen and bottle of ink. "Now, on to our next bit of business."

Raising his hand, Paul pleaded, saying, "It's freezing outside."

Momentarily exasperated, Adams agreed to let Oliver inside, saying, "We aren't going to reveal any dirty secrets today anyway."

Hancock offered, "Actually, this might help the young man understand our righteous cause a little better, and we'll be able to see how he responds from head to torso to toes."

Revere went and opened the door, and beckoned Oliver, who came in and headed straight for the fireplace to warm up.

"That's a good place to sit while we talk, Mr. Atkinson," said Hancock. Oliver pulled up one of the sitting chairs with a seat made of twine and warmed up while listening closely to everything the men discussed. And drank more sugar-laden coffee.

The three adults went on to speak freely about how they felt the previous night's activities with the tea could not have gone better. "Three full uninterrupted hours!" Adams said excitedly.

"If we weren't marked men before," Hancock added.

"We are now," Revere finished.

As Oliver listened, he wondered whether these men were criminals against the Crown or not. But it all came back to the right for these men to have representation in England and be more than British economic slaves. The talk continued for a while, heated at times, jovial at others, but mostly serious. These men were on a mission to have their voices heard by King George himself.

"What do you think they'll do?" asked Oliver out of nowhere. He had been sitting quietly for two hours, though he could barely sit still. He concluded that too much coffee was not such a good thing after all.

The adults' heads swiveled as one towards the young man, then looked back at each other. It was obvious they were tickled by this question, one they hadn't yet considered.

"Well," Hancock offered, "it's quite possible that they will seek a truce of some kind, some diplomatic agreement by which the thirteen colonies will get a representative with full voting rights in Parliament, and we will go back to building our lives here. Our mission will have been successful at that."

"Rubbish," said Adams, who rose with his right finger piercing the air above his head. "This will bring on the wrath of the Crown like we've not yet seen. They will not allow the colonies to continue to throw destructive tantrums that add to their insolvency. No, they will scrape their coffers to teach us a final lesson and send many thousands of Redcoats to our shores and try to scare us into submission, force upon us more severe laws, and bleed us of every pound and penny they possibly can."

"England, all of us, could end up destitute. I give us odds of one in ten in being able to beat them back," Revere said.

"Are you suggesting that we fight the most powerful army on the planet, Paul?" asked Hancock.

Revere rose from the bench and motioned for Oliver to do the same. Revere walked to the back door, opened it and whistled, waving his hand. "Unless we dissolve our mission and surrender within a year or so, we won't have a choice."

All four in the room were now standing, as Oliver followed Paul to the front door.

Hancock shook his head in concern. "Our militias are not prepared. We'd get slaughtered."

Pausing at the door, Revere and the young man turned to their hosts. "We knew this was a possibility all along," Revere said as he shook each man's hand.

"Diplomacy, diplomacy, diplomacy! This is why I herald it with such vigor. What would be left of us in the end?" Hancock asked rhetorically.

They paused for a moment before Adams grabbed Oliver by the shoulders, then looked at Paul Revere. "Do as he says lad. You'll have a good life if you do."

"Not if the Redcoats come!" Oliver retorted, sending each man into hysterics.

With that, Revere and Atkinson mounted their horses and sprinted east away from the declining sun.

Their horses rested, Oliver and Paul Revere began a hasty trek back to the Revere home in Boston, wanting to get there before dark to eat dinner with the family and relax. The next day would be an important day for Oliver's standing with Paul and the Sons of Liberty. But first, he needed to discuss what the young man had overheard in the meeting that just ended with Hancock and Adams.

Oliver summarized the discussion well as they bolted down the Bay Road back to Boston, asking at various spots about points that didn't make sense to him. He quickly guessed that Hancock wanted a diplomatic solution and asked exactly what that might look like according to Hancock and those in agreement with him. He also questioned why violence would be necessary.

"Are you a pacifist?" Revere asked.

"I'm not exactly sure what that means. Admittedly, I just got here and know little about the colonies, Boston, or your cause. On the surface, it seems we might have some similar issues and experiences that point to shared vigor against what appears to be unrighteous servitude. You, to the Crown, and me, to a Baron from whom I never borrowed a penny. To add, this is a law upheld by the Crown and Parliament. So, to a degree, I probably understand more than I can comprehend. Honestly, Mr. Revere, it's a little overwhelming to me. I just arrived, thinking I was a dead man, and now I am somewhere in the middle of Massachusetts discussing matters way over my head."

"Did you attend Oxford?" Revere asked facetiously.

"The university?" asked a confused Atkinson. "Ha! No!"

Like Baron Effringham, the Vicar of Derby, the retired professor, and almost everyone else he met, Revere marveled at this young man's ability to process, understand, and verbalize complex issues. He thought the young man would quickly gain a thorough understanding of this moment in time and history with a simple retelling of the story of the colonies from the time of the French-Indian War to the present, and he did as they rode.

They discussed many things along the trek home. But Revere withheld mentioning the stockpiling of guns, bullets, and gunpowder at various locations in Massachusetts, or of anything similar happening in the other colonies. The uncertainty of the actions and political and self-ruling aspirations of other colonial entities were not so much his concern here, and he didn't want to muddle the boy's understanding of their immediate goals and concerns. There would be other times for an expansive discussion, for a more robust picture. For now, an overview had to be presented, understood, and agreed with before much else could happen in their relationship.

In a moment of silence as the two rode east, it suddenly struck Revere that if young Atkinson was not agreeable to their cause, what was he going to do with the boy? Turn him over to the authorities to be sent back to England? Release him to the streets, to a pastor, an orphanage? None of those options seemed to please him. He grabbed his stomach as if sore.

"Are you well, Mr. Revere?"

Revere's agitated heart and conscience couldn't raise his concern.

"An awful belch, that's all."

Paul continued with his history lesson. The boy asked a few questions. It was clear to Revere that his mind was a whirl. He had to be wondering "How in the world did I end up here riding with a man who is talking about taking on the King of England? In America!"

He then went on to teach the boy about himself and his family.

His first wife, Sarah, with whom he had eight children, died earlier that year. Soon after, he met and fell in love with Rachel. Up to this time, Revere hadn't participated in any violence committed by the Sons of Liberty and didn't consider the Tea Party a violent act as humans were not physically hurt. He wasn't a pacifist. He always stated he'd fight if the fight was inevitable. His question to the boy about being one was to get a further read on him.

"Would you like to learn a trade?"

"What? Who doesn't dream of being a stable boy for life?"

They both laughed. Paul continued.

"Paul Junior is excelling as a goldsmith, but I need help in my printshop. I'm away more than ever on Sons of Liberty business and yet the print shop is booming. Your gift with words should make this natural for you. What do you say?"

Oliver was quiet as they walked their horse's home. Paul looked over after a moment and saw Oliver wipe what he thought was a tear from his eye.

"I'll even show you how to create insignias like the Liberty Tree. You'll help create Sons of Liberty materials in support of our cause."

A liberty tree was a designated area where the Sons would meet to discuss business, hang effigies of Stamp Act supporters, and rally people to their cause. The Boston Liberty Tree was near the Commons and was easily accessible by most in the area. Liberty Trees began springing up all over the colonies, and the elm became a subtle symbol of their cause. Every colony shared a common cause that was energized by injustices that affected them all, from the shopkeeper to the silversmith to the farmer, lawyer, and landowner. The pursuit of liberty united them.

Paul Revere was also a printer and had been creating political cartoons that in an instant would say as much as a piece in the *Boston News-Letter*, or even the Sons-friendly *Boston Gazette*. His cartoons were designed to evoke outrage against the inequities of the Crown against its subjects. To be an Englishman was not the problem. To be treated as conquered subjects without total citizenship was.

"Yes."

"I'm sorry, Oliver?"

"Yes, Mr. Revere, I'd like that very much. What is happening to me?" He began to openly cry. Paul pulled up next to him and their horses stopped. Giving the boy a hug, not unusual for his affectionate family, he said nothing with words.

Continuing on after a moment as the sun said "goodnight" to Boston, they entered Boston-proper, steering their horses to its northside where the Revere home sat.

"I've shared a lot with you today," Revere said. "Perhaps, too much."

"I'm fascinated, sir. This time yesterday I was a prisoner on *The Beaver*. Now I'm discussing liberty from the tyranny of the Crown with complete strangers."

"It is quite an unlikely life, Oliver Atkinson."

"As I mentioned, my father was here. That's eerie. We crossed the ocean for different reasons and ended up in Boston. May I not let his memory down."

"He would be very proud of the young man that you are, so bright and intelligent, resourceful, a survivor, an outstanding horseman. He would see you as I see you, as Adams and Hancock see you, as a young man with a great destiny. Providence brought you here for a reason." Revere paused for a moment. For an instant in the moon's growing reflective wash, he saw a halo around the boy. And just as fast, it was gone.

CHAPTER 6

Their faces frozen from the brisk ride, and their lungs cold from inhaling modestly more air from their chatting, their horses knew where to go at this point and led the two back to the stables behind his home. Paul Junior came running out of the house and looked at Oliver with a half-smile while taking the reins. His father gave him a big hug.

"The wedding invitations were picked up. The lady cried. The man shrugged his shoulders."

Paul Senior laughed and said, "You're very good at what you do. Thank you, son," reassuring Junior that he hadn't lost his favored son status.

"Hello, Paul," Oliver said.

"Hello, Oliver. How was your ride? Did you keep up with Dad?" he said grinning.

"He might be a better horseman than me, son."

"I'm sure," Junior said insincerely.

Senior noticed. "Why don't you two play some checkers after dinner?"

Junior shrugged his shoulders.

"I'd like that," Oliver said sincerely.

"Let's get washed up so we don't have a repeat with Mrs. Revere as we did last night!" he said, chuckling. The two walked into the home as Paul the younger, known as Junior, situated the horses for the night.

Paul Revere's family sat in front of the fireplace a week before

Christmas. A few British Regulars, along with a major general, visited their home earlier that evening to question Paul yet again about what he knew about the destruction of the tea at Griffin's Wharf the night before.

Sitting next to the fireplace, Oliver was playing checkers with Paul Junior, who began to warm up to their guest.

Loud knocks rattled the door. "Open up in the name of the King!"

Paul Revere stepped outside into the cold night to speak with a new group of soldiers. Oliver was anxious, knocking over the checkers board as fear pulsed through him. "When will they get around to asking about a missing boy?" he wondered. He never came up. In fact, because the boy hadn't any papers and the ship wasn't hired to bring him to the colonies, there was no official record of him. Had one spent a few minutes reading the captain's log, they would've read about a young boy that had been aboard their ship as a stowaway, but little else. Surprisingly, Captain Coffin never entered any details. No name, no description, and nothing that Oliver volunteered to the captain over their discussions during the remaining part of the voyage.

Oliver didn't exist.

Revere was back inside with a hot coffee in hand in the company of his family minutes later, where they began singing songs and telling stories. Oliver decided to sit back and listen. His time was the night before, and he didn't want to dominate but learn and be a part of the family. Junior noticed, and this helped soften his heart towards his guest.

* * *

In another part of Boston at that hour, the Tea Party dominated discussions between Governor Hutchinson and the rest of the Massachusetts British brass. They decided to send a descriptive message to the King and Parliament about the destruction of the tea and who they thought was responsible. They would impatiently await their response. However, there was no mention of a young stowaway.

Deep into the evening, the young ones were put to bed, the kitchen was cleaned, and the family living space was tidied up. Everyone had a part. Even Oliver forced his way into service, though he was told at first that he was an exempt guest. Paul and Rachel were quite pleased with the boy and his demeanor, politeness, and intelligence. Their kids seemed to like him, including Paul Junior. They would soon become the best of friends.

Mr. Revere asked Oliver to remain downstairs once everyone retired. They faced each other sitting on two chairs by a fire reduced to the smallest embers, ashes scattered and mostly doused.

"Would you like to learn more about the Sons of Liberty after what you saw today?"

"Very much. But I want you to know, I don't hate England, sir. It is my country."

"We all consider ourselves English, Oliver."

A moment of silence ensued before Oliver broke it.

"I'm delighted my work in printing will help advance our cause," the recruit stated.

"Our cause? You catch on quickly!" Paul said laughing. He rose from his chair and began walking towards his bedroom and Rachel. "I have many other things to teach and show you, much of it involving your riding skills."

Oliver stood up, and said, "Oh?"

Revere nodded. "Get a good night's sleep. We'll talk more tomorrow."

He was halfway through his door when Oliver asked, "What about Paul Junior?"

The grown man smiled. "Tomorrow." With that, he entered his room and closed the door.

The boy raced up the stairs and was in his bed in seconds, forgetting that his steps might wake someone. The comfortable bed was once again so heavenly that he felt he could stay there for days if they'd let him. He rolled and turned and twisted over every inch looking for the most comfortable spot, but they were all equal. Closing his eyes, his mind didn't wander or process the day. The day's travels and excitement exhausted his mental reserves, and within a moment, he was off into a slumber's pleasant womb.

After breakfast, Paul Senior brought the young guest and new apprentice into his print shop to begin his training. Oliver began spending large amounts of time with Paul Revere. It was the leader's opportunity to learn not only about the boy's competence to do the job, which wasn't in doubt, but to further examine and judge his abilities and uses with the Sons of Liberty.

Paul explained in detail his commercial business that created books, pamphlets, and newsletters for various businesses and organizations, and designed and printed personal stationery for many of Boston's well-to-do citizens. But their primary mission had morphed into being an underground voice for the Sons of Liberty.

The British tried suppressing critical voices to the Crown, imposed taxes on newspapers, and occasionally confiscated printing presses. Smuggled paper was used to herald messages for mass persuasion as well as to create unity between the colonies. Couriers would ride copies up and down the East Coast to distribute to key people, most of whom were sympathetic to their cause, or downright enmeshed in it.

Revere wasn't the only one doing this. Benjamin Edes, the publisher of the original *Boston Gazette,* was also one of the Sons of Liberty. He became a mouthpiece for the rebellion, was arrested for sedition, but later escaped nine miles away to Watertown, Massachusetts, where he continued printing throughout the Revolutionary War. These men were not competitors, but complementarian to each other's work with the same goal in mind: Liberty, freedom of the press, and proper representation in Parliament.

Oliver picked up on the work quickly and learned easily from his mistakes. He wasn't paid a penny for his work. The Revere's provided him with room, board, clothing, and a trade.

"I think that's more than fair, sir," Oliver stated.

The young man was content with this and never asked for money. Occasionally he'd find a small sum on his pillow. He saved almost every penny he made, but would occasionally buy a sweet, or a birthday gift for someone in the large Revere family. If he splurged, it was on books.

By the spring of 1774, he was entirely dedicated to the Sons of Liberty. Beyond political reasons, Oliver was now convinced that God had allowed the struggles and injustices of his early life to prepare him for this glorious service and cause.

The print shop was called a "chapel" because of the large windows surrounding the interior on every side so that natural light could easily shine through to help the printer see what he was creating.

The light was important for another more serious reason: candles burned with fire, and fire near paper could be disastrous. Their work would often begin at sunrise and end before sundown for this very purpose. It was work that required great concentration and attention to detail. One wrongly placed letter, or word could alter the meaning of an important point, and cause confusion, not to mention embarrassment for the publisher. Their work, if continuously fraught with errors, would go elsewhere and they'd soon enough end up closing shop.

However, Revere was known for excellent work both in his print shop and smithing, and Oliver wanted to perpetuate that good will.

Oliver's contributions were noticed immediately. As an apprentice, after a few major mishaps early on, he quickly mastered typesetting and printing, but instead of moving on to continue training under master printers in New York, Philadelphia, or Charleston, Oliver stayed in Boston to work on behalf of the great cause. Sam Adams occasionally stopped by and would then leave after a minute and simply mouth, "Providence."

Oliver's print mastery allowed Revere more time to work on his goldsmithing with Paul Junior, who himself had become a superior craftsman with precious metals, designing fabulous works of art, jewelry, tea sets, and more, so that by the time the fall of 1774 arrived, Paul Senior basically spent his time as more an overseer than as one ingrained daily in the craft of either the print or goldsmith shop. This allowed him to continue in greater measure his smuggling business, as well as to begin creating networks of contacts within two hundred miles of Boston that would provide and trade intelligence regarding British troop movements and endeavors of the Crown.

The Boston winter of 1773-1774 was like any other, though Oliver was shocked at how cold, icy, and snowy it was, adding as many layers as possible before going outside.

"You walk like a duck, Oliver!"

"A snow monster!" said another as he threw an ice ball at the boy from Derby, only to see it bounce off of him without causing any pain.

His new friends realized that the extra layers absorbed blows from ice balls. Soon, all of them wore extra clothing when they played in the snow.

The rain he was used to, but not these other elements,

especially if he was near the harbor when the wind blew in from the sea. It cut right through the coat the Revere's gave him. So, if he had an errand, was out exploring, or playing games with some of the youth around his age, he would pad his body as thickly as possible. He waddled like a worm. He didn't care.

CHAPTER 7

Oliver and Junior were out on an errand for Mrs. Revere which required them to walk past Griffin's Wharf. Docked ships from the East India Company and private shippers filled the harbor, hoping to offload their goods before tensions got worse between the colonials of Boston and the Parliament. A couple of British warships were moored near the harbor's mouth to remind everyone who was in power.

As they were within thirty yards of one of the ships, Oliver noticed that it was *The Beaver* and froze. He tried lifting his legs to run but they seemed as heavy as cannon balls. Instead, he began shivering at first before a full-body shake took over.

Junior was carrying on about a chandelier he was creating for some so-and-so who worked for the governor when he realized Oliver wasn't at his side. Looking behind him, he witnessed his friend fall to the ground, shaking. He ran to him then he saw his frightened stare. Looking in that direction, he noticed the ship and knew it to be the one Oliver had stowed away on.

Junior knelt at his friend's side and wrapped his arms around him as if to shield him from any onlookers from *The Beaver*.

"I've got you, Oliver. You're safe with me. No one is looking."

Oliver began emerging from his state of mind, turning his head to Junior with pleading eyes.

"It's true. You are safe."

He lifted Oliver to his feet, while alternatingly looking back at the ship, put his arm around the terrified boy, and led him home.

Rachel rushed to his slide as Junior mostly carried the traumatized boy through the front door. They led him to his bedroom, where he crawled under the covers.

"Go get your father!"

She knelt at his side, clearing a wisp of hair from his face and dabbing his moist brow with a small green towel. She then prayed for him. "You are Jehovah Rapha, the healer of our mind, heart, and memories. Relieve your young servant, Oliver, this day, of his suffering, and restore him to wholeness according to your mercy and grace. Amen."

When Senior arrived, Oliver was of sound mind again, instructing him to take the rest of the day off.

Oliver avoided the wharf for the next year.

He loved his new life in Boston, though feared less and less about being sent back to Baron Effringham's estate, or to India, which he'd learned enough about to not ever want to go. Nothing he experienced was similar to anything else he had seen or done back in England. He even began attending an Anglican church with the Revere's that was just a few blocks from home. Sunday became Oliver's favorite day of the week—no work, which he still loved, but rest, play, a feast, and church.

At The Second Church, also known as the Old North Church, Oliver was introduced to a formal version of Christianity. Paul Revere was raised in a puritanical home, but he preferred the order and ritual of the Anglican Church, though never abandoned his puritan roots thoroughly as he would occasionally take Junior and Oliver to hear a fiery pastor at a Congregational church. Oliver heard about Jesus Christ, the Holy Spirit, and Father God at the Old North Church, but he heard the gospel for the first time at a Congregationalist meeting and thereafter became a passionate daily reader of the Bible.

The eager learner sadly discovered there wasn't a public library in Boston but still managed to find books to read wherever he could, even gathering them from perfect strangers by knocking on doors and asking if they had any they would like to discard, at no cost, he would emphasize. This way, he got his hands on all kinds of books. He quickly discerned within a few pages whether it would hold his interest and attention. And this method permitted him to save more of the money the Reveres gave him.

Though informative, he found many history books to be unnecessarily dry. Those that weren't excited him. He saw in them recurring themes: war, migration, authoritarian rule, and mass oppression. These were the constants of history. He saw its form in the relationship between England and America. Scriptures seemed to tell him that the human heart is desperately wicked, and that greed, and power drove the wars and caused many of the migrations. It gave more credence to the history he read. He wondered what point of this historical cycle he was in the middle of in the colonies. It seemed different, unlike any period he had ever read about. He quickly became aware of its uniqueness and would converse with anyone willing on this subject. Paul Junior was a fun friend but did not share his intellectual interests. Even most adults weren't interested in these conversations. This surprised him. That is not to say that no one had an opinion on the times in which they lived. But deeper dives into history and what they could learn from it to help them forge their path to liberty quickly got too deep for most.

That is, until he met John Adams, the second cousin of Samuel Adams, and also one of the leaders of the Sons of Liberty. John, whose piercing bright blue eyes seemed to know the thoughts of everyone he looked at, including Oliver, was considered one of the finest lawyers in Boston. This short, portly man, with a funny form of hair that made Oliver think of hair ear muffs that stretched high over his head while leaving a big bald spot on top, was so good at law and in the courtroom, he, much to the displeasure and vexation of his fellow patriots, successfully defended eight British soldiers who fired upon a group of citizens in self-defense in what became known as the Boston Massacre. In fact, his host, Paul Revere, created a famous print of the massacre that went up and down the colonies and was used to further invigorate opposition to England and the Crown.

Adams said the most important duty he could exhibit as a patriot was to uphold the rule of law. Without it, whatever they were hoping to achieve would be impossible, as "the law ... will not bend to the uncertain wishes, imaginations, and wanton tempers of men."

Oliver was fascinated with this man who was dismissive of young Atkinson, at first, mostly because he had little time for him due his work and family obligations. Adams' opinion of the "Boston Curiosity," as John labeled the boy after hearing second hand of his travel tales, pleasantly changed following a stroll one day.

The morning rain ended and the clouds vacated the sky, giving way to a cyan blue backdrop, giving Oliver opportunity to drop off personal stationery Revere's shop created for Mr. and Mrs. Francois Laurent, Boston's leading couple from France. Upon his return, Oliver ran into John Adams while on his daily constitutional.

"Mind if I walk with you, sir?"

"Of course, young Atkinson! I'd be delighted to have your company."

After asking John Adams about the trial, the boy told John, "Philosophically and practically, to be a civil society, fair trials are required, especially for your enemies and causes you stand against."

"And what law school taught you that bit of wisdom, young

Atkinson?"

Oliver shook his head and shrugged his shoulders. "I think I first thought of this when getting unfairly blamed for the breaking of a porcelain basin at my cousin's house."

"I see," the attorney said, cocking his head while his right hand upheld his chin. "Would you like to be a lawyer someday?"

"No, sir. Life as a printer suits me fine."

"That makes sense as I understand you work for Mr. Revere and like books?"

Oliver nodded. "Yes, sir, Mr. Adams. Very much."

Having arrived at the Adams home, the boy's new friend said, "I'll set out a few recommendations in my home study for you to read at your leisure."

When John wasn't home, his wife Abigail would allow him entrance into the study, always having cookies ready for him. All books had to remain in the room.

He got the feeling that while he was welcome, it was a busy home and didn't want to get in the way of the family. He didn't want to end up being tolerated and then despised being a constant presence. Occasionally, he would bring Abigail wildflowers he had picked on the way to show his gratitude. She'd quickly put them in a vase in the front foyer for all guests to see, which delighted him.

Oliver began reading books left out by Adams: Rousseau, Voltaire, Montesquieu, though he was already familiar with Locke, Hobbes, and Hume. Apparently, these philosophers influenced many in the Sons of Liberty, but not entirely.

John popped in during a quick stop at home and asked what his nose was in.

"I must confess, Mr. Adams, I don't understand much of what I'm reading, but to take a stab at it, it seems these writers keep trying to find the divinity of man in self-rule while being bound by their limitations. Most seemed not to care about the divine but instead emphasized reason and science. This is silly to me, no offense intended, sir."

"None taken, and I think you understand more than you realize."

"One more thing, if I may?"

"Please..."

"If law and society were to truly provide freedom to its people, that its people had to come under God's greater rule. Providence had to be submitted to. This means religion could not be governed by any civil government, or it would be tainted, twisted, and aberrant. God would be excused from service, and mankind would become abusive in His name."

John walked over to his writing desk and grabbed a pen and paper and motioned for Oliver to sit there. "Would you mind writing what you just said?"

He looked at the lawyer as if to say, "Me?"

"Please, Oliver."

Minutes later, as the last crumb of the last cookie entered his mouth, Oliver completed the task asked for by John Adams. His brain was full as his tummy was. Now, he hoped he could find some friends to play with.

CHAPTER 8

Except for the freezing weather, though, the boy from Derby loved living in Boston. It was so much nicer than Derby, he thought, and more exciting. Every week held new adventures for him. His favorite playtime thing to do was get kids from the neighborhood to have a snowball fight. Oliver didn't have the strongest arm for throwing snowballs, but he was accurate.

At times he and some friends would go to where they knew some Regulars were during or after snow and start a snowball fight, intentionally sailing their "ice rocks" over their opponents' heads to plunk a soldier. Of course, the soldiers would chase them off, and the boys would race through the crazy streets of Boston laughing until they found another group to do the same to. Oliver reasoned that they were just having fun, but his friends were made up of sons of the Sons of Liberty, so he knew there was more to their snowball wars.

During one particularly heavy snowfall, Oliver and his harmlessly mischievous crew of five boys were out for a walk. One of them a boy of African descent named Benjamin Kent was named after a white lawyer who took up the case of a slave against his master and won in 1766. Benji, as he liked to be called, was the son of a freed slave from Georgia who had migrated north to work in a factory that made hemp ropes for ships. These boys were walking the streets of Boston looking for a snowball fight with some boys from another neighborhood, or preferably, a few Redcoats to pummel. It was all in fun, and a few times some of the younger soldiers would laugh and toss snowballs back. However, that was a rarity.

This day was a day none of them would forget.

As they walked down King Street, the boys spotted ten British soldiers keeping warm by a contained fire in front of the State House, waiting their turn to police the streets when the other soldiers returned from their shift. Oliver motioned for the boys to halt before they exposed themselves to the men.

Paul Junior peeked around the corner of a brick building to see the soldiers and turned with a wicked smile to the crew. "Perfect," he said. "Sitting ducks!"

The excited young men began to quickly make snowballs and pile them upon each other as one would stack cannonballs. Once each of the boys was supplied, they nodded to Oliver, who then took another peek around the building and gave a thumbs up signal. "On the count of 'three,'" he commanded. And with his woolen-gloved fingers, he counted down from three to one.

All at once, the boys stepped out from the side of the building into an open area at a main thoroughfare on King Street and bombed the soldiers with snowballs. The unsuspecting soldiers couldn't discern between an actual attack and a snowball fight and raised their guns as one to fire.

"Stop!" a screeching voice shouted out of view from everyone, causing both groups to pause. "Stop now! Put down your guns this instant!" Paul Revere and Sons of Liberty founding member George Trott came racing into view, standing between the Redcoats and the boys. The soldiers held their aim steady as the boys dropped their snowballs and shook in fear.

Revere told Trott to go find their superior officer, who then took off running down Congress Street.

Looking at the soldiers, Revere shouted in a commanding voice, "Put down your arms! They're just boys who wanted a snowball fight."

The tension dissipated and they slowly lowered their weapons. Once Revere was satisfied, he speedily moved to the boys and dragged them around the corner and out of harm's way.

"Do any of you remember March 5, 1770? Do you?" Junior's father shouted angrily, glaring lastly at his son. "You remember, Paul, you remember! Your friend Christopher Seider, he was just like you boys, was shot and killed during a skirmish in which soldiers were antagonized, some with snowballs. Five colonials died from that massacre!"

"The Boston Massacre!" Oliver mumbled to himself.

The boys were scared out of their minds. They seemed frozen not because of the falling temperatures, but because of the sight of loaded muskets being pointed at them by young men thousands of miles away from home who were also afraid. Revere's wrath added to their state.

"These are unstable times, boys. We must all be careful how we engage the Regulars and their superiors." He paused for a moment, and his voice softened. "No more snowball fights with the Regulars. Go home to your families. Go!"

The boys took off in different directions, except Paul Junior and Oliver. Shaking, Revere looked down upon them with a combination of unnerved love and anger.

By now, Trott and a superior officer arrived at nearly the same spot as where the Boston Massacre had occurred, and where the soldiers stood before a fire. Paul and the boys stood ten feet away.

"What happened," the officer asked the men?

"The boys were throwing snowballs at your soldiers for fun," Revere explained. "Seems your soldiers took offense to this playful act and raised their guns to fire at the defenseless children. You should train them better."

The superior officer was offended at his remark, and spoke

firmly, "And you should teach your children history. You know what happened on this very same spot, Revere! Wars have started for more ridiculous reasons."

Paul and his boys turned away to leave, Trott saying, "We'll conclude our task tomorrow, Paul."

Revere nodded and walked off, motioning for the boys to follow him. No one said a thing as they walked home to the north side of Boston. The boys never forgot this near-death experience, but it was a settled matter in the Revere home, and once something was settled, it was never brought up again.

* * *

Most of Oliver's friends who were in his age range, give or take five years, were less concerned about liberty and freedom than they were pleasing their parents in school and catching the eye of the young girls they knew. Actually, that was the most important part of any of their days.

They were consumed by the thought of falling in love and marrying Sarah, Deborah, Martha, Jane, Alice, or Abigail. Even he began wondering what it might be like to hold a girl's hand or, dare he consider it, kiss her. He didn't know whether he needed to first fall in love to participate in such exotic acts, or that love would follow them.

The idea of romance made him anxious, causing his heart to beat a little faster, especially when around Molly Braddock.

One day, while Oliver was undergoing this awakening, Molly and her family sat in front of the Revere family at church. Suddenly, he noticed her. She smiled at him while sitting. Her mother noticed and glared back at Oliver, who quickly looked away. But during the service, he could not stop thinking about her. As the congregation sang, he began counting the auburn hairs on the back of her head that he would like to have run his hands through. He wondered if it would be alright for him as a boy to like pink the same color as the ribbon holding her brown locks together. During the transition from singing to sermon, Molly glanced back at him and smiled. He wanted to get up and run out of the church as fast as he could in fear for his life, thinking his heart would explode right there during an "amen," with pieces of his heart splattering the parishioners and pastor.

Oliver squirmed the entire service. Rachel and Paul thought he had to go to the bathroom. Junior knew it was about Molly.

Still, he resisted, and over time was able to slow down his heart rate enough so that when she smiled at him, he could smile back instead of looking at her in shock.

"How will you fight against the Redcoats if you can't even look at Molly Braddock without falling apart!" Junior would tease regularly. That is until Oliver caught him having the same episode while looking at Maggie Ashmore, who was visiting Junior's sister Deborah, and laughed until his sides hurt.

Maggie ran out of the house because of the two boys, angering Deborah who said Maggie wasn't "going to return until they stopped acting like children!"

Though an orphan, young Atkinson grew more accustomed to his daily life as an adopted Revere.

While sewing together some torn clothes, Rachel caught him staring into the fire one late afternoon and asked what he was thinking about.

Without looking up, he spoke solemnly. "My Dad and mum. How different life would've been had they not passed."

"May I sit next to you?"

He nodded, "Yes, Ma'am. That would be nice."

Their bond grew as Rachel placed an arm around his shoulder, rubbing his arm.

"And then I think about what my life would be like without you and your family." His head fell against her shoulder as mixed tears of loss and gain edged out onto his cheeks. A moment later, as he rubbed his face with a sleeve, he continued, "I think about England, but I don't miss England. Boston, America, this is my home. This is where I belong."

England receded to being only his birthplace, his origin. He felt the British system was designed to profit few, hold down most, and limit one's divine right to pursue life, liberty, and happiness. Like most of the rest of his fellow patriots, he still considered himself British, but increasingly he and the Sons considered themselves first citizens of Massachusetts, and then Americans.

The idea of the colonies uniting as one was at the fringe of their political and philosophical discussions. They all shared things in common, but instead of uniting as a confederation, they supported each other's right to self-governance. This would change soon enough, but not all at one time.

It didn't matter whether day or night, at the Liberty Tree near the Commons, the Green Dragon Tavern, or any secretive place, the Sons of Liberty seemed to meet more frequently than in the past. Tension between the colonies escalated with each day.

The loyalists, colonials who sided with Parliament and the Crown, continued in opposition to everything the patriots did. Families and churches were splitting. A Tory family would stop visiting Liberty families on holidays or to celebrate birthdays. But as time went on, with every egregious act, more seemed to be won to their cause. Walking the streets of Boston, conducting business, going to church, was becoming a social oddity, an uncomfortable experience for many. Tension between loyalists and patriots escalated.

CHAPTER 9

As the Sons of Liberty, and patriots from the thirteen colonies awaited England's response regarding the Tea Party, Paul Revere thought it best in the late winter thaw of 1774 to train his printer apprentice how to use a gun.

The patriots began stockpiling munitions in Concord at an armory, as well as in a few churches, and Revere was asked by John Hancock to perform a frequent inventory on the weapons and powder stored there. Not that they expected to go to war with Britain in 1774, but it was simply a matter of preparation in case something foolish happened.

Plus, Hancock would use his wealth to fund various needs of the Massachusetts militia, and this included munitions. Hancock approached this like he did all of his businesses and liked to plan for both the best and worst-case scenarios.

At the end of the day, Revere and Junior came into the printing office just as Oliver was cleaning up from a hard day's work.

The apprentice held up yellow 3x5 pieces of paper. "I fixed my error on the invitations for the John Lowell-Susanna Cabot wedding. You can take it out of my pay." Oliver smiled.

Paul walked over and grabbed his right shoulder and playfully tussled it. "How kind of you to offer since I don't pay you any money. Perhaps we can take it out of your meals?"

Junior added, "Yes, instead of five a day, we can move him to two until its equal value is paid off. Which could take months."

"We?" Paul asked, looking at his son, to which they all laughed.

Oliver took off his apron. "How about you consider my mistake a reasonable part of my training and let it go? Even five meals a day doesn't seem to be enough for me, much less two! I think I'd waste away."

"I couldn't allow that to happen. That would mean I'd have to return to my print shop fulltime and suspend all my other considerable activities," Paul said, winking at the boys. "Speaking of which, have you ever fired a gun, Oliver?"

"A gun? No, no sir, I haven't," he said, placing the invitations in a folder.

"Then you should learn. The three of us are riding out to Concord tomorrow. There are some outstanding places near there where I can teach you how to fire a musket."

"Who knows," Junior injected, "you may need to learn to hunt for your food if you keep making printing mistakes!"

"It was one mistake!" the apprentice replied with a sharp smile. He turned to Mr. Revere and said appreciatively, "I think I'd like that very much, sir."

The next morning before the rooster crowed, the three sleepy patriots saddled their horses and readied to ride. Paul Senior handed a wide-eyed Oliver a musket. "Our gift to you. We'll show you everything you need to know about owning this weapon. Take possession of it seriously."

Oliver took it in his hands, his eyes boring as deeply as the pre-dawn light allowed into every line of the five-foot-long musket.

"It's as tall as I am!" Oliver marveled. The Revere's proudly watched as he motioned with his hands up and down as if he were weighing the piece, then asked, "How do I carry it while riding?"

Junior showed him how to carry it across his lap and pointed out the little leather strap on his saddle to secure it. Paul handed him a wooden cartridge box covered with leather and a long deerskin sash to put over the head and carry across a shoulder.

"The cartridge box holds thirty rounds of shot and powder," Paul explained. "We'll show you how it works when we finish our duty later today."

Oliver chose to carry the musket on his lap. He figured this would be a smart exercise to learn as the musket would be a common tool of his. He wanted to get the feel for it, and eventually learn to shoot while riding.

With that, the excited little band turned south to Boston Neck on their way to Concord. Paul had a few quick stops to make along the way and wanted to be home by nightfall.

As they rode with the eastern sun at their back rising from its slumber, the details of the gun became clearer. Oliver studied as best as able while riding at a modest trot. "Other than the vicar's Bible and adoption into your family, this is the best gift I've ever been given."

He'd never really thought about firing a gun until every Regular he saw carried one. A few citizens did as well. He'd hear gunfire occasionally, and just assumed someone was shooting at a snake, some wildlife that had wandered too far into town, or that some drunken idiot fired his weapon randomly.

But as he held this beautiful "barking stick," as he heard an Indian call it once, his mind began judiciously considering its use for good or evil, for peace and for war, and not just to put food on the table. Guns were best held by hands who wanted peace. Otherwise, trouble for many would surely come, he thought. He couldn't wait to fire it. He wanted to be a peacemaker.

With gravity, young Atkinson wished out loud. "I hope I never have to fire this at another human."

Along their route to Concord, Paul made a few brief stops to update a few of the Sons of Liberty on recent happenings in Boston. The three travelers arrived at the armory about 10 a.m. Paul did his audit and was concerned by what he saw and didn't see. The stockpile he hoped to find was nearly gone. He learned that citizens had been "borrowing" weapons without returning them. Revere left strict orders for the armory to suspend this practice.

The three then departed southeast of Concord to a wooded area Paul knew was sparsely inhabited and still had some game left. Just in case.

"Game becomes scarcer the closer one gets to Boston," Senior said. "Hunters who make their living providing meat and skins have to increasingly go further west to find game. This intrusion into Indian-held lands has ignited tensions. Sometimes hunters don't return."

They steered their horses to a lake about five miles north of Concord. A few minutes later they came to a small clearing bordered by woods on either side, and the lake in front of them. No one else was in sight. They dismounted and walked their horses to some bushes and gently secured the reins to a Virginia rose bush.

Over the next hour, the Revere's showed Oliver how to break down and put the musket back together, how to clean and preserve it, and explained how often this should be done and why.

Once Oliver showed he understood what he was being taught by doing it by himself twice without coaching. He lifted the gun and said, "Can we get to shooting now?"

Paul laughed and said, "You will need to come up with a name for your rifle at some point, which is most often a woman's name."

Paul Junior opened the pan on top of his weapon, then took a cartridge from his pack with his right hand while holding the musket parallel to the ground with his left. He then lifted the cartridge pack to his mouth and bit it open, tearing it across with his teeth before spitting out the waste. Next, he poured a portion of the powder into the pan and closed it, before dropping the butt of the flintlock musket to the ground to pour the remaining contents of the pack down the barrel. Once this was done, to Oliver's surprise, Junior then stuffed the paper into the barrel. "This will help keep the ball and powder in the barrel while readying to fire."

"Where's the ball?" Oliver asked.

"At the bottom of the paper tube," Junior answered.

"Ahhhh," the novice responded.

"Now, draw out your ramrod from under the barrel, and jam it into the barrel a few times to make sure the contents are tightly packed. Do not lose your ramrod," Junior said intensely, "or your musket will be useless." Oliver nodded. "Replace the ramrod, take the hammer to full cock position, then shoulder your gun like this," demonstrating how to place the curved butt onto his right shoulder while pointing the gun at the intended target. "Fire by pulling the trigger."

Junior looked for a target, seeing a squirrel on a tree fifty paces away. "Supper."

Instantly and simultaneously, a deafening explosion shattered the serene environment as a wave of white smoke and sparks burst upwards from the hammer, clouding Junior's face, as the barrel nose spit out smoke, fire, and paper.

A squirrel fell from a tree branch to the ground dead.

"You're still the best shot in the family, Junior," Paul said. "Give it a try from start to finish," he said, looking at Oliver.

Oliver went through each step carefully, looking up at them a few times as he glanced at their faces for signs he was doing it correctly. Finally, he fully cocked the hammer and only then began looking for a target while waving his gun.

"Stop. Stop!" Junior yelled.

"What?" his friend asked.

Paul, more calmly, said, "Never point your loaded and cocked weapon without intention. Once it's loaded and cocked, you should be ready to fire. If it accidentally goes off it could kill someone. Hold it up and away from people until you have your target."

Oliver nodded as he looked for a target with the gun pressed against his shoulder, barrel pointing away from the Revere's. Eyeing a squirrel twenty paces away, he pointed his gun towards the creature, steadied the gun, and caught the fox squirrel in his sight. Then nothing. No kaboom from the musket. Silence. Oliver's hands began to shake, and the weapon with it. His tutors saw signs of stress on his face as the boy lowered his rifle away from them.

"What's the matter?" Paul asked.

"This is a weighty matter for me. I've never hurt anything in my life. The overwhelming sense of power and responsibility of what I'm about to do might be too much for me now."

A sullen silence hung in the air for a moment. Just as Senior was about to speak, Oliver continued. "Would you mind if I took my first shot at something other than a living animal? I'll get there, but I think a stationary target would be best this round." He wasn't really asking permission.

The sensitive young man surveyed the area and decided on running to an azalea bush thirty paces away. He took off his upturned brim-tricornered hat and placed it on top. Returning to their side where he first stood to fire, Oliver lowered the rifle to his shoulder, locked in on his hat through his sight, and fired.

The explosion knocked him backwards, tripping as he fell through the wafting smoke and landing on his backside as he watched his hat fly off the bush. Paul and his son were in hysterics, as Oliver rose quickly, dropped the gun and ran to his hat. There was a hole right in the center of it. Holding it up to show them, he smiled while running back. "You'll not believe this!"

The Revere's were amazed at his perfect shot. "Luck," Junior ribbed him. "Try again!"

"That's the best first shot I've ever seen," Senior said.

Oliver couldn't wait to show Molly Braddock, but by the time he had the courage to speak with her, she had moved her affections on to Jimmy Williams.

Still, the hat became a fantastic conversation starter, developing a legend all its own.

For the next hour, they practiced loading and shooting. As Oliver became more comfortable with the process, they then began to coach him on speed. Mr. Revere said, "A good musketeer should be able to get off three shots a minute." Each of them shot a squirrel, including Oliver, then cleaned them before they headed home.

As they rode, Oliver took off his hat a few times for a glance, shaking his head and smiling. Paul told stories as the boys listened intently, before they entered a period of discussing Sons of Liberty business, and the possibilities of a coming war. Paul somberly reminded them that he hoped it would be avoided, and they'd be free to rule themselves under the Crown.

By the time they reached the Revere home, they were hungry and tired. Rachel took the squirrels and roasted them with herbs and rendered pork fat, so that by the time the three had washed up, dinner was ready, and the Revere family gathered to say grace and eat.

CHAPTER 10

On June 1, 1774, there came a loud pounding at the Reveres' front door. Presuming once again a few Regulars were there to harass him as they often did, he waited a few minutes to open the door. He hoped the thick sheets of rain and thunder and lightning popping a few trees nearby would annoy them enough for them to seek shelter elsewhere. Instead, the thumping on the door continued.

"Revere, open up! It's Swan!"

Revere's mocking smile fled his face, and he rushed to the door and let in a soaking wet James Swan.

The man with the softest voice Oliver had ever heard for a man, boomed, "Paul, even I would've let in a Redcoat in this weather! Good gracious, man!"

"No, you wouldn't have," Paul smugly countered.

Swan paused, then agreed with a smile as he removed his drenched coat and handed it to Rachel, who graciously took it to the back porch to shake it off, then placed it next to the fireplace in their living room to dry.

The men walked a few feet across a newly installed yellow pine floor covered with various lightly-hued rugs to the pleasant, inopulent living area. Paul sat on a Windsor Chair while Swan took a Ladder-back chair with a seasoned-brown leather seat as sixteen-year-old Deborah Revere brought them coffee. Paul Junior and Oliver left their checkers game upstairs and raced downstairs when they heard a new voice in the home.

"Might we have some coffee, too, my sweet sister?" Junior asked. As much as she didn't want to cater to her brother, out of politeness because of the company, she smiled and poured the boys each a cup. Oliver added maple syrup to his as pure sugar had become scarce.

Paul and James sat opposite each other with the boys behind Senior. Out from the inside of his jacket pocket wrapped in oil cloth was a document. He leaned forward and handed it to Revere, who took it and removed the document from the cloth. The boys tried reading it over his shoulder as Swan sat back and quietly sipped his beverage.

It was titled, "The Coercive Acts, Boston Port Act, March 25, 1774." Revere read, his face tightening with anger. He looked up at Swan and was about to speak when his visitor interrupted.

Pointing to the document, Swan said, "That's the first reason why I am here."

"And the second is?" Revere asked.

Standing, Swan announced, "The blockade of Boston Harbor has already begun. Today, in fact."

Revere stood, then the boys.

"Adams and Hancock have called a meeting at The Green Dragon Tavern for 10 p.m. tonight." Swan grabbed his coat, nodded to Rachel and Deborah, and headed for the door. "I have a few other visits to make. I'll see you there." And he was out the door and into the storm.

Rachel came to Paul's side, touched his arm, and asked, "What does it say?"

Reading it again, he turned to her and looked at his children and Oliver. "The British have decided to make Boston pay for the tea that was destroyed and have blockaded the harbor allowing nothing in or out until both the cost of tea and the customs fees England would have gained from its sale have been fully paid."

The house was quiet. Paul walked to one of the front windows and looked out as lightning flashed against his face through the window. Turning to his family, he smiled and said, "This will be good for my smuggling business, and even better for liberty. But dark days are coming to Massachusetts. I hope the colonies unite with us."

"Mr. Revere, sir," Oliver said. Paul looked at the boy without speaking. "May I go with you tonight?"

Junior blurted out, "Yes, father!"

"Rachel?" Paul deferred to his wife.

She hesitated at first, then nodded.

Paul walked over to the two best friends and said, "Welcome to the Sons of Liberty. It has mostly been philosophy until now. Tonight, it becomes as real as life." The excited boys cheered. "We will go the long route to avoid the usual Redcoat posts. We leave in an hour." To the boys he said, "Ready the horses."

The boys raced outside through the back door and into the softening rain, Rachel calling out to them to first put on their coats. But they were gone. Paul turned to Rachel, "Would you mind packing some food and drink for us? We might be there all night."

An hour later, the boys had the horses ready to ride and had changed into dry clothes, each wearing a coat. Rachel had prepared a meal for the three Sons of Liberty: Pork, corn, biscuits, and a canteen of water were placed in blue and white checkered cloth bags.

The boys kissed Rachel on her right cheek as they exited the home. Paul stopped and gave her a big kiss on her lips, his eyes showing his deep love for her.

"This is serious, isn't it, Paul?" she asked.

"Parliament and the King are determined to make us enemies. They are after our money. We are after freedom. Who do you think will win in the end?"

They kissed again before Paul raced out the door and into the night. Rachel heard three horses galloping away as Deborah came and held her mother's hands saying, "It was a different world when we woke up this morning," the girl said.

Rachel hugged her and said, "May God have mercy on us all."

* * *

All the Sons of Liberty were on time and arrived without incident to the rustic Green Dragon Tavern. The noisy pub was lit by dozens of lanterns, revealing faces of both fearful and excited men sitting on simple benches at long, worn-out wooden tables. Patrons usually drank ales, beers, and ciders heavily from various pewter mugs delivered by young maidens in ceramic pitchers, but tonight, solemn sobriety kicked gaiety out the door.

Hancock and Adams stood on benches, and without fanfare, got everyone's attention. As the loud hum dissipated, Hancock was the first to speak.

He held up a copy of the Coercive Act regarding Boston Harbor with his left hand and paused, all eyes upon the document, then finally said with a smile, "Diplomacy!" The serious souls in the Green Dragon Tavern suddenly erupted into laughter.

Adams slapped his friend Hancock, the leading voice for diplomacy, on the back, and proclaimed, "In the annals of Boston, nothing ever more egregious than this has been forced upon us!"

The crowd shouted, "Hear! Hear!"

"To summarize, because of a few ruffians..." He paused as the men laughed again. "The English Parliament and our Mad King George III, has decided that all of Boston is to reimburse the British East India Company for the tea lost during our glorious three-hour party, and the Crown for the customs they would've earned on said tea."

Men shouted various things, like, "How dare they!" and "My

wife wasn't there!"

Hancock raised his hands, quieted the men down, and continued.

"The Royal Navy has closed the port until the debt has been settled. Nothing comes in and nothing goes out. This will obviously have an impact on us economically, so we must be committed to our cause. Is your will for freedom greater than their will for your money?"

The men shouted all at once a hearty approval.

Hancock continued. "As you know, a few of us run operations that skirt the port and its customs, and we will be more reliant upon them than ever. Simultaneously, England will be more determined to shut down our smuggling operations. I'm going to ask Paul Revere to appoint men to keep an eye on all naval and soldier movements, as well as keep an eye on Parliament-appointed officials. We need to be able to bring in and smuggle out goods for our survival."

"As you wish, John. Many of my sources are already in place." Revere said confidently.

"Ahhh, yes, The Mechanics!" Hancock offered. Revere nodded as Adams carried on.

"I understand that Parliament is considering more acts against the colonies, so don't misconstrue this as being our darkest hour. It's not yet war, men, but something must give, and it won't be us!"

The men hollered approvingly once more, then quieted down when Adams raised his hand again.

"Does anyone have anything to add? Any questions?"

Remarkably, the room remained silent for thirty seconds until Oliver raised his hand and stepped forward. Adams and Hancock looked at each other, before Adams said, "Many of you know Paul Revere's young protege, Oliver Atkinson." Looking at the boy, he calmly said, "Please, Oliver, share with us your questions or thoughts."

"Well, sir," the young man cleared his throat, "It seems logical to me that the prime minister, Parliament, and the King have done this for more than punitive reasons to recoup the costs of the tea and the following customs." Oliver looked around to see if he had lost any listeners.

"Go on," Hancock said.

"From what I've learned and witnessed, our noble group has grown in recent months, but not all Bostonians are in agreement with us. In fact, many are in full support of the King. Forgive my possible heresy, but even some who might be sympathetic to our cause could have their arms twisted hard enough behind their backs economically to finally turn against us when the pain gets too much."

"Are you suggesting they are trying to create a civil war between Bostonians, perhaps between those of this region?" asked a young man from Connecticut named Benedict Arnold. Arnold spent much of his time in Boston, and specifically at the tavern, to coordinate his arms and ammunition-smuggling operations to supply his fellow patriots in the north.

Oliver cleared his throat again and swallowed hard before continuing with all eyes upon him. "Without knowing what other acts are being considered and will ultimately pass in Parliament, and I understand I am not nearly as educated in these matters as you fine patriots, and am but a mere youth, but I would venture to guess that they will enact legislation that will reduce whatever autonomy and rights all of the colonies are chartered for as a show of might, strangling us and turning us against one another so we give up and willfully return to the tyranny that will certainly await us in greater measure. They are counting on us coming to our senses to see that there's no way our different colonies could unite, muster forces, raise money, and be committed to taking on the world's strongest nation." The boy paused for a moment. "That's what I think, sirs." With that, Oliver stepped back to Paul Revere's side, with both he and his son putting their hands on one of the protégé's shoulders and squeezing.

Hancock and Adams, as well as all men present, were stunned by the astuteness of this new Son of Liberty. He was right, they thought. This was as much about dividing the colonies and setting them against each other as it was about dividing Bostonians and people in Massachusetts.

Hancock then said, "Paul, get your printing press humming and meet with the mechanics quickly." Revere nodded his head. "These Coercive Acts..."

"Intolerable Acts," boomed Sam Adams, with all men cheering on his response.

Hancock continued while nodding. "These Intolerable Acts cannot be allowed to divide us. They must unite us! We have our work cut out for us, men. We need riders and those with boats that can sail down the coast to take copies to major ports in the thirteen colonies. Immediately. We must see how they respond to this. Adams and I will write an accompanying letter to each colony to be included with these Intolerables, with much appreciation to Mr. Atkinson." Hancock gave a single nod to Sam Adams before taking a step back to indicate he was finished speaking.

Adams entreated the men to continue discussing this change in history, and to figure out what their roles were to be for the next chess move between themselves and the British Empire. By three in the morning, all the men had returned to their homes.

Indeed, it was a different world.

* * *

Paul Revere had his printing press humming as Hancock ordered first thing that morning. Other like-minded printers did as well.

While Revere still took business orders, as he needed to provide for his family, much of the print work and engravings were devoted to heralding the cause of liberty. The hour was never more crucial than the present to convince and recruit for the cause of freedom in Massachusetts and their sister colonies. While a few colonies already had a branch of the Sons of Liberty, the work now was to help awaken those who were otherwise still loyalists.

The patriot leaders knew they weren't going to convert all the Crown's loyalists but were certain these new laws from Parliament could be used to drive more sensible thinking citizens realize that what was occurring was unjust, economically destructive and punitive, and that they should be able to run their own lives.

It was commonly agreed on that while a revolution and war against England was becoming a frightening possibility, the general hope remained for representation in Parliament, or autonomy and self-rule under the Crown. If neither were granted, then it might well necessitate something more drastic. If it came to this, they understood that they weren't ready. Not even close.

As the messengers flew by horse, boat, and foot up and down the coast, from east to west, the Parliament continued releasing more Coercive Acts designed to flex their power and dishearten colonial citizens to the point of putting down the uprising in their own statehouses.

All of the Coercive Acts had been passed and posted in the colonies by the summer of 1774. Joining with the Sons of Liberty was a growing number of sympathetic patriots who called these the Intolerable Acts. They were a series of four laws designed to enact punishment and inflict economic harm to Boston, primarily, and the colonies in general, as a disciplinary response to the Tea Party.

"We really kicked a hornet's nest, didn't we?" Sam Adams asked his cousin John while dining at a family member's birthday celebration.

"A hornet's nest doesn't have the British army or navy at its disposal," he retorted.

These Intolerable Acts included the authorization of a blockade of Boston Harbor to stifle the commercial hub of the city and beyond. It didn't take long for the colonists to feel the pinch. They couldn't ship anything out to foreign ports, and the only incoming freight were provisions that supplied British officials and the army. Until full restitution was made, the harbor was closed for business.

The next part of the Acts was the Massachusetts Government Act, passed on May 20, 1774, that dissolved the elected Massachusetts Council and replaced these men with appointees of the Crown. It gave the British Governor of Massachusetts the power to choose judges, sheriffs, and jurors at whim, removing from the colonials the ability to police themselves, create local laws, and rule in the court system. The Sons of Liberty, and the growing number of those who sympathized with them, saw this as a direct attack on what modest representation they had.

Also passed on May 20, 1774, was the Act for the Impartial Administration of Justice. This allowed the Massachusetts Governor to arbitrarily move trials to another colony, or even to Great Britain, eliminating the right to a trial by one's peers. This obliterated an English right dating back to the Magna Carta, one that Oliver recognized when reading this act.

The Quartering Act was passed on June 2, 1774, and was the only one of the four acts to directly affect all thirteen colonies. Massachusetts was no longer alone in the grand suffering the Crown intended to impose upon the rabble rousers in America. Housing British troops had been a long-standing issue between Britain and the colonies. Up until this point, troops were often made to live an inconvenient distance away from where they kept an eye on the colonists. Now, senior officers were allowed to take over any uninhabited building, barn, outhouse, or stable, to quarter their soldiers. Sam Adams remarked, "Why not my marital bed, too?" This put British troops right in the midst of the colonists, eliminating privacy, commandeering property that the owner could no longer use for their own purposes, and turning their properties into military bases.

As more Americans learned of and understood The Intolerable Acts, public opinion clearly changed and growing sentiment to the cause of liberty replaced indifference and loyalty to the Crown for many.

While no one had been injured, no fires had been set, and no ships had been destroyed, the musket-free Boston Tea Party became the catalyst that set off the American Revolution and would lead to Lexington and Concord ten months later and the infamous "shot heard around the world."

CHAPTER 11

With these acts, a powder keg had been rolled out into the town square by the British, daring the rebels to set it off. The Sons of Liberty and the leaders of the thirteen colonies knew they had to respond to the Intolerable Acts. Though originally suggested by Ben Franklin, the Virginia Committee of Correspondence advocated that delegates elected by the people or legislatures from all thirteen colonies attend a convention in Philadelphia. All agreed to participate except Georgia.

A new day was gifted to the cause of freedom. The sun was about to rise after yet another late meeting at The Green Dragon Tavern attended by the leaders of the Sons of Liberty to update and discuss with each other the blockade's current impact, when Mr. Revere woke Oliver and asked if he'd be interested in doing something different that day. "We haven't any current orders that need immediate fulfillment. Would you like to go for a ride? I'll see you at the stable." The Sons of Liberty leader was halfway out the door before he could respond.

The groggy young man dressed and ambled downstairs as his fog dissipated. He stopped only to grab a few strips of bacon and biscuits that Rachel had readied for him. "Thank you, Mrs. Revere," he said slurring as he stepped out the back door.

Though June, cool morning air enveloped his face. Once he smelled the scent of horses, their manure, he awoke fully and raced to his horse that had been readied by Paul Junior and hopped on like a show rider. As soon as his backside hit the saddle, Paul

Senior was off like a musket ball, laughing as he went.

"You're as good a rider as my father. Go prove you're better!" Junior said.

"Checkers tonight?" Oliver hollered as he sped away, with Junior calling out after him.

In a minute, Oliver caught up to Revere and flew past him, thinking they were going to leave Boston-proper by the usual way of the Boston Neck at the South End. But Paul turned right across a small field and cut through the yard of sneering loyalist Simon Williams, waving to him as he raced past. Oliver wheeled his horse around and headed to Fox Hill at the edge of the Charles River. The slight incline was traversed easily by the horse. It led to a decline to the water's edge, where he caught up with Revere.

A man with only a few teeth, wearing a thick pea coat and wool hat, waved them over to a small rowboat. Oliver followed Paul's lead and got off his horse. Looking to their right, they saw a few British ships sitting still in the harbor. The boatman said, "They came in yesterday. General Gage has brought in the four-thousand new troops our beloved King George promised in hopes of teaching us a lesson."

"Message received loud and clear, King George," Revere responded.

A different man wearing all green came from around some bushes and grabbed the reins.

Paul greeted him. "Isaac."

The man nodded while looking at Oliver. "Your return, Paul?" he asked.

"Today before sunset," the Son of Liberty responded. "Isaac Edwards, this is Oliver Atkinson."

"Mr. Edwards."

The man with few teeth climbed on board the skiff, as did Oliver and Revere, and without saying a word, proceeded to row across the unusually choppy Charles River.

Oliver had learned when to speak and ask questions and when to observe. He learned by listening and observing, not talking. Silence also allowed him to think through what was happening and going to happen creatively and circumspectly, look for clues, interpret coincidences, but most of all, enjoy the adventure that had become Boston, the Revere Family, and being part of the Sons of Liberty.

It was for this purpose that Paul Revere had chosen to take the teenage boy with him, because he had proven himself trustworthy to Adams, Hancock, and the others in their rebellious band. Paul felt it was time to elevate the boy's experience and understanding.

Today was to be a special day for young Atkinson, Paul believed. He originally planned to introduce Oliver to some members of his growing spy ring, a group less-than innovatively known as the "The Liberty Boys," though Revere preferred the name, "The Mechanics," which is what they preferred as well. It gave them some anonymity from the Sons of Liberty while being a subgroup of them.

The Mechanics were craftsmen, artisans, small businessmen, and farmers, men just like Revere, who were increasingly longing for self-rule and the removal of British forces and governmental appointees from America altogether.

Paul Revere had established the first patriotic spy ring in existence, designed to keep track and gather information and intelligence on the British army and their movements, as well as that of British officials in and around New England, with a focus on Massachusetts. It was secretive to the point that Revere didn't discuss their activities with most of the members of the Boston Sons of Liberty.

To meet them, Revere would ride out to the Charlestown area, about three miles from where he'd come ashore, to a secret meeting place that changed every month. However, it wasn't unusual, especially once the Intolerables were enacted and they got further into an increasingly tense 1774, that special meetings would be called not only in Charlestown but other locations around Boston to be unpredictable.

Once they arrived at the opposite shore, a man met them with two horses. Revere and the man only nodded. Oliver did the same, and it was returned by the stranger. Climbing on, they rode off to Charlestown.

A short distance from the embarking point, Revere disclosed to the boy what they were going to do as they walked their horses toward their destination.

"This isn't just a fun ride in the country. I have a meeting with The Mechanics you can't attend. That may come in time. But let this demonstrate a measure of confidence I have in you to bring you this far."

"Thank you, sir. What will you have me do while waiting?"

"I need you to be a lookout. There is a feeling that some loyalists have got wind of our gatherings, which usually occur at night—hence our day visit. If you see a group of any size moving with seemingly bad intentions, you immediately ride as hard as you can two hundred yards south of here yelling, "Disperse!" Do you understand?"

The boy felt equal pride and humility. "I will remain alert, sir."

It seemed to Oliver that the cool morning was all-at-once a typical hot June day. He found a large oak tree for shade and waited three hours for Mr. Revere to conclude his business. He saw nothing to concern The Mechanics.

However, he kept looking at a dozen African slaves in various duties in a field not far from him. A white man on a horse rode around them barking out orders and cracking a whip. Until that moment, he'd not considered how their cause of freedom intersected with the plight of black people. It had never been addressed by the Sons of Liberty in his presence. It also occurred to Oliver that he hadn't seen any black people at any Sons of Liberty meetings. He intended to ask Mr. Revere why.

Principles were important to Oliver and to the men he looked up to regarding the cause of freedom. It seemed they would be equally concerned about the rights of blacks to be free and full active participants in government and society. He reasoned that there had to be more to the story that he just didn't understand. He committed himself to finding out if the Bible had anything to say on this matter.

Oliver's thoughts were interrupted by the prettiest girl he'd ever seen as she rode past him in a small open carriage with an older woman at the reins. The girl gave him the biggest smile he'd ever received. For a moment, there were no Mechanics, no Sons of Liberty, no Beaver, Tea Party, Baron Effringham, no Molly Braddock—his crush for her ending that very instant, or the town of Derby. It was as if the sun and sky fled away, along with the homes, scenery, and even the slaves, and only she was left. He stood and nearly tripped over his feet but caught himself while watching her giggle in his direction. The adult woman gave her a stern look, but the girl turned back once more for a final glance.

His dream-like state was intruded upon by a familiar voice.

"Oliver!" The boy turned to see Mr. Revere approaching him in a trot from twenty yards away. Paul stepped into a stirrup and up he went, ready to ride. "Are you as hungry as I am? There's a tavern a short ride from here."

After linking their horses to a post outside of a large two-story brick and wooden home, Paul Revere and Oliver Atkinson took off their hats and knocked dirt off their shoes before entering. The inn had a large, stone fireplace to the right that crackled with the sound of seasoned wood. A small bar was in the back left. The walls were empty except for two aged tapestries on the wall opposite the fireplace. Three twenty-foot-long tables were perpendicular to the door, each having three sets of six-foot benches on each side. A few feet from the fireplace were stairs that went upward. Another door was square in the middle back that led to the kitchen. The place was empty of patrons.

The two sat down and were served a meal of sugared bacon, a ham sandwich, and coffee by a woman who walked as if gliding across a ballroom floor and looked like the one he'd seen a short time earlier on the carriage. Voraciously the two ate, until out of the corner of his right eye, Oliver saw the girl from the carriage emerge from the kitchen with a plate of fresh rolls and butter. She was wearing a sky-blue dress bordered with white lace, and a pink apron. The boy stopped chewing, dazed as if by an unseen punch. She almost dropped the rolls as her heart skipped a beat when she saw the young man. Composing herself, she walked to their table and presented the items. "Please enjoy. May I get you anything else?" she asked as she stared at Oliver with eyes as blue as her dress, who stared back, open-mouthed and still in mid-bite.

Paul noticed, then nudged the young man. "Oliver, aren't you going to answer?" he said, looking at the girl.

"Pardon me. My name is Clara Cole. My father is the owner of this tavern."

As well as beauty, Oliver thought she had the sweetest voice he had ever heard. He swallowed and stood up, then spoke in his deepest voice to appear as manly as a fourteen-year-old could.

"My pleasure to meet you, Clara Cole. My name is Oliver Atkinson. May I introduce you to…"

Finishing his sentence, she said, "Paul Revere. He's a friend of the family."

Paul kindly nodded his head with a smile. "Hello, Clara. Turning his head toward the kitchen, he pointed with his eyes.

"Well look who it is!"

All eyes turned towards Paul's object of speech, as Charles Cole, short and wiry with arms the size of butter churns, approached with a wave and a smile.

"Chased out of Boston by General Gage again?" the tavern owner jokingly asked.

"We do the chasing, Charles," Paul retorted.

Oliver shook Mr. Cole's hand as Clara stood close, glancing between her dad and Oliver. "My name is…"

"Oliver Atkinson. Yes, I heard you speak last June 1. A young patriot, indeed!" Mr. Cole said. Oliver looked surprised he knew him.

"You know him, Daddy?" his mannered daughter asked. This made her even more interested in the young man.

Her father saw the obvious crush she had on Oliver, so he turned to him and said, "The next time you are out this way, perhaps you will join my family for dinner?"

Oliver swallowed hard while looking at Clara's pleading eyes. "Yes, yes, sir, I think I'd like that very much. If Mr. Revere agrees?" His head swiveled to Paul.

"Of course. And let there be a standing invitation to you and your family to join us in Boston for dinner," Paul offered.

What Oliver didn't know was this was a part of Paul's plan for the day. He wanted the two to meet. So did Mr. Cole. He was so incredibly impressed with Oliver's speech at the announcement of the Intolerable Acts that he made a beeline for Paul to inquire about the boy.

Paul thought to himself, "So this is what 'love at first sight' looks like" from the outside. He'd felt the same when he met his second wife Rachel. He had seen her cross a street one day and his heart was undone.

The two youngsters stole glances and traded sweet smiles as the men ate. Once the two had finished their meal and paid, Revere saw Oliver stand and stare at Clara. "Go say goodbye, Oliver," Revere said.

Oliver mustered up all the courage he could, walked up to Clara, and said, "I'm going to marry you someday," to which she inhaled a short breath, put her hand to her chest, then let out a muffled squeal of joy, before recomposing herself. Her father, and mother Trudy, watched from the kitchen door. The suddenly gallant young man took her right hand and kissed it, then turned and ran out of the tavern as fast as he could. Paul was waiting for him, already saddled and ready to go.

"I think she likes you," Revere offered to a red-faced Oliver Atkinson, as they turned their horses back where they had come from.

"My heart feels like it's about to explode!" Paul laughed. "No, seriously. I might need medical care!"

It was a relatively short ride back to the waiting skiff that would take them back across the Charles River. The excitement of meeting Clara overwhelmed him, but the question of slavery bored its way back to front of his mind. "May I ask you a question, Mr. Revere?"

"About Clara?"

"No, about slavery."

"Oh. Well, yes, of course. But are you telling me after meeting Clara this was the first thing you wanted to talk about on our journey back home?"

"Strange, I know. If I may be honest, I think I'm going to marry her someday. And she will attend to most of my thoughts for the next few decades. I hope, of course. But I was so burdened thinking about Africans and slavery while waiting for you as I watched a few being mistreated by a man with a whip. Frankly, if I may be blunt, sir...?"

"Go right ahead, Oliver."

"It seems hypocritical that we are fighting for our freedom while keeping a people in bondage simply because we can. Please help me understand. What don't I know?"

They rode across an open fallow field in silence for a few minutes before Paul spoke up.

"I saw a man, an African man, a slave, hanged for murdering his master a few years back. His name was Mark. His master was abusive, wouldn't sell him to another master, and was violent towards him and a few other of his slaves. Tiring of this and seeing no way out, the slaves were driven to murder John Codman. You and I have ridden by that hanging tree on our way to Concord and Lexington a few times. You haven't noticed but I look at it each time and ask myself the same question you just did."

He paused for a few seconds as Oliver painfully listened.

"There have been many private discussions among the Sons of Liberty regarding this matter, and we are convinced Massachusetts is, hopefully, but a few short years away from abolishing slavery once and for all time. However, as our problems with Britain escalate, we realized we need all thirteen colonies to unite if we are to be successful in overcoming our own bondage to the Crown. If we press slavery as an issue, we will lose a few of them and we will be further driven into our own bondage, unable to free anyone. It is the hope of many in the North that Christian reason will win out in the South eventually. But until then, for the sake of liberty for all men, slaves included, we must be victorious now and stay this course. This is where our moral energy is spent, and our lives offered for its sake. Morality shouldn't come in grades, but it often does. We are but broken men relying upon Providence to direct us, trusting His will be done in this fallen world. We must fight this battle before we can move on to the next one. This answer may not satisfy you, Oliver. I simply don't have any other."

Oliver thought about what Revere had just shared and finally spoke. "Thank you. I am going to have to think about this further."

"As well you should," Paul encouraged. "When you have developed a more formal opinion on this matter, I'd appreciate hearing it," his mentor said.

"Now, what can you tell me about Clara and the Cole family?" the teenager asked.

* * *

The Revere printing press, mastered now by Oliver, kept humming along, running off manifold pamphlets, documents, notices, and papers, almost all having to do with the business of liberty and the mounting aggression of the British empire not just upon Massachusetts, but all thirteen colonies. Their dissemination was handled by runners who raced their horses to villages, hamlets, and cities as far south as New York City. What seemed worthy for continued circulation south was then reprinted under the banner of a local printer and hustled further south by pony.

Boston had become such a troublesome port for those seeking redress against the Crown that they employed other ports, even small docks, from which to get their materials onto ships sailing south, using Dutch and French vessels to do so. They would run these materials to Alexandria and Norfolk, Virginia, Wilmington, North Carolina, Charleston, South Carolina, and Savannah, Georgia.

Oliver had some help now; Benjamin Kent, the son of a freed slave who was with him when he and his friends were nearly shot by Regulars after pelting them with snowballs, and Tristan Beckwith, an older boy of sixteen who walked with a limp and was deaf. Paul's pastor asked him to teach Tristan a trade. "Grant that he learns the printed word, my dear brother Paul, because apart from a miracle, he will never know the spoken word," he requested.

Tristan quickly caught on and even taught the other two boys some sign language, which Benji mastered over time.

The extra help was needed because of the increasing volume of work, but also because there had been discussions among some of the leaders of the Sons of Liberty about the future need to print their own currency if there was war with Britain. It was planning at its best, with all still hoping for a peaceful resolution.

Besides the prospect of printed money and the ongoing aspect of his business, Revere saw Oliver's role with the patriots changing, especially after a conversation he had with John Adams one evening while both took a casual stroll together on Boston's cobbled streets. Adams was heading to Philadelphia in early August. Fellow Massachusetts citizens Sam Adams, Thomas Cushing, and John Hancock were representing their colony at the First Continental Congress.

"We need someone reliable who can act as a local runner to keep us in paper and ink as well as be a lookout. Someone young but mature, with proven allegiance to our cause, who has superior riding skills would be of great benefit in case we need to quickly get word back here. Do you have any recommendations, Paul?" he asked smiling.

Revere paused with a chuckle before continuing the stroll. "At fourteen he's less likely to be a threat to any roaming bands of Redcoats and nosy loyalists. I'll ask him if he's interested."

On August 1, 1774, Paul Revere poked his head into the print shop as Oliver demonstrated a printing technique to Benji and Tristan and called for him.

Excusing himself, he followed Revere outside, who said, "John Adams wants to have a word with you." Oliver looked concerned. "No, Oliver, you've done nothing wrong. At least that I know of!" He laughed. "Go clean up and then head over to his office. He's expecting you."

With hands on his hips, Oliver smiled at Mr. Revere and said, "What are you two brewing now?"

"You do love adventures, don't you?" This perked the boy up. "Go. Go on. I'll help the boys today."

Oliver sprinted to the house, washed up, changed into his church clothes, and was out the door and off to John Adams' home office in mere moments.

CHAPTER 12

PHILADELPHIA

Oliver ran the half mile to a row of large brick homes adorned with ornate glass windows that held box planters, each filled with a variety of flowers. It suddenly dawned on him that he didn't want to be sweaty in the Adams' home, so he slowed to a walk.

Spotting the home with the large forest green door, Oliver took a few breaths as he measured each step that led to a gray stone-slab stoop. The white trim looked freshly painted. A large brass knocker in the shape of a pomegranate beckoned him to knock.

Abigail answered the door in a modest dark blue dress and white smock with her usual warm smile and invited him in. "Master Atkinson, I saw you through the window. My husband is expecting you."

She led him down the hall, whose walls were covered with landscape paintings and a few silhouettes, past the library he'd been in more than a few times, and turned right into John Adams' office, which the young man was seeing for the first time.

The room had nearly as many books as his library did. "He'll be with you in a moment. Please sit down," she said while drawing her right arm toward one of two green velvet chairs placed in front of a large desk. He obeyed as she left the room. It smelled like leather and lilac, and all the furniture, from his desk to the paneling and bookshelves, was a rich, burnt mahogany. An open law book sat on his desk next to a quill and ink bottle. He gazed at the many books on the shelves behind the large, polished desk and high-backed chair.

John came in and welcomed the boy by playfully saying, "You probably now think I've been holding out on you by not giving you access to this part of my library." Oliver shot out of his chair and extended his hand which Mr. Adams took. "Please sit. Thank you for coming on such short notice."

"I'm happy to, sir. Is everything alright?"

Adams chuckled as he motioned behind and over his head to the leather spined tomes and law books. "I use these in my law practice. I must confess, in spite of your ambition to be a printer I've been secretly hoping you'd be interested in the law."

"Upon meeting you, sir, I momentarily considered the law, Mr. Adams. But Mr. Revere has graciously chosen to teach me a skill and vocation that I can earn a living for the rest of my days. I quite like it."

"Well, that's fine, very fine, Oliver. It is a gift from God to be able to follow our hearts desire. I guess I'll not try and persuade you to consider my profession, then."

Abigail entered with tea and a plate of Cry Baby cookies, made of plum puree, oats, and a little butter. She placed them on a small table next to her husband's desk as he and the boy thanked her for the treats. They helped themselves. They were so delicious Oliver noticed he ate the first two faster than was polite, though he wanted to consume the entire plate. John sat back and looked at the young man while nibbling on one.

Wiping crumbs from his mouth, Oliver asked, "How can I be of service to you Mr. Adams?"

Leaning forward, the lawyer asked, "How would you like to travel with me to Philadelphia next week?"

The boy paused his eating, his eyes wide – "An adventure!"

"Of course, we will be traveling with my cousin, Sam, Mr.

Hancock, and Mr. Cushing. Have you heard of the Continental Congress that is gathering there?"

"I have, sir. You want me to go with you?"

"Yes, we all do. Mr. Revere is in full agreement with us," Adams assured him.

"I would be honored, Mr. Adams! What would you have me do?"

John Adams went on to explain to the boy loosely what his plans for him were. "It will require you to travel great distances alone in harsh environments under stress. Your life could be called to account. What we are doing will be considered treasonous by Parliament and the Crown. We will need riders to quickly deliver messages to key publications and people not attending this congress and then return for the next wave of dispatches. It will be difficult, tiring, monotonous, and dangerous." He sat back and looked at the boy's face and posture, seeing exactly what he thought he'd see: confident competence and juvenile excitement all at once.

"I'm certain it will be everything and more that you've described. How can I not have confidence in myself to accomplish all you ask, if you say so, Mr. Adams?"

John Adams was quite pleased, but not surprised, at Oliver's response. "You often speak like an adult," Adams offered.

"My parents said the same thing when I was five."

Adams nodded as if to say, "Of course," then went on to explain what he'd need to bring. He would be coached on unique travel methods through the colonies, secretive ways to connect with those patriots in the know, and where to get fresh horses, housing, and food. He was also told what to avoid, what to flee from, and what, where, and whom to fight if it ever came down to it.

"Welcome to our inner sanctum, young man. Without sounding too dramatic, we are entrusting you with secrets and with our lives." He reached out his right hand, which Oliver excitedly shook for a moment, saying nothing.

"Any last thoughts before I get back to work?" the gentleman patriot asked.

"I've never been so speechless in my life. Thank you. Thank you, sir, and thank you to Mr. Hancock, and Mr…" John cut him off.

"I'll be sure to express your gratitude to them all, Oliver."

The handshake finally ended, and Oliver floated dreamily out the door, passing by Abigail, who handed him a small cloth bag full of Cry Baby cookies, with a "Goodbye, Mrs. Adams, and thank you!" as he let himself out the door four hours after arriving.

He didn't head straight for the Revere home or the print shop next door, but down towards Griffin's Wharf to where *The Beaver* had first docked. It was the first time he'd been able to be this close without having an anxiety attack. Yet he was still one-hundred yards away. A new ship was in its place.

He took a panoramic view of the area, trying to remember everything from the night Paul Revere freed him from the brig and brought him into his life, his world, to America. The young patriot fell to his knees and thanked God for His providence in bringing him from Derby to this land. Then rolling waves in his chest pushed out burning tears on his rosy cheeks. As his heaving subsided, he looked up and noticed people staring at him from about twenty yards away, and a Regular approaching him.

"Are you alright?" the Regular asked.

Oliver got up and brushed off some dirt from his knees, then brushed past the Redcoat without saying a word and headed home, not before looking back for one last glance at his point of entry into America.

The trip from Boston to Philadelphia would take nearly three weeks. Had they all traveled by horse and not carriage, as the delegates did, they would've been able to shave a week or so off the trip.

The night before departure, Mr. Revere sat with him on the front porch drinking apple cider. "Listen a lot, say little, watch how these men act, their manners, how they speak to one another, how they agree and disagree, and how they relate to the fairer sex. Absorb all you can. This is the most serious mission these men have ever undertaken, so let it be yours as well."

"Yes, sir, Mr. Revere." They sat there quietly for a few minutes until Junior joined them, sitting with Oliver in the middle. "I'm going to miss my family. Very much." The men embraced for what seemed like an hour before rain forced them inside.

* * *

The early August sun seemed to sit on their shoulders. Oliver could never understand why any human being would wear wool in such conditions, which is why he wore as much linen and cotton as possible. Still, there was little anyone could do to stay cool in the summer sun amid the onslaught of humidity that prevailed from sun-up to late at night. Mosquitoes were everywhere, more pervasive than the flies that followed the horses. He wouldn't let on to his discomfort, as it would have made him the first to do so in the party.

These men proved they were strong physically and with character by not mentioning the obvious annoyance of these natural factors, and saved their complaining for Parliament and the Crown, not to mention the loyalists who were constant pebbles in their shoes.

The natural annoyances made Oliver thank God repeatedly for the gift of becoming a printer and working indoors where he could control the environment some, rather than having to work in the open air.

Oliver was fascinated by the scenery, terrain, and the many

towns and villages they passed through. He kept mental notes of everything he saw. One of the things Revere instructed him to do on this trip was to learn everything he could about everything he saw. It would come in handy as the patriots expanded their network.

His training continued after the men stopped for the day, and Oliver got a fresh horse to ride through the area off the main roads. He was somewhat seasoned in escape and knew that life and death might be determined by his awareness and knowledge base.

Life and death? Those are two words he'd not considered up until then, but something seemed quite real about them. This was indeed an adventure, but not a game. These were serious men with a serious cause on a serious mission, and he needed to be as serious as they were, just like Mr. Revere advised.

His rides at dusk, often with someone around his age, or a man who knew the area well, were usually informative. He began to see certain rock forms, brush, trees, valleys, and woods, and knew what to expect as a rider on the run through them. He loved riding and being outdoors, but knew he wasn't a farmer, and preferred large towns. He loved being around people.

Since arriving in the colonies, he'd not been more than fifty miles away from Boston, and now he was two hundred miles away with another one hundred to go.

As they drew closer to Philadelphia, Thomas Cushing decided to ride a few miles with Oliver as he didn't know him as well as the others.

'Cushing,' thought Oliver, 'has a trustworthy face, yet his words rarely give away his truest thoughts.'

"The City of Brotherly Love, which is what a loose translation of Philadelphia means in the Greek, has twice the population of Boston. But not close to the one million people in London."

Sam Adams leaned out the window upon hearing this and said,

"Oliver, if we ever get to London, perhaps you might give us a tour?" To which everyone laughed.

"You know I've never been!"

Along the way, the men made a few stops to see others of their kind, fellow Sons who updated them on what was occurring in their realms, the attitudes of the people regarding various patriotic positions, and see who would attend the congress.

The men from Massachusetts were deeply concerned over Manhattan's overwhelming allegiance to the Crown. The Sons there worked diligently to convince the masses there of English tyranny, but because New York City was so dependent on English trade, leaning towards the Crown was smart economic sense. The Boston men understood this and knew that something dramatic would have to occur for those in New York to embrace the cause of liberty with the patriots.

Riding through New Jersey, the Massachusetts party visited William Franklin at the request of his father, Benjamin Franklin. Benjamin had corresponded with John Adams in preparation for this gathering, asking him to visit his son William, the royal Governor of New Jersey since 1763, and see if they could convert him to the patriot cause. William was a staunch loyalist and resisted discussions with his father regarding liberty.

The stern-faced governor in formal dress reluctantly received the men, and only momentarily as he was sitting for a portrait. The agitated man met them on the porch of his residence before sitting on a cushioned chair as if on a throne sipping lemonade under a broad brilliant white awning, swatting away flies who were attracted to his drink, while never offering the men refreshments. With an Army Regular standing on each side of the governor, menacingly looking at the unwelcome visitors, Benjamin Franklin's son spoke.

"I've no intention of abandoning the Crown, so I offer you my most sincere pardon for the waste of your time, but my father's ploy at convincing me through you less-than-esteemed gentlemen is yet another of his failures in our relationship. Frankly, you are all edging towards rebellion and hanging if you continue your nonsensical proxy on behalf of ungrateful and stupid 'patriots.' Tell my father his heart is to remain crushed as mine eternally belongs to England. Now, be gone, all of you, at once!"

The heat pressed upon the men as sweat began showing through their suits. Sam Adams glowered at Franklin as the other men turned back to the carriage. Franklin stood and waved at Adams, as if to unceremoniously dismiss him. The sentries cocked their rifles and raised them.

Not taking his eyes off the governor, Sam promised, "We will convey your message to your father. You will not hear from us again."

A few steps later, Adams turned back one step towards Franklin and said, "But be sure, Governor, whatever the thirteen colonies decide to do, we will accomplish. You may end up having to flee to England if you don't first lose your head!"

He turned and walked to the carriage, ignoring the Governor who shouted at him.

"Are you threatening me? Are you threatening the Crown? Answer me!"

Sam jumped in and they sped away, leaving William Franklin steamier than the hot August air.

* * *

Situated between the Schuylkill and Delaware rivers, residing just north of the center of the colonies, Philadelphia, established by William Penn in 1682, had blossomed into the commercial and cultural heart of colonial America. Philadelphia had become the third most important port to the British Empire after London and

Liverpool. The confluence of two rivers, its centrality in the colonies, its astute Quaker business folks who would bring in coal, farm goods, and ore assets needed for the nascent iron industry, and its shipping to both the West Indies and England, created this boomtown.

It was also a city of freethinkers, the most notable being Benjamin Franklin, who embraced the exploding new thought of the enlightenment going on in Europe and the New World.

Oliver had long ago abandoned some of what he considered the "darker" elements of the enlightenment thinkers who, in his opinion, were looking to distance themselves from the belief in a Supreme Deity while convincing men that they were their own gods. This was his rendering, and he felt quite strongly about it. He would gladly discuss these thinkers with anyone if they had read them. Otherwise, he would, most often, graciously steer the conversation to something lighter.

He would find this difficult in the coming days but knew that it was not for him to engage the delegates at this convention unless asked to contribute. He was certain that this was larger than a meeting of the Sons of Liberty in Boston, where he felt free to speak. Here, he was only an invited outsider performing odd jobs to support the Massachusetts delegation while in Philadelphia.

What's more, Hancock explained his role as a runner to various points, primarily New York City and Boston, with updates from the congress. A couple of printers would print the notes. John Adams would give them to Oliver, and then Oliver would be off with the finished product to New York and Boston, unless directed otherwise. He was not a delegate. He was to speak only when spoken to.

Coming to the top of a ridge, Thomas Cushing asked the driver to stop their carriage. Once halted, the men exited, stood side-by-side, and looked down upon the second-largest city the still-mounted Oliver had ever seen. Two miles away lay Philadelphia. The men looked at each other solemnly.

Sam Adams said, "We pledge our heads to heaven, gentlemen."

After a minute of quiet, reflective thought, they climbed back into the carriage and continued their slow ride into the cauldron of freedom. Unbeknownst to them, word had gone out of their arrival. Soon, a throng of well-wishers and patriots greeted them along the streets on the way to their lodging, making their entrance more a parade than the end of a long, tiring trip.

Nearly three weeks of travel brought them to the brink of treason.

This gathering of gentlemen patriots was unsanctioned by the Parliament and the Crown. Had they known this congress was occurring, surely, they would have shut it down with ferocity, arrested the attendees, and brought even harsher penalties down upon the colonies. England, however, was too smug, and their intelligence network failed them miserably.

The men rode to one of the finest inns in Philadelphia, the City Tavern. This would be their lodging while attending the congress. Oliver helped the driver unload the delegates' luggage and place it in each room, before tending to his own affairs. His room was upstairs in the far back just above a pig pen and stable.

Upon entering, he felt his face punched with a concoction of dirty pig, horse manure, and chemicals from a soap maker next door. The August heat cooked the stench in the air, and with a constant breeze aimed at his window, he decided to protect his health by wearing shirts across his face to limit the odor's ability to enter his nose and mouth. He spent as little time in his room while in town.

Still, he was more excited about this adventure than anything he'd ever experienced, so the room could've been in the pig pen for all he cared about.

That night, the Massachusetts men would connect with numerous delegates from the participating colonies, some they'd never met or heard of, and others, like Patrick Henry of Virginia, they already had great admiration for. Almost immediately they got down to business despite the first gathering not being until the next day.

Oliver was allowed to sit among them at long tables and plain benches during dinner and was introduced to everyone in attendance. They even asked him a few easy questions about the current state of affairs in Boston just to show off his acumen and acute grasp of all things patriotic.

Oliver understood that he was entertainment for them, to a degree. Sam Adams was the orator he looked up to, but Oliver knew his own personality didn't have the same fire. And once he heard a Patrick Henry monologue on liberty for twenty straight minutes, despite his oratorical skills, it made the pen, paper, and press his preferred method of communication.

When he had spare moments between duties and sleep, Oliver spent time writing bits of his story down. His preferred distraction was Clara, though. He would replay the day they met over and over again, with her flinty voice on loop in his head. They had met only once, he reminded himself but allowed his imagination to chart the rest of his life with her.

Clara had been thinking the same things having heard from Rachel Revere why Oliver hadn't visited her, nor was he there when the ladies of the Cole household called upon Mrs. Revere one day. Understandably, Clara was disappointed, but now she was in love with a hero.

CHAPTER 13

On September 5, 1774, men from the thirteen colonies, minus Georgia, gathered at Carpenter's Hall to discuss the future of America under British rule. Within a short time, all delegates were present and seated. The two-story cross-shaped brick building had three prominent Palladian windows on the second floor and was crowned with an elaborate cornice and large cupola. Located just off of Chestnut Street, it was a trade guild for carpenters.

The Georgian interior featured displays of carpenters' tools and a few portraits. The delegates sat on Windsor chairs at tables typically used by guild officers, surrounded by tall windows that provided natural light for them to work by.

Oliver made sure the Massachusetts men had ink, quill, and paper, and kept their water jug filled with cool water from a spring close by that Oliver had been told about by one of the black slaves that served at the Hall.

Young Atkinson was told to stay close by in case the men needed anything and was also able to serve the needs of others present if they didn't conflict with the wishes of the Massachusetts men. A gentleman from Delaware quickly learned that being rude to Oliver was the same as being rude to the Massachusetts men, though he would snarl at Oliver when the men weren't looking. The boy thought the man was a child and would snarl back.

He was to sit outside of the room in the main hall or on the steps that led to Chestnut Street. He was to be a lookout for Redcoats, royal officials, loyalists, or any other uninvited guest. He could hear much of the discourse, their arguments, occasional laughter, much fury, a few insults, as well as, reason and compromise.

But what stood out to Oliver that first day was when Thomas Cushing made a motion that the congress open with prayer, John Jay of New York, and John Rutledge of South Carolina rejected it because they were divided on religious grounds, though all were professed Christians.

Attendees were Baptists, Anabaptists, Quakers, Anglicans, Presbyterians, and a few Congregationalists. While all believed the others to be Christians, each considered their movement truer than the others. The arguing continued until Samuel Adams rose and said that he was "no bigot and could hear a prayer from any gentleman of piety and virtue who was at the same time a friend of the country."

On September 7, 1774, Oliver was told that an Anglican priest, Jacob Duche, was allowed to enter the chamber to open the First Continental Congress with prayer and a reading of Psalm 35, which was the reading that day in the Anglican psalter.

After the gentle pastor read several prayers from his prayer book, he read Psalm 35:

Contend, LORD, with those who contend with me;
Fight against those who fight against me.
Take hold of buckler and shield
And rise up as my help.
Draw also the spear and the battle-axe to meet those who
pursue me;
Say to my soul, "I am your salvation."
Let those be ashamed and dishonored who seek my life;
Let those be turned back and humiliated who devise evil
against me.
Let them be like chaff before the wind,
With the angel of the LORD driving them on.

Sam Adams rocked in his seat, his countenance alight with great satisfaction. Samuel Ward from Connecticut fought back emotion as the priest continued.

Stir Yourself, and awake to my right
And to my cause, my God and my Lord.
May those shout for joy and rejoice,
who take delight in my vindication;
And may they say continually, "The LORD be exalted,
Who delights in the prosperity of His servant."
And my tongue shall proclaim Your righteousness
And Your praise all day long.

After a few short prayers from the Episcopal prayer book, Reverend Duche spent the next two hours piercing heaven with his prayers, interceding on behalf of liberty and their shared cause. This was not the usual length for any of their practices. Many said later they had not heard sweeter words in their lives. Before they could make a request of God, they wanted to be aligned with His will and were certain after this that they were.

When Duche had finished, those doubting Providence's approval of their ambitions no longer did. It was agreed later that no more perfect Psalm could have been read for the state of relations and their mission.

Patrick Henry asked the Anglican priest what led him to choose this particular Psalm.

"I didn't choose it," Duche replied. "It was scheduled for this day in the Anglican psalter. God prepared many years in advance what would be read today for our gathering." The attendees were in awe and sat silent for a few moments to absorb this revelation.

Strengthened and encouraged, they then got to work.

The men from Massachusetts expected their fellow Americans were there to learn about the condition, opinion, and level of appetite for liberty of all the colonies. Yet, they were wise enough to know that each had their pet interests and wanted to have their own way. Oliver was learning that in politics, negotiations came at a price.

Compromise may not always be the best result for all but may be the best result for the day. This would allow them to continue onward and upward towards loftier ambitions.

The Adamses, Hancock, and Cushing hoped the delegates were there to unify the colonies to see themselves ultimately as one bargaining group and not thirteen disparate entities. Ultimately, if they couldn't unite, Massachusetts was in trouble, and it would be hard times for the rest as well.

During preliminary deliberations, mostly an airing of each colony's perspective and aim, John Hancock stood and waited until the hall became silent.

"Men, you have traveled many miles to this gathering because in your hearts we know that we must find a way to unite against the Crown, to build solidarity, and to agree on a common goal. With the brilliance found in this room, surely, we can put our minds together and respond to these Intolerable Acts with a reasonable recommendation which will lead to peace and prosperity. I fear that if we do not unite and instead place our individual colonies above the greater good, we will soon see our blood dripping from the edge of a British bayonet."

For the day, at least, this seems to bring the congress back on task.

* * *

When not assigned tasks and responsibilities, Oliver worked on his journal of life recollections or wandered the streets with Peter, a young slave he'd met at Carpenter's Hall where he worked a few hours a day keeping it clean.

Wiry thin Peter didn't have a last name, but when he was pressed, he gave the last name of his master, Armstrong. He also had no idea how old he was. Having been separated from his mother at birth, and already sold twice, he estimated he was around sixteen-years-old. He had one leg longer than the other and walked with a limp. This kept him from being a useful field slave and he was moved from Georgia to Philadelphia to serve at the home of Archibald Armstrong and his wife.

Mr. Armstrong was an importer and exporter, and one of the wealthiest men in Pennsylvania who was known to treat slaves like human beings, not property. This came from his Quaker beliefs, many of which he had strayed from, but in this area he couldn't. He was fond of Peter, as was everyone who met the ever-smiling boy.

At times when life became difficult, Armstrong would call for the boy just to see him smile. He always had candies for him and gave him more leeway than many slave owners might have.

Peter's English wasn't very good, but Oliver, like everyone else, was drawn to his smile. Instant friends, they talked mostly about food, a little about girls, though Peter never spoke about liking white girls. That was forbidden, he was told and could get him into trouble he'd not want to experience.

They went fishing, something Oliver hadn't done before, or just walked the city streets and talked. Little of what they spoke about carried much weight and had little bearing on the meetings being held at the Hall, which was fine by Oliver, who at times just wanted to be a boy and surrender his future to adults for a short while.

What's more, it was hard on his conscience to speak about liberty and the philosophy that all men were created equal to one bound in chains, real or figuratively. It was the only life Peter had known, and he didn't seem bothered by it.

Peter didn't know how to read or write. So, thinking nothing of it, Oliver asked him if he'd like to learn the alphabet and a few words. Enthusiastically, the teenager said yes. Oliver brought his writing materials down to the dining area of the inn because of the outside smell that invaded his room, and because they were hungry. He ordered food for the two, then set everything out and the instruction began. One of the innkeepers obviously disapproved. Delivering their ham sandwiches, he called Oliver off to the side.

With quiet sternness, the innkeeper said to Oliver, "Young man, if this boy's master wanted him to know how to read and write he would've taught him by now. Don't interfere with his raising!"

A stunned Oliver told the man to mind his own business and angrily walked back to the table. He didn't have to say a word to Peter, who closed his writing journal where he had been practicing the letter "P."

"I'm sorry, Peter. Let's finish our food and find another place." The slave friend's eyes lit up until he saw the innkeeper glaring at him. His eyes lost their light for a moment as he looked down while grabbing his sandwich. "Race you to see who finishes first!" And with that, the two stuffed their mouths with their food. Oliver was pointing at his full mouth then raising his index finger to signify he was first. Peter objected wildly by standing up and putting his empty mouth in his friend's face and saying, "I win!" Oliver nearly choked with laughter.

The innkeeper asked, "I think you boys are about done here."

Oliver threw down a few coins, grabbed his writing equipment, and the two raced out the tavern door whooping and hollering as they went.

* * *

It went on like this for weeks. Oliver had been expecting to make a mad dash on his horse north to New York City and Boston, but as of October 25th, it had pretty much been a dull routine with no travel. Not that he wasn't enjoying himself, but after nearly seven weeks of being in Philadelphia, his adventure needed a boost.

Things began to change when he met George Washington and Patrick Henry, both of Virginia, during some down-time at Carpenter's Hall. Oliver had returned early from lunch to find the Massachusetts men still absent. Oliver stood by the desk when Washington entered the hall.

Oliver gasped at his height. Mr. Washington was taller than most men, standing at a broad six-foot-two. His tied-back reddish-brown hair allowed his handsome face with high cheekbones and prominent nose to stand out. Patrick Henry was also tall at six feet. Oliver surmised men from Virginia were giants.

Oliver was finally going through a growing spurt, which he concluded was due to eating regular, healthy meals, and to not being so stressed. He arrived in Boston at five-feet as a thirteen-year-old and now at fourteen, stood five-foot-five, a long way from the height of men from Virginia.

There was something regal, commanding, and calming about Washington, the veteran Lieutenant Colonel of the French-Indian War. Like most, he took an instant liking to Oliver, especially when Samuel Adams told him the boy's story. Washington loved Oliver's hat with the hole in it, and mentioned that if told properly, his hat could become a heroic symbol for their cause. He also went on to say, "I might have great use of your intellect and skills someday soon, Mr. Atkinson. Do stay in touch."

The boy's mouth dropped open. "Indeed, I will, sir."

Patrick Henry had a passion for colonial liberty equal to any of the Boston men. When he wasn't firing off a speech at Carpenter's Hall or his gun on a hunt outside of Philadelphia, he could be found playing his flute or violin in revelry at a tavern near the docks that many first-generation immigrants from Scotland frequented. He was drawn to these Scotsmen, as his father came from Aberdeen. He, too, loved Oliver's stowaway story of breaking free from the confines of what he considered a ridiculous British law where one man could be forced to pay the debt of another.

John Adams allowed Oliver to go to this tavern with Henry once and only once. The young man had never been drunk before. Three ales later, his legs gave out as the room spun around him. He was sick the entire night—like being on *The Beaver*, and nearly useless the next day. It was the only time in Oliver's life that he ever came close to inebriation.

John Adams appeared tense as he summoned the boy to his spacious room on October 25 and told him to get ready to ride the next day. Some drafts needed to get to Boston promptly. Firmly, he went over with him places where he could get fresh horses, sleep, eat, and how to safely carry the intelligence he would be given. If he was stopped by bandits, or worse, Redcoats, especially close to the cities, he was to burn the papers. There'd be many other copies to follow. He made the boy repeat everything back to him, tracking every word and body gesture. Oliver had not seen him this way before.

"I realize that you've been sedentary and haven't made all the glorious rides to-and-fro since arriving." He let that linger for a moment before continuing. "You've been very patient and very helpful, nonetheless. Are you ready to ride alone and perform this invaluable duty for America?" Adams pointedly asked.

"I am ready, sir. I won't let you down."

"We know you won't, Oliver," Adams said kindly as he handed Oliver the documents. The boy reached out and grabbed them as if holding something sacred. "We are quite proud of you. I bet you'd like to know what the First Continental Congress has concluded.

Tomorrow will be our last day for now, but we've agreed to meet again to gauge how our demands and efforts have either furthered or failed us."

John Adams went on to give Oliver an overview of what had been decided by the defiant colonials.

They were prompted by The Coercive Acts, or, as Oliver corrected him, with a laugh, The Intolerable Acts. "You are one of us," Adams chortled. He explained that men from twelve colonies were drawn together, at the behest of the delegates from Virginia, to discuss what the effects on all of them these Acts would cause.

But before they dove deep into this discussion, it was imperative that they support the Suffolk Resolves. Next, they created the Continental Association, by whose final decisions all would be bound.

Having done this, it was next vitally important that they called for a ban of all British imports to the colonies and exports from the colonies to England. Enforcing this would be difficult, so each colony had to create committees of inspection to get merchants, shippers, and colonialists to refrain from doing business with England. Knowing this would harm the colonial economy, men knew they'd have to stir up and inspire patriotism among their citizens, convincing them that this would do damage to England's economy as well, and lead to full restoration of rights and, hopefully, representation in Parliament.

Their aim remained peace and full rights as British citizens.

It was also agreed that a Second Continental Congress be held the next spring to determine what any of their decisions had produced for or against them. This would give Britain time to respond to their demands.

These patriots knew there were fewer and fewer avenues of redress to make the colonials whole and permanent citizens of the British Empire. It just might come down to a war for independence. As such, it was agreed that each colony would form, supply, and train militias just in case.

The sober truth was, most of the men knew that war would be impossible to avoid. They also knew they weren't ready to take on the greatest military force in the world. They would be destroyed. Even preparing for such an inevitability, they knew that.

While the delegates took a short break, Sam Adams told Patrick Henry and George Washington that, "Providence would truly have to be on our side to see liberty and emancipation perfected. To accomplish this, I fear, much blood will be required of many brave patriots, and, hopefully, many more brave British soldiers and sailors."

"Hear! Hear!" they replied.

Once Adams had finished explaining the documents and resolutions of the congress, Oliver was released from his duties at the Hall and immediately ran out to find his friend, Peter. He hadn't seen him at the Hall all day, so he ran to his friend's home, then to a few places he knew Peter liked to play, especially as it pertained to a pretty girl he said he was in love with: Maggie. She didn't know where he was. Finally, he ran down to the river where his friend had taught him to fish and found him downcast.

Without looking up at Oliver he sadly said, "I heard the meetin' was getting over tomorrow."

"I came to say goodbye, Peter."

Peter dropped his pole just as a fish was biting. He grabbed Oliver around his waist and hugged him. "You the best friend I've ever had. Now you goin' away." The boys began to cry. After a minute, Peter stepped back and asked, "Is there goin' to be a war to free all men?"

It was the most soul-crushing question he'd ever been asked knowing what the answer was.

"Some believe war is inevitable. It would be for freedom, but

I'm afraid not for you. Not yet anyway. Many men want Africans, being God's creatures, to be liberated. I was told that first things had to come first."

The sadness on Peter's face doubled as he buried his face in his hands, before he rose in anger. "Why, Oliver? My master is a good man. But I know it ain't the case with most. Why can't ya'll wrap up our cause in yours?"

"The only answer I have is unsatisfying for both of us, my brother."

"Am I ever gonna see you again?" the slave asked.

"I've already been praying that Providence will reunite us, both as free men."

With that, they hugged each other again. "I'll be gone before the sun comes up."

Peter reached down and grabbed his pole. On it was the biggest trout he'd ever caught, alive but not flailing. They both looked at each other and back at the fish wide-eyed. "I'm gonna give this to Maggie. Maybe she'll finally fall in love with me!" The boys laughed as they headed back into The City of Brotherly Love.

CHAPTER 14

Before learning of his departure, Oliver had spent a few days creating a compartment for carrying secret documents. At least, he hoped it would be a secret compartment. He found a way to remove a part of the saddle where the cantle rests, that would allow him to place up to an inch worth of documents without making the area look bulkier than normal, while also disguising any obvious manipulations of the seat.

After dinner as guests of Pennsylvania lawyer and delegate John Dickinson, John Adams briefed the young man again as they made their way back to the Yards Inn. Oliver respectfully remained quiet but was really quite agitated. He didn't like being told two, and now three times, what he was supposed to do.

Back at the Inn, Hancock, Sam Adams, and Cushing were there to thank him for his outstanding work, and to wish him godspeed. His orders were to ride as hard as he and his horses could ride, what he should do if captured, and to return to his apprenticeship at Revere's print shop when the mission had concluded. There he would wait for his next assignment, if he wanted to continue with them. Oliver cocked his head with a grin as if to say, "If? Seriously?"

He packed food and a few canteens of water the night before but could barely sleep. It was one thing to be brought to this congress, which he understood to be an honor and a privilege, but now the very thing he'd been waiting for was upon him. His adrenaline was high, his senses keen, his awareness broad yet sharp, and his zeal at its peak. It was time to ride. It was time for adventure!

As the morning star went to hide in the rising sun's glow, Oliver was off, riding as hard as he had ever ridden. He soon was saddle sore, something he remembered from his earliest days on a horse at the baron's estate. The constant pounding of his backside as he kept his horse running as hard as he could started to bother him, and he was only on the second day of the journey. He had switched horses twice already and planned on two more stops before ending his day somewhere in northern New Jersey.

So far, his trip was uneventful. The one time he saw Redcoats was in Princeton, but they were too busy playing cards to be bothered with a teenage boy.

The next few days were more of the same. A horse was readied for him about every fifty miles, as was a meal and freshwater. The stops were at homes of sympathizers to the cause of liberty, and except for his final stop of the day where boarding was provided, all he would tell those helping him was that the thirteen colonies agreed on what they hoped would be peaceful redresses to the King. He wasn't allowed to show them the documents Adams had given him.

Truly, they weren't aware he was carrying anything of importance.

While rising to relieve himself in the middle of the night on his third day he saw a shadowy figure pass through a moon beam near the barn where his gear was. Oliver opened a window and shouted, "Hey you!" The figure fled as the young messenger hurried downstairs and out to the barn.

He slept against his saddle for the rest of the cold night, using his saddle blanket as a cover. He slept like this each subsequent night until he delivered his package.

By six p.m. four days later, just as the sun was setting, Oliver's last horse pulled up to the Revere home.

He rode back to the barn while shouting, "I'm home!" Paul and his family rushed out to greet him. The women and the young one's button-hooked back inside quickly when they realized how cold it was.

Paul Junior took care of the horse, as he always had done, while Oliver opened the saddle and pulled out the documents.

"John Adams said you'd know what to do with these," Oliver said, handing them to Mr. Revere.

"Thank you, Oliver," Revere said, clutching the treasured papers as he touched the young man's shoulder while heading to the house. "I'm very proud of you."

"We all are," said Junior.

Oliver's pride pushed aside his exhaustion for a moment, spilling out upon his face.

"Tell us about your travels at dinner, will you?" Revere asked as they entered the home.

Oliver held their attention for an hour as he regaled his adventure and answered a few questions. He spoke of William Franklin, the celebratory public reception along the streets leading into Philadelphia and got laughs when telling of the inn where they stayed and how stinky his room was. He mentioned the tasks, chores, and errands the Massachusetts men had him do, always being respectful, even giving him money for them. He did not tell them about his journaling. He did not want anyone to snoop around for it, not that he had anything embarrassing in it. It was private, for now. He then concluded by talking about his slave friend, Peter, who taught him how to fish as he taught him how to read. "Well, not exactly read," Oliver offered, but "just how to spell his own name."

Nine p.m. was fast approaching, and Paul bundled up to head into the freezing temperatures to a meeting at the Green Dragon

Tavern.

"Oliver, you're staying here," Paul said smiling.

Oliver didn't contest him.

"Checkers?" Junior asked.

Mr. Revere was out the door before Junior's one word question was answered.

Oliver nodded no. "I'm headed to bed. Tomorrow?"

With that, Oliver Atkinson said goodnight to the Revere clan and headed up to his bed, where he fell asleep on his covers without climbing under or taking off his clothes. He slept for the next twelve hours.

Paul Revere allowed him to rest the next day as well, but on the following day, he had his apprentice up early and fed, walking him to the print shop to explain what the next few months were probably going to be like.

"Our public printing business is doing well. We're busy and the guys have been doing really well. But I want you to focus on Sons of Liberty and congressional work."

"Yes, sir."

"I'm also going to involve you more with The Mechanics, so you'll be back on your horse regularly."

"I'd like that, sir."

Oliver's runs to connect with The Mechanics increased after Christmas in 1774 and through the winter of 1775. He was given more responsibility and always delivered.

On more than one occasion he was stopped by Regulars who simply wanted to harass a colonial. These occasions ignited fear and fury in him. The odd mix of emotions were barely tethered to wisdom as he often wanted to lash out and humiliate them. There were usually two to four soldiers at these check points, so he couldn't take them on physically–his still developing physique was just strong enough to maybe take on one fellow. So, he hid the growing rage in his heart and complied calmly with every bit of strength he had.

These emotions were new to him. His personal passivity remained, in general. But as the days became darker and it was clear that war was probably inevitable, he had incidental ideas on how he might be a catalyst to just get it started and over with. He wasn't sure he liked this side of him and wondered if it were the adult in him emerging from adolescence.

At one stop, he was pulled from his horse and interrogated, accused of being affiliated with the rebel cause.

Jerking him off his horse to the ground, a Redcoat barked, "Get up and hands up, American!" He complied.

Oliver kept assuring him he was just a simple tavern boy from Hingham.

"Hingham? I know Hingham," said the eldest. "Which tavern? And if you're lying there's a good hanging tree right there," he said pointing to a mature oak.

Two men just slightly older than him searched his riding gear and his pockets.

"The Oyster Bed Tavern. Mrs. Sculley's place." Oliver forced his eyes not to betray anything special about his saddle. "The secret saddle compartment" was about to get its first test, he thought as he fought against the slight tremble of his knees.

"Ahhhh, you've never been to Hingham, McDonald," said one going through his pockets. "I have. Mrs. Sculley makes the best..."

"Seafood stew," Oliver interjected.

"Yes, yes, indeed!" The boy soldier responded. "Nothing here," he said, pushing Oliver away. "You can lower your arms now" as he studied Oliver's face.

The young Mechanic couldn't breathe easy just yet. Another soldier with terrible acne yanked his saddle off Oliver's reddish mare and began to inspect it.

"Why so anxious, American?" the frisker asked.

"Wouldn't you be if you were me?"

"Only if I were hiding something," he said with an evil grin.

If they found the order from Revere in his compartment, death would quickly follow, Oliver reasoned. Surveying the land, there were no paths of escape on foot, nor could he reach for one of their weapons as the fourth man kept a loaded musket aimed at him the entire stop. His brain calculated one thousand outs and outcomes to this search, and all he saw was his skeleton buried in a shallow grave never to be found.

"Perhaps we'll just shoot you as the law allows," said the grinning soldier with the gun.

"He's clean. Just a pub boy," the boy with acne said disappointedly. To Oliver, he said, "You can go. Next time we might not be in such a generous mood."

Oliver was forced to resaddle his horse and did so in record time. Moments later, he rode as fast as a projected musket ball away from the four Redcoats, hearing their laughter getting dimmer and dimmer. He was shaken up. When well out of range of his temporary captors, Oliver hopped off his horse and threw up. When he finished, he wiped his mouth to reveal a satisfied smile. His compartment saved his life.

* * *

In February of 1775, the Parliament declared that Massachusetts was in a state of rebellion. This gave Gage and the military even greater power over the colony, allowing them to shoot rebels at will. Oliver knew this. With this in mind after his last stop and frisk, Oliver regularly carried his musket, which he had decided to call "Belle," as in "Clarabelle," the love of his life.

Oliver received an invitation from Captain John Parker, with a friendly nudge from Paul Revere and because he had proven himself in Philadelphia, to join the Minutemen. He was underage by one year at this point but was granted admission and would train two days a week. These were the best of the militia and were prepared to fight in the field or the woods at a moment's notice.

Atkinson returned home from his two days of training with a report on the armory and the men. He had great respect for these fellows, and they encouraged each other with philosophy, scripture, and homespun wisdom.

On an "errand" with Paul Senior, a word used by him when telling Rachel that he was going to meet with The Mechanics, Oliver confessed that he felt overwhelmed with the physical training, insecure about his skills with the musket, was not physically strong enough for prolonged close quarters combat, and felt dismissed because of his age.

"Why am I with these men?"

As usual, Revere paused his thoughts, but not his steps, as he considered his answer. "You are smarter than any of them, Oliver. Even Captain Parker. I've heard the reports back. I know these men. They are gifted in so many ways and are great patriots and family men. But you ride faster, think more quickly, assess more soundly, and scheme more astutely, than these brave fellas. We all bring our strengths to the cause."

The boy who thought and assessed more quickly hesitated to respond, but instead soaked in what Paul Revere said.

"No response?" the elder Revere asked.

"I think I understand."

"And don't worry about them dismissing you now. You'll earn their respect."

The errand that they ran turned into a two-hour walk, covering a host of subjects, including Clara.

"I need to see her. She must hate me by now."

"Mrs. Revere is working on something, but I understand how

you feel."

They passed by the Commons and the Liberty Tree and began their march towards home as the moon showed in the still sunlit sky.

"One more thing," Paul said, as he went on to explain that The Mechanics had heard General Gage was readying a plan to destroy the Massachusetts rebels by first commandeering their weapons, powder, and balls. "Be available and be ready. I may have to send you back sooner to help prepare the men for any engagement."

* * *

An early thaw began in late March 1775, as the love affair between Oliver and Clara also heated up. Paul had allowed him to visit Clara a few times since his return, but an abundance of work prevented his visits from lasting more than a day, always returning before dark.

Oliver was pleased to learn one Saturday morning that Clara Cole and her family were visiting Boston for the weekend to spend time with the Reveres.

Oliver was so excited that day that he bathed twice, changed clothes three times, until he realized he couldn't get cleaner, and that most of his clothes looked the same. Junior made fun of him until Oliver gave him a look that said, "You were justified the first few times. Enough!" Junior kept laughing as he walked downstairs.

Oliver was concerned that Junior might fall in love with Clara and said so to Deborah.

"Not to worry, Oliver. She's rebuffed him, kindly I will add, a half dozen times. He knows it's not meant to be."

The Coles arrived just before lunch. It was more like a family reunion, especially because of what was brewing between Oliver and Clara.

Oliver greeted the Sunday best-dressed Coles upon their

entrance. He especially showed deference to Trudy, Mrs. Cole, which pleased the hopeless social climber very much, a lofty ambition for the wife of an innkeeper. He then retreated to the kitchen entrance waiting to catch a glimpse of Clara, who came last through the door in the same pink dress she wore the day they met.

It was a loud house anyway but now it became louder as everyone seemed to be talking all at once. Except Oliver and Clara. They stood on opposite ends of the home as hugs and cheek kisses were spread around.

Spotting Oliver by the kitchen, Clara's left hand grabbed a basket of food from her mother's hand to add to the basket of food in her right, saying, "I'll take them to the kitchen," just so she could brush against Oliver upon entering. As she did, she whispered, "My hero" while their fabrics grazed, sending heart stopping flames through their beings.

The Reveres had borrowed chairs from the church and set them out in a circle so they could see each other and catch up on the latest news.

After a brief time in the living room, they moved to the dining room, which had been set by Deborah and Clara. Clara insisted on helping to show Oliver she could be a good wife, knowing how to properly set a table. If Oliver had been asked if this was a concern of his, he would have answered that he figured she already knew, having worked at her father's inn, and, well, it's just something all women knew.

The two prospective love birds were seated opposite each other at the narrow end of the long dining table that displayed their meal of wild boar, vegetable salad, a variety of breads, various cheeses, porridge, ale, cider, and coffee, followed by a few candies Rachel had been saving.

Every chance each had, they stole looks. Occasionally the thieving would occur at the same time, causing each's heart to trip over itself. Junior became strangely jealous, not because he believed he could ever win Clara's heart, but because it seemed Oliver was touched by a divine grace superior to his regarding everything he did. But he hadn't any skills as a goldsmith. Probably because he hadn't tried, reasoned Junior.

"Clara, how do you like the candlesticks I made?" Junior said pointing to a new set styled after a Greek leafy Corinthian column he had recently finished.

Oliver shot him a nasty look, but Junior didn't back down.

Paul spoke up to cover for an extremely uncomfortable Clara. "Junior, you are the best goldsmith in Boston, better than me..."

"And better than I could ever be," Oliver chimed in.

"Yes, probably in all of Massachusetts colony," Paul declared.

With that, Junior slunk down in his seat, and Rachel turned the conversational corner to updating the Coles' on how the rest of her children were doing.

Oliver heard very little of it. He couldn't stop his hands from sweating. He rubbed his sweaty hands on the tablecloth that rested on his lap until it was soaking wet. He was certain everyone knew. His face alternated from fascination to fear, from Clara to embarrassment. He then moved onto a napkin. Deborah did spot this and quietly placed a few more napkins near the boy.

Mr. Cole asked him about his Philadelphia trip and what his thoughts were on the current state of affairs. Clara hung on every word as he briefly regaled his adventure before he gave a thoughtful response about what he saw happening in the colonies and where things might be going.

"War," the lovestruck boy calmly said. "It's inevitable. But who will start it?"

Mrs. Cole asked, "Are we really at such a dreadful place?" She looked at all while continuing, "I'm scared to death every time my husband leaves the inn. I don't know what I'd do with him gone."

Mr. Cole gently grabbed her hand to comfort his wife before saying, "I'm not going anywhere, darling."

"Paul," Rachel asked, "Is there no hope for a compromise, for a return to things as before?"

Paul Junior asked, "Mum, do we really want a return to before?"

"I'd like a new nation," chimed Mr. Cole. "The old one doesn't fit so well anymore."

"That necessitates a war, Mr. Cole. The question is, which side is willing to suffer the most to gain the most? If we can endure the bloodshed sure to come, we will have our nation," Oliver offered between bites of wild boar. "This is the best boar I've ever had, Mrs. Cole!"

Noticing a sudden pall at the table, Senior suggested that "Supper is probably not the best time to discuss this matter. But we are in the right, and we must trust that God thinks so as well."

Oliver looked to see the gloomy faces at the table. No one was eating, their utensils sat on their plates. Swallowing, he tendered, "I know Mr. Hancock and the Adamses are working diligently with the congress to avoid inciting the King any further. Restored rights and a return to normalcy—whatever that looked like for you all since I arrived in the midst of this, is preferred so we can all get on with our lives."

Gently, Rachel suggested a pause of such heavy topics until after they digested their food. Paul laughed and heartily agreed.

With the conversation turning to lighter topics, Clara spied her hero. This young boy was a man. She was going to marry him. She knew it. He knew it. Everyone else at the table by then knew it. The mothers agreed, "Those two have the kiss of heaven on them." The plan was for them to try to spend more time together.

After a long day, Mr. Cole, having awakened from a snoring nap by the fireplace, and his family prepared to leave for a local inn to stay for the night. Oliver asked Mrs. Cole if he could walk with them. She and Mr. Cole agreed.

"Next to Clara?" Oliver clarified.

Mr. Cole burst out laughing as Trudy elbowed his ribs. "Yes, you may, Oliver."

Both beaming, they walked behind the couple and their two other children as they strolled towards their lodgings.

It took a minute, but Oliver finally spoke softly at Clara's closest ear. "You have the prettiest smile in the world."

"Thank you, Oliver. And you are the bravest man I know," she responded.

Man. She called him a man, he thought. "You did a really good job setting the table. And Mrs. Revere said you made the salad. It was the best I've ever eaten."

Smiling, the pretty teen said, "Come visit and I'll make you another." Lifting her head she yelled ahead, "Mother, when can Oliver visit?"

Trudy kept walking, hand in hand with her husband, and said, "Anytime he wants to."

Grabbing his arm she excitedly asked, "Can you come next weekend?"

"I don't see why not, unless Mr. Revere has work for me."

"I'm going to pray every morning, noon, and night that he won't."

Letting go, their hands brushed against each other, and both were hit with a bolt of unfamiliar joy that shot out from the place of contact throughout their bodies. Then it happened again as they walked. And again.

Trudy looked back occasionally because the kids were now walking in silence. They couldn't find words once the contact started, and this made her curious.

Finally, the group arrived at the inn, and everyone went inside except Mrs. Cole and the two infatuated kids. They stared at each other for a moment. Mrs. Cole finally said, "Go ahead and kiss her cheek again. You've already done it once!"

"It was my hand, Mother!" Clara barked, embarrassed.

Oliver froze for a second, then spoke. "Mrs. Cole, since you are allowing me to kiss Clara, would you mind facing the door?"

Containing her laughter, she did as requested.

Oliver grabbed her hands, tenderly looked her in her eyes, closed his, then bent in for a soft kiss on her cheek. Instead of wanting to run this time, he wanted to kiss her again.

Turning around. Mrs. Cole said, "That's enough for tonight, Oliver Atkinson." With that, she grabbed Clara's hands from Oliver's and pulled her inside the inn. Both smiled at the boy as mother closed the door.

Oliver felt more like a man than ever. Turning toward home, he heard a knock from a window of the inn to see Clara waving at him. She then blew him a kiss. That was his favorite remembrance of her for the rest of his life. He floated home and then struggled once again to fall asleep.

* * *

The following Monday was a typical day at the print shop. While instructing Benji on a project, the unmistakable sound of rapid hoofbeats came closer until they stopped right outside the shop door. An unknown voice called out from his horse, "Paul Revere? Are you there?"

Oliver stepped outside, wiping ink from his hand on a towel, and asked, "What is this about, my good man?"

"Sam Adams asked me to deliver a message to Mr. Revere."

"He's at home. Do you know the way?"

The man nodded, turned and was gone before Oliver could offer to meet him there.

A moment later Junior heard the same rapid hoofbeats and rose quickly from the dinner table where he was being tutored on math by his mother and looked out the front window.

"Paul Revere! I've a message from Sam Adams," came the voice from outside.

Turning to his father, he said, "I've never seen him before."

Paul rose from his reading chair. "Stay here," and in a flash he was out the door.

Entering quickly through the back door, Oliver joined Junior at the window. Both gazed at the stranger who spoke to Mr. Revere excitedly.

"Who is it?" Deborah asked.

Simultaneously, both boys said, "Shhh!" Yet they still couldn't hear.

The stranger reached into his saddle bag and produced what appeared to be a scroll and handed it to Paul. Revere undid the bow and began reading as the man turned his horse and sped off.

The family gathered around Paul by the fireplace as he spoke.

"The horseman was a courier from New York. This," Paul said, holding up the scroll and showing it to all. "This is exactly what we needed to hear from a southern colony. Listen to this from Patrick Henry of Virginia." Paul cleared his throat, and read: "Is life so dear, or peace so sweet, as to be purchased at the price of chains and slavery? Forbid it, Almighty God! I know not what course others may take; but as for me, give me liberty or give me death!"

A solemn silence fell upon the simple home. Paul turned to his family. "It is an honor to join with men who have everything to lose because they recognize that life without liberty isn't living at all."

CHAPTER 15

THE SHOT HEARD AROUND THE WORLD

On April 18, 1775, Paul Revere asked Oliver Atkinson, the once-indentured orphan from Derby, England, who stole away on *The Beaver* only to end up in Boston to become a critical part of the Sons of Liberty and the cause of freedom, to ride to Lexington and give a dispatch to Sam Adams and John Hancock, who were staying at the parsonage of Reverend Jonas Clarke, the witty husband of Hancock's cousin, Lucy Bowes. All Revere would tell Oliver was that the Redcoats would most likely be on the move to dismantle the Concord armory the next day or so and that Adams and Hancock should consider moving to a new location.

By now, Oliver carried his musket Belle with him everywhere he went, meaning he'd often have to ride greater distances to avoid regular Redcoat positions in and around Boston. Dressed in his minuteman uniform, topped with his bullet-holed hat, he set off immediately for Lexington to deliver the message.

He found himself holding the reins more tightly than usual as he rode to the person's home. Competing ideas for what this could mean and lead to pulled and tugged for dominance as he rode fiercely west. Something dramatic was about to happen, he knew. Life in the colonies was about to be altered forever, and he wanted to be a part of it.

As he crossed the Charles River, he vacillated between riding to Clara's for a short visit or focusing only on his duty. His mind juggled thoughts of her beautiful face and their hands touching, and the urgency and seriousness in Mr. Revere's eyes to the degree he'd not seen before.

His soul was being torn as if by competing lions.

If this meant war, he would be called off to battle and might not see her for a while. Could either of them endure that? If he died a hero, wouldn't she want one last look at him? It was only a few miles out of his way, and he wasn't due until later in the afternoon.

The pull was unconquerable. He'd not seen this kind of weakness in himself before. But the lure of love from the purest Siren was calling, and he could no longer resist. Changing direction slightly, he steered his mare to his right towards the Cole's while grimacing over his decision. "Five minutes with her and no more," he told himself like an adult giving into their child's tantrum.

Riding hard from the shore, he arrived at her family's tavern and inn twenty minutes later, hopped off his horse, and burst through the front door almost dislodging it from its hinges.

A stunned Trudy Cole nearly dropped the plates of food she was delivering to a table of men, and said, "There are more acceptable ways to enter a tavern, Mr. Atkinson!"

Breathing hard, he said, "My apologies, Mrs. Cole. I'm on urgent business and I only have a minute."

"She's in bed sick with a fever. Go around to see her," she said motioning with her head towards the back of the inn.

He raced past her saying, "Thank you, ma'am." Cutting through the kitchen he yelled out her name. "Clara! It's me, Oliver!"

Hearing a weak voice coming from a room, he knocked and entered, seeing Clara under a stack of quilts, her face pale, and her brow damp with perspiration.

"Oh, Oliver. I prayed you'd come to see me. Now I know I'll be better," his love struggled to say.

He knelt at her bed, grabbed her hand and kissed it, holding it tight. "I can't stop thinking about you, Clara."

"Nor I you, Oliver."

"I've only a minute, or I'd stay until your fever goes away."

"Father told me you'd become a minuteman. You are an amazing man, my love." She tried sitting up with difficulty.

"I'm going to pray every second I can for your healing, Clara. You will be made whole again. You will be my bride."

They stared into each other's eyes, falling more in love with each passing second.

"I could get lost in your eyes and never return, my love, but I must leave."

He arose a moment later, disciplined to offset the weakness caused by her magnetic beauty that led him there, conquering the urge to stay while dragging himself toward the door as he reminded himself of his promise.

"My dear Clara, dark times are upon us. I don't know when I'll be able to see you again, but you will never leave my thoughts. I'll return as soon as I am able."

"Please hurry back, my dear Oliver," she said while trying to sit up.

His heart beating a thousand times a second, the boy minuteman left as quickly as he came, brushing past Mr. and Mrs. Cole, proclaiming over his shoulder while exiting the tavern, "I'll be back for your daughter as soon as I am able!"

Oliver mounted the horse he named "Courage," a proud, chestnut brown female quarter horse who would carry him for many days thereafter. "Huhyah!" Oliver shouted as he made haste for Lexington.

* * *

Mr. Revere had warned Oliver about the proliferation of Redcoat scouts to the north and west of Boston. The British army was forced to cross the Charles River on the north side to get anywhere in Massachusetts as the brave militia of this colony had set up fortifications at the Boston neck that prevented them from moving inland via that route. Not seeking confrontation at that time, Gage and his generals chose other routes to perform their duties in policing the colony.

On a high after seeing Clara, the young patriot rode on the wind towards his destination, dreaming of her face, praying for her healing, and imagining what being married to her might look like. He was so lost in his fantasy that he hadn't noticed a group of five Regulars ahead just north of the town of Medford. Suddenly, a wall of red appeared twenty yards before him. "Halt!" boomed a lieutenant.

Oliver pulled on the reins slowing the obedient Courage down to a walk, as he whispered in her ear, "Be ready, big girl." The horse nodded her head and whinnied he understood.

"I said stop," barked the oldest of the five. Courage was now ten yards away and had come to a near stop.

"Apologies, but my horse has a mind of its own," Oliver offered.

"Then perhaps she needs a better trainer," the elder soldier retorted.

Oliver said, "You're probably right. She's been asking for someone new for quite some time. I keep insisting I know what I'm doing, but she just looks at me funny." She was now ten feet from them. "Let me demonstrate." With that, he thrust the insides of his heels into Courage's sides, yelled, "Now!" and lifted the reins, turned and sprinted away from the soldiers, laughing.

The soldiers were momentarily stunned.

Only one horse was available to them, and, once awakened to the situation, the commanding officer was on it in a flash, directing it after Oliver who by now was thirty yards away, zig zagging to avoid the musket balls that flew past his head.

After a few looks over his shoulder, Oliver noticed that the soldier was gaining on him. By then he was far enough away from the musket's effectiveness, that he sprinted on a line forward to go faster. Courage occasionally would toy with horses when racing them, displaying deep intelligence and a mind of her own. "Now's not the time for games, Courage," an anxious Oliver said. Courage interpreted his laugh as a time for fun and games. It most assuredly was not. He needed to remember not to do that again when in a serious situation, so now his voice articulated gravity and concern.

His mount got the message and rushed headlong into a forest where Oliver felt he could lose the Redcoat. But looking behind him, he was shocked his opponent was still following at about the same distance, if not gaining a little.

Courage danced around trees, leapt small streams, and burst through brush for about ten minutes until, when looking back again, Oliver saw the Regular knocked off his horse by a low hanging branch that hit him flush across his neck. Oliver slowed Courage down, then turned her back for a look. The soldier was writhing in pain while holding his neck. Oliver looked in the direction he had to be going, then back at his adversary. He looked up at the sun to determine time, then cautiously rode back to where the man was, his anguished whimpers fighting for release through his crushed windpipe. The Redcoat struggled to breathe.

Oliver hopped off his horse and lifted the man to a sitting position. Atkinson didn't know what to do, except offer him water from his canteen and pat him hard on his back thinking something might be dislodged to get him breathing normally again. It didn't help. The gash on his neck bled profusely, and the boy soldier removed a handkerchief from his rival's saddle, laid him back down, and squatted to apply pressure to the wound. Yet blood flowed and the breathing became more difficult.

The minuteman lifted the lieutenant to his feet and gently said, "I know a doctor close by who can help you." His limited physical strength was barely able to get the grown man up and across his saddle. His blueish face gave Oliver pause. He'd never seen a dying man before. Mounting Courage, he took the reins of the officer and slowly led him to the home of a loyalist family who the Reveres had created pitchers, bowls, and a tea set for.

The ride should've taken five minutes but took fifteen instead. Never learning the man's name, they finally arrived at the doorstep of the loyalist home. Oliver shouted for help, and in twenty seconds, the plump Dr. Ward came rushing from behind his home with an ax in hand until he saw Oliver and the Redcoat.

"I found him in the woods. Please take care of him, sir."

Oliver rushed off as Ward shouted unanswered questions at the boy, before turning his attention to the soldier.

Atkinson was running behind due to two unplanned stops. Love and compassion. Truly biblical, but in this case, misapplied, perhaps, he wondered. He kicked and congratulated himself at the same time. The face of Clara and the soldier competed for his inner vision. He felt guilty either way.

Because of the lateness of the day, he opted for the main road to Lexington and the parsonage. But after knocking on the door, calling out their names, and walking around the homestead, he saw that no one was there in spite of signs of life as the chimney coughed out gray smoke. Like a punch in the chest, his first thought centered around his tardiness. "Have the Regulars arrested and taken them away already? What about the Parson and his family?"

He waited for an hour, and still no one came. He paced the property wondering what to do, kicking himself over his poor decisions. "Is saving the life of your enemy really a poor decision, even in the current climate?" he wondered. "Where does compassion enter into war–an imminent war, and what if it conflicts with duty?"

His ruminations were relieved by the high-pitched jangly sounds that approached from the road south of the parsonage that led to Bay Road. Through the lengthened shadows of midafternoon appeared the reverend and his family, as well as Misters Adams and Hancock, singing hymns in a style they'd heard from some of the African slaves.

His friend, the young slave Peter, had taught him a few African hymns, clapping with various rhythms depending on verse, refrain, or melodic emphasis. They were very different sounding yet had some of the same great doctrinal power of the hymns of Charles Wesley, Isaac Watts, John Rippon, and Ann Griffiths.

Adams spotted Oliver first, and called out, "Ahhh, Mr. Atkinson. What a jolly picnic you've missed!" They then saw the messenger's face.

Going inside, Oliver explained what had happened on his trip while handing them correspondence from Mr. Revere. Reading it with growing concern, Adams passed it to Hancock, whose furrowed brows revealed his soul's disquiet.

"What do you think, Sam?" asked Hancock.

"I think Mr. Atkinson needs to alert Captain Parker and the local militia to prepare for trouble that may be headed this way, and that you and I should move our living elsewhere."

"Tonight?" John Hancock asked.

After a brief pause, Adams hesitatingly said, "At least before the rooster rises. I'm not accustomed to running, John. But until we get what we rightfully deserve or until we can't run any longer, by way of age, jail, victory, or death, this might be our standard for a time. Besides, we need to return to Philadelphia."

The seated men looked strangely at the fire in the hearth, before rising from their seats.

"Gentlemen, I need to go. I'll look for you before heading back to Boston. I'm off to brief Captain Parker," Oliver rose and headed for the door.

"Oliver." Hancock said as he stood up and extended his hand to the Minuteman, who uneasily took it. "Thank you."

The boy nodded, turned, and was gone.

* * *

Oliver found Captain Parker at the Buckman Tavern. Travelers, locals, militia and Minutemen ate, slept, and held meetings in this building desperately in need of repair and a whitewash.

By now it was nightfall, and many of the men had gone to their homes for the night. Oliver found the captain taking care of his bill. Doing a double take at the concern on the young man's face, the captain leapt up without seeking his change and walked with Oliver outside and away from nosy ears.

"I've word from Mr. Revere. It's serious, Captain. Orders have been given for seven-hundred Regulars to march in the next few days to the Concord armory to remove all weapons, powder, and musket balls. Everything. And take them back to Boston."

The always decisive captain said, "I'd do the same thing, Oliver. The men are ready. As you know, we've been expecting this. Go alert the locals and have them meet us here before sunrise. We must do this daily until we know differently." The stout jaws of the man's face became gentle for a moment. "Afterwards, come back here. I'll arrange a meal and a room for you."

"Thank you, sir. I'll see you in the morning." The young man sprang in one motion into his saddle and was off into the last remnants of dusk.

It took Oliver about three hours to ride around the immediate area and deliver the captain's orders. He asked a few men on the outer bands of Lexington to go tell others further out, and to tell them to do the same. He had learned more than a few things from Paul Revere and Captain Parker.

As he trotted the equally exhausted Courage back to the Buckman Tavern, he thought back to his journey's start in Derby. He was now wanted in both England and America, by the same Crown, but for different reasons. He didn't consider himself rebellious by nature, but quite conforming, though he did expect rights, justice, and truth to guide him in whatever situation or nation he was in. "I don't recognize myself," he muttered as he concluded this passage back over the prior sixteen months he'd been in Massachusetts.

Other than growing physically, his ideas about what it meant to be British had evolved. He was now an American. When asked, he would say he was British, but he stopped believing this a few months back when Massachusetts was deemed a rebel colony.

In the final mile of his return, it dawned on him that a force had taken over the world. It was as if both sides were driven by an unseen hand toward conflict, and neither side could prevent the inevitable. War. Both sides knew the colonials weren't prepared for military conflict. But they had something the British soldiers did not have: a passion for freedom. The Redcoats and their officers were fighting because it was what they did. And they were the best in the world, but to them it was still a job. As his father told him once, "It's a living, Oliver." The Americans would fight to cast off the bonds of oppression and tyranny to live as free men. The British, because they got paid or had no other skills.

As a tired Courage was settled for the night, he paused while looking up at the heavens. He gave thanks to God for a life worth living, hoping He would be glorified by him in all he did. "I don't even know what that really means or looks like. I just hope to do it," he said as he opened the tavern door.

As he sat down, a furious rage of hunger boiled within, his thoughts turned to Clara, wondering if she was feeling better. He prayed for her, as promised, for perhaps the hundredth time since leaving her earlier in the day.

He finished his meal quickly and the innkeeper guided him to his room. He was delighted it didn't smell like the one in Philadelphia. Despite his exhaustion, Oliver struggled to fall asleep.

CHAPTER 16

Dr. Joseph Warren was considered the best physician in Boston, though it was his brother John who founded Harvard's Medical School. Being true to the Hippocratic Oath, Dr. Warren attended to both patriots and loyalists. He was also quite active in politics and was the author of the Suffolk Resolves that rejected the Massachusetts Government Act and called for a boycott of British goods, the organizing of local militias, and for the colony's citizens to refrain from paying taxes to the Crown until their rights were restored. The Suffolk Resolves was later adopted by the Continental Congress.

The widowed Dr. Warren was also a master spy. He gave important information to the Sons of Liberty but never let on who his sources were. Some suspected he had one source. An astonishing rumor bandied about Boston was that the American-born wife of General Thomas Gage–Margaret Kemble Gage–fancied the handsome young doctor. It was said that she was torn, but ultimately her allegiance was with the patriots. Hence, the intelligence, often meticulous and accurate, that Warren received was thought to have come from her. She was playing a dangerous game, if the rumor was true. It could have cost her head, and possibly General Gage's.

A messenger arrived at Paul Revere's home at mid-evening directing him to Dr. Warren's practice, where he often worked late into the night, and where Revere had put a filling into Warren's mouth one day. Goldsmiths were known to do that. When Revere arrived, he was met by William Dawes at the door and brought inside to a waiting Warren.

At first it looked like no one was home, but knocking once, as he was instructed to do, Paul Revere entered the chilly home that had a lone candle lit, providing just enough light for him to see Warren sitting in a back corner.

"Join me, Paul, William," Warren invited as both men pulled up a stool next to the doctor. He then went on to brief them.

Paul thought, "Wherever his latest intelligence came from, it was time for action."

The good-looking doctor paused before saying, "An arrest warrant has been issued for Sam Adams and John Hancock."

"Having heard something similar, Joseph, I dispatched Oliver to alert the men."

"Well done, Paul." Now smiling, "But I'm certain we don't share the same source on this one."

Paul and Dawes returned his smile before Revere changed the mood. "I think this is it, gentlemen. Ten more years wouldn't make us any more ready."

"I agree with you, Paul." He paused again before revealing, "In addition to the warrants, the collision between nations has arrived. Patriotism is at its peak in Massachusetts and it's up to us to spread the fire to the other colonies. Gentlemen, seven-hundred British are marching on Concord tomorrow, though we don't know if by land or sea."

The meeting was quick. Moving toward the doors, Revere looked at Dawes and said, "I'll cross over the Charles on the north side and head towards Lexington and Concord and alert our men along the way. I want you to ride through Boston neck and alert the men along that route."

Dawes dashed out into the night without another word. His horse's galloping became faint as he disappeared into the night.

Warren said, "One if by land, two if by sea, correct?"

Revere nodded. "My men are ready."

"Godspeed, Paul." The men shook hands, and Revere was out the door as fast as Dawes and was gone into the broad pale moon night.

Stopping by his home, Paul told Rachel what his mission was, put on his riding boots and overcoat, kissed his wife, and was gone.

He headed north to a preset location to meet his choice boatman. He also had arranged through The Mechanics to have a horse ready for him once he landed across the river.

Once on the opposite side, Revere pushed his horse as fast as it could run, though he slowed down when passing Mark's tree, where the slave had been hanged some years earlier. He thought for a moment that he could end up with a noose around his neck as well, but for a different reason. Perhaps freedom would soon come to all men instead.

Remembering his mission, Revere stopped outside the home of every militia man, minuteman, or sympathizer, he passed, awakening them to the coming Redcoats, shouting, "The Regulars are coming! The Regulars are coming!"

Passing through Charlestown Neck, he came upon two British officers sitting on horses under a tree on the road to Medford, and he took off, asking his horse to give him everything it had. One trailed him while the other raced ahead to cut him off. Paul outmaneuvered them both. Knowing the terrain, he led the one in front into an area where he knew was full of marshy clay, making it impossible to ride quickly through. The officer took the bait and got stuck. Paul sped on, with only one glance behind him, satisfied he was no longer being chased.

In Medford, Revere stopped at the home of one of the leaders of the minuteman and explained briefly what was happening. He instructed him to get his men to Lexington while employing a few riders to head into northern Massachusetts and even into Vermont and New Hampshire and alert friendlies.

Finally, Revere arrived in Lexington and went straight to the reverend's home where he found Adams and Hancock sitting before a fire in Reverend Clarke's living room.

"I hoped you'd be gone by now," Paul said.

Adams said, "Consider us gone before sunrise, Paul. We appreciate you sending Oliver ahead."

"The news is worse. The Regulars are coming for the armory in the morning."

"Yes, that's what we surmised from Oliver," Hancock confirmed.

Paul and his horse needed a quick rest. They heard a horse approaching. Paul lifted his weapon and went to the door. It was Dawes.

They went inside for thirty minutes, discussed their plans, and thanked the reverend and his family for their hospitality before continuing on their mission, but not before Paul sternly told Adams and Hancock, "I'll be back for you before daybreak. I'll tie you up and drag you by my horse away from here if I have to!" to which the men chuckled.

Their next stop was Concord, and they were soon joined by Dr. Samuel Prescott, an esteemed Son of Liberty. "There are many more coming," he promised Dawes and Revere.

Revere led the two men by thirty yards. But just before Concord, a command pierced the night: "Stop, or we'll blow your brains out!" Four British soldiers came out from under a tree where they'd been hiding, weapons pointed directly at Revere. Dawes and Prescott were a short distance behind Paul and decided to make a run for it in the dark. Dawes fled one way and Prescott another.

Dawes' horse, to him, seemed slower than usual and felt he

couldn't outrun the Redcoats. He stopped at a house, hopped off his horse in a dark area, and yelled, "I've got two of them! Go after the other!" This trick worked on his pursuers, so that both he and Prescott were able to escape.

Not so Paul Revere. His midnight ride had come to an end.

Prescott was the first to warn the people of Concord that the Regulars were coming, as Paul Revere sat bound, captive of the patrol.

They took his horse and weapon and interrogated him by the side of Concord Road for the next few hours. Without being smug, Revere assured them they were all "dead men," that "patriots from as far away as New Hampshire were gathering in Lexington to inhospitably welcome the coming British army. Your young boys from Sussex, Manchester, Leeds, and Bournemouth are going to wish they had chosen a different occupation!" His captors stood wide-eyed, the firmness and conviction of his voice unnerving. To be sure, they escorted him to Lexington where they saw no signs of a rebel buildup, then released him without his horse or weapon and returned to their post.

All the while, men from all over Massachusetts were sounding the alarm to gather in Lexington, if possible, or along The Bay Road that the Redcoats would travel on to and from Boston.

Paul ended up back at Reverend Cole's home, where the next day, before a certain shot had been fired at Lexington Green, he helped the two Sons of Liberty leaders steal away to a safe place at 4 a.m., just an hour before the British troops marched through.

* * *

Oliver wrestled with his thoughts and smelly sheets all night, not finding comfort, especially since he was being eaten alive by bed bugs. Having had enough, by 2 a.m. he took the curtains down from the window, grabbed a pillow from a sitting chair, and plopped himself on the warped, wooden floor to sleep. Two hours later he heard noises and looked out the east-facing window to see patriots assembling outside.

He went downstairs, following the smell of biscuits and bacon, to the dining room of the tavern and ate breakfast with a growing number of militia and Minutemen from all over the region, and within twenty minutes, not one more soul could have fit into the establishment.

The growing boy scarfed down his meal and scooted out into the cool morning air to find Captain Parker. The patriot leader came riding hard towards the men shouting, "The Regulars are an hour away!"

Seventy anxious men spread out feet apart on the expansive green behind trees, stone walls, and along a riverbank on a crisp, clear chilly morning. Much of the ground was still wet from a rain the night before making footing a possible issue. Word got back to Parker that the muddy conditions caused by the rain prevented the British from bringing their cannons. Still, Parker was concerned that their overwhelming numbers would make that moot.

The colonel rode up and down the line, commanding his men to "Stand your ground. Do not fire unless fired upon. But, if they want to have a war, let it begin here!" A rallying cry went out from the men "Freedom!"

Captain Parker found Oliver in the open field on the far right of the line and ordered him to move to the rear and be ready to provide supplies and help, having never been in battle.

"Sir," Oliver asked, "How many of these men have ever been in battle?"

The captain dismounted his horse, and an aide took the reins and led the horse away.

"Mr. Atkinson, if you fire your weapon, you'd better hit at what you are aiming." His serious growl turned into a smile. Pointing to the bullet hole in his hat, he said, "Be sure to aim about eighteen inches lower than this." Oliver smiled wistfully.

At 5 a.m., the growing sound of walking thunder pulsed through the cool morning air. The noise ricocheted through the woods and up the lane from Boston more loudly than he heard on his first visit to Lexington. It was announced that seven-hundred men were approaching. A few minutes later Major John Pitcairn arrived with the advanced guard of nearly two-hundred and forty British soldiers. They stopped one hundred yards away and organized as a line infantry.

Seeing this number, Parker knew they were going to be slaughtered if a battle ensued in the open with no covering while facing the best trained army in the world. But he refused to show weakness.

Pitcairn loudly ordered Parker and his men to lay down their arms. Every brave patriot turned to their concerned commander looking for direction. After a moment's consideration, Parker responded to Pitcairn first, saying, "We will not lay down our arms for we will not surrender to you today or any day."

An agitated Pitcairn looked at his men as if to say, "Be ready!"

The proud patriots stood poised for battle.

Oliver's heart raced as he asked himself for the twentieth time that morning if he were "ready to kill more than squirrels." Eyeing the British soldier directly across from him one hundred yards away, unable to see the details of his face, helped him decide. "Yes. I am ready."

Parker's bravado masked his fear for the lives of his men. In the strange silence of the new morning, with the birds seemingly refusing to sing, Parker took a few deep breaths, faced his mean, making eye contact with each, then said meekly, "Wisdom counsels us to disperse at this time, brave patriots."

The patriots hesitated at first. "C'mon, men. This imbalance requires us to stand down for now. Our time will come."

Slowly, Americans from all over Massachusetts and beyond began to depart the field. Then it happened.

The unmistakable blast of a musket being fired shattered the air.

Next, a British pistol went off. Suddenly there was mayhem and war.

Redcoat guns opened on the disbanding men, who quickly recovered and returned fire. Smoke hung thick in the air as muskets barked out death and injury.

As men fell around him, Oliver's shaking hands still allowed him to fire three times, struggling after his first shot to load under pressure. His instincts were to flee, but his conscience kept him in place.

Finally, having loaded his weapon again, he fired, hitting the British soldier he spied moments before square in the chest. Watching the young soldier's arms fly forward as his chest caved in while falling backwards made him want to throw up. He fought through this quickly as the patriot soldier fell dead next to him. The boy got off one more shot before the battle ended.

The British advanced on the Americans, who by now had fled the green and sprinted or rode to Concord.

Oliver rushed back to the tavern for Courage and was about to head to Concord when he heard Captain Parker yell his name and wave him over.

Galloping to his commander's side, he told the young man, "Don't go to Concord. The British won't get what they're looking for. We've moved most of it. Plus, we have many more men there ready to engage the British. This is what we're going to do." Parker went on to explain that groups of patriots would dot Bay Road back to Boston to ambush the Redcoats on their return. "They marched all night and now must march all day back. They will be easy prey. Follow me."

CHAPTER 17

Parker and Atkinson sped off across the green past the dead and wounded. Women already tended to those still alive. Off they flew into the woods on a semi-circular route to avoid the rest of the British troops. They began seeing militia and Minutemen at various points along the Bay Road hiding strategically behind rocks, brushes, trees, and outgrowths, waiting for the return of the Regulars. The men were ordered to attack with a few rounds before fleeing through the woods to another spot to support the next ambush, and to do this for as long as they had breath in them, all the way to Boston.

As the captain and Oliver settled behind a large stone that would provide perfect cover for them, Parker asked, "What was it like for you to see a man fall by your ball?"

Atkinson hadn't processed that yet. He paused, his eyes moving quickly side before exhaling heavily. "In the blink of an eye, it put to the test a year and a half's worth of rhetoric, speeches, subterfuge, spy work, propaganda, and truth I had been convinced of. In a moment I had to decide if I really believed it all."

After checking on his men along the road, Parker was back after an hour having ordered Oliver to stay put. They ate lunch and as they finished their last bite, they heard British soldiers approaching. Parker was about to tell Oliver to load his gun, but he was already prepped and was positioning himself for the best aim and cover.

"Remember, fire three rounds, then get on Courage and sprint a mile south to join the men for the next ambush," the captain ordered.

All told, there were about 400 men stationed in prime ambush spots along the road. What they couldn't do with numbers, overwhelm the Regulars, they would do with cunning learned from Native American warriors.

"Wait for the front of their line to be at our side where we have a clear shot. Then fire and go!"

Oliver nodded. Thirty seconds later the Regulars came into view. An adrenaline blast added to his courage as he breathed deeply a few times to steady his hands. Unlike on the Green, he had time to mentally prepare. He was ready.

Captain Parker raised his weapon and fired, dropping a Redcoat. Oliver did the same. Confusion rattled the Redcoat ranks as a sudden volley of hundreds of lead balls pierced the air, most finding Redcoat body parts, while others struck branches, trees, or rocks. Blood spurted as men shrieked in pain while falling to the ground wounded or dead.

British officers shouted commands to regain order among their troops. Adding to their fear, they couldn't see any Americans. They only knew their general position. A major told a group of Regulars to charge into the direction from where the guns were fired, only to find the area bare of men, who had fled, including Oliver and Parker, having fired three shots each.

Dozens of men fixed themselves in secure spots along the Bay Road back to Boston. Oliver had never seen so many patriots in one day, all ready to die for the cause of liberty. Most of these men he had never met, but many had heard of the "patriot stowaway" being apprenticed by Paul Revere, who wore a hat with a musket ball hole square in its middle.

Oliver met about fifty men on the south side of the Bay Road for the next deadly barrage. They were close enough to see fear in their opponents' eyes. The Redcoats were exhausted and afraid yet still impressed the Americans with their disciplined marching.

In his heart, young Atkinson wanted to wound them, not kill them, though he knew they would kill him without hesitation. A wounded Redcoat might still kill one of his colonial brothers. He fought the tenets of compassion and gave himself over to the reality of a war for freedom. Only the death of a Regular could expedite that. He refused to be a conscientious coward.

The militia's captain told them to be ready for a quick response from the British, having been ambushed again.

Atkinson found a cairn like his earlier hiding spot, and it was high enough to allow him to stand and fire, swivel back behind for cover and reload, then fire again. Three times. Then flee to the next spot.

"Have you ever been in hand-to-hand combat, son?" Asked a grizzled man of about forty who took up space next to him.

"No, sir," Oliver responded.

"If they break through our first volley and come upon us, they will use their bayonets and musket butts to attack us." Oliver gulped deeply as his brow pressed up into his scalp. "Do you have a knife?" Oliver pulled out a small knife that wouldn't pierce a Regular's uniform. The massive man shook his head.

"I have a hatchet," Oliver said, hoping it would be approved. The man nodded his approval.

"In close combat, it will be more valuable than your rifle. Keep it at your side." He then went back to eyeing the road as Oliver pulled his hatchet from his saddle pack.

The young rebel learned that the man's name was "Big Mike" Downham, that he lived in Cambridge, was a tanner, and had a wife named Lynn. No kids. "But we keep trying," Big Mike said, as he smiled and winked at the confused boy.

Just then they heard a few horses approaching from behind. They were Redcoats sent ahead to scout the area for any other ambushes. This caught twenty patriots off guard. The British fired off a few rounds on their side, killing two men and wounding three, before a platoon came running up the road at the sound of gunfire.

Oliver and Big Mike pivoted around to the other side of the cairn, and each got off a round before swords were brandished and the horsemen from England rode straight into the hive of Minutemen.

A cavalry soldier came right at Big Mike as he reached for his knife, wielding his silver saber and bringing it down on the new friend's shoulder. Lifting his sword to swing again at him, Oliver took his hatchet and swung as hard as he could against the man's leg, causing him to scream in agony and drop his weapon. At this, Big Mike picked up his enemy's blade while rising and thrust it through the Redcoat officer's chest. The man collapsed dead before falling from his horse.

Their senses at peak, they turned to see the platoon bearing down on them. Men who had been stationed fifty yards away came to their defense and repelled the British. A few cavalry men turned and galloped back towards the main group, undoubtedly, to report what happened.

Big Mike was bleeding badly. A stain developed through his leather jacket increasing in size. "Oliver, will you get my horse for me?" Oliver did. When he returned, he saw Big Mike had removed his coat and saw where his left arm was dangling by a few tendons. "I'm going to lose it, Oliver."

Oliver and a man who claimed to be a doctor helped clean the wound and wrap the arm to stabilize it as best as they could. "I need to go see my wife, fellas." He struggled to get on his horse and finally managed with a push from Oliver and the doctor, and he rode off across the road, howling in pain every time his rear hit the saddle. Young Atkinson watched him until he was gone. When he turned around to speak to the doctor, he was gone attending other wounded patriots.

"What is happening?" Oliver agonized for a moment.

He knew he needed to get to the next gathering of patriots when a man he'd never met before approached speedily on horseback and asked, "Are you Oliver Atkinson?"

Startled out of his macabre thoughts, Oliver nodded.

"Paul Revere says he wants you back in Boston immediately." In an instant, he was gone.

The young man looked around him and saw death, pain, and rage, hearing the groanings in an otherwise quiet wood. All wildlife close by had scattered. Now it was time for him to do the same on orders from his American father.

Mounting Courage, who he thought he heard blowing loudly and whinnying during the battle as if begging to join the fray, he rubbed her cheeks for a moment and fed her a couple of carrots he'd pocketed the night before from his meal at the inn. Whispering in her right ear, he said, "Go!" And off she went, piercing the smoky, stale air of the previous battle, and made a beeline for the Revere home on the north side of Boston.

* * *

Oliver beat Mr. Revere home. "I can smell the battle on you," Junior said before the Minuteman changed into clean clothes. Rachel fed him after he washed up. By the time he finished eating a second helping, Paul Revere walked through the door.

Looking straight at Oliver before greeting anyone he said, "I know you're exhausted, but I need you to head to Philadelphia tonight."

He was exhausted. He knew Courage was the same.

Revere saw dread in his eyes. "Get a couple of hours of rest, then meet me at the shop."

Riding hard home after leaving the field of battle, the only thing on his mind was safety, staying alert to any Redcoats along the way.

He hadn't time to process the carnage he'd just been a part of, and as he finished his last bites, his mind felt secure enough to wander into those new memories to figure out what to do with them. Now he was being ordered back into the fray. Looking down at his plate as if the weight of his chin made it difficult to raise his head, with the entire family waiting for his response, he muttered, "Yes," as gunfire and the cries of wounded and dying men, some at his hand, fought for dominance. Lifting his head, he looked at Paul Revere in his eyes, nodded and assured him he'd be ready.

Leaving the emotional care of the boy to Rachel, Paul fled back to his print shop. After Lexington, he sprinted home and printed out what had happened so Oliver could pass copies out to the Massachusetts Bay group, which once again included John and Samuel Adams, Thomas Cushing, and John Hancock. "Our brothers gathering for the Second Continental Congress need to know, the world needs to know, that innocent blood has been spilled by the British!"

Mrs. Revere prepared a few days' worth of food and packed a few pairs of clothes and sundries to take with him. Junior watered and fed Courage, who laid down and was quickly asleep.

Two hours later, after having not been able to sleep a wink as he replayed the battle repeatedly, he walked into the print shop to see candles burning to provide light. Oliver curiously looked at them.

"Obviously, this is an exception. Are you ready?"

"I couldn't sleep."

Paul Revere solemnly said to Oliver, "I understand. You'd better pass through Boston Neck before the British return." The boy nodded, and within two and a half hours of arriving home from the battle, having fully debriefed Mr. Revere, he dashed out the door and headed south in hopes of catching the Massachusetts men to alert them that war had come to the colonies.

CHAPTER 18

THE SECOND CONTINENTAL CONGRESS

Courage was not happy. She was downright mad being forced to rush right into the night, as it had been a long forty-eight hours for her as well.

Noting her belligerence at being disturbed from her sleep, Junior suggested an option. "Perhaps you should leave Courage here and take another horse?"

"I know her. I can get her to Philadelphia."

"I'm not going to tell you what to do, but as hard as you need to ride you may be forced to leave her somewhere along the way. Seems leaving her here would be preferable, no?"

Oliver answered by mounting his bold steed. "Please get word to Clara where I've gone." And he galloped away.

He passed through Boston Neck and into the undulating countryside. Night had come. The moon wasn't helpful, sitting concealed above the grayish white blanket of clouds that seemed to be lower in the sky than normal. Riding would be difficult. Hiding along the road behind trees and brush to accost him would not be. Surely, he thought, Redcoats would have alerted every regular from there to Connecticut.

His temples, and everything in between, hurt. The galloping only exacerbated his suffering. Believing himself to be dehydrated, Oliver emptied one of his canteens in three swallows. It didn't help.

His sense was that Courage could outrun any Redcoats for at

least one mile in her condition, but she had to hurt, too. He didn't want to injure his friend and knew how dangerous night riding could be at such a pace. But after witnessing what he did earlier that day, he knew he had to get word to Adams, Hancock, Cushing, and everyone else attending the Second Continental Congress. They needed an eyewitness account in addition to what Mr. Revere had printed.

Oliver's eyes adjusted to the night. He looked for low-hanging branches, potholes, as well as the British. He knew the further south he got from Boston until just above New York City, his problem would not be the Army, but loyalists. In retracing his ride from Philadelphia before with the First Congress's response to the Intolerable Acts, he stopped by the same places and slept in the same barns. Fortunately, the weather was milder, and he didn't freeze.

This time, he brought a little company with him in the form of a Bible he had purchased. In some of the homes he stayed in he was granted privacy, so, without being unsocial, he read.

He was learning to pray as he slow-rode but still didn't know if he was doing it right. Some of the men he'd been around had strong Puritanical backgrounds and were mostly Congregationalists.

He was drawn to their pursuit of holiness and passion for glorifying God through their lives, to what little degree he understood both. It was their personal, individual cause. Everything in his world seemed to be a cause. He was also intrigued by some of the Anglican churches' formality. But he really loved listening to Presbyterians and their talk of the Providence and sovereignty of God. Night after night he would read Genesis and then go into the gospels, so by the time he arrived in Philadelphia ten days later, he'd finished the gospels and most of the first book. Some passages made no sense to him, even after reading multiple times, while others jumped off the page and were like the voice of God spoken directly to him.

Skirting around New York through northern New Jersey, he stayed to the left of the mountains and rode through some of the most beautiful country he'd ever seen. Western New Jersey seemed to be its own little Garden of Eden.

Painfully, he decided to stable Courage a few days into his mission. His valiant friend had little left. It could be costly for both, so he willingly resigned to riding a new horse. Courage was quite jealous seeing Oliver on another beast. "I'll be back for you, my brave buddy," he gently assured her as he fed her some apples, "I just don't know when."

Cutting south through Roxbury Township, Oliver picked up his final horse in Princeton one morning after an all-night, yet cautiously slow, ride. After eating and sleeping for two hours, he was back on the road for only ten minutes when he came upon the carriage carrying John Adams, Thomas Cushing, and Robert Treat.

Halting the carriage, Oliver handed the surprised men copies of the testimony Mr. Revere had printed. "And what is your addition to this, Mr. Atkinson?" Thomas Cushing asked.

John Adams asked over Cushing, "How many patriots died?"

"I don't know, sirs. But I'm certain there were more dead Regulars."

"What was battle like, son?" Treat asked.

Without hesitation, as Oliver had thought much about it on his ride, he replied, "If you're asking if I was scared, the answer is, 'yes.' But not so scared as to understand why it must be. The inevitable has arrived, sirs. To me, the question now is, how soon until we proclaim independence? Or do we await the obvious response from the King, who will surely bring the wrath of his empire down upon us?"

The three delegates looked at each other, then Treat said, "These are the very questions that will create a political and philosophical logjam among the attending loyalists!" Turning to John, "How did they get invited?"

"Rhetorical, Oliver," John said looking at the maturing boy. "Each colony sent their own delegates. None asked for our opinion, Robert."

Cushing interrupted and said, "Okay, we must get going. Oliver, give us your account as we ride."

The Massachusetts radicals pulled themselves back into their carriage while telling Oliver to ride ahead and look for Hancock and Sam Adams, who they suspected were already in Philadelphia and who would tell him what to do next.

"Same Inn?" the young messenger asked with a grimace.

John laughed and said, "I'd heard about your previous accommodations. I even went to smell them for myself." Chuckling, he continued, "I've arranged for you to stay with Peter at his home. His master approved of this even before we left last fall after we'd decided to come back this May. We weren't sure if you'd be with us, but just in case. It pays to plan."

Delighted, Oliver thanked them and turned his horse south to the City of Brotherly Love. He couldn't wait to see Peter again. He couldn't wait to witness history, either.

* * *

Many of the delegates had arrived by the time Oliver crossed into town. He didn't find John Hancock or Sam Adams, who were still in Massachusetts compiling as accurate an account as they could about what happened at Lexington, scouring through testimonies in hopes of determining if it was indeed the British who fired the first shot. They would be along soon enough.

The men from the Old Bay State knew well that almost every other colony expected the Massachusetts colonials to provoke the British into war, and Hancock and Adams wanted as sure proof as possible that the patriots were fired upon first. They learned that the patriots stood down, disbanding and leaving the green when the shot was fired. The battles that ensued along the Bay Road were, then, justified, and the Boston patriots could now convincingly report this to the new congressional gathering.

Oliver offered the same testimony when asked, independent of anyone else's account.

Young Atkinson was now fifteen-years-old and still growing in height, but not necessarily in physical strength, something that concerned him. His hours on end in the print shop didn't build muscles. He was not a man of the earth but of the mind. But he wanted to be both, at least enough to help him in battle. He decided that during whatever free time he might have during his visit to Philadelphia, and beyond, that he would exercise and build physical strength. He could ride a horse like no other but needed to get stronger. He wasn't exactly sure how to do it, but he was going to find a way.

He kept an eye out for Sam Adams and John Hancock, men he had grown very fond of. After being in town a week he'd cycle through the City Tavern to the livery where the carriages and horses were kept, but there were no signs of them. City Hall was a regular stop on his cycle, so he ran there as part of his exercise program.

Atkinson saw no one except a rotund gentleman sitting in the room where the men had congregated before. He sat where the Pennsylvanians had been. A cane leaned against the table to his right. His hair was long and thin, and though short, he was bulky and broad. Hearing a noise behind him, Benjamin Franklin turned around to see Oliver, whom he didn't recognize at first. Oliver stepped away from the door but leaned back in across the painted white frame as if on a hinge and took another look, his eyes squinting. Franklin looked over his shoulder as if spotting something familiarly unfamiliar.

"Mr. Franklin?" Oliver wondered aloud with one foot in the sacred room.

Franklin, who loved being noticed, pivoted in his chair to get a better look at the young man.

"I know you," Franklin said. Now rising. "Yes, we've met, but where?" Oliver took one step into the room. Ben grabbed his cane and waved it towards him, smiling while adjusting his glasses, and said, "Baron Effringham. Yes! At his estate, am I correct?" he asked pleasantly surprised.

"Yes, Mr. Franklin, that is correct," he said, swallowing hard, suddenly realizing that Benjamin Franklin was the only person in the colonies that knew them both and was frightened he might be turned over to the English and returned to the estate.

"You did escape! How delightful! It almost makes this whole bloody mess worth it!"

"You inspired me, Mr. Franklin."

"Come, come sit over here and tell me your story before bloviators from all thirteen colonies swoop down on us and ruin good fellowship. How in the world did you get to Carpenters Hall?"

Oliver said, "Sir, I must first find Mr. Hancock and Sam Adams..."

"They haven't arrived yet. Come sit down," Franklin beckoned while sliding out the chair next to him. Hesitatingly, the young man sat down, and after a few light-hearted comments from this wise old man, Oliver asked him where he wanted to start.

"Where all good stories start, at the beginning!" Franklin replied.

For the next hour, Oliver, being prodded for details and clarifications, began to tell his story from Derby to the present. Franklin was fascinated.

"You know, Effringham was deeply shaken by your escape. He

admired and loathed you all at once. Great powers will always fear greater intellect and power."

Atkinson finished his story, and the marveling Renaissance man sat back pensively, his right hand to his chin, and finally said, "This should be in print!"

Oliver smiled at the familiar words, and said, "Not until the story concludes on its own merit. I'm hoping and praying for a satisfying ending."

Laughing, the bespectacled man said, "Don't we all want that! Look, if the men of Massachusetts fail you in any way, you are welcome to come work for me!"

"Ha!" A loud laugh came from behind them. It was John Adams. He walked over to Oliver and put a hand on his shoulder and said, "You're not one to pilfer, Ben, unless they are wonderfully scented and wear the latest French fashions, of course."

Franklin stood and the men shook hands. "Ben, we were unable to convince your son to join our cause. I'm very sorry."

The aging patriot sorrowfully nodded as he returned to his seat. "Some things are thicker than blood, John, but nothing breaks a heart more than being on alternate sides of freedom. We've all sacrificed something. I'm afraid we've only just begun."

John looked at Oliver and asked while swiveling his head towards Ben, "Did you tell him about Lexington and the Bay Road?"

"Indeed, sir."

Adams handed Franklin a copy of Revere's print. "A fuller report is on its way. I've learned that Sam and Hancock stayed behind to collect evidence and testimonies regarding the day so they could bring a convincing report to us all."

The three talked for the next hour about what this could mean for the thirteen colonies and how it might affect this congress. Suddenly, they realized they were hungry and left Carpenters Hall for an early evening meal at Franklin's home. Once dinner was over around six, Oliver left for Peter's home while the men talked late into the night.

CHAPTER 19

It was warmer than usual for an early May night in Philadelphia. Having frozen for two straight winters in Boston, Oliver felt he might need until June to fully thaw and be properly limber.

From two blocks away, he saw Peter in the dimming day standing at his front door, looking across the landscape of his section of this great city, waiting for a long-lost friend, having been told Oliver was back in town. The young slave spotted his best friend riding out of the dropping sun as a silhouette first, and then with detail. "Oliver!" Peter shouted as he jumped off his three-step porch into Oliver's arms upon dismount in mid-trot. "You stayin'n with me, Oliver. My master seen to it!"

"You're taller than me, now!"

Peter helped his friend unpack his goods and bring them into his princely room upstairs in the main part of the mansion. A pleasant fragrance hung in the air.

"Where's your room?" Oliver asked.

"Oh, I have a nice room, I do. It be in the main servants' cabin out back," his friend joyfully said. "Moved into last fall right after you gone back to Boston."

"Oh." Oliver put away his things and asked if he was allowed to go down to the river.

"I dug up some fresh worms just today! We gots maybe an hour fo' the sun go down."

The boys sprinted to the river. They talked about what had transpired over the last six months, including the exciting news that Peter had a girlfriend.

"I already proposed to her," Peter confidently said.

"How'd you feel when she said 'no'?" Oliver joked.

Punching Oliver in the shoulder while laughing, Peter said, "Maggie said her mama wouldn't let her get married for 'nother year, so we gotta wait. But I am the one. Her mama said!"

Peter then listened to Oliver talk about the girl he was going to marry, Clara Cole.

They talked about anything and everything except revolution, impending war, or even freedom, liberty, and the men from thirteen colonies gathering in the City of Brotherly Love to discuss what their response to Britain would be. They were just young men enjoying one another's company, joshing, laughing, telling stories about odd people they'd met, and fishing, until they realized the moon was up, the sun was down, and the fish weren't biting.

They caught nothing and they could care less.

By the time they got back to the home, a large black woman was standing on the doorstep, arms folded with a rolling pin in one hand.

"You know you don't be out too late, Peter," she said angrily, eyes piercing Peter's. "There's bad people out there. Now get on back to your room!"

She turned to Oliver, who swallowed hard as his friend smiled and whispered "t'was worth it!" and split around the house to his cabin.

As warm and sweetly as she could, the lady with the rolling pin turned to Oliver and introduced herself.

"Mr. Atkinson, my name is Netta, but you can call me Mama Net. So pleased to have you in the home." She broadly waved with the rolling pin in her hand towards the door. "Do come in." Oliver eyed the rolling pin in her hand as he entered the magnificent home. If it was only to get a point across, he got the message.

He went straight away to his room, shut the door, and laid back on his bed. It was now about 9 p.m., he figured, and brutally hot. He left his window open hoping for some cool overnight air. He didn't bother climbing under the covers but took off all his clothing except his drawers. He was exhausted, and though he had to use the loo, he was so tired he hoped he'd be able to sleep right through the night until early light before his bladder burst. Fortunately, a bed pan was close by on a mahogany dresser.

As always, his last thoughts of any day were about Clara. Oliver Atkinson entered a deep sleep as he envisioned kissing her cheek.

* * *

The delegates from Massachusetts moved from the expensively elegant dwelling of The City Tavern to a more comfortable location across the street: Mrs. Sarah Yards Lodging House. That's why it took Oliver a little more time to find the men that morning.

John Adams, now 40, was coming down the stairs when he saw Oliver and said, "Thirty shillings a week in Philadelphia currency, my good man Atkinson. The City Tavern wanted twice that. I'm not here for a vacation. Now, had the beautiful Mrs. Adams accompanied me, well," he said, standing with his hands on each of Oliver's shoulders, "that would be a wholly different story." He smiled and patted Oliver's head as he walked by to the dining area where Mrs. Yard had a spread of food ready for the Massachusetts men.

As John fixed a plate of eggs, bacon, and biscuits, he opened his palm and thrust it toward the food, as if to say, "Are you hungry?" Oliver prepared a plate. "How was the smell in your room last night?" Adams asked, laughing.

"I was so tired, I didn't smell a thing. I awoke this morning in a pool of sweat from the heat but refreshed, otherwise."

"I imagine most of Philadelphia awoke in similar puddles this morning. My favorite almanac said that it will be hotter this summer than last. I hope we get our work done quickly," John said between bites.

Having just arrived from their fact-finding mission, Sam Adams, and Hancock, 38, joined them with food and sat down at the long table. Oliver remembered Paul Revere's admonition to listen when among great men, and speak only if asked, or if something obvious is missing from a point, but to never embarrass anyone when doing it.

At least, not until he became voting eligible.

Like many parts of the Bible, the young man would occasionally get lost when these men wrestled with ideas that floated somewhere above the clouds. It wasn't just philosophy they had bandied about over a few pewter mugs of ale at the meeting house, but ideas that had consequences for their fortunes and very lives.

Though foolishness ended up at the center of many arguments over the next few months, Oliver recalled the first to take center stage the previous year was an argument on where the delegates would meet.

The loyalists and the less radical representatives wanted the gathering to convene at Pennsylvania's State House. Sam Adams demanded a more neutral meeting place. Not wanting to give these weaker delegates a victory from the onset, he prevailed. It was settled that they would continue there. One major battle out of the way. Sam Adams won.

"This is what adults fight over," Oliver wondered. He didn't understand all the nuances or the tug of war over such matters, but, yes, he concluded, the debates, disputes, and diatribes were only going to get worse with such high stakes.

Now that the Second Continental Congress was meeting, Sam Adams and his band thought it better to give the loyalists and moderates a win at the onset as a tool to use them to concede to greater things later. Politics was about strategically compromising certain points for the greater goal, Oliver was noticing. Besides, Sam confided, they needed more space, and the State House was their best option. Sam wins again.

John asked Oliver to remain close by during their sessions to run errands just as before. He had to familiarize himself with the new place. It also meant he wouldn't be seeing Peter during the day.

Entering the House from the street, Oliver carried a few leather bags on behalf of the Adams and Hancock and were led to a table by a porter where the Massachusetts delegation had been assigned. The men chose which seats they would occupy, and then Oliver removed everyone's things and placed them before their seats on green tablecloths. Some writing paper and ink and quills were provided, as was a candle for each table. All the chairs were the same type, except for the chair where the soon-to-be elected president of the congress would sit. It was kingly.

The room was a brilliant white, ornate, with a few fireplaces and plenty of windows for natural light to enter. Men from other colonies began settling in, some with helpers like Oliver, while most just came with their delegates. Conversations among the delegates that had started the previous few days continued until order was called.

"Go get some lunch at Mrs. Yards," John Adams suggested kindly. "Come on back when you're finished."

The always-hungry young Atkinson ran to Mrs. Yards Inn a roundabout way. He noticed the construction of a new building three blocks from the State House and asked the foreman if he could lift some of the heavy buckets of cement for a few minutes a day to work on his strength. He thought the young man was joking before realizing it was a genuine request. Humored, the man said it was fine, if he didn't get in the way or waste any materials. So, until he left Philadelphia, he did this every day during his lunch break.

On the first day he went on too long at the work site, so that by the time he got to the inn, it was full of people getting lunch. After about twenty minutes, Penelope, Mrs. Yard's fifteen-year-old daughter, finally appeared with his bacon sandwich, and was instantly in love with the boy.

"Thank you, Miss," he said without looking at her as he grabbed the food and raced out the door, and back to the State House. Day after day he returned for lunch, or to visit the Massachusetts men, and she fell more deeply in love with him each visit. Yet, he paid her love no attention. In fact, he didn't even notice her. His thoughts were always with Clara when not on duty, and even then, he battled not being consumed with her. The Boston patriots knew about Clara but teased him about Penelope.

"Your minds and my heart don't share the same sense of humor," he finally told the esteemed men. They stopped teasing him immediately.

The number one topic of discussion around Philadelphia was about the battle at Lexington, and the Redcoats bloody return to Boston. Since he was a witness and participant in both, he became a minor celebrity, and everywhere he went people gathered around him to ask questions, listen to his unembellished story, and see his hat.

It was at this time that the legend of his hat started to grow among the masses. They believed the bullet came from the gun of a British Regular, and that it wasn't luck that prevented the bullet from going through the skull of this young patriotic hero, but Providence Himself. People asked to touch it, asked if they could cut off pieces of it for luck; one man even offered him a large sum of money to purchase it. "Yes," they could touch it, even try it on. "No," they could not take threads or cut off pieces of it, and it was "absolutely not" for sale at any price.

He caught himself enjoying the attention a little too much and remembered one night as he was thinking of his recounting of the battles and the applause he received, about humility. Humility was the key to life, first before God, and then before men, a puritan minister once said. Exhaling, he cut himself some slack. He was just a kid, after all, he told himself, confessing that a little was O.K.

After several attempts to quash this legend, Ben Franklin, 69, and more rotund than Oliver could remember, pulled him aside and told him not to fret about his celebrity nor the legend, as they could be useful for him at some point. His integrity was intact, having pushed back against the growing myth. "But now you've glimpsed the goodness of what the tide has brought in. Don't throw it back out to sea," he warmly counseled Oliver.

The fury over Lexington and Concord was not limited to the Massachusetts men. The colonies were electrified with anger. Loyalists among the delegates knew that the Crown would do everything it could to snuff out the rebellion, so they continued pushing for diplomacy. Militias in the various Colonies recruited from this news, and divisions among the colonial citizens grew ever wider.

Patriots couldn't understand why the loyalists would give up their rights, while the loyalists couldn't understand why the patriots thought they had any chance to overcome the British Empire in war. Families were divided along these sentiments. Ben Franklin knew this firsthand. Cities and towns did as well. Some Colonies, like North Carolina, did not have overwhelming support to cast off the Crown, and were evenly split between loyalty and patriotism. This would eventually change for all the Colonies.

The delegates brought their ideas, ideals, questions, concerns, and with the news of Lexington, their fury of the injustice of this assault on men who were leaving the green, disbanding, retreating from any potential fight, only to be forced back in by the British Short Land pattern musket, the British infantry's standard weapon.

Waiting for one of the sessions to begin, Thomas Cushing whispered to John Adams that, "this wildfire rage among the fence sitters is exactly what will fuel our ambitions for independence."

"Diplomacy died in Lexington," John Adams replied, as Cushing nodded, while Hancock seemed to ignore the comment.

Oliver knew the patriot's language, their influences, their objectives, and how they proved the faith and object of their pursuit by their willingness to lay down their lives. He stood right next to them. This gave him boldness to begin openly telling his story as one who had "been in bondage in mother England to a system that forced me to pay a debt that wasn't mine, with no recourse or representation, only to escape to America as a stowaway and be fired upon here for the very same things!"

As comfortable as he was speaking at that level, he also realized he was a social oddball at times, and didn't always enjoy certain galas, and despised going to balls. Twice Ben Franklin coerced him into going with him in order to "make" him a man. He hated them. He didn't like the drunkenness, for one, nor the devolving conversations that appeared a few hours into imbibing. He had few "proper" social skills and saw the well-to-do's pointing and laughing at his expense. Franklin saw this and told the boy, "Don't use manners. Use charm! And wear that hat next time!" Oliver wondered if he was Franklin's prop.

Jolly Ben Franklin was amusing the remaining delegates in Independence Hall after a day's work. As Oliver was leaving, he called out to the young hero to become a man by attending a ball with him that night. "It's well past time for you to know a woman, Oliver!"

Oliver's gaze pierced Franklin's eyes, he asked him, "Is Clara going to be there?" Staring down Franklin for a moment, the men around Ben burst out laughing.

Ben was the last to get it. "You, indeed, my friend, are a man. No more foolish talk from me." He quickly gathered his papers and left.

"Mr. Franklin!" Oliver ran after him and caught him on the street. "I apologize for what I did in front of the delegates. I should've been more honorable and tactful when insisting that your invitations to get drunk and meet strange women stop. I really was trying to be funny, but it was too aggressive."

"You did the right thing," Franklin answered as he turned and headed towards his home. "I was boorish, lascivious, and imprudent towards you, Clara, and your faith." Stopping, Franklin turned to face Oliver. "I spent years being close friends with the greatest revivalist Christian preacher since St. Paul himself. Have you ever heard of George Whitefield?"

"No, sir, I haven't," Oliver confessed.

Franklin continued walking with Oliver at his side, offering to carry the heavier materials, which the aging Pennsylvanian appreciatively handed the young man. "Thank you. He had some theatrical training before God got a hold of him," Franklin said of Whitefield. "I've never seen nor heard a more powerful, more enjoyable orator in all my life. I told you he was a close friend. I occasionally traveled with him to towns and cities to hear him preach. I helped support some of the orphanages he established. We corresponded for some time, though I hadn't seen him in years when I received word he had passed in 1770. Yes, George was a close friend." Franklin paused as if seeing something play out in his mind before continuing with a sigh. "Tragically, though, in my heart I was more like the mockers at Mars Hill than the believers at Thessalonica."

They arrived at Franklin's doorstep. Silence Dogood, for that's what he called himself when writing anonymous letters to his brother's newspaper many years earlier, faced the boy and said after opening his door and taking his materials from him, "I think the gift of spiritual faith tired of waiting for me a long time ago and alighted on someone else. Any residue of faith left behind I now place in the ideals of America. I can smell its earth. I cannot the Kingdom of God's. Your nostrils are full of the Kingdom, as are your eyes and your heart. The Kingdom of God is yours, young man." Franklin paused for a moment before gently, briefly, touching the boy's face, and saying, "Wait for your dear Clara."

The man he met at Baron Effringham's estate two years earlier entered his home and closed the door. That was the last conversation they ever had.

CHAPTER 20

The main discussion among the delegates to the Second Continental Congress on May 10, 1775, was whether the big event in Massachusetts was enough for them to pursue independence at this time. Certainly, the Massachusetts delegates, and their more radical friends, believed it to be the perfect time to make this declaration.

To add urgency to their argument for independence, they received word from Colonel William Prescott from a courier sent by Revere that General Gage had declared martial law in Boston to be in effect starting June 12. Any person helping the rebellious Colony of Massachusetts would be shot as a traitor to the Crown. Additionally, the courier gave John Adams a report of a battle that occurred on Breeds and Bunker Hill.

After digesting the missives in his room, Adams walked the few blocks to their meeting house, and, after Hancock called the gathering to attention, he stood and proceeded to inform the members of the battle he hoped would spur them closer to declaring independence.

"Colonel William Prescott sent me a battle report about an event in Boston you must hear about. I will summarize. Led by Dr. Joseph Warren, the patriots in Boston began to fortify Bunker Hill and Breed's Hill a few months before this righteous convocation. If any of you had been to Boston, no doubt you would have chosen this perfect location to keep an eye on the British warships in our fair harbor. Sadly, it became a battleground. On June 17, the

British attacked a band of one thousand patriots with twenty-four-hundred of their own men. Because the militia had limited powder and shot, the patriot soldiers were ordered by Colonel Prescott to "not fire until you see the whites of their eyes!" Every shot had to count. And they did, as the British sustained more than a thousand casualties while the Americans sustained four-hundred-and-fifty. In the end, however, our patriots lost, overwhelmed by the Redcoats third charge up Breed's Hill. Our good friend Dr. Warren died. There is much sorrow among the Massachusetts men who knew him well."

Oliver entered the hall with fresh bottles of ink and additional parchment just as Adams sat down. The gravity on the faces of those present alarmed him. He dared not ask what happened, but as he placed the items down on the Massachusetts Men's desk, John Adams whispered that he'd explain later.

After a moment passed, Button Gwinnett from Georgia shouted from his seat, "Men, I think it's time to get back to work!"

Breed's Hill helped spur on the spirit of compromise among them all, agreeing on July 5 to make one last plea to King George III for peace by appealing to him with the Olive Branch Petition. A young delegate from Virginia, the handsome and shy Thomas Jefferson, noted more for his written word rather than his spoken word, was assigned the task of authoring a letter to King George of the colony's loyalty to him while asking him to intervene on their behalf with Parliament. They hoped this peace offering would de-escalate tensions between the two groups, allowing them to rejoin in meaningful discussion about the contentions both sides made. The petition read in part:

"Knowing, to what violent resentments and incurable animosities, civil discords are apt to exasperate and inflame the contending parties, we think ourselves required by indispensable obligations to Almighty God, to your Majesty, to our fellow subjects, and to ourselves, immediately to use all the means in our power, not incompatible with our safety, for stopping the further effusion of blood, and for averting the impending calamities that threaten the British Empire."

It went on to plead with the King for a reduction of forces and reconciliation. But the King would have none of it. They later learned that he refused to read it. By August, King George declared all the Colonies to be in a state of rebellion.

Assuming this might inevitably be the case no matter what they proposed to King George, the delegates agreed each would create militias, while also establishing a Continental Army ahead of sending the document.

By June 10, the forces in and around Boston, made up of men from several northern Colonies, were deemed members of the Continental Army. A general was needed, and by June 16, George Washington, a gentleman planter from Virginia who had served as Lieutenant Colonel in the Virginia Militia for England in the French and Indian War, agreed to lead the new army as its general. Washington didn't hide his ambitions. He had worn a perfectly tailored military uniform he had created just for this purpose every day to Independence Hall.

Men from every Colony would be sent to serve under Washington. Congress then issued "bills of credit" to help pay for this army, with each of the Colonies promising to pay the debt incurred.

* * *

Standing outside Independence Hall on May 10, Oliver saw the most noble, regal man he'd ever seen approaching in calm confidence on the tallest horse he'd ever seen. He seemed like a giant of a man, sitting tall in his saddle, nodding to passersby and tipping his hat to a few gentleladies. He was dressed in a military uniform unlike any in all of Philadelphia that Oliver had seen. The young man was instantly captured by his presence, and as the man came to a halt at the steps to the Hall, Oliver asked if he could help him in any way. Smiling, George Washington replied, "You can help me in every way, young man!"

George Washington dismounted his horse as gracefully as any rider Oliver had ever seen. In one fluid elegant motion, the uniformed man swung his right leg back over the saddle and in the blink of an eye he had two feet on the ground, gently landing, seemingly without disturbing the dust on the street.

"My name is Oliver Atkinson, sir."

Mr. Washington cocked his head towards the boy while unleashing a leather case attached to his saddle. "Oliver Atkinson. I know you and your hat! We met last year."

"You remembered," Oliver excitedly asked.

"Of course! You're one of the heroes of Lexington-Concord and the skirmishes along the Bay Road." He handed his case to an eager Oliver while a stable hand took the Virginia planter's horse.

"There were many heroes that day, sir," he responded.

This caused Washington to pause and reflect solemnly for a moment. "Truer words, Mr. Atkinson."

Oliver followed George Washington as he climbed the few steps that led into Independence Hall and placed his leather case down at the seat designated for him among the Virginia delegates. The Hall was starting to fill up for the session.

John Adams approached the two and said of Oliver to Washington, "He belongs to us, Mr. Washington," and slapped Oliver on the back, to which they all laughed.

"Not for long, Mr. Adams. How is Abigail?" the tall Virginian asked the diminutive Bostonian.

"As always, making me a better man at everything. How is Martha?"

"I confess the same as you," he said with a sincere smile.

Adams gently tugged at Oliver's waistcoat and said, "Come along, Oliver, before he tries to turn you into a southern gentleman!"

Washington laughed and said, "It is the finest life, Mr. Atkinson."

Adams walked Oliver to the Massachusetts desks and instructed him on his duties for the day. Turning to go outside of the Hall into the foyer and wait to be called for errands, he spotted Mr. Washington looking at him. The elder nodded to him, and he smiled and nodded back. Oliver was thrilled to no end.

Once the forty-three-year-old Washington was made Commander-in-Chief of the Continental Army, John Adams pulled Oliver aside during a break in a session due to the overwhelming heat that sat upon each man at their desks, and asked him to a small room in the back of the Hall.

Oliver heard Stephen Hopkins of Rhode Island complain to John Jay of New York as they abandoned their seats that he'd never had to step outside on a summer day to cool down.

Uncertain of this peculiar beckoning, the young man followed Adams apprehensively, wondering what he might have done wrong. Nothing came to mind as they both entered the room and sat opposite each other at a small table. The green curtains were tied to the side so air could circulate, but this room was hotter than the main hall.

Exhaling as he leaned forward with his folded hands clutching a handkerchief that he kept dabbing his sweaty face with, Mr. Adams said, "It has come to my attention that you have been impressing people here." He paused.

"Is that a problem, Mr. Adams?" the wide-eyed young man asked.

"Remember I told Mr. Washington, now General Washington, to stay away from you. That was done in jest, of course. You know that, right?" He continued without waiting for Oliver's response. "Well, he is leaving us tomorrow to head for Cambridge to take command of the Continental Army and has requested you be the junior aide-de-camp on his staff. I assume you will be doing much of what you've been doing here with us, but more formally as an army soldier. He's quite aware of not only your familiarity with the Boston area, but the skills you acquired and demonstrated as a Minuteman. You would be quite valuable to him and to our cause." Adams finished and leaned back in his chair.

Oliver stood up and walked to a window, looking out for a moment. After a moment, he said, "My loyalty is to our Colony, to you men who took me in and breathed life back into me."

Adams responded, saying, "You recently told me that you are now an American."

"I did," he said, turning back to Adams.

"Joining General Washington for what will be a near-impossible task may be the greatest opportunity to be an American you'll ever have." Adams stood and faced Oliver. "But it's purely your decision. You will not be judged negatively by either of us."

"No one else knows?"

"No, one. You can seamlessly continue working here and no one will be the wiser." He moved toward the door. "There will be other opportunities for a young man with your intellect and talents. But I believe Providence is giving you a promotion."

"When will I see you again? The others?" Oliver asked, his upper lip shaking while fighting back tears.

"Only Providence knows that as well." He came in to embrace the young man, who wept on his chest. "We can only pray sooner than later, and in the finest of health."

The young man pulled back finally, and upon catching his breath, said, "I should go tell Mr.–uh, General Washington, that I'll be leaving with him in the morning. I need to let the other

Massachusetts men know as well."

Suddenly it hit him. "Peter." At this he became emotional. He stepped back from the embrace.

"Yes. Go see the men now and spend the rest of your afternoon with Peter. We are dining at the Yards' Inn tonight. I shall see you there."

John Adams quickly turned and walked away just as a fiery hot tear escaped down his cheek.

Immediately, Oliver sprinted back to the home of Peter's master to see his friend. He wasn't there. Nor did Oliver find him at Carpenter's Hall. The concerned young man ran to their favorite fishing spot on the Delaware, but the spot was vacant. Peter was nowhere to be found. Then it dawned on him that he could be at Maggie's home, or somewhere nearby, because apparently Maggie's mother wasn't yet ready to allow those two to be together unsupervised, though Peter had confided in Oliver that they had sneaked away a few times to a large cherry tree on a fallow farm just outside of town.

Almost no one came out that way, so it was their safe place to talk. It turns out Maggie did in fact love Peter. They'd pick cherries and eat them until they felt sick, laughing and carrying on as young ones do. They even kissed once, but it scared them both so much they agreed not to do it again until they were married. "Not that it was a bad feeling," he confided in Oliver while fishing, "It wasn't fear because it was bad, Ollie," as he called him, "but because it was too good. If something happened beyond that and we got caught, we'd be separated for life."

Oliver didn't find them at her house, so he ran back home and got on his horse and rode out to the cherry tree. His physical fitness had never been better, but, frankly, he was tired of running and burning adrenaline as time was limited. As he approached the magnificent black cherry tree, he saw the two sitting back against the trunk and giggling, until they heard hoof beats. Looking up with concern, they saw Oliver nearing, wildly waving a hand. Peter shot up and ran to meet him as Maggie rose and brushed off a hundred cherry pits from her apron.

"Every'ting right, Ollie? What you doin' out here?"

Oliver hopped off his horse as it came to a halt and placed the reins over a bush. Standing two feet away, Oliver said, "I'm leaving in the morning. I don't know if I'll ever be back."

Peter stepped back in anger, his face clenched. Oliver wasn't sure how to interpret this. Maggie wasn't sure what was happening. Suddenly, Peter rushed him and hugged Oliver so hard as if to say he wasn't going to let him go. Stepping back while holding each's forearms, Oliver explained his story.

"I'm going to work for General Washington and the Continental Army. We're headed to Massachusetts."

"Promise me you'll come back, Ollie. Don't let no Redcoat shoot you, O.K.?"

For the next thirty minutes the three of them sat under the tree laughing between gulps of cherries. By then, it was late afternoon and Oliver needed to pack and meet the Massachusetts men for dinner.

"If I have room. I think I ate too many cherries."

Hugging one last time, with Maggie joining in, Oliver rode quickly back to Philadelphia.

* * *

At the candle-lit Yards' Inn that night, the Massachusetts men, including Oliver, gathered for dinner and were soon joined by General Washington. As soon as the tall Virginian entered the fragrant dining area, his presence drew everyone's attention, momentarily quieting the hubbub. Whatever awe men had of him before, now that he had been made the Commander of the

Continental Army, their esteem for him approached kingly status.

Washington took off his hat and placed it between his arm and side, nodded to a few people, and was congratulated by a few more. The loud discussions resumed as he zig-zagged his twisting body past crowded tables and chairs to one in the back hosted by the Massachusetts men. Present also were Patrick Henry, Richard Caswell from North Carolina, and Thomas Mifflin from Pennsylvania. The Virginia gentleman's plate of food arrived at the same time he did. Warm greetings followed before the paused conversation restarted.

To be sure, Washington wanted an update on the situation in Massachusetts. The Bostonians explained in as much detail as they could what had happened and was happening in Boston and in the Massachusetts Colony. The general asked questions about the militia. How many men? How were they trained? Did they have munitions, and what about cannons? The answers he heard were disappointing. Oliver sat and listened, as he had been taught to do.

Finally, General Washington, who was sitting across from the quiet young man, faced him and asked, "Are you prepared to help us accomplish the impossible?"

"My life the last couple of years has been a manifestation of the impossible. I don't doubt that with your leadership on the battlefield, combined with the leadership of great men like those present at our table, we will inevitably be approved of, and empowered, by God Almighty Himself, and that our righteous aims will lead to victory."

"Hear, hear!" the men shouted.

"Either a preacher or politician you will be, Oliver," Caswell merrily projected.

"I've been nudging him towards the law," an amused John Adams offered.

"No, no, not me, dear sirs. Frankly, from what I've seen, I don't like politics, though, mind you with no disrespect, I understand its necessity. I've not felt the heavenly tug to the pulpit, either. What I'd sincerely like to say to all present here is, I am an orphan boy, a stowaway, who finds himself among kind, generous, brave men who were born for such a time as this. Dark days are here. Let's bring His light."

Washington sat back, marveling at Oliver. He had just heard more from young Atkinson than he ever had because Oliver always seemed silent in his presence. He later learned this was the direction Paul Revere and the Massachusetts men had given him for his two trips to Philadelphia.

"We may have just won the war by assigning Oliver Atkinson to my staff!" Washington said, with cheers, laughter, and toasts following. Oliver blushed and fidgeted uncomfortably.

Shortly thereafter, Washington needed to leave to meet with some other delegates. "I need you men to work diligently to secure funds for this army. I can promise you, whatever is decided upon, we will need four times as much. I'm counting on you." Turning to Oliver while rising to leave, the general said, "Be prepared to spend months on end in a saddle. We leave before the rooster wakes."

Oliver stood and saluted someone for the first time. "I will be ready, General Washington." The men at the table stood and said farewell to their commander-in-chief, as all eyes followed the tall planter out the door.

CHAPTER 21

General George Washington

On June 23, 1775, Washington headed north. Another sleepless night fired by the excitement over his elevated role under Washington and because he was headed back to Clara.

Morning had never been so peaceful to the new Continental recruit. The richly dark sky covered the sleeping metropolis like a blanket, its shimmery stars faithfully watching over all. The roosters hadn't crowed yet.

He was on his horse and ready to go when General Washington pulled up to the departure point at Independence Hall. The head of the newly formed Continental Army was dressed handsomely in a stately blue and buff uniform, perched immaculately upon the whitest horse Oliver had ever seen.

General Washington, it appeared to Oliver, could've conquered any army in the world dressed as he was, including the British.

As the last man of his traveling party arrived, General Washington solemnly looked over his entourage, and after a moment of silence, addressed them: "I have chosen each one of you because you understand what we are embarking on, what the loss and gain might inevitably be. Our fight is before us, except for Mr. Atkinson here, who has already engaged the British on the battlefield. Be resolute in your affections for your family and for freedom and self-rule, and we will ultimately have victory because we won't face one British soldier who is fighting for the same thing."

With that, the general gave the order to move out.

They were an hour into their journey north to Massachusetts before a rooster crowed.

Accompanying them were two Majors General, Charles Lee and Philip Schuyler. Additionally, Thomas Mifflin, Washington's primary aide, a few officers of the local Pennsylvania militia, a stableman to take care of the horses, and General Washington's gregarious slave valet, William "Billy" Lee, who was with him constantly, completed the staff. Extra horses were brought along with provisions, ammunition, and a light phaeton carriage he had recently purchased in Philadelphia.

Also, there were twenty-five members of the Philadelphia light infantry that joined to provide protection all the way to New York.

Oliver thoroughly enjoyed the camaraderie but understood the gravity of the mission they were on, especially as he listened and learned more during the trip to Cambridge, Massachusetts.

The Virginia planter did not ask Congress for a salary, but that all of his expenses be reimbursed at the end of the conflict, which amazed Oliver because he kept hearing Charles Lee, who had politicked for the role of Commander-in-Chief, cursing up a storm, the likes he'd never heard before, demanding what many considered an exorbitant wage to assume this responsibility.

Charles Lee was a British-born officer in the Seven Years War, who had sold his commission afterwards, serving for a time in the Polish Army. Returning to the Colonies in 1773, he bought an estate in western Virginia and waited for what he saw was the inevitable: war with England. He saw himself as the logical choice to lead its army if the conflict occurred. But when the Second Continental Congress appointed the American-born Washington instead and was then relegated to third-in-command below Artemas Ward, he raged.

Washington always "handles himself like a gentleman," the young man thought, and aspired to be as gentlemanly as he. He had adopted the daring of Paul Revere, the temperament for liberty of Sam Adams, the hope for diplomacy of John Hancock, and the wisdom and intelligence of John Adams. Now, Oliver would add "gentleman soldier" to his being.

Oliver knew very little about Washington except what he had gathered from conversation with others and overheard from just outside the main hall as the delegates discussed his potential command. Other than the one conversation with Delegate Washington at the start of the Congress, and the evening at the Yards' Inn, he hadn't conversed with him.

Befriending Billy Lee on their long ride north, Oliver learned that General Washington had been a surveyor, and a Lieutenant Colonel in the Virginia Militia serving the British Army during the French and Indian War, before becoming an elected official in the Virginia House of Burgesses. He married Martha Custis in 1759, becoming a plantation owner in 1761.

Washington enjoyed tinkering with crops, looking to create new types of plants, and rotating crops to see how various strains adapted to the soil. He grew assorted types of corn, wheat, turnips, potatoes, hemp, flax, watermelon, squash, beans, cabbage, parsnip, cotton, and oats.

He turned from tobacco to various kinds of wheat in the 1760's. This was a strategic economic decision as there was already an abundance of tobacco farms all through the South. English merchants controlled the price of tobacco and dictated the market, which created a debt-economy for many farmers. With wheat, he could sell whole wheat locally or mill it into fine flour and sell it both locally, regionally, or export it, without the same competition or merchant issues tobacco created.

"General George is a smart man. A good man. Never know him

not to succeed," Billy Lee said of his master.

Until Billy Lee rode up to him a couple of days into the journey, Oliver mostly rode alone. He was not a part of any of the traveling groups yet, though found no one unfriendly. Many of the men seemed to know each other, and he was a young man still finding his confidence. So, he listened. What did he have to add? He waited to be approached to have a conversation. This was a good exercise, he thought to himself. Washington had chosen him personally. He had plans for him.

There would be plenty of time to get to know some of these people, but unlike being a part of the Sons of Liberty, where personal relationships were more important than connecting professionally, Oliver discerned with this group that professional relationships mattered more than personal ones.

He observed everything he could. From physical and social mannerisms to the language of the military, how each rank interacted with each other and with the general, he read from a living book.

They spent the night just north of Trenton, New Jersey, and were back on the road early the next day, slogging their way across the rain-soaked, muddy roads full of potholes and slippery rocks.

Washington feared Providence was telling him this campaign they were embarking on was going to be perilous through to conclusion, though he told those around him to "pray that this unhappy controversy come to an honorable and speedy end."

After a few days of hard travel, the military party crossed into New York, but not before Washington had sent a messenger ahead to alert the friendlies there of his pending arrival. Oliver had hoped for that assignment, but he didn't get it.

"I'm fine with it," he told Billy Lee. "It gives me more time with General Washington."

Billy Lee smiled with an exaggerated nod, and said, "Not a

better privilege in the world!"

Before crossing the North River, later to be renamed the Hudson River, General Washington put on a satin purple sash and switched his travel hat for one with a large plume befitting a Commander-in-Chief. The boat that took the general across didn't have enough room for his entire party, so Oliver said he would take the second boat, an act of humility Washington noted as the other men were jockeying for a spot with him.

On the other side, Washington and his party met nine militia companies and a considerable number of patriot citizens of all ages. This impressed Washington very much as he understood that New York was still primarily devoted to the Crown. Rewarding Oliver for having volunteered to take the second boat, Washington asked him to ride beside him through New York on the parade route to their destination north on Broadway to Hull's Tavern, where they dined and rested for the night.

"Turned out real good for you, now didn't it, Mr. Oliver!" Billy Lee exulted as he galloped past.

Along the way, Oliver was able to reunite with his horse, Courage.

Finally, they arrived in steamy Cambridge, Massachusetts, on July 2, 1775, to a ragtag group of soldiers numbering around fourteen thousand. They were untrained, undisciplined, and lacked provision. Washington thought that fighting the British would be difficult enough as it was, but how much more with this lot of unprepared patriots? Nevertheless, the men greeted him respectfully and were eager to learn how to be soldiers.

Many loyalists had abandoned their homes and mansions in the Cambridge area due to the proliferation of patriot militia. Including Harvard's buildings, these would become makeshift barracks during their time in this small, overwhelmed town. After establishing his HQ at the abandoned Vassall House, Washington began their training immediately, having the men build earthworks, trenches, and forts around the Cambridge area. Washington chose this area to support the siege of Boston and send the British the strongest possible message that the colonies were ready to fight, though he knew his undisciplined men weren't due to lack of experience, little-to-no training, and a shortage of supplies.

This "dirty and nasty lot" stressed the general. But he was encouraged by these proud men's willingness to become a united fighting force for the nascent union.

CHAPTER 22

Depending on the general and his staff's needs for the day, Oliver either trained with the soldiers in Roxbury, where many were staying, and the Vassall House, or on standby at the general staff headquarters. At first, his role was primarily that of a courier. But after a couple of weeks, he was summoned from Roxbury to see General Washington at Vassall House, who asked the fifteen-year-old young man if he was ready for something more substantive to do.

"I am, sir, yes, I believe so," Oliver said seriously.

"You believe so? That's not the typical Oliver I've come to know," Washington stated.

"I'm still learning soldier etiquette, general," the youth said, eliciting a chuckle from his boss.

The general moved from around his desk and put a hand on his right shoulder and said, "I understand you enjoy riding around these parts?"

With that, Paul Revere, now 41, came into the room. A stunned Oliver hadn't seen him since before he left for Philadelphia a few months earlier, now being mid-July. Revere was about to shake Washington's hand when Oliver ran up and hugged him tightly, with Revere returning it while Washington laughed. "Protocol, Oliver," Revere said with a warm smile as Oliver let go.

"My apologies, sir. As I said a moment ago..." Oliver offered, embarrassed.

"Nothing to be ashamed of, Mr. Atkinson," Washington said as he shook Revere's hand. "Shall we take a ride to Boston's perimeter?"

Revere, Oliver, Washington, and a few of Washington's staff, surveyed the land around Boston, visiting the areas where the siege that had begun two days after Lexington was under way.

During their ride, Revere told the general what his spy network had learned about the Crown's current intention for Boston.

"What are your expectations for the siege, Paul?" Washington asked.

After pausing, Revere responded, "To chase the British out, dry up their resources from our land, choke off access to Massachusetts, and gain a reprieve to our citizens."

"Where do you think they'll move their forces?"

"Hopefully north to Canada, but if I had to guess, it would probably be to New York City and its friendly environs."

"Putting them in a position to divide the colonies?" Washington asked.

Revere silently nodded.

"Mr. Atkinson, do you have any thoughts on this?" Washington invited.

Surprised, Oliver hesitated for a moment, gathered his thoughts, then offered, "Right now, I believe the colonies need victories anywhere it can get them."

Both men agreed with him.

At the end of the review of the siege, Washington asked Oliver not-so-seriously if he had any idea where they might get "twenty or so cannon?"

The young man perked up. "I'd heard yesterday from a new recruit about a group of men calling themselves The Green Mountain Boys led by a man named Ethan Allen from Vermont. Some of their fellows fought at Lexington and along the Bay Road. He mentioned a British fort they'd overrun called Ticonsomething."

"Ticonderoga," Revere finished.

"That's it! Someone in Roxbury said they had at least fifty cannons there along with powder and balls."

Revere spoke up and said, "This happened in late May, sir. I made a request that they give us some of the guns but was told, "no." According to current protocol, I mentioned this to Major General Schuyler and asked him to tell you. I thought he had. My apologies, sir."

An angry Washington barked, "From now on, I give you permission to speak to me directly with news at this level, Paul. Timely information at this time is as important as shot and powder."

"Yes, sir, General Washington," Revere humbly responded.

The siege seemed to have some positive effect for the patriots, and for now it was enough, but he wrestled with this as well. The British still had unimpeded access to the sea, meaning, at some point the King could send even more troops and overrun their positions on the perimeter. He knew that sometime soon he would need those cannons, but for now, he gave his primary attention to training his army.

His first dilemma was how to instill discipline, build morale, and keep their eyes on their objective: victory over Britain and the liberty that would follow. Many of these citizen soldiers were there at their own expense. Washington pressed congress to elect a Paymaster General. He didn't want his men worried about feeding their families. He wanted them focused on becoming an army that could stand up to the British. Presently, the better prepared British army could mow right through his brave volunteers, and he had to change that as quickly as possible.

Oliver trained with the general army until he learned the basics of being a proper soldier. He had a head start on many of the men because of his semi-formal training with the Minutemen.

He was then moved to the calvary as a mounted troop. His riding ability, and skill at shooting his musket Belle accurately while in full gallop, not to mention his background serving Revere's spy network, made this sensible. However, Washington wanted him to remain close by for special courier runs.

General Washington admired the young man's discipline, willingness to learn, and immediate response to orders given by both him and his staff. Only occasionally was correction needed, and it was not a result of Atkinson being undisciplined or disorderly, but lacking understanding, technique, precision, and accuracy in certain duties and military protocol.

During this time, Oliver secretly hoped that he would be given a commission as an officer. He was a natural leader, and men more than twice his age respected him and followed his lead throughout training, including during combat drills. But he knew he was too young at that time.

"I'm certain you will make a fine officer at some point, but for now I have other plans for you, Mr. Atkinson," General Washington told him one night as he dismissed the staff who had gathered for the day's debriefing. "Much of your work in the near future will be solo, and will include long hard rides into areas you've never been before, carrying important dispatches from me and the staff. The first of these rides will have you headed to Mount Vernon, my home, where you will find two men, a Mr. Diggs and a Mr. Betancourt, who help manage my plantation. You will give Mr. Diggs this list," the general handed him a sealed envelope, "and ask him to gather these military history books, and have Mr. Bettencourt bring them to me immediately, along with winter clothing, extra glasses, etc. It's all there," he said pointing to the envelope.

"Yes, General Washington," Atkinson said. He looked at the

general who seemed to have something else to say.

"I have been debating whether to send you to North Carolina to connect with certain militia down there. You don't know the land, have never been further south than Philadelphia, and are still..." Washington paused.

Oliver completed his sentence. "A boy."

Walking from behind his desk, the giant man looked down with fatherly tenderness and said, "You stopped being a boy a long time ago. You are a man, Oliver. I'm simply concerned if I am putting too much on you too soon."

"I can handle the travel, sir, and so can Courage," Oliver confidently said.

"Oliver," Washington said as he placed a hand on his shoulder, "the colonies are full of danger. Loyalists and Tories will be on the lookout for couriers from me. If caught, you will be considered a spy and shot. Do you understand this?"

"I could have been shot at Lexington and along the Bay Road, your Excellency. With the additional training I've received, I'd like you to consider going with your first instinct. Let me take the cause of freedom as far as I am able. I'd ride across the ocean on Courage to take London by myself if I could!"

Washington's head snapped back in laughter, and he returned to his desk. He sat down, picked up a quill and began to write. "You are not one given to bravado, but I appreciate your sentiment, as I would join you!" Looking up at Oliver, who was still standing at ease before the General of the Continental Army, the Virginia planter said, "I want you to take these messages to North Carolina. The Colony is split. The militias there are concerned with the larger loyalist and Tory militias that have come together. I want them to know that they are not alone, that we are thinking of them, and will support them as best as we can with prayer, as well as influence on their colonial leaders to side with us, while persuading Congress to get them ammunition, uniforms, and pay."

Washington finished writing his messages, sealed them in envelopes with wax and his personal stamp, then handed them to Oliver. "For your secret compartment."

"Thank you for your trust, sir," Oliver said.

"My aide-de-camp George Baylor will give you further instructions in the morning. Christmas is approaching, and it is sad to say but you will be traveling and not with the Reveres or your lovely future wife, Clara. Please go and spend two days with them before leaving but check with me before you depart."

Washington opened reports from his officers with a look Oliver had seen many times, meaning their conversation was over and the general was on to his next task.

Oliver and Revere exited the home. Standing on the expansive porch, the Son of Liberty leader put a hand on each of the young man's broadening shoulders. Oliver's heart raced with excitement over the new duty he had been assigned to but suddenly pivoted to concern as he saw the eyes of Paul Revere well up. The goldsmith, printer, Mechanic, and patriot, paused while noticeably gathering himself.

"You are no longer the boy I met on *The Beaver*. You are a man, Oliver."

Oliver tightly grabbed Revere's upper arms, trying to resist the sudden appearance of emotion that had been closeted away for the last two years.

"From Derby to Roxbury..." Revere's voice trailed off for a moment before continuing. "An unlikely life, indeed."

Oliver pushed aside his patron's arms and wrapped his tightly around the man's chest as a curious lieutenant walked past and into the house. Stepping back, Oliver composed himself as best as the moment would allow, and simply said, "Thank you," and turned, bounding down the steps.

"Supper at our home before you leave!" Revere called out, which Oliver acknowledged with a wave as he turned the corner and was gone.

* * *

Each time the door to her father's tavern opened, a hopeful Clara's head would turn instinctively with such great force that once she hurt her neck. And if it wasn't Oliver who came through, her sadness would deepen. All day, every day, the young girl dreamed of her heroic Oliver's hand holding hers, of his kisses on her cheeks, alternating them on the left and right with each visit, of his breath on her neck when he would whisper in her ear.

He tried being funny but was only funny for trying. He also wasn't romantic, yet, but not because he hadn't tried. He was young, a novice, and didn't have a father to look upon for guidance on how to woo a girl. Paul Revere was his father figure and taught him the language of patriotism but wasn't one for teaching him the language of love. At nearly sixteen, he was already a man in so many ways, but not in this area.

She had patience for him growing up in other ways. After all, as much as she loved him, she was afraid to love him too much until the colonial conflict was over. She cried so many tears of fear in her mother's arms.

Walking by the river with her mother one day after a prolonged absence by Oliver, she said, "My faith seems choked by an invisible tie. I'm struggling to pray and read the Bible. Oliver suggested I pray the scriptures and keep me in his prayers, but I am so consumed with fear for his life that my mind goes blank when I try. In some ways it's a strange respite, and in other ways it scares me."

"As it does your father and I. You are still quite young and are forecasting emotions meant for someone a few years older. He isn't God. Don't make him an idol."

With that, they finished their walk in silence.

Christmas was two weeks away and she had a special gift for her love. Clara had taught herself to dye wool that she'd bought with money she'd saved from her job with the family, as well as from times when she watched a widower neighbor's children when he was away delivering leather goods he made to surrounding towns. Clara took the wool to a weaver who made a beautiful purple and green blanket that she couldn't wait to give Oliver. It was delivered to her the same day that General Washington's special aide walked through the door for the first time in a month.

Clara stared at Oliver until her heart returned to her chest, while her mother grabbed the blanket off the table and quickly retreated to the back to hide it.

"Clara, my love," Oliver said tenderly as he confidently strode towards her, his arms extended, when in a flash, she was upon him squealing joyously, holding him so tight he thought he was going to stop breathing. Finally, she relaxed her grip, and he kissed her on her lips for the first time. Clara pulled away pleasantly stunned, then went back in for another. Neither knew what they were doing, but they were enjoying it until Mr. Cole came out to the dining area where they stood and cleared his throat.

Loudly. Twice.

Embarrassed in his bliss, the Continental soldier shot back a step from the tavern owner's daughter as Clara cleared hair away from her rosy face and brushed down her apron. "Mr. Cole. How do you do, sir?"

Smiling, he said, "Good to see you, Oliver." He approached the young man extending his hand, which he took. Motioning for him to sit on a bench seat at a dining table, Oliver did. "Go see what help your mother needs," with a glance at Clara.

Clara turned and rushed into the back of the tavern shouting, "Mother, Oliver's here!"

"How long are you here for?" the man asked.

"Until the day after tomorrow, assuming you have a bed for me?" Mr. Cole nodded. "Tomorrow, I'm going to see the Reveres in Watertown where they are living now. I'd like to take Clara with me, if I have your permission. I promise to have her home by dark."

His eyes pierced Oliver's as he said, "You two have never been alone together."

"Perhaps, you and Mrs. Cole would like to join us?" Oliver hastily asked.

"Mrs. Cole and I would enjoy that," he responded with a wink.

"Good," Oliver said with a heavy swallow. "I'm delighted to hear that. The Revere's will be doubly joyful."

At that, plates of food and drink were brought out by the mother and daughter, and they feasted and talked about the army, General Washington and what he was like, the condition of the army, the patriots and the siege of Boston, all the while laughing, crying, and praying.

Soon, it was time to shut down for the night. Oliver helped clean the tavern while the women cleaned the kitchen, before Clara fixed Oliver's bed.

The lovebirds were given one minute to say goodnight to each other. They stared at each other while holding hands, looking as deeply as they could into each other's soul, hopelessly in love.

"Clara!" her mother called.

"Coming!" Clara responded.

Oliver leaned in and gave her the softest kiss she could imagine. It wasn't a busy kiss; it wasn't wet; it wasn't searching; it was the tender heart of a boy who had become a man assuring her that all would be well. "I love you, Clara."

"When can we get married?" she excitedly asked.

"CLARA!" her father now called.

With one quick kiss, she bolted from the room, stopping in the doorway, turning. "Goodnight, my hero."

"Goodnight, my love."

The tavern keepers and guests departed around 8 a.m.– the Coles in their carriage and Oliver on Courage, arriving at the Revere's temporary home in Watertown around 10 a.m. It was roughly ten miles from the Cole home. Normally, it wouldn't have taken as long, but despite the patriot's siege that surrounded much of Boston, the Sons of Liberty and those serving under Washington knew that loyalists remained on the outskirts of Boston, many working as spies. Others would be perfectly happy to find Paul Revere and his ilk to end them with a musket ball. This meant that the Cole party had to take a northerly route for a few extra miles before heading south into Watertown.

Mrs. Cole asked, "Is this really necessary? You know I hate traveling as it is."

"The loyalists that remain know Revere and I are friends. Don't want to be followed and expose him. And especially don't want a bullet between his eyes or ours," Mr. Cole stated matter of factly.

"Father!" a frightened Clara blurted out. "Now mother will never leave the home!" Causing Mr. Cole to laugh.

"Horrible! Horrible!" Mrs. Cole said. "You are not funny, Mr. Cole!"

"It's not loyalists we have to worry about around Cambridge," stated Oliver, "But new recruits who can't shoot straight. We might have to duck musket balls for the next mile or two!"

Mr. Cole howled with laughter as Clara shot her man an angry look.

Clara composed herself before saying, "At least I get to be with you, Oliver Atkinson, even if you are being as horrible as my father!"

Truly, Clara watched intently everything Oliver did. He acted so much like a man, a mature man, a brave man who could protect and provide for her and all the children she planned on having. She was awestruck. He was on General Washington's staff. He worked for Paul Revere, was a Son of Liberty, a spy, had been to Philadelphia and served the Adamses and John Hancock at the First and Second Continental Congress. How could a girl not be in love with him?

And he had eyes for her alone, was crazy in love with her. He told her every time he could, every way he could, even sending her a few letters from Pennsylvania and Cambridge because he couldn't get away while training. She felt she was the luckiest girl in the world as they pulled up to the Revere home.

They were ready for their guests. Warm greetings and hugs were passed around.

"Sorry to burst in on you like this!" Mrs. Cole said out loud.

"Don't be silly. We're delighted. We knew Oliver would bring you," Rachel assured them.

It was a wonderful reunion for all, except Junior was nowhere in sight.

"He's in Boston, protecting the family property," Paul said.

Oliver was sorely disappointed, so Clara took it upon herself to console him. It allowed her, within her mother's gaze, to offer an affectionate embrace that lasted about twenty minutes, until Revere and Cole beckoned Oliver outside. This irritated Clara, who was not usually given to moodiness.

They ate heartily in the sparsely outfitted home. "Other than cooking equipment and a long table Paul had built for us to eat our meals, we're making due with what the Tory family that lived here left behind," said Rachel.

"They burned most everything they didn't take," said an irritated Paul. "The children are sleeping on straw on the floor. We only had time to bring a few things from home."

As Rachel stood to replenish the pewter jugs of water, she humbly said just above a whisper, "Mind you, we are grateful to the

Lord for what we have. Now," she said with more pep, "let's not allow this day to be anything but mirthful gratitude!"

Much to the delight of all, most of the talk was about family, crafts, the business of the tavern, print, and goldsmithing shop, how the children were doing and learning, and how everyone's health was. And very little about the conflict.

Grabbing their guns, they exited the Watertown house and walked to a small pond in a field at the back of the property. The temperature was beginning to drop as the men stood by the water and talked. The flat, serene water was usually filled with migrating birds twice a year but now was devoid of life above the surface.

They shared rumors and intelligence that they'd heard. Revere and Cole wanted to know what was happening at Cambridge with Washington and the army. Oliver squirmed a little as he wasn't sure how to answer. He'd never been the one with information before and he hadn't been briefed on what was private and what wasn't. After a moment, he reasoned that what he knew wasn't for general dissemination, but these were Sons of Liberty men who had placed their heads on a block for exactly what was being accomplished by the men in Philadelphia and Cambridge.

Still, just before he spoke, Oliver remembered Paul Revere's warning when he'd introduced him to The Mechanics and sent him on his first assignment: *a man may be trustworthy, but that doesn't mean he needs to know.*

In an instant, Oliver resolved to tread carefully. Until he better understood what could be shared and what must remain guarded, he would say only that the men were being trained by an exceptional leader, that recruits were arriving daily, and that Washington was still assembling his staff. Congress, he added, seemed to quarrel, drink, and compromise in equal measure—yet even so, there were brilliant minds at work in Independence Hall. And, Oliver concluded, the longer the struggle dragged on, the more it would favor the patriots' cause.

In the end, Cole and Revere smiled at themselves, with Cole saying, "You trained him well, Paul. He just spent ten minutes telling us a lot without telling us a thing!"

"I'm proud of you, Oliver," Paul said while rubbing his head. "And I'm freezing, let's get back inside."

The men turned back to the house, "Not to mention that we need to start back home. It's been a good day, Paul."

The two adults put their arms around each other's shoulders and headed back to the house, Clara still watching them from the inside.

That night, Oliver kissed Clara goodnight and said, "I don't know if I'll be able to write, I mean, where I'm headed, I don't know if posts come up from there." She looked sad until she produced a small pair of scissors and smiled.

"I want a lock of your hair!" And before Oliver knew it, she clipped off a clump of his shoulder length brown hair. "Oh no," she said laughing while dangling it before him.

"CLARA!" her father called.

They gave each other one last quick kiss, before she skipped away.

Early the next morning as Oliver prepared to leave, he found a scented note on the bedside table that simply said, "I love you, Oliver Atkinson, Yours affectionately, Clara Cole (The future Mrs. Atkinson.)" To the side of it was a lock of her golden hair tied with a red ribbon, lying on top of the blanket she made him. His day could not have begun better.

Downstairs, Mrs. Cole had awakened early to get him some breakfast.

"Ma'am, you really didn't have to," he politely said.

She sat down next to him, her eyes anxiously darting about as she squeezed her cup of coffee. The hungry young man didn't notice as he stuffed his face, being in a rush to see General Washington.

Finally, Mrs. Cole said what was in her heart. "Every time my husband leaves on a mission, my heart fearfully races until he finally walks through these doors." Oliver swallowed the last morsel and looked at her. "You are a good man, a brave man, Oliver Atkinson. Please come back for Clara."

The young man saw the painful pleading in her eyes as she grasped his hands. "Mrs. Cole," he said, rising from the table, "Pray for me. Pray for us all that we all return to our families before too long." He bent over and kissed her forehead and was out the door into the freezing morning, off to see General Washington before turning south.

CHAPTER 23

THE LONG RIDE

Oliver entered George Washington's tent as flurries fell from a gray sky. He was surprised to see a short, attractive, middle-aged woman with brown hair he'd never seen before with her arm around the sitting general's shoulder.

Washington said, "You are back and have been briefed?"

Oliver nodded "Yes, sir."

"Good, good." The general stood and grabbed the right hand of his wife, Martha Washington. "Oliver Atkinson, I'd like you to meet my wife, Martha Washington, who has so graciously decided to visit for the winter to make sure I'm running the army properly."

The young man bowed, "Pleased to meet you, Mrs. Washington."

"Likewise, Mr. Atkinson," the short forty-four-year-old woman with hazel eyes and evidence of graying hair responded. "I assume you've been keeping my husband in line in my absence?"

Not knowing her sense of humor, Oliver didn't know how to respond at first, until the Washington's couldn't keep a straight face any longer.

"He pretends that I am! I'm sorry I won't be able to draw from your military expertise, ma'am, as I am actually heading to where you just came from."

They chuckled as General Washington handed him another piece of folded paper. "Add this to the list of things Mrs.

Washington and I will need from Mount Vernon."

Taking it, he replied, "Yes, sir. If there isn't anything else, I'm off."

"I've added Philadelphia to your circuit. Stop by on your return. Godspeed, Mr. Atkinson."

Oliver saluted the general and bowed to Mrs. Washington and left Cambridge on a western route.

Junior came to mind, and missing him, Oliver allowed a rare series of questionable thoughts to entangle his mind until wisdom gave up. He quieted reason and decided that no one would be the wiser if he crossed the Charles River into Boston and saw Junior. For a few minutes. The Revere family property was on the north side where he would land. He knew where the boats were hidden and could easily visit Junior and be back on the road in an hour. After all, what was that for a trip that would last two or more months?

Not using the same good judgment as he did at the pond the day before, Oliver convinced himself that it was only slightly impetuous of him to cross into Boston and see Junior. So, he button-hooked around Harvard Town and headed for one of the spots on the river where he knew boats were kept.

Twenty minutes later he'd learned that all the boats were gone. The brush that covered them during the spring, summer, and fall had lost its leaves, leaving them exposed. The boats were most likely found by loyalists and destroyed. "Perhaps, they had been repositioned somewhere else by The Mechanics. But where?" he asked himself before trekking further north along the banks until he saw a flat-bottomed vessel fifty yards ahead about to launch across to Boston. On it were a carriage and a few men, as well as a few barrels of something. Oliver wore civilian clothes.

He rushed towards them and called out, "Wait! Wait for me!" They were about to push off but waited as he requested. "Do you have room for one more?" He'd never seen the men before and didn't like the way they were looking at him.

"Who are you?" asked the scruffy man with a long oar.

Suddenly he realized that these men might be loyalists as they were doing trade in Boston. "Tristan Nottingham."

"Never heard of you." They eyed the boy for a second. "Why are you going to Boston?"

Without thinking, he said while sitting tall in his saddle, "Good sirs, I've never seen you before either, but if you have room on your vessel, I will gladly pay for my crossing, but my business, though absolutely benign, is really none of yours."

As they got to the Boston shore, Oliver asked, "When will you be going back?"

"In an hour or so," the man with the long oar gruffly said. He kept an eye on Oliver the entire trip across. The courier couldn't hear their quiet conversation over the sound of the waves splashing against the side of the ferry. The boy began questioning his decision as his anxiety grew, working its way out by shuffling his feet, rubbing his hands, and avoiding eye contact with the men.

As he said "Farewell" to stony faces, he and Courage leapt off the ferry and onto the dock, darting away without looking behind. While the cold air blew against his face, he kept trying to recall anything about them that should give him cause for concern. He'd never seen them before at any Sons of Liberty gathering, they were not a known part of The Mechanics, and they did not know who he was. At least he didn't think so despite becoming a minor celebrity in the last two years.

On his return, he would stake out the area to see if there were any Redcoats waiting for him. If there were, the only way out was crossing deep into Boston and making a run through Boston Neck, hoping that the men participating in the siege didn't think he was leading an attack, especially if he had regulars chasing after him on foot and horse.

His folly reasoned that a horse wouldn't have kicked himself any harder than he was doing at this time. "What a foolish decision!" he spoke angrily to himself.

Riding hard for a few minutes, he pulled behind the Revere home and found Junior wasn't there. He rode to the silversmith shop and the print shop but wasn't at either. Time was running out for him to head back to the ferry, when he decided to circle back to the Revere home, and pulled up just as Junior was closing the door, his hands full of items he'd purchased at the market.

Junior threw the goods onto a kitchen prep table as Oliver gave him a huge hug.

"What in the blazes of Hades are you doing here, Oliver? Did my father send you? Is everything alright?" Junior popped his head out the door and scanned the area, then closed it.

"I saw your family yesterday. They are fine. Great, actually. But I missed my best friend."

Junior moved quickly through the bottom floor of the house and closed all of the curtains. "You do realize that you are wanted by the Redcoats? A British official often stops by to ask the whereabouts of you and my father. You know I'm not good at lying, Oliver."

"You won't have to, as I won't tell you where I am going or who is sending me."

The two sat down and looked at each other for a moment.

"Your army work can wait—tell me about your love with the prettiest girl in Massachusetts!"

"I'll be standing before General Washington in his tent or surrounded by the most important men of our movement, and I have to fight off thoughts of my beautiful Clara! What about you?"

"Sadly, romantic opportunities have mostly fled to the countryside as I remain behind in Boston, the faithful protector of the Revere empire. I haven't got it in me to be a patriot Romeo to a loyalist Juliet. Please hurry and end the conflict so the girls will return, Oliver. Please! I'm going crazy!"

The young men were catching up when Oliver asked what day it was.

"It's December 17," Junior said. "Why? Oh, December 17! My goodness, Oliver."

The last two years flashed by in Oliver's mind. He fell to his knees suddenly, and instead of weeping, his soul let forth a joyous shout of praise and thanks to God! "As your father has said, 'What an unlikely life!'"

Out of the corner of Junior's eye he thought he saw something moving by one of the front windows. "Oliver, it might be time for you to leave quietly out the back door."

He saw the seriousness on Junior's face and quickly rose with his musket in hand.

"As soon as I get to the front door, go out the back, close the door gently, get on Courage, and walk her as quietly as you can out the back alley. I'm going to just walk out the door as if headed for the silversmith shop in the opposite direction."

"Junior," Oliver began.

"Go. Now," his friend firmly said between his teeth.

They timed the departure and door opening perfectly. Oliver's head was on a swivel as he slid away to the small stable and climbed on Courage.

Meanwhile, Junior opened the front door as if on a mission and walked outside into two Redcoats who were about to knock. They grabbed him, and he knocked their arms away, as he kept walking down toward the silver shop. They followed, peppering him with questions about Oliver, saying they'd received word he'd come into town, and naturally it made sense for him to stop by the Revere home.

Junior turned left on Green street, a block away from his home, slow walking to buy more time for his friend's escape. "It would be an obviously stupid thing for either he or my dad to come back to the residence."

"We know it was Atkinson. We should arrest you simply on suspicion of harboring a traitor," said one of the Brits.

Walking up to the shop door, he thrust the key in its hole, turned it, and shoved the door open. Junior turned to boldly face the Regulars, saying, "Then arrest me. Otherwise, I must finish a tea set for General Gage's mistress by this afternoon, or I will be in worse trouble than what you can give me. And so will you two."

With that, he slammed the door in their faces, and they departed.

In the meantime, Oliver walked his horse quietly in the opposite direction. "Great decision, Oliver," he grumbled to himself. He knew he couldn't go back to the ferry.

His only way out of town was through Boston Neck. There were four thousand Redcoats stationed on this modest peninsula, and they were everywhere. Of course, not all knew him, but many knew of him. Oliver guessed that they would be on the lookout for a young man matching his description.

He wondered whether it was smarter to race away or casually walk Courage out of Boston? His decision was made for him as he was spotted by two British cavalry soldiers fifty yards away.

"You there! Halt!" One of them shouted.

Instinctively, he turned to see them joined by a few other men on horses who charged at him. Adrenaline rocketed through his body, sending invisible signals to Courage who got the message. Quickly arriving at top speed, he had to slow down to turn right onto Batterymarch Street and then left onto Hawes Street before going west on Boston Road. His eyes aching from the cold blasts against them, Oliver could see his mounts flaring nostrils as it sucked in as much of the cold air in as possible, squeezing out every bit of speed he could. "Go, girl, go!" Oliver yelled into his ear.

Each time he looked over his shoulder, it appeared that more cavalry had joined the chase. A series of trumpets were blown, alerting more soldiers throughout the area to be ready for action.

Oliver raced forward at a pace he'd never gone before on any horse. Even as he zig-zagged, Courage kept up the speed. The siege works were one hundred yards ahead.

Kaboom! A musket ball whizzed right past his unfazed head. Then another.

Patriots stirred on the first hill in front of him loading their muskets as they witnessed about thirty Redcoats galloping towards them, being led by a man not in uniform. One sharpshooter from Waltham had lined up the front rider and was about to fire when he heard the rider yell, "It's Oliver Atkinson! Don't shoot!"

General Washington happened to be at that location while performing an inspection of the siegeworks and to build the men's morale, when he heard Oliver's voice first, then saw him. His courier was being fired upon. "Don't shoot! Do not fire any weapons!" the general commanded as he rode up and down the line.

Suddenly, Oliver came into clear view of the patriots with the Redcoats thirty yards behind him. The Redcoats stopped their chase once Oliver cleared the battle lines and safely into friendly territory.

He was immediately met by both a cheering crowd and a furious General Washington, who demanded he follow him away from the men. Climbing off Courage, who was catching her breath after his half-mile sprint, Oliver had never felt fear quite like he did at that moment, and thought his career was over before it began.

Flanked by his junior officers, Washington paced two steps to his right before coming back two steps to his left. He then stopped in front of the frightened young courier and said with controlled fury, "What were you doing in Boston, Mr. Atkinson? You should be halfway to Connecticut by now."

Blood ran from his brain, causing him to feel lightheaded. Oliver quaked, losing the ability to form words at first. He'd never been in a more fearsome presence than at that moment. His chin attached to his chest, he shamefully said, "I wanted to say goodbye to my closest friend, Paul Revere Junior. I am shocked by my lack of discipline and judgment, General Washington."

Paul Revere rode quickly to their side then halted. Oliver looked at him, "Mr. Revere, I just wanted to see Paul Junior!" Then he looked back at the steaming Commander-in-Chief.

"Give me the dispatches and lists. Now, Oliver," Washington furiously demanded.

The young man dismounted Courage and opened the hidden compartment on his saddle and shamefully handed them to his commanding officer.

Paul said to Oliver, "What was Junior doing?" Washington looked at the seals to see they had been broken.

"We met at your house when he dropped off some things from the market and planned on going back to the shop to finish a tea set for one of General Gage's mistresses. That's what Junior told me. I was only there for fifteen minutes. Once in deep, I realized how stupid it was of me. You know, Mr. Revere, I've never done anything like this before." Turning to face Washington, "Sir, I am trustworthy. I will never deviate from any orders ever again. Please let me continue this mission. Please, sir."

The general huddled Revere and his accompanying staff a few feet away as patriots manning the siege looked on. Washington turned to his officers, then looked at Revere. "Paul, you are the spymaster here in Boston, what do you think?"

Pointing to the seals, "They're not broken, sir. He's not a spy.

Spies don't get chased and shot at by their own. He's also correct about Paul Junior finishing that tea set today. If you consider the time it took him to get to this point from the time he left camp this morning, I don't see how he would've had time to do anything else. He is typically trustworthy. This is a youthful aberration, sir."

Washington stood pensively for a moment before nodding to himself, then motioned for Oliver. All the color had left his broken face. He stood before the greatest man alive and had been foolish enough in one decision to last a lifetime. Washington extended his hand with the letters and lists and offered them back to the stunned young man. Oliver took them, hands shaking, and said, "Thank you, sir. I'll never let you down again."

"I know you won't Oliver. I did something once around your age that I regretted terribly and learned a life lesson from it. I'm certain you will as well."

"Thank you, General Washington," Oliver humbly said. "I'll see you in a few months."

"Mr. Atkinson," Washington said, pausing the young courier's ascent on Courage, "if you do anything like this again there will be severe consequences. Do you understand?"

At that, Oliver felt like his soul was trying to leave his body and flee. "Yes, sir, General Washington, I do."

"I hope so."

Oliver saluted Washington, before mounting Courage and bolting south towards Connecticut.

As was proven during his escape from Boston, Oliver knew that Courage could run short distances faster than any horse he'd seen. But he wondered if she was a horse that could ride a great distance. Philadelphia proved she could, but they were both about to find out if she could withstand a trip three times that long.

Courage was a dark black three-year-old with attitude and confidence, traits needed for short-distance horses and warfare.

Though he talked with Courage as if she were a person, a horse could not understand the gravity of the mission, its honor and privilege. But Oliver was convinced Courage grasped the tone of his voice and intensity of his words, which was why she was such a responsive creature. When riding her, they operated as one.

Washington's rebuke stung him for the next few days. The Virginia planter's personal testimony of a similar event in his life at about Oliver's age showed great compassion and reserve. The General of the Continental Army hadn't time to babysit him or hold his hand, no matter how zealous and sincere Oliver was for the cause. He was willing to give his life for their shared ambition.

As the sting wore off, he asked himself if he loved the idea of America more than the reality of Clara. This thought sobered him even more and gave it his strictest attention until he reasoned that it was because he loved Clara and wanted the best future for her that America had to have his all at this time.

CHAPTER 24

While Clara kept most of his thoughts company on this lonely ride, troubling intrusions about Peter and the issue of slavery beckoned for attention.

In 1773, a group of slaves in Massachusetts unsuccessfully petitioned the government to be freed. He remembered sitting outside the main hall when the First Continental Congress vowed to discontinue the importation of slaves, and last year, in 1774, he recalled, Connecticut, Rhode Island, and Georgia did, as well. Perhaps there was reason for hope.

Oliver thought about some of the private conversations he had had with Paul Revere and others about the hypocrisy of this fight for the freedom for all men when people with a dark skin color were excluded. He understood their reasoning, begrudgingly accepted it, but remained a bitter point in his soul.

"One stage at a time," he was frequently told.

"Wait and see how our language develops as we move closer to independence," a young Thomas Jefferson of Virginia told him. Jefferson was a slave owner. "If we press this issue now, we will lose the southern Colonies, the war, and our heads. Keep an eye out for the language, Mr. Atkinson."

He arrived at the home where he was to stay this bitterly cold December night. He decided to sleep indoors believing no one would be so foolish as to be out in this weather and rummage through his things. Then it dawned on him, that's exactly what the enemy would have him think. Revere taught him how to think in reverse, and so, young Oliver Atkinson slept in the barn with about ten blankets on him, the top one being Clara's gift. Two grayish woolen caps covered down to his ears, both provided by his host after warm stew and biscuits. He lay under and on top of a bale's worth of hay. He made sure Courage was as warm and then went to sleep. At least for a little while.

As cold as it was, he overdid his coverings and began to sweat. He knew that it could be dangerous when mixed with freezing air. He took off a few blankets and put them on Courage, relieved himself, and went back to sleep.

He was on the road before the sun broke the horizon. His goal was to make it to the outskirts of New York City on the New Jersey side in a week. He felt good about his progress, especially as Courage responded to the pace well.

While he was tempted to take a day of rest in Philadelphia to see Peter and the Massachusetts men, General Washington had advised him to avoid the distractions and not rest until he arrived at Mount Vernon. The wound at Boston Neck was still healing. Philadelphia would have to wait.

Day after day he and his horse pierced the bone-chilling cold at a fair rate of speed. Oliver was beginning to believe that the cold weather was a friend to Courage. She had already grown out her winter coat and constant movement kept her blood warm. He stopped frequently during the day for Courage to graze for a few minutes, and once a day during their traveling period Oliver would take the saddle off and rest for an hour. He was worried about cold rain and sleet that could get under her winter coat, which could lead to sickness.

Oliver had asked for and been given extra blankets by the owners of the Worcester home from his first night. He kept an eye out for sweat under the saddle blanket and would change the blanket regularly. Every night he would brush her coat while feeding her carrots or apples that the homeowners offered during their stops. He told Courage a few stories, but the horse looked at him with disinterest or exhaust. Oliver couldn't tell which.

He spent Christmas night with a family named Coates in Princeton, New Jersey. Mr. Coates was a tanner. They lived sparsely because he and the Mrs. had a child a year for sixteen straight years. All but three made it into adulthood. Their home stayed warm in the winter because of the body heat they all created. The dinner was simple: turkey, ham, cranberry sauce, loaves of warm wheat bread, and pumpkin pie. It was so tasty that this became Oliver's chosen Christmas meal from then on when he could influence the menu.

Passing Philadelphia to the east, Oliver eventually made it to the home of Charles Carroll of Carrollton in the Colony of Maryland on January 31. While not yet a delegate from Maryland to the Congress, Carroll would travel back and forth to Philadelphia to see what progress was being made. His estate was an expansive ten thousand acres and had three hundred slaves operating it. Oliver had met him briefly at a dinner at the Yards' Inn and invited him to stay with his family "if ever in the area."

Hancock whispered in the young man's ear that Carroll was the wealthiest man in the Colonies, "perhaps the world."

It was as if the very proper Mrs. Molly Carroll had anticipated his visit. After bathing and being given a new set of clothes, Oliver was treated to the most sumptuous meal he'd ever eaten. He dined with her two young children, Charles Jr. and Mary, and an assortment of relatives ranging in age from newborn to eighty. There must've been twenty people at the long mahogany table. Half of the food he'd never seen before, but he remembered the manners Rachel Revere and Abigail Adams had taught him at their homes. "Smile and eat what is before you. Assure the host it is the most delicious meal you ever had," they had coached.

Each person bombarded him with non-stop questions about the elite of Boston, the army, General Washington, and England. His answers weren't energetic, but short. After a while, it dawned on Molly that his vagueness wasn't rudeness. The boy was simply tired.

He decided to sleep inside. He felt secure on the estate, and he was allowed to bring his saddle into the house in an area used for changing when coming in dirty, and because he laid down for a nap before dinner on the most comfortable bed he'd ever been on; even more so than the Revere's. He felt comfortable leaving Courage in a massive barn greater than Baron Effringham's. He was told it was constructed to stay relatively warm in the winter and cool in the summer. He didn't ask how this was accomplished, but standing there as he gave the reins over to a slave, he felt the temperature to be cozy and knew this would help rejuvenate Courage. He could use some rejuvenating himself.

Before bed, the family and the slaves gathered outside to watch fireworks that one of their paid helpers, a white man named Billy O'Toole, had made. It was New Year's Eve. One of them exploded a little early, detonating ten feet in the air with a blast radius of about fifty feet, showering everyone with colorfully hot particles. Billy got singed but laughed it off as he tilted a bottle of whiskey skyward and swigged heartily.

Oliver checked one last time on Courage before heading to his guest room.

Despite going to bed so late, Oliver felt refreshed when he woke, and before anyone was up, even any slaves, he was off in the darkness headed toward Great Falls, Virginia, where he would cross the Potomac River at a spot that didn't require a boat, before turning south along the river thirty miles to George and Martha Washington's estate, Mount Vernon.

He knew there was no way he could make this one-hundred-mile leg in one day, so he didn't push Courage, who seemed reinvigorated after the comfortable night. They made great time, and were two days ahead of schedule, an amazing accomplishment in this cold weather. He considered Molly's invitation to stay an extra day, but decided to use the extra time at Mount Vernon, instead. Plus, it was his birthday, and he felt conscientious about letting it slip, not wanting anyone to make a big deal of this day.

* * *

General Washington wanted Oliver in North Carolina by the beginning of February, to ride from the western part of the state to the east with the dispatches for men and militia groups. He also wanted Oliver to bring back reports from them on their well-being. His early arrival would give him a few extra days of relaxation in Mount Vernon, which the general approved. He planned on taking advantage of it, despite the urgency of his mission.

As he made his way toward Great Falls, his mind wandered to the siege in Boston. How was it going? Did General Henry Knox, his favorite book seller in Boston, get the cannon from Fort Ticonderoga back to Boston? He didn't know it would be a few more weeks before this happened.

Not being musical, he rarely hummed songs or hymns. His entertainment was his mind and memories, as well as his thoughts of a future in a free land with Clara. He would send her a letter from Mount Vernon, he decided, the energy from the thought warming his body. He hoped Washington's men wouldn't mind delivering it to her since they would be going to Cambridge with the things the general ordered. He'd never written a love letter before, so he began writing it in his head to kill time as he slow-walked Courage toward Great Falls. He searched his memory looking for a reference point in literature from which to be inspired, nothing came to mind.

Philosophy, history, law, maps, and the few novels he'd read didn't lend well to the prose and poetry he was hoping to write.

Late that morning, he began to feel ill, his stomach churning. His face was pale due to more than the cold. He wondered if he'd eaten too many oysters and crabs the night before. The answer to that was, "yes." But not only the shellfish, but the blackberry and mincemeat pies really did him in. He could feel his stomach churning to the point he knew he needed to vomit. Fighting back a few onrushes of regurgitation in his throat, he nudged Courage to move quickly to a patch of trees and gave up what contents remained while still saddled. Dismounting, he continued his heaving as an unconcerned Courage ate and paid no attention to him. But after his third round of throwing up, his horse came over and bent its neck down to nudge him, as if to ask if he was all right.

Oliver leaned back against a large oak tree and waited for his fourth vomit to come, but it never did, though not without effort from his gurgling stomach. He even stuck a finger down his throat hoping to induce unwanted fare to come up, but it only caused a dry gag, which felt worse than vomiting. He was done and decided to rest for a while and refill his body with water.

He was going to come short of Great Falls by about fifteen miles. The weather demanded he find an inn of unknown allegiance as he was not aware of any friendly homes in the area. Given his habit of sleeping outside with his horse and saddle, he realized it would appear odd to a loyalist innkeeper, who could then alert some of his loyalist cronies, overpower him and take the dispatches. Or he could sleep out under the stars in freezing temperatures. He had a few days' rations with him, so food wasn't an issue. He had to decide as he approached the small farming village of Rockville, Maryland.

Then came snow mixed with sleet. This settled the matter. They needed cover. Trotting south into the small village from a knoll, he saw a man driving a mule with a cart attached that was topped with bundles of wood and kindling. The man, who looked as if he were wearing multiple coats, stopped as Oliver approached.

"Hello, sir," a nodding Oliver said to the stranger.

"Young man," the man returned his nod with a hesitating look on his face and asked, "Who are you and what are you doing out in this weather?"

He employed the cover story Washington and Revere helped Oliver come up with in case he was stopped by a suspected loyalist, interrogated or quizzed by a nosy person.

"My name is Tristan Nottingham, sir. My employer is a mapmaking company from Hartford, who has hired me to meet one of their surveyors in western North Carolina, so I am headed there."

"During the winter?" the doubting man asked.

With a slight chuckle, Oliver replied, "Oh, no, sir. Our work doesn't begin until spring. If you must know, I'm an orphan and had no place to go for the holidays, so I thought I'd get a head start."

The man gazed at Oliver and asked, "Whose side are you on?"

"Whose side? You mean the colonial conflict?" He chuckled and continued, "I don't care about politics. All I want to do is work and hopefully marry and have children one day. This is one of the reasons why I took this job, so I can be as far away from all this nonsense as possible."

The man nodded his head slightly. "All right, then." Looking at the sky before returning his gaze back to Oliver, he said, "It's getting late. I'm bringing this wood to the local innkeeper. I imagine you need a place to stay for the night. Help me unload this wood there and I'll see about getting you a room."

"An Inn? Oh, very good to get out of this weather. That's very kind, thank you," Oliver responded.

"He's my brother. My name is Allan Bryant."

Oliver was introduced to one-eyed innkeeper William Bryant, while offloading the wood, but insisted he remain outside with his horse, saying, "I'm training myself for the frontier if it's all the same to you. May I take a meal in lieu of the room?"

The brothers talked among themselves while Oliver ate in silence. They were the only three in the inn. The wood deliverer disappeared in the middle of Atkinson's meal, and William came over to ask him some similar questions. Oliver knew he was being tested. He also knew that he was in the inn of a loyalist. The Union Jack on the wall gave that away. He began wondering if maybe it wasn't a good idea for him to stay there. Perhaps he should be polite and wait until just after nightfall and then sprint out of the village and head south.

This decision was taken out of his hands when he saw out the window several men on horseback approaching in the pre-dusk light, from about one hundred yards away, led by Allan Bryant.

"Where's the outhouse, sir? I've had a bout with vomiting all day," Oliver queasily said, bending slightly at the waist with an arm across his stomach. He knew where it was because he surveyed the area when approaching the inn. It was near the stables. This excuse would give him a few more seconds head start to the trouble that was nearing.

"Outside to the left," the innkeeper said, quickly standing.

Oliver moaned as he exited the inn. As soon as he was out the door, he sprinted as fast as he could to the stable. Fortunately, he hadn't yet prepped Courage for the night as his discernment warned him to be cautious. He would trust that voice from now on as he undid the rein attached to a stall gate. Finding a stirrup with his left foot, Oliver heaved himself up onto his horse, turned his horse to face the exit, and whispered, "Hyah."

Bolting out of the small stable, he saw the innkeeper pointing to Oliver and the men bearing down on him at a fast rate. The courier squeezed Courage's sides with all his might, and his partner took off like a musket ball. In seconds he was one hundred yards away from the inn, but the men remained on his tail. Not knowing the territory, a certain disadvantage, he went on instinct as one who had ridden in the dark from England to Massachusetts under frightful and dangerous conditions. He trusted his horse and his skills, but could his friend stay on his hooves on the icy terrain?

What he could not have known was that the woodman was a colonel in the local loyalist militia, and while he didn't disbelieve Oliver, his story seemed too perfect. He became alarmed when he insisted on sleeping in the barn, as if he was protecting something.

The chase went on for ten minutes before the men gave up. Oliver had not required Courage to go full tilt for several days, and this may have been what kept them from being captured, because those men had good horses, as well. But they didn't have Courage.

The snow continued to fall as he slowed his pace and made tracks for Great Falls. A full moon was out and the moon's reflected light off the snow made his travel safer and easier.

About one a.m., Oliver arrived at the patriot inn completely exhausted. It was further than he wanted to ride that day, about seventy miles, but it had to be done after his near capture in Rockville.

The owner was from Kilmarnock, Scotland. He moved to Maryland when his entire family died from a plague that swept through the country. He was twenty at the time. He got a job working the docks in Baltimore before saving enough money to purchase this inn. It turned out to be a money-maker because it was situated near the easiest crossing at Great Falls on the Potomac River. He didn't like to be awakened from his sleep, but this bull of a man with the reddest hair the young man had ever seen warmly greeted Oliver and got him situated for the rest of the night. In case the men continued tracking him, he was given permission to bring his saddle into his room.

"If any of them come, we'll just have to blow their loyalist heads off, now won't we, Oliver?" He asked, laughing at the prospects of such a thing. "Keep your musket loaded by your bed. Goodnight." With that, the man with the biggest chest he'd ever seen sauntered to his room while scratching himself and closed the door.

Oliver replayed his cover story a few times and thought he had done well during the threat in Rockville. He concluded that sleeping with his horse for the purposes of preparing him for the frontier set off an alarm that needed further investigation. It made sense, and it should have. It was still a good story, and he decided to stick with it just in case. Or just keep moving on.

CHAPTER 25

MOUNT VERNON

With only three hours of sleep, Oliver crossed Great Falls at dawn. The weather warmed as if it were a spring day, creating a difficult slushy mud to travel through on his way south along the Potomac River, becoming wider until it seemed a mile across.

He came to Little Hunting Creek just north of Mount Vernon, having entered Washington's estate two miles earlier, and crossed at the narrowest point of the creek as it led out into the Potomac.

There, Oliver came upon some twenty male slaves who were walking north in grayish clothing carrying agricultural tools. He assumed they were to work in the farming area he was passing through. On a horse was a white man riding behind them. Oliver couldn't hide his frown.

"Where are you headed, young man?" The white man stopped next to Oliver. He then looked at the continuing slaves and yelled, "Stop!" And in an instant, they did. He turned his attention back on Oliver.

"General Washington sent me from Cambridge to hand off a list of things he wanted brought to him."

"He did, did he?" The man snorted and spit to his left away from Oliver.

"Yes. I am going to see a Mr. Diggs and a Mr. Betancourt. The general has also graciously granted that I stay on a few days for rest."

"You'll find Diggs at the main residence. You'll be there in a few minutes. I've no idea where that idiot Betancourt is." With that, he trotted away, yelling, "Git!" to the slaves, who immediately restarted their walk.

Oliver took one last displeasing look over his shoulder before continuing to the main residence.

Arriving at Mount Vernon, he was at once in awe of its beautiful cream-colored exterior and its slate blue roof shingles. He did not recall seeing anything like it in England or in Boston. It seemed about one-third the size of Effringham's residence, and one quarter the size of Charles Carroll's mansion. It had less of a noble quality to it than a comfortable one that bespoke success but not excess. It was immaculately landscaped with gardens of roses, lilacs, hibiscus, black-eyed Susan, Cherry tree blossoms, and more. While it was winter and the plants weren't in bloom, he could still tell what kind they were, having read numerous books on flowers, trees, and gardens.

He didn't see anyone right away, so he wandered around to the back of the home and saw its dominating view of the Potomac.

As he was admiring the glorious sight, a voice came from a distance behind him. "You there!" Oliver turned to see a man wobbling rapidly towards him waving a hoe. "You! Who are you?"

Oliver met him halfway and introduced himself to the bearded man.

"Ah! My name is Diggs. Pleased to meet you, Mr. Atkinson. Come with me." The man began wobbling back from where he came and brought him into a small shop thirty yards from the residence. "This is my shop. I manage the property." Motioning to Oliver to sit, he said that he needed to get his horse first and would be right back.

Returning a few minutes later, Oliver produced the lists General Washington had given him. Diggs read them, nodding his head, "Yes, yes. Yes," He sat back and looked at Oliver, after taking a huge swig from a jug. He offered the bottle to Oliver "We make it here." Oliver smelled the whiskey fumes and passed.

"The general has asked that I put you to work with the Africans for a week." Thinking he was funny, Diggs burst out laughing. Oliver didn't join him. Diggs stopped suddenly. "You're right. It's not funny. You'll be staying in the main residence. The house cook will feed you, and every comfort you need will be provided for you. If you'd like, I can take you on a tour of this magnificent eighteen-thousand-acre plantation."

"Thank you, but no. I plan on staying out of the saddle for a few days, though I wouldn't mind a walking tour of the immediate area tomorrow," Oliver replied.

Diggs brought him to the front door of the main residence and knocked. Marcus, a serious African man about fifty years old, dressed in a finely tailored suit, answered the door. Diggs explained Oliver's presence.

"Mr. Atkinson, sir," Marcus motioned, "Please come in."

Diggs walked away saying, "You know where to find me, Mr. Atkinson."

Rumbling down the stairs came a young man about twenty-two years of age. He stopped at the bottom of the stairs, and looked at Marcus, then at Oliver. "Who are you?"

The house butler introduced the guest. "This is Oliver Atkinson. He is here on behalf of your father."

"Your parents, actually," Oliver added.

At this the young man lit up and became pleasant. "Jack Washington," as he stuck out his hand, which Oliver shook. "How are they?"

"I saw them last about three weeks ago. Your father, the general, has a monumental task on his hands. Your mother's presence seems to be helping him get the Continentals ready,"

Oliver assured him.

Jack looked at him in silence for a minute before announcing that he was off to see Eleanor Calvert and wouldn't be back for a few weeks. "Mr. Atkinson, my apologies, but I'm in love," he said. "When you next see my father, please tell him that I still want to join the army, and if he won't let me, I will marry Miss Calvert before he returns," he said smiling. "Threats never work with either of my parents, but you'll enjoy the look on their faces."

With that, Jack Washington was out the door.

Marcus led Oliver to his room and asked for his clothes so they could be washed. Within twenty minutes, an African woman named Betsy had prepared a hot bath for him and a meal of bacon, eggs, and corn grits, which he'd never had before. He loved them instantly.

He slept most of the next two days, taking time to eat and walk the property for a few hours, enjoying the unusually mild weather. It felt good to move his legs. He had not been able to keep his fitness up with all the riding he'd been doing, so this exercise gave his legs some strength back.

Towards the end of his first day, Betsy appeared at his door as Oliver was rising from one of his series of naps and announced that Mr. Bettencourt would meet him in General Washington's library. In an instant, Oliver was dressed in his new clothes and downstairs.

Hastily entering the library, the wiry thin Mr. Digby Betancourt looked over his glasses, narrow chin down, and sized up the young guest. He was the curator for the estate, overseeing art, letters, books, and the like, for the Washingtons.

"While you slept," Betancourt cleared his throat from an imaginary obstruction, "I prepared the books General Washington requested. They will be packed and shipped immediately, along with all other requests of his listed here," he said holding up the piece of paper. He noticed Oliver's wide eyes as he glanced around at the many volumes lining the four walls. "The general has graciously asked me to allow you to spend as much time here in the library as you want. All I ask is that you put the books back exactly where you find them, and that none leave this room."

"Yes, of course. Thank you, Mr. Betancourt."

Betancourt looked him over again, before turning and exiting the library.

Over the next few days, he spent about six hours in the library. He'd randomly choose a book, flip open to a page, and if it didn't interest him, he went on to the next one. He also made time to write Clara that love letter, but he hadn't found anything in the library to inspire him. He ended up simply saying what was on his heart.

He visited Courage a few times a day, took her for a few walks on the property during an unusual mid-winter warm front, letting her run wild with other horses in a large, fenced field. Oliver was curious as to how this independent and confident horse would get along with the others, but he didn't see any issues. Horses could be so moody.

On the third day, Betsy brought him a mid-morning snack of strawberry jam and biscuits as he laid on his bed, and said to the young man, "You look bored, Mr. Atkinson!"

He sat up and thanked her as he grabbed the silver tray of food. "I am bored. Men are preparing for war, and I'm being pampered. It doesn't seem right."

"But you on General Washington's order," she stated.

"Betsy, he gave me two days. I'm starting my third day although I arrived here two days ahead of schedule." He popped up out of bed, and between big bites of biscuits lathered with jam, he began to dress to leave. "Please help me get my things ready to go. And may I inconvenience you for a few of your delicious bacon sandwiches?"

Within thirty minutes, Oliver Atkinson had saddled Courage, packed his clothing, resupplied his bags, loaded them on his horse, given Betancourt a letter for Clara, and was off to North Carolina on the nicest day of the winter. He knew it wouldn't last, so the sooner he got southward, the less cold it would be for him and Courage.

CHAPTER 26

NORTH CAROLINA

He was warned that Royal Governor Lord Dunmore had fled with some of his officials to a ship on the Chesapeake Bay, but that there were still many loyalists in Virginia. And even more were in North Carolina. He carried the order and letters from Washington with him in his secret saddle compartment, so he had to be even more alert to those he came across along the road to Yadkin Valley in western North Carolina.

The path was more difficult than any he had taken yet, not because of trouble from loyalists, but as he went west into the mountains, the terrain became downright dangerous to navigate in certain areas. He had to climb over outcroppings of rocks, some covered with ice, as the winter reappeared, and watch for sudden crevices in the earth and cliffs.

He made his own trail much of the time, feeling wholly inadequate as the surveyor he was pretending to be. His trek uphill was becoming increasingly cold. Oliver took his time and often got off Courage and led her at treacherous points on the route. Neither had been up a mountain before, and Oliver immediately didn't like it. Looking in Courage's eyes he could tell she hated it and may have been angry at her partner.

One night, as he built a lean-to to sleep under and got a fire going, he sat back to rest and was suddenly awestruck as he looked over a high drop off into a wide, emerald-green valley. It was as beautiful a natural sight as he had ever seen, especially as he watched birds fly swiftly below him as the mountain shadows grew long to the east until the valley was dark. Despite this, he simply did not like the mountains. Plus, as he looked over the edge, he learned that he was afraid of heights. "Atlantic storms are more preferable," he jokingly lied. "The sooner I get out of the mountains, the better."

He arrived in Yadkin Valley, North Carolina, on February 1 without incident nine days after departing Mount Vernon. Despite the two days of rest at Washington's home, he was in a constant state of exhaustion. He oddly craved vegetables, for his diet consisted mostly of meat. While he normally never tired of bacon, he was eager for carrots, broccoli, green beans, and even... "spinach," he groaned.

Oliver had never heard of Daniel Boone. He was told Boone was a militia officer for the patriots and the man for whom the next letter was destined. The young man's presence brought a few people out of their homes, one being a man of about forty holding a musket, dressed all in deer skin. "What can we do you for?"

Oliver stopped Courage, then turned back to see the man, and said, "I'm looking for Daniel Boone."

The first man was joined by a few similarly dressed men of various ages brandishing rifles.

The courier sized up the distrustful men.

"I won't ask again," the first man said, raising his weapon.

"Are you Daniel Boone?" A couple of the men laughed. Oliver allowed an uneasy little smile to form. Fighting back anxiety, he continued. "I was told by General Washington I could find him here."

"General Washington? What for?"

"I don't know the message, only that I was to deliver it to him. I rode down from Massachusetts."

"Let's see the message," the man demanded.

"Are you Daniel Boone?" Oliver asked.

"I am."

Oliver didn't believe him. "Then surely you know the password you and the general arranged at a meeting of the Virginia militia last year?"

The man said firmly while holding out his left hand. "You can give it to me, and I will give it to him."

"Respectfully, sir, if you were patriots you would understand. Do with me as you will, but I am bound by duty and oath. If you are going to kill me, you might as well know who you are killing. My name is Oliver Atkinson." The courageous boy stared down the mountain man for a moment, until Squire began to laugh.

"Now this is a good young patriot. A loyalist spy would've given us the letter and skedaddled out of town if he knew who Daniel Boone was!" He reached out his hand and Oliver shook it, as the other men lowered their weapons. "I'm Daniel's brother, Squire. Welcome to North Carolina, Oliver Atkinson. Daniel is away in Kentucky dealing with Indian problems but should be back in a few days."

"Is he close by? I don't have the time to wait as the general has given me orders elsewhere also. Where can I find him?"

"There's been an outbreak of Indian fighting on the borders England created to keep us from moving west. Some brave settlers have been ambushed, and Daniel went to settle the score and get back a few women who had been kidnapped. He could be anywhere within a hundred miles of here. My guess is you don't know this country, so I recommend you wait for him." Turning to the five men that had gathered around the stranger, he asked, "Any of you want to go look for Daniel?"

A chorus of "NO!" went up from the residents.

Disappointed, Oliver asked how long it would take him to ride to Wilmington, North Carolina. "Perhaps I could go there then return?"

When he learned that it would be more than a two-week round trip if he moved quickly, he decided to stay and wait for Daniel to return. Oliver's patience was severely tried as Boone didn't reappear until February 15. Oliver stayed at the home of widow Margaret McCartney, and her two young girls. Her husband, William, had been ravaged by bears the year before, Oliver learned, when out looking for wild mushrooms and onions.

He was afraid that the delay might make the information obsolete in the other letter destined for a militia leader on the southern coast of North Carolina. He knew well from his time with The Mechanics that information delivered with speed was the most helpful. If the news had become outdated, and caused death and loss, then how would he feel? Washington would fire him, his reputation ruined, or worse. They said there might be delays of unknown origin, that plans often changed at a moment's notice, but that he must stay eagle-eyed on his duty the best he could.

Every morning, he would ask Squire if his brother had returned. With every hoofbeat he would look out the widow's window hoping it was Boone returning. The agonizing was too much. The people of the town began to tire of him and his ever-diminishing fuse. After nearly getting in a fist fight with a man who stared menacingly at him at dinner one night, who he realized would have whipped him, he apologized to Squire and the tavern owner and said he'd leave in the morning and give the letter to Squire.

In the bedroom mirror that night, he shook his head and questioned himself asking, "Who are you?"

While saddling up the next morning, to his undying relief, Daniel Boone appeared in the foggy mist from behind him.

"You looking for me?"

Oliver turned to see a blond-haired man of average height, with radiant blue eyes, with the most ferocious presence he'd ever been around. The hand off was made, and the no-nonsense Boone took the letter, opened it, read it, nodded to Atkinson, and said only, "Tell the general that we're building the militia the best we can, but that our colony is torn." Oliver nodded. "Do not return the way you came." Boone pointed to the opposite end of the street. "Ride south to a trail that splits an hour away. Go left down the mountain, and you should avoid most towns that are predominantly Tory. Godspeed, young man." With that, Boone disappeared back into the morning fog.

* * *

This stretch of travel was as cold, wet, and icy as any other part of his trip. His greatest battle wasn't the weather, but his attitude. Waiting on Daniel Boone affected Oliver more than he first believed.

"I was lied to. The south isn't warmer. I'm tired of icicles forming on my nose!"

His bitter state made him question whether Washington had sent him on this "ridiculous mission" just to get rid of him.

Adventure. He was beginning to tire of endless miles with little company. He wondered if there were better uses for his skills. He checked his pride, remembering words about humility, the greatness of the cause that he was serving, and the scripture that told him to do everything, whether eating or drinking, as unto the Lord. But these were being severely tested.

He defused this ruckus by reminding himself that he didn't have musket balls whizzing past his head, as his brave brothers did up north. This was his part to play, his role, in the Colonies' hopeful march toward liberty and self-rule.

Clara elbowed out all other thoughts. He began hearing her

voice. In his mind, she reminded him of his promise to marry him as soon as the conflict was over. So, Oliver Atkinson swore to himself not to complain, to do his part to hasten the end of this revolution, return to his beloved, marry her, and have as many children as possible.

He had been warned by some patriots of a loyalist enclave ahead, so he crossed over into South Carolina.

The courier wasn't paying attention while passing by what appeared to be an abandoned farmhouse about fifty yards to his south. Though Courage whinnied and jerked her head up twice, Oliver's mind was numb. Another day. Another mile.

Suddenly he and Courage broke through ice on a small pond and ended up in four feet of water shocking them both. Courage became anxious and flailed about. Oliver gathered himself and spoke calmly to his mate, "Quiet Courage. Shhh." A minute of that got the horse to stop, allowing Oliver to lead Courage safely out of the pond.

Oliver knew he and Courage could not continue while soaking wet, which meant they'd need fire and shelter. The courier took another look at the farmhouse. He didn't have any other options. Time was of the essence for both, especially Courage. The temperature outside would kill his wet horse, so he steered his steed to the home.

Hopping off, Oliver raced up the three steps to the front door and knocked a few times, calling out, "Hello!" The place looked abandoned. It wasn't dilapidated but seemed like it had not been cared for in a while. It was then he noticed on the door, written in soap, "Gone to fight the British."

He pushed the door open and entered. Sparse, dusty, without a woman's touch, he checked the two rooms and kitchen. Abandoned. The small living room had a fireplace, a rug, and one chair. The ceiling corners connected dust-laden cobwebs. The bedroom had a straw bed and nothing else. Looking out the back window, he spotted a few cords of firewood and a small barn, so he got to work.

Pulling a flint and steel from his saddle, he had a fire going within minutes. He quickly brought Courage inside and had her stand before the fire, which suited her.

Oliver cleared space in front of the fireplace for his horse to lie down in front of, and she did.

Next, he looked for bedding and towels, which he found, to dry Courage with because she had been submerged more than himself. Once he dried the horse as best as he could he changed his clothes. He found riding boots close to his size. He took his socks off and clothes and hung them by the fireplace. He then took the rest of his wet gear, including spare clothes, and hung them up as well, then lay next to Courage to share warmth.

As the fire blazed on, the home quickly warmed up. In about fifteen minutes he saw Courage had calmed down and seemed to be enjoying herself as she relaxed while being stroked. Five minutes later the horse was asleep. Then Courage began to snore. Smiling, Oliver grabbed beef jerky he'd been saving and ate and then decided to take a nap, as well.

Their traveling for the day was over, even though it was only about noon. They had to dry off, and he needed to make sure Courage wasn't so spooked it would take days for her to be willing to have a rider again. He'd seen other horses do that, but he didn't think his horse would. Still, he needed to be sure.

Agitatingly, this would delay their arrival in Wilmington even more.

After a nap, it occurred to him to check the dispatches and see what condition they were in. Cautiously opening his secret compartment, he was relieved to see that they were not damaged at all. This gave him renewed energy to explore behind the cabin and the small barn, in spite of being dressed only in long underwear. He hoped some livestock had been left behind, as there wasn't any food in the kitchen.

He put on his warm, dry clothes, and as he did, Courage got up. His girl was all right. Oliver led her out back to eat from a patch of tall grass. Courage apparently didn't like eating through a layer of thin ice on each blade and followed him to the small, unpainted barn. The courier spotted a few bales of hay, and broke one down so Courage could eat to her heart's content. He wasn't surprised to see there weren't any chickens or hogs left behind. At least he had lots of deer jerky that the widow McCartney had given him.

Later that evening as he rekindled a dying fire so that it would last through the night, Oliver Atkinson and Courage fell asleep on the floor.

The next morning, Courage seemed ready to go. Everything that had been wet was dry, and the two rested travelers went into the freezing morning air once again to continue their expedition, but not before Oliver put out the fire and wrote in soap on the door, "Thanks for the night. A patriot from Boston." He then pocketed the soap.

* * *

Three days later on February 25, 1776, Oliver Atkinson arrived in Wilmington, North Carolina, a beautiful town nudged between the Atlantic Ocean and the Cape Fear River. He saw patriot flags hanging outside of homes and businesses, including the familiar Pine Tree flags of the Sons of Liberty he'd previously only seen in Boston.

He asked a few people where he could find Colonel James Moore, and no one knew. He didn't believe them.

"If you see him, tell him I'm here on behalf of General Washington." He saw the eyes of a few light up at that.

After paying for a room at an inn, Oliver found a livery to take care of Courage, allowing the horse to rest. The livery owner rented him another horse to ride until he found the colonel. Oliver removed the dispatch when the man wasn't looking, stuffed it in his leather satchel, and went back to the inn for a meal.

As he consumed the last bite, a deep, unfriendly voice came from behind him as he heard a gun being cocked.

"Why are you looking for James Moore?" the voice demanded.

Oliver slowly stood before turning around, eyeing a massive man with a square jaw, who looked like he could wrestle bears by himself. "You must be Colonel Moore. General George Washington has sent me."

Moore lowered his gun. "Pleased to meet you, young man. I'm Moore."

Oliver stood and shook his hand. "Oliver Atkinson. Please follow me."

Back in his room, Oliver produced the dispatch and handed it to the colonel, who read it while shaking his head. Finally, he looked at Oliver and said, "Please tell the general that we are working hard to convert the North Carolinians to the side of righteousness, and will send as many men as are available to join him as soon as possible. But we have an immediate problem here in Wilmington. I just received a message from a loyalist courier who instructed me and my small militia to lay down our arms because a force of sixteen-hundred loyalists is preparing to attack Wilmington. They want to make way for British General Cornwallis to arrive to use the port here to help cut the Colonies up."

"What did you tell him?" Oliver asked.

A huge grin stretched across his square face. "I blew my nose in the loyalist's demand for surrender and handed it back to the runner." His face turned serious. "We could really use your help.

Can you stay for a few days until we end this?"

Oliver squinted his eyes and pursed his lips before saying, "Two days. Three at most."

"You rode from Massachusetts?" Oliver nodded. "Has anyone figured out who fired the first shot at Lexington?" he asked while looking at the hole in the courier's hat.

"I was there. Our captain had told us to leave the green when the shot occurred. I turned toward the sound and saw a plume of smoke ascending over a Redcoat, so there you have it."

"You were there! Is that where you got the hole?" he asked as he put his finger in it.

Moving his hand away and smiling, Oliver responded, "It's a legend I'll allow to remain a mystery. But I did fight there and along the Bay Road. I'd be glad to help you."

"Good. Meet me here tomorrow night as the loyalists won't be here until the morning of the 27th. We have a tactical advantage and have built up some earthworks to maximize the terrain overlooking Moore's Creek Bridge. They must cross it to get here." Smiling again he said, "It's going to be like pharaoh and his army crossing the Red Sea!"

Courage was resting, though not happy when she saw Oliver mount another horse at the livery and head out. Oliver had time to explore the area. He had not seen anything like it in his life. He wandered the small, elegant town and then rode out to the beach. He was so taken with this area that he promised himself that once the conflict was over, he would marry Clara and bring her here to start a printing business.

The night of February 26th, Moore grabbed Oliver at the inn and asked, "Ready?" Oliver nodded, jumped on Courage for the first time in a couple of days, and they raced out of the city, as men joined them by the dozens.

While riding next to Moore, Oliver learned that he had been one of the original members of Wilmington's Sons of Liberty and had been waiting for this day for years. Oliver shared some of his stories regarding Revere, the Adamses, Hancock, and Washington. Moore was so impressed, he felt like a private and not a colonel next to the boy.

"After we win the war, you would be welcome to make Wilmington your home."

"I've already decided that. I've even picked out the perfect spot." Oliver joyfully added.

After their eighteen-mile ride north, they inspected the lines and earthworks. Each was satisfied. The militia was ready for battle. They and the two Sons of Liberty waited in silence behind a wall of logs and dirt, looking down upon the bridge. The militia of sixteen hundred loyalists was expected to be there by first light.

By 5 a.m. right before dawn broke, the loyalists were spotted.

"Bayonets and swords. They think they can overwhelm our force with six-hundred-fifty men," Moore quietly said.

Oliver began feeling the same adrenaline he felt before the battle up north when he shot at and killed men for the first time. There wasn't any moral conflict in his mind or heart this time, and he wasn't afraid. He thought, "This is for you, Clara," as the loyalists began their charge across the bridge.

The men under Colonel James Moore opened fire, spitting out a volley so thick it appeared the musket balls were linked together. Cannon erupted, and smoke mixed with the morning mist as loyalists' bodies were shredded. The bloody barrage surprised the loyalists so much that after seeing their two leaders killed, they turned and ran from the battle.

It was over in minutes. Many were caught and taken prisoner.

As the militia hooted and hollered, Moore turned to Oliver.

"I guess I didn't need you after all." They both laughed.

Oliver later learned that this decisive victory inspired most of the North Carolina Colony to join the patriot cause. When he later reported this battle to General Washington, it could not have come at a timelier moment because by the time Washington's forces reached New York City, he and the Congress needed some good news.

The young man from Derby didn't leave Wilmington immediately after the battle, as the loyalists were headed in the same direction he was. Moore advised him to wait a day and take a northwesterly route toward Raleigh before heading north through Richmond, Virginia, and Mt. Vernon, before landing in Philadelphia.

They went back to Wilmington and ate another grand meal by the hands of the vivacious and plump Mrs. Jane Moore. While dining, James Moore asked for Oliver to share his story beginning in England. He closed his story with falling in love with both Clara and Wilmington. Mrs. Moore didn't touch her food during his monologue, and turned to James excitedly and said, "You know a great wedding gift from us to Mr. Atkinson and Clara would be a parcel on that piece of land overlooking the Cape Fear River by downtown that we thought once to build a house on!"

Mr. Moore was used to his eager wife blurting out wild things, but an offering like that to a man they'd just met topped them all. "Yes, Oliver. We'll revisit it if you both move here. Let's end this war first."

They bid each other goodnight as Oliver thanked them for their generosity and hospitality and retired to his room in Moore's home.

CHAPTER 27

THE JOURNEY NORTH

The next day, February 29, 1776, Atkinson said goodbye to Colonel Moore at 6 a.m. Having decided before going to sleep the night before, Oliver explored the area one last time before heading north. He fell even more in love with the area. He could smell the ocean everywhere he went. It felt like it could be his home. "Not my parents, the uncle's, Effringham's, or the Revere's, but mine and Clara's."

Philadelphia was five-hundred miles away. The weather had warmed and the ice disappeared. The sky was clear and the sun bright as he rode past Raleigh. He expected to run into some loyalists but chuckled to himself that they were still running from Moore's Creek Bridge.

After staying the night in Richmond, Virginia, Oliver was back on Courage for a ride to Mount Vernon, where he had arranged to stay on his return in case General Washington needed him to bring him something.

Oliver found himself exhausted, in need of a nap, somewhere between Richmond and Fredericksburg. He could tell that Courage, too, was tired. He was amazed at the stamina of his faithful friend but wondered of her usefulness beyond this trip. Oliver could have swapped horses along the way and shaved a few days off on both sides of the journey, but he loved his familiar sidekick. He was proud of Courage.

Without any towns, villages, hamlets, or farmhouses in site, Oliver decided to build a lean-to among the trees and brush about thirty yards off the path he was on. He typically did this so a passerby would not easily find him and steal his horse or possessions. The sky gave no indication of rain to complicate his night.

As he walked Courage to what he considered a perfect patch of trees, he came upon a group of people who also thought it a perfect spot. Seeing movement in the brush ahead of him he stopped, loaded his musket, and called out, "Who's there?"

The movement in the brush ten yards ahead of him stopped at once, though he could hear a whimpering sound as if coming from a child. He called out again, but no response came. His heart picking up speed, he cautiously walked toward silhouetted figures that were partially concealed by brush and shadows. He stopped Courage, and raised his gun, and forcefully demanded, "Make yourselves known or I'll shoot!"

An unarmed African man in tattered brown slave clothing, about thirty-years old, walked into the remaining light of the day. His hands were up, and he was visibly shaking.

"Sir, please don't shoot. You got us. We sorry. Just me 'n my kin. You got us. We go back." As he spoke, a woman about his age, two men around twenty, and three children, emerged from the shadows behind him, each frightened seeing the white man with a gun pointed at them. "Just me 'n my kin, sir. We sorry."

Oliver began to shake as well upon seeing their condition. He slowly lowered his musket, and they stared at each other for a moment.

"Don't mean to cause you no harm, sir."

"You are slaves, yes?" Oliver gently asked.

The first man looked at his mates puzzled before answering, "Yes, sir, we slaves, but don't want to be slaves no mo'." One male runaway moved to Oliver's left and another to his right. Gravely concerned, Oliver looked back and forth over the frightened people before him and barked at the men to step back. They paused and looked at the one talking. Oliver raised his gun and pointed it at their leader. The women and babies retreated back into the brush.

Staring at the gun pointed at him, he bravely said, "We ain't goin' back, mister."

Nature had ceased speaking. The quiet wind carried no sounds as if holding its breath.

Lowering his rifle, Oliver gently assured them, "I'm not here to take you back. Are there any others with you? Do you have food, any weapons?"

"No, sir, we alone. Little food, no guns, sir, but we've knives." he admitted. "We come from six days away. Long way."

"Where are you headed?" the formerly indentured servant asked.

"Some man in a red coat came by our hut one day and was chased off by our massah, but he tol' us we get free if we fight for da British. Gotta make our way to Pennsylvania. Told we get freedom if we fight."

An unnerved Oliver was in a moral tug-of-war. He completely understood their desire to be free, having escaped his own type of bondage from Effringham's estate. But they were going to fight for the British. If they had the good fortune of making it to Pennsylvania and joining a loyalist militia, one of their musket balls could kill Oliver or a fellow patriot. He also hated with a passion that any man in America be in bondage to another, and for a moment he thought of Peter and how his bondage was not nearly as inhumane as those who he was speaking with that moment. Did he turn them in and send them back to slavery, a sure whipping, and possibly death? Or did he help them escape to freedom only to become his enemy on the battlefield?

The slaves remained still, silent, afraid, as Oliver processed his competing thoughts.

"You okay, sir?" the African asked.

Finally, he spoke, telling them, "Every human being has the right to fight for their freedom." He paused and questioned himself for what he was about to say and do. "I'm letting you go. I have no right over you."

"You not turning us in?" The man began to shake, not from fear, but joyful relief, as did the others. A woman cried as he hugged her.

Curling in his lips and pressing down his eyes, Oliver fought back raw emotion, turning away for a breath, before regaining his composure. He gave them some food and wished them God's will be done before they thanked him and quietly disappeared into the night.

He couldn't sleep for a few hours. He was deeply disturbed by this experience. Once again Oliver resolved to make this his issue after the war in whatever small way he could. Oliver was no longer naive about the age in which he lived, but besides his personal experience of bondage, there seemed to be a moral societal shift regarding slavery, with a growing call for its end. At least in the North.

He still knew little about the South and its culture, but he was disturbed by some glimpses. His last thoughts before his eyes forcibly shut on him from being wiped out emotionally and physically were the slaves he saw at Mount Vernon. He didn't see abuse. He didn't witness anyone being punished. He hadn't heard any cracking whips. No screams in the night. Yet it seemed wrong. Very wrong. He was determined it wouldn't affect his opinion of General Washington, and it didn't, in part because Diggs told him that upon Washington's death the slaves would be set free and receive a large piece of land for them to live on and work.

Oliver had considered leaving Courage at Mount Vernon. He knew his friend was tired. His gate was slower, and the young man couldn't match the speed he demonstrated earlier in the trip. In the end, he wasn't ready to part with his faithful friend.

As he was about to leave Mount Vernon after a two day stay, Betancourt ran after him that early mid-March morning shouting, "Mr. Atkinson! Mr. Atkinson! I nearly forgot to give this pamphlet to you." As the morning-robed man breathlessly caught up to him, Oliver took it. The cover read: "Common Sense." Its author was a man named Thomas Paine. Oliver had not heard of him.

"Thank you," Oliver kindly said, stuffing it into his vest.

* * *

Directing Courage north, he followed the Potomac River back to Great Falls and crossed into Maryland. He bypassed the Carroll home. He enjoyed the bed and their company, but the rich food didn't sit well with his stomach. He aimed east, away from the loyalist area he had narrowly escaped, so that within four days he was once again in Philadelphia, arriving late afternoon.

He rode by Independence Hall only to find it empty except for a delegate from Rhode Island arguing with a delegate from South Carolina about whether true gentlemen should powder their wigs white after their hair had turned gray.

"I'd hate for the coalition between the Colonies to fall apart over this issue," Oliver thought to himself as he rolled his eyes, backed out of the room, and returned to Courage. His next stop was The Yards' Inn, a brick and timber working man's locale that was simple in appearance, accommodation, and food. But the beers and ales were quite superior, according to those who enjoyed such beverages.

He found Samuel Adams alone in the quiet tavern-area of the inn finishing a pint of his favorite afternoon ale and learned that the rest of the Massachusetts men were off doing 'What only Providence knows.' "So good to see you again, Oliver. You've really grown. Sit. Regale me with tales of General Washington and your travels."

The two sat down, and just as Oliver began to speak, he noticed that Sam was wiggling his nose as if smelling something bad.

"Tell you what, Oliver. You've managed to upstage the typical sweat and spilled rum smell of this place. There's a room for you upstairs and a change of clothes as we knew you'd be coming soon. Go take a bath for the sake of the cause!" They both laughed. "So, you don't have to tell the same story a dozen times, we're meeting here for dinner later and you can share with all of us then."

"Yes, sir," Oliver said as he got up and went outside to give relief to Courage. He'd been unable to leave Courage at Mount Vernon even though he knew the good care she'd receive there. Oliver settled her in the stable, went to his room, undressed to his soiled undergarments, and fell back in his bed asleep. He was shocked awake an hour later by a knock at the door. It was one of the young Yards girls, Emma, who alerted him that his bath was ready and that dinner would be served in thirty minutes.

Clean and dressed in proper clothes, he dined with the Massachusetts men, Thomas Jefferson from Virginia, Charles Carroll from Maryland, whose home he had stayed in, Nathaniel Folsom from New Hampshire, and Allen Jones from North Carolina. Jones was most excited to hear that his good friend Colonel James Moore had routed the loyalists.

"If the Redcoats fight like the loyalists, this war will be over before you can say "Independence!" Jones bellowed over the din of the packed dining hall.

It was clear to the delegates that an exhausted young man sat before them, using what remaining energy he had to share his travels and news. He had served the interest of their cause bravely and with excellence, and now it was time for them to release him to his room. John Hancock told the young patriot to take a few days off from anything that seemed like work. "Don't even run the simplest errand for anyone. Stay away from Independence Hall and all the vultures there! We are awaiting word from General Washington and his orders for you. Until then, relax. Go see Peter. Catch some fish."

The young courier didn't argue. Once the food settled in his stomach, his mind began to shut down. The recent intensity and stress were much different from both his escape from the English estate, his voyage on *The Beaver,* and his fighting at Lexington and along Bay Road. This exhaustion went deeper.

Laying on his bed, he thought of Junior, his friends from Boston, and the games they played. His memories of playing as a child before his parents died was foggy. He'd had so little time to be a child. It was too late now, he thought. As he intended every night as his eyelids met, he wanted his last waking thoughts to be about Clara, and they were.

The sun was up when he awoke. Oliver found an envelope on the dresser that had a pink bow tied around it. He smelled the scent of the perfume Clara wore only for him. This was her response to his letter that instructed her to write to him in care of John Hancock in Philadelphia. He read and reread the letter a dozen times. She swore her undying love and patience in waiting for the bravest man in the world to return from fighting for freedom and God.

"I have to make it through this war," he said, smiling to himself.

During his downtime, he read Thomas Paine's *Common Sense* no less than ten times. It seemed everyone in Philadelphia had a copy, so everyone was talking about it. It spoke not only of the tyranny of the Crown towards Americans, but the tyranny that all Crowns throughout history have imposed upon subjects. It did so much to solidify the resolve of patriots, and to enlighten and turn many loyalists against England and join the cause for liberty. It stoked calls for independence from Britain, and the revolutionary radicals used it to drive this matter before Congress. Oliver kept his ears open, and his mouth shut on those days he hung around Independence Hall or was in social gatherings among great men.

The independence he had hoped for was at hand, he believed.

In early April, a courier arrived from Boston to report that the British evacuated Boston with their ships. The siege worked. The Massachusetts men, along with Oliver, celebrated late into the night. The courier had been a part of the story, he told the men.

"Colonel Knox was ordered to haul fifty-nine cannons to Boston to help with the siege. Many in Boston said it was the cannon that drove the British out. My parents' home was near the fort at the base of Cook's Mountain when he recruited me to the cause. We, with the help of oxen, hauled the artillery three hundred miles over frozen lakes, rivers, and mountains. Didn't lose a single gun! The English saw all those cannons staring down at them and hightailed it from Boston, they did!"

The jovial night came to a close with Thomas Cushing calling for quiet. "Our families will now be safe at last. Now, let's finish our job so we can all be safe once more!"

Oliver penned a letter to Clara that night reminding her of his love, sharing some of his journey, and asking her to keep praying. It was working.

Peter was kept from seeing Oliver for the first two weeks he was back in town, being punished for having been caught running off with Maggie a few times without permission. His friend confessed that he was afraid he might be sold to a master down South where he heard they are "wicked mean to their slaves. I got it good here, Oliver. I'm just so 'n love wit Maggie."

Weeks after his return, there was still little for Oliver to do on behalf of Congress, as the Massachusetts men had new people in place to serve them. So, he and Peter went fishing often, and when his friend was working, he would continue his physical exercise and go for rides in the Pennsylvania countryside.

While fishing one day Oliver asked Peter if he knew how much he cost.

Peter looked at him strangely.

"I'm sorry. I don't know these things nor the language. But if I were to buy you, how much would you cost?" Oliver asked, fearing he had offended or wounded his friend.

Peter stared at him for a moment, then said, "Why you asking? Gonna try 'n buy me on your private's salary?" Peter's face finally broke and the two laughed.

"Who knows? Maybe I'll discover a treasure chest full of gold, silver, and jewels! Or I'll become a successful businessman and make lots of money."

"You don't seem like the greedy kind, Oliver."

"A man has to make a living."

"I'll find out my price, Oliver. But I hope you don't be a mean master!" he laughed.

Oliver turned serious. "I wouldn't buy you to own you, Peter. But to free you." he said with tears gathering in his eyes.

Peter patted his friend's shoulder. They fished silently for an hour until the sun began to disappear in the West and the young man with new hopes left for home before he got into more trouble.

CHAPTER 28

Private Atkinson began to think General Washington had forgotten him. It was late June and the only thing he had heard from his camp was to abide until he was summoned. He felt that he was wasting away, as he wasn't really a part of the Congressional matters or the war effort. He spent much of his time reading, writing Clara, working on his physical fitness, dining with the Massachusetts men at The Yards Inn, and going on rides with a rejuvenated Courage out in the lush green hills of the Pennsylvania countryside.

And staying as cool as he could. It was yet another blazing summer.

Oliver got word that Thomas Jefferson had been tasked to write a declaration of independence to unite the thirteen Colonies and create a new nation of thirteen states.

Sneaking up to Jefferson's small, rented room where he was diligently writing and rewriting his draft, Oliver knocked on the door only to receive a sharp, "Who is it?"

"So sorry to disturb you, Mr. Jefferson. It's Oliver. Just stopping by to see if you needed anything?"

The door swung open, kicked by a sitting Jefferson's foot, and Oliver saw a now beaming, but exhausted, thirty-two-year-old Thomas Jefferson sitting at his desk. He showed Oliver an early draft of what he was working on.

"The United States of America." Oliver said out loud.

"I keep vacillating between that and using 'United Colonies.' I can expect criticisms either way I choose. What do you think?"

"You're asking me?" Jefferson nodded. "I think 'United States' has a strong, dare I say, majestic, ring to it. We've been colonies. Our revolution demands evolution. Let's become states."

Jefferson thought he was looking at young version of himself for a moment. "I think you're exactly right, Mr. Atkinson. I will press for this name."

Oliver took a deep breath to soak in this moment.

"Remember what we talked about before concerning slavery, Oliver? Watch for the language."

It was a momentous undertaking in history that had never been done before. Serfs, slaves, and subjects didn't shake off kings, popes, and pharaohs to create new nations. It just didn't happen. Rebellions that were marginally successful almost always failed in the long run.

But this was different. Every true believer knew it. Freedom or failure. Life, liberty, or death. This was so true that Charles Carroll of Maryland not only signed his name on the declaration, but underscored it with where he lived, as if to say, "Come and get me, King George!" No one had more in the terms of material and earthly wealth than this man, and here he pledged everything. Oliver was constantly reminded that he was in the company of greatness.

If Lexington was the "shot heard around the world," what would a Declaration of Independence from England be?

They would soon find out.

On July 3, Private Atkinson received orders to meet General Washington in Manhattan, New York, post haste. Washington had learned through his spy network that British General William Howe was on his way to New York with four hundred ships and thirty-two thousand men. Washington needed every able soul. It was time for Oliver to say his "goodbyes," pack, and leave.

Making his rounds, he interrupted John Adams at Independence Hall, who told his young friend, "You may want to wait until tomorrow."

"But I have orders to leave immediately!" Oliver exclaimed.

Whispering to young Atkinson, he said, "How delighted would our esteemed general be if you arrived with a copy of our declaration of independence in hand?" Adams sat back and gave the wide-eyed private a cheshire cat grin.

Late the next afternoon, a runner about Oliver's age found him in his room, writing to Clara. He told Oliver to join the Massachusetts men at Independence Hall. Packed and ready to go like the Minuteman he was trained to be, Oliver rushed down to Courage, saddled her, secured his goods, and raced to the Hall. John and Samuel Adams met him at the door.

Excitedly, Samuel said, "Stay right here, Oliver. The document has been adopted. A printer is working on a copy for you to take to General Washington."

The jubilant men said they had to get back inside and make sure that things didn't blow up, but not before sincerely thanking the boy for his help for more than two years. As the grown men walked back into the Hall, they looked at each other and simultaneously said, "Providence."

An hour later, in the simmering heat of a pale Pennsylvania afternoon, a runner approached him with two copies of the Declaration of Independence, waving them in the air so the ink would dry. Taking them from the boy's hand, Oliver placed one of the copies between four large Princess Tree leaves that would protect the document from the abrasive leather on the inside of his secret compartment. He then carefully placed them in his leather case. He then read the other copy.

"We hold these truths to be self-evident, that all men are created equal, that they are endowed by their Creator with certain unalienable Rights, that among these are Life, Liberty and the pursuit of Happiness. That to secure these rights, Governments are instituted among Men, deriving their just powers from the consent of the governed. That whenever any Form of Government becomes destructive of these ends, it is the Right of the People to alter or to abolish it, and to institute new Government, laying its foundation on such principles and organizing its powers in such form, as to them shall seem most likely to affect their Safety and Happiness."

Tears rolled down his face as he finished reading the document and covered it with leaves, as he did the first, and gently placed it in his leather bag. Oliver mounted Courage and they were off faster than a musket ball, nearly knocking down a man crossing the street.

"Sorry!" he yelled through his mucus as he glanced over his shoulder.

The adrenaline was back, and Courage never felt better.

As Washington's army entered Manhattan, roughly one-third of the residents of the city fled the battles that they knew would come. Those citizens who remained were divided between loyalty to King George III and the patriot hope in George Washington. The wealthy city was now at the center of a revolution.

Washington and his army of nineteen-thousand men entered New York City in mid-April. This allowed him to strengthen batteries that protected the harbor and construct forts on the north end of the city and across the East River in Brooklyn. The general was convinced that although British troops moved from Boston to Nova Scotia their next strategic destination would be New York City.

* * *

The general didn't have a fully established spy network yet, as he would by 1778. For now, he relied on intelligence provided by fellow patriots and members of the Sons of Liberty, who had a strong presence in New York. Word came by late June that General William Howe was on his way with four-hundred warships and thirty-two-thousand men, prompting the general's call for Oliver to join him. He needed every man.

As Oliver rode Courage past New York Harbor on the New Jersey side, he was awed by the number of British ships. He paused for a moment, his heart quickening its pace while his breathing shortened. The task before them suddenly looked too daunting to overcome. A show of force this size, Oliver feared, would prompt the half-hearted patriot to flee. Their only hope was the leadership of General Washington and the men's preparation and indivisible commitment to fight for liberty. The document he carried, he hoped, would help blow out any flames of fear and ignite the flames of freedom.

It appeared that British soldiers were disembarking on Staten Island, so he continued north to just above the island's peak and crossed into Manhattan by ferry from Powles Hook.

General Washington was in a staff meeting at his new headquarters when Oliver arrived. The young courier was warmly greeted by those in the meeting who knew him and he received the warmest welcome from General Washington.

"I received your reports, Corporal Atkinson," Washington said, signifying that the young courier had been elevated from private, "and found the news about Moore's Creek Bridge to be quite encouraging. Well done."

Oliver pulled out the declarations and handed them to his commander-in-chief, and said, "These might encourage you further, General."

Washington opened the leather case to find two copies of the declaration and read silently to himself at first, and then offered a copy back to Oliver, asking him to read it to those present, an honor Oliver never forgot. It was as if the room shook from the shouts of joy and foot stomping that followed. People from other parts of the headquarters came running to learn what the jubilation was about and joined them.

Washington raised his hand, and the room instantly became silent. "I want to get as many of these printed as possible and hand them out to every officer for them to read to the men under them. I want them to be available to the public. In fact, I would like a public reading of this Declaration of Independence to be made tomorrow night, July 9, at 6 p.m. Invite our soldiers! Invite our citizen patriots. And be sure to invite every loyalist and British official you can find. Tell them all to meet at the Common. We will have a grand celebration! May God bless America!"

The room erupted again with joy and hallelujahs. It was later said that it may have been the drunkest night Manhattan had ever experienced.

At the first public reading of the Declaration of Independence, Oliver met a zealous young patriot who reminded him of himself. His name was Private Joseph Plumb Martin. He was a couple of inches taller than Oliver with about the same build.

"I'm from Milford, Connecticut. Threatened to run away and join the American Navy if my grandparents didn't allow me to enlist in the militia."

"I did run away from England to Boston."

"Sounds like there's a story there."

"A most unlikely one."

Martin had just arrived in New York City to serve under George Washington days before Oliver rode into town. The corporal and the private became instant friends, though they didn't see much of each other because they were training in different locales for different purposes.

Oliver trained with the cavalry for the next few weeks. His training with the Minutemen was basic warfare as a foot soldier, but now he would be doing most of his fighting from Courage's back. His horse seemed to take to the new training well. Although she could be temperamental, his long journey with Oliver had softened her occasional moments of stubbornness. Her vigor remained strong, she was as fast as ever, and like Oliver, Courage had matured over the last eight months.

CHAPTER 29

DARKNESS

While Washington was convinced that Howe would attack Manhattan after the army he saw land on Staten Island, he, nonetheless, sent much of his force to Brooklyn. Oliver was put under General Israel Putnam at Brooklyn Heights for the time being and would be his primary courier between the two men until his orders changed. Oliver rode with his new commander to survey the area. Putnam assumed Howe would come in from the west and the south.

They proceeded by Jamaica Pass, a forested valley thorough a ridge of hills in Brooklyn, northeast of the main forces for both sides. Oliver noticed that Putnam hadn't given any orders to secure the area other than leaving a few men. This concerned the young corporal.

"Permission to speak, general?"

He nodded without looking at Oliver.

"Would it be a good idea to reinforce the Jamaica Pass so as not to expose our flank?"

Finally, Putnam looked at him, smirked and said, "The battle will come from the south. That's where Clinton is. It would be foolish to waste resources there, Corporal Atkinson."

And with that, he galloped off.

A few loyalists saw the same thing and alerted the British army of this opportunity. On August 27, the first shots of the Battle of

Brooklyn rang out. Washington immediately took a boat across but went no further than a redoubt on Cobble Hill.

Oliver suspected that the German Hessians, mercenaries hired by England, to attack on the main line of the American forces from the southeast and a smaller British force's attack on Major General William Stirling and his Maryland 400 on the southwest were ruses. After firing his musket and hitting a Regular in the chest, Oliver turned Courage north to investigate his hunch and raced towards Jamaica Pass while reloading his rifle.

Musket balls whizzed past his head, he instinctively ducking, "as if that will help," he amusingly would say to himself to help minimize his stress. Passing through the ranks, he spotted his friend Joseph Martin and shouted for him to give the Redcoats the "Milford musket!" The Milford Musket was a model of musket that Spain produced and provided to the Continental Army. Martin waved his gun and shouted something as Oliver sprinted by.

As he approached Jamaica Pass, the sound of British cannon burst before him, coming from the direction of the Pass. Just as he thought. Large copper and tin balls rocketed by overhead falling viciously upon Americans, eliciting screams heard over the gunfire.

He shot up a hill close by and saw at least ten thousand soldiers coming through the unguarded Pass. Furious, he turned Courage and flew back to where Putnam should have been, but he had left the area, he assumed to see General Washington. Oliver found Washington, but not Putnam on Cobble Hill and explained what he saw.

While he reported to General Washington, General James Sullivan commanded his troops to retreat as the heat of the battle against Cornwallis at Flatbush Pass was too much.

Oliver raced back to the battle to help General Stirling and his force at the Red Lion Inn with the Gowanus Bay to their right. No other reinforcements came to the aid of Stirling and his men, who fought valiantly to hold off the British on their flank for an hour so that the soldiers to the south of them could retreat. Stirling ordered Oliver to report to Washington what his intention was. About two hundred and fifty of Stirling's four-hundred Marylanders and Delaware militia members died, and he was taken prisoner. Their heroism spared many patriot lives.

And then for unknown reasons, the battle stopped.

British General Howe ordered his men to dig in around the Continental forces and resume the battle the next day. He thought that Washington and his men had nowhere to go. They were trapped from all sides, including the East River.

As a glum Washington paced the area with his officers, he wondered aloud what could be done, as they were trapped along the East River, and seemingly doomed. These men knew that if Howe pressed the battle this day, the war for independence would be over.

While Oliver waited for orders, he could see several boats on the banks of the East River on the Brooklyn side.

After being offered suggestions by a few officers, Washington half-jokingly asked Oliver if he had any ideas.

Oliver paused for a moment while looking down at the shore, then said, "We can't stay and fight, sir, that much is true. But we can leave by the river." He pointed to the river's edge. "See those boats?" Washington nodded.

An aide burst out angrily at Oliver. "Oh, come on little boy! We have thousands of men! How will those few boats evacuate the army? General Washington, we have serious business to discuss."

Washington shot the aide a look that almost stopped the impudent man's heart. He then looked back at Oliver, who moved a few steps closer to the river.

"There must be dozens of boats within a short distance of us. At nightfall, we can leave our campfires burning along our lines, giving the British the impression that we're still hunkered down, and move the men off the lines to the boats to ferry them across. The first group that gets there can recruit help from our friends to bring even more boats across until every man is safely in Manhattan."

The boy paused for a moment as Washington stared down at him, then over at the boats, and across to Manhattan. Oliver, having no idea what he was thinking, asked. "May I add one more thing, General?" Washington nodded. "We not only have to be quiet while crossing, but, frankly, we will need a miracle fog to descend on us for cover as we cross, so I suggest all of us pray," he said while looking at the condescending aide.

Washington put his arm on Oliver's shoulder. "Your plan might just work, Sergeant Atkinson," he said, giving Oliver a promotion on the spot. "I don't think we have any other options." He told his officers to get the word out to their men. "Have them keep their fires going for as long as they can."

"General Washington, sir?" Oliver said.

"Yes, sergeant."

"I'll stay to the end to make sure the fires remain lit and will go on the last boat out."

"That means you will be riding with me, Mr. Atkinson."

Along with the officers present, Oliver headed out with orders to the commanding officers on the lines to prepare their men to evacuate Brooklyn. "Keep the campfires burning until you leave!" Oliver instructed.

The first men to move out were from the front line. Oliver spent the next few hours tending to the deceptive flames, stealthily moving up and down the lines, adding anything flammable he could find to keep them going.

The lines thinned out as men departed for Manhattan on

anything that floated. He knew the night would soon come to an end and he had hoped for a report from Washington's camp on the evacuation's progress, but none had come during the previous hour.

Every thirty minutes, Oliver visited Courage, who he kept twenty yards behind the front lines. His horse seemed calm, and Oliver began to relax, thinking they were going to pull off a miraculous escape. The last news he'd received had been an encouraging report. And just as he and the officers had prayed, God saw fit to roll in a night fog as thick as anyone could remember.

He paused to take a drink of water while he lay on his belly overlooking part of the British first line. Everything seemed so peaceful, though he knew the English would awake soon and resume their assault. He decided to make one last run through the southernmost part of the Continental line before he returned to Washington's camp. This should get him there by the break of dawn. Still, why didn't anyone come to check on him? Maybe they thought he would have returned on his own?

He had to hurry. So, for his last examination, he thought it wise to ride Courage to the area. He felt the sound of hoofbeats might add more credibility to their ruse. Surveying the fires, he felt confident that they'd be out just as morning appeared he would then rush back to the exit position.

Over at the exfiltration point, as the last of the dark of night gave way to morning's first light, the last of the men, including General Washington and Oliver's new friend Joseph Plumb Martin, reluctantly boarded a dinghy that held ten men. A concerned Washington looked back hoping to see Oliver appear on the shore, but all he saw were the fading flames of the fires that his young sergeant was supposed to have stoked.

"The British will discover our scheme any time and within

minutes have their dragoons upon us, general. We must leave," a major firmly suggested.

Washington knew this was true and grievously gave the order to leave. The last boat made its way quietly into the East River and aimed at fires that lined the opposite shore so the rowers knew where to go. Washington kept his eyes on the Brooklyn shoreline until the fog disallowed visibility.

Exhausted and hungry, Oliver spun Courage west in the early days light for the short ride to the beach where the evacuation was staged when three Regulars jumped in front of him. He heard their muskets cock before seeing them, and he immediately halted Courage. There was no way to escape. He'd be shot if he tried. Suddenly, a few more Regulars appeared, all equally stunned at the absence of their enemy. One of them said to another, "General Howe needs to see this." A Regular ran back to the British position.

As Oliver was yanked off Courage, he saw a face he thought he recognized. As a young man slightly older than him came into better light, he saw that it was his cousin from Derby. Shocked, they stared at each other speechless until Oliver's cousin forced him up against a tree and told him to hug it. While searching him he whispered in his ear, "Effringham came back and replaced you with me, then sold me to the army. I hate you."

Not finding anything on him or his horse, they bound his hands behind his back and turned him to face his interrogators.

A stunned captain demanded, "Where is everyone? Where is your army?" Oliver remained quiet not knowing how many men were still on the Brooklyn banks. He needed to buy them as much time as possible.

Some of the Regulars, including his cousin, were ordered to go check the other American lines, being warned to "Be alert. This could be one of Washington's traps!"

Just as these men were reporting back to the captain, Howe's armed contingent of cavalry and Regulars rushed him to where Oliver was being held.

An incredulous, shocked, Howe surveyed the area as the day's sunlight lit the empty battlefield.

One of the searchers reported, "They're gone, General Howe."

"Gone?" the disbelieving general asked. "What do you mean, gone?"

"The rebel army has disappeared. Not a soul left behind 'cept this one, general."

Turning to Oliver, he asked, "Where has General Washington's army gone, corporal?" Oliver remained silent. "I command you to tell me." Howe said. Oliver remained quiet, staring at the general's eyes.

Howe dispersed his cavalry to search for Washington's army.

Looking back at the insubordinate American, he ordered Oliver to be flogged until he told them what happened. Two Regulars wrestled the liberty fighter back to the tree where they frisked him, tore off his uniform coat and shirt until he was bare, and secured his hands around the tree with rope so he couldn't escape. Taking a riding crop, a Regular lashed Oliver every thirty seconds per Howe's orders until he gave up his men. Howe amused himself with the beating as if watching lawn bowling.

After ten lashes, the sound of a few rounds of British muskets was heard from the exit zone. Howe and his men quickly rode to the shores only to see one final boat three-quarters of the way across the East River. The volley couldn't reach them.

A furious Howe rode back to Oliver and demanded he be untied and sent to one of the prison ships in New York Harbor "with the other rebel captives."

Howe rode through the empty American camp, wondering how the entire army could have vanished. He just kept shaking his head and muttering to himself, "It's impossible. It's just not possible."

* * *

Bound, Oliver was led to a boat that was to take him to a ship in the harbor. About a thousand other patriot soldiers awaited the same fate. It was mid-morning, and the weary, dirty, bloodied captives were commanded to remain quiet as they waited to be taken to the prison ships. Oliver, being the last one brought to the defeated collection, was last to get on a small boat. He was ordered to sit silently at the threat of being butted with a musket or whipped with a leather strap.

British sailors mocked the "losers" and warned them of the great horrors that awaited them. "It'll not be a cruise along the Thames, I promise you!" one jokingly said, while another quipped, "Hope you had a big breakfast as I don't recall seeing much food on board for prisoners."

The taunting continued until they pulled up to the converted 8-gun fireship HMS *Scorpion*. It didn't look seaworthy, Oliver wondering how it stayed afloat. Perhaps the Brits intended to load the ships until the weight sank them to the bottom of the harbor, or use them for target practice?

There was a dark presence on board. It felt like the opposite of what he'd experienced at church. The sailors had black saucers for eyes and seemed only part human.

The captives were lined up in rows across the deck. A short, impossibly thin lieutenant approached the men as a midshipman placed a box fifteen feet in front of the prisoners. He stepped up on the box and contemptuously surveyed his new inmates before clearing his throat twice and saying with a high-pitched voice, "Welcome to the HMS *Scorpion*. Your home for the rest of your natural life. Your commanding officer General Washington and his army have been routed. Therefore, you have nothing left to fight for, and as rebels, you now have nothing left to live for. My promise to each one of you is, and I speak on behalf of the King of England, you will all die here. Welcome to hell." He gingerly stepped off the box with the assistance of a midshipman Oliver's age and disappeared toward the back of the ship.

The men were stripped naked and forced to stand at attention for ten hours. They were not allowed to have bathroom breaks, water, or food. Oliver stood in the very back. He immediately began thinking of escape, but being tied to the men around him there simply wasn't a way. If they all jumped overboard, they couldn't swim being bound together. They would drown.

After three hours, one man fell from heat exhaustion, causing his line to topple with him. Guards stood by with whips and swords to punish anyone out of line, and these men were brutalized for a few minutes; the first man to fall was pierced through his abdomen with a sword. He was then untied from his line and thrown overboard. The guards didn't have to make threats. This was enough.

Oliver keenly observed everything the captors did, looking for any weakness, any area he might be able to exploit. He prayed for wisdom, reprieve, escape, and survival. And he did nothing to draw attention to himself. He had to survive. He had to get back to his army. He had to get back to Clara.

The patriot prisoners fought to remain motionless. The young sergeant's consistent workouts helped him remain strong, but his muscles were straining, cramping, as pain moved in waves through his thighs and calves. He hoped this would be the worst of it, having expected the very proper British to adhere to some form of decency and honor. But he soon discovered, as the captives were sent single file into the bowels of the converted hospital ship, that this was not to be.

When the hatch was opened, a stench, unlike any Oliver had ever encountered, rose with volcanic force from below. If smells could feel like a sucker punch in the face, this was that. He could taste it. It was a mixture of sweat, body odor, human discharge, and rotted flesh. Oliver, along with most of the men, threw up on each other while being led down into their holding area.

After adjusting his eyes to the dim bowels, the captured Continentals discovered to their horror that some male citizens and patriots were already present, at least one hundred by Oliver's estimation. And shockingly not all of them were alive. They were stretched out on the deck, some moaning from wounds, others looking white and sickly in the little light that existed.

The prisoners were directed to find a place to "call their own," and that would be their sleeping quarters. Except there wasn't any room. The British intended for them to sleep one on top of the other, to their amusement.

Oliver made a spot near the hatch that led to the main deck. He figured this might give him shots of fresh air and sunlight when it was opened. A Marylander named Arnold Curtiss was on his left, and Thomas Mayfair, a man from Rhode Island was on his right. They waited for the guards to leave before speaking to each other.

Oliver went first. "We have got to find a way off this ship."

Mayfair angrily responded, "There's no way off this ship." He pointed to the mass of bodies in the dark. "If there was a way off, don't you think these poor souls would've found it?"

"Not necessarily," countered Curtiss. "I can't imagine it's easy, but we need to look for weaknesses in their operation here. Perhaps there might be a way out through the hull of this rickety boat."

"I wondered the same thing," said Oliver.

But it wasn't to be. For the next six months the three men would descend into a Hades that Dante could not have imagined. Oliver wondered if he had missed a sign on the hatch through which he descended that said, "All hope abandon, ye who enter here."

The horror guards caused their prisoners personified the worst of humanity. More men were added over time, both soldiers and citizen patriots. The astonishment, the cries for relief, the process for each person seemed to be the same. Because of the lack of food and water, and rations being sparsely given with the intention to starve and dehydrate these men to death, many men capitulated. Including that of Mayfair, whose greening body oozed liquid onto Oliver.

Four days after Mayfair's Death, Oliver and Curtiss were allowed to take his decomposing body up to the deck and throw him overboard into the harbor. This happened every day with other men. Besides starvation, death from dehydration, disease brought on by the dead bodies, and rats that feasted on them claimed man after man.

Oliver and Curtiss fought to keep their sanity by discussing books they'd read, including the Bible, with one prisoner overhearing a particular discussion on the resurrection. A nearby prisoner called the resurrection a myth. Oliver told him he didn't fear death because he knew the resurrection to be true. The man mocked him more. The next morning, the heckler was dead.

The two friends also talked about the girls they loved, and what they planned to do after the conflict.

One man across the hull overheard this and told the two to, "Shut your bloody faces up! We're not getting off here alive. There is no hope in Hell!"

"No hope." Oliver's ears pricked up as these words cut through the air. "I'm not dead yet."

The two men continued their conversation. Curtiss offered that he would return to grow corn, build a mill, and never get on a ship again. Oliver tried laughing at this, but there was no joy left in his soul to harvest it from. Oliver said he wanted to print a weekly newspaper and publish books. He wanted a simple life.

Atkinson tried keeping track of the date, but his mind wasn't working so well after nine months of captivity. He looked around and didn't recognize many of the faces. He was losing his wits and had no idea how he had survived.

All of the soldiers that came aboard with him were dead except Curtiss. He was shocked that they hadn't died yet. He could see his ribs, and his arms and legs were bony, with little muscle definition left. He attributed his survival to his physical regimen. That and Providence, though he was struggling gravely with His goodness at this point, becoming angry at the perpetuation of the injustice of his prolonged suffering. "What was the point?" he would ask.

There came a time when Oliver quietly begged God to kill him and take him home. Quietly, because he couldn't scream. God didn't grant this request. Instead, as he cried waterless tears, his buddy, Arnold Curtiss took his last breath and died, falling on Oliver's shoulder. Oliver tried getting mad at God, but he couldn't, but he didn't want to talk to Him anymore. He was empty of everything good he used to know. The world was wicked. While contemplating this, he fell asleep. As soon as he was under, he had a picture in his mind of Jesus hanging on the cross. This shocked him awake. It didn't console him, encourage him, or give him any hope. He still wanted to die.

Three days later, a guard kicked his feet. "You!"

Startled, Oliver awoke, "What? What?" and sat up.

Pointing to Curtiss, he said, "Get this man out of here." The guard then barked at a prisoner who had recently arrived to help Oliver with this task, and they both stood slowly, forcing their atrophied muscles to stretch.

Why him? He was a skeleton and hadn't any strength. This man would be doing most of the hauling. With great difficulty, they hauled Curtiss up through the latch and onto the main deck.

Oliver was first on deck. Though blinded by the light for a moment, the warm, soothing breeze reminded him he was alive.

And that meant hope. He tried laughing at himself for thinking that. But as his eyes came into focus, he could see the sky to the west had splashed bright streaks of orange and blue across the horizon. What really caught his eye was the private fishing boat near the HMS *Scorpion* headed towards New Jersey.

He and the unnamed helper dragged Curtiss to the rail. "Goodbye, my friend." Upon releasing the man to the bay, Oliver summoned what remained of his strength and began calling out to the fishing vessel while waving his arms.

"Unless you want a musket ball in your back, you'd better get back below deck!"

The emaciated soldier turned and looked briefly with recessed eyes at his slightly older English counterpart, then quoted Jonah 2:2 with a chalky whisper: "I cried by reason of my affliction unto the LORD, and He heard me; out of the belly of hell cried I, and thou heardest my voice." And with the strength Oliver had left, cast himself off the ship, crashing into the harbor.

Shocked guards fired their muskets once at him until an officer barked at them not to waste the shot. "There's no way he survived the fall, no way."

Oliver hit the harbor hard feet-first then sank ten feet into the water before he floated to the surface. The cold water shocked him into clarity. "I'm not dead! I'm not dead!"

Refocusing, he looked for the fishing vessel, and began waving his arms, shouting with what little air he could force through across his vocal cords. The vessel seemed not to have noticed him and sailed past. No way he'd make it to shore two-hundred yards away. His only chance, he thought, had just sailed by.

Someone at the back of the fishing boat had spotted him and steered back.

Suddenly he heard voices calling out, "You there, are you alright?"

As the vessel came alongside Oliver, the three men on the fishing boat were horrified, unable to move for a moment when seeing the condition of the man before them. One broke out in tears, before forcibly shutting them off.

Gently lifting Oliver on board, they laid him on the deck. Oliver motioned with his head towards the prison ship, and the men quickly moved away from the HMS *Scorpion*. He was given water and dried fish, then covered with a blanket, and added a cushion for his head to rest on. They didn't ask him any questions, though they knew he was a captive of the British. Their sunken hearts knew to let him rest. They also knew they needed to get distance from the harbor ships and to a doctor as fast as possible.

CHAPTER 30

Two days later, Oliver woke up to see through a haze an unfamiliar face standing over him in an unfamiliar pink festooned bedroom talking with an unfamiliar woman. "He's awake," she called out anxiously excited.

Feet were heard running up some stairs, and within seconds, one of the fishermen who pulled him from the water came through the door and knelt before a weak, but alive, Oliver.

The bright sun coming through an east-facing window caused the sixteen-year-old boy's eyes to recoil and close.

"How are you, son?" he asked.

Oliver tried to sit up, but he was too weak. He then tried speaking, but his voice was hoarse. He was on a small bed dressed in clean sleeping attire. He knew not how he got there or where he was.

"Keep giving him fluids when awake. Don't give him cheese or bread for a few days, but vegetables in broth for food, maybe a little meat when his swallowing eases up," said the man holding a black leather case. "I'll check back tomorrow."

He turned and left, his footsteps descending until they were no more. The fisherman put his arm around his wife's waist and pulled her in close.

The patient mouthed, "Where am I?"

"My name is Abraham Blossom, and this is my wife, Mary. You are in the colony of New Jersey, in Sandy Hook. This is our home. I and some men pulled you from the water a few days ago."

Oliver tried to speak but no sound came forth. They leaned in closer to hear what he was saying. Oliver took a sip of water, and didn't fully swallow, but allowed it to rest in his throat. After a few seconds, he swallowed, then tried speaking again. The couple leaned in a little closer.

A faint sound and a wisp of air came from between Oliver's lips. "Thank you." The couple looked at each other as if to ask if they understood him.

"What did he say? What did you say?" asked the grizzled man.

Pushing additional air out this time, his throat better after another swig, Oliver said loud enough for the two strangers to hear. "Thank you." He then weakly coughed and leaned back on his pillows and closed his eyes.

Mary tugged on her husband's shirt and led him toward the door. "Let him rest, Abraham."

A few days later, the woman brought him more vegetable broth that had a few small pieces of chicken in it. As she came through the door, she saw that he was sitting up in bed. Some color had returned to his face, but until now, he hadn't been able to speak. His senses were also returning.

Receiving the meal, Oliver clearly said, "Thank you." Shocked, she called out to her husband to hurry. "This smells so good, Mrs. Blossom."

As Abraham came through the door the boy asked, "What happened to General Washington and his army?"

Abraham cleared his throat. "New York City has fallen to the British."

"But General Washington and his army? Were they destroyed?" His eyes looked for hope and truth in theirs.

"General Washington and the army escaped, but the British have New York."

Relieved, Oliver lifted his head from his chest and spoke with mist in his eyes. "The gratitude I have for you two cannot be expressed in words. My name is Oliver Atkinson. I was a sergeant in General Washington's army, in the cavalry. I was captured in Brooklyn as the army escaped back across the East River. I've been on the prison ship since."

"Oh, my goodness," Mary said, nearly fainting. "That was nine months ago."

They brought him up on current events until he had to rest again. Later, Doctor Vernon Warner returned to check on his condition and make recommendations, as he did every day for two months.

Oliver learned that the Blossoms were patriots, though they kept it private now that loyalists were turning in "rebels." He was a fisherman, as was his father, who he was with when they found Oliver in the harbor. She was his wife of two years. The pink bedroom was for a daughter that died shortly after birth right before he arrived. He wanted to join the army but was not allowed to enlist because of his poor eyesight. "I shall yet make my mark on this war," Abraham proclaimed.

"Perhaps you are doing so right now nursing me back to health."

After a month, the sergeant from Derby began going on daily walks, then daily runs. He began lifting anything heavy he could find, and after three months felt he was nearly back to full strength, though anyone looking at him would think otherwise had they known him before. He hadn't regained all his weight, and he was prone to suddenly waking at night from horrifying dreams. He'd be covered in sweat, soaking through his bed so many times it was ruined and had to be replaced.

The Blossoms learned to endure the night terrors and stopped rushing in to see him after the first week, knowing it was something he'd have to work through alone, not understanding the mental devastation he'd endured and lived with. They politely didn't ask. And he didn't offer.

Oliver was glad these didn't occur nightly, because the day after one he'd emotionally have to fight back through darkness into the light of hope, zapping him of all energy. Adding to his depression were his missing hat, his missing army, his missing Courage, and, most of all, his missing Clara. He knew that he'd never see his hat or Courage, but Washington and Clara, yes.

The ambitious boy began to believe he was ready to go find General Washington and the army again. He wondered if fighting and killing a Redcoat would rid him of the nightmares.

He wrestled with his sense of duty and his love for Clara and the burning in his heart to go to her. Her face looked upon him every day while aboard the ship. He convinced himself that he felt her prayers, though she couldn't have possibly known where he was. Did she even know he was alive? He recalled almost verbatim some of the letters she'd written to him that were stripped from his leather bag after his arrest. It was the fantasy that countered his reality day after day.

It was now July 15, 1777. Oliver told the Blossoms he would be leaving but needed help. Doctor Warner advised that he remain there a few more weeks.

"I need to go. I also need a horse," Oliver said. "The fastest horse you can find me. Send the bill to Congress as an officer on Washington's staff needs it. I also need to know where the general is camped."

Within two hours, Oliver had his horse, a dappled mare he named "Speckle," a musket with plenty of powder and shot, food, a canteen, an extra set of clothing, two blankets, and a new tricornered hat. After an emotional goodbye, he thanked the Blossoms and Doctor Warner and made haste for Washington's Pennsylvania camp.

CHAPTER 31

THE RETURN TO WAR

The sergeant from Boston gradually learned the capabilities and willingness of his new horse. Oliver's experience was that riding a new horse for the first time was more like a tug of war for control, but that eventually the beast, no matter how rambunctious and determined it might initially be, would ultimately give in to its rider if its rider treated it with kind authority. He felt little pushback from Speckle after the first ten miles. He kept whispering warm words into her ear as they rode, just as he did the other horses he'd ridden. This tactic worked every time but once.

Atkinson was told General Washington was headed to Philadelphia to report personally to Congress on the perilous state of the Continental Army. So, he aimed Speckle south along the routes he felt were safest and quickest.

Some members of Congress, who now questioned their choice of the Virginia planter, believed Washington was on his way to exploit them for more money, arms, clothing, and such. Others, meanwhile, trusted the general's words, and knew he spoke the truth. None, however, believed his motivations impure.

Ultimately, Congress had no power to tax its people and raise money. They hoped Ben Franklin would be able to work his charm in the French courts to continue raising money and eventually persuade them to send their army and navy knowing that if there was one thing the French elite loved doing more than making love, it was beating the British in war. The truth was, everyone knew the Americans needed a signature win for them to open their treasury even further, and offer up their ships, arms, and sons.

Oliver settled back into the Yards Inn. A room had just opened. He unpacked and walked over to Independence Hall and was jubilantly greeted by the Massachusetts men, who had not yet heard of his tribulation on the HMS *Scorpion*. When he told his story, all listeners in Congress were aghast, angered, and determined to help General Washington in whatever way they could, even those who were initially reluctant.

Listening to his story was a young man from France who had just been elevated to the position of Major General to the Continental Army. Nineteen-year-old Marquis de Lafayette, one of the wealthiest men in France. He sailed to America for the sole purpose of beating the British and avenging his father's death by their hands at the Battle of Minden in 1759.

Soon, General Washington and his entourage arrived in town. Sergeant Atkinson went to the Hall to hear his report. Oliver stood quietly off to the side by the Adamses as Washington entered the Hall as if needing to ask permission first. The general always respected authority. He first saw Lafayette and shook his hand. And as he was about to speak with Thomas Jefferson, Sam Adams loudly cleared his throat. Washington looked to his left to see Oliver standing at attention. The eyes of the commander-in-chief swelled up as Oliver broke protocol and rushed to him. As the young man was about to salute him, Washington bent at his waist to hug him, pulling him in tight for a moment. Tears from thirteen colonies flowed.

Later after dinner when the delegates had departed, Oliver told General Washington the shock of getting captured and his time on the prison ship. Washington was speechless until he said, "This is why we fight. If this nation will do this in war, there will be no peace for us if we are not victorious."

Washington gave Oliver orders to support General Gates in New England as the general thought that the British would attack from Canada, and Oliver's experience could best be used there. "Gates is assuming command from General Schuyler and could use you. But do stop off in Massachusetts first to see Clara for a few days, will you?"

Oliver paused before answering, and asked, "When was the last time you saw Mount Vernon, sir?"

"Not since before the conflict commenced. Why?"

"When you head home, then I will as well. Clara understands this."

An admiring Washington smiled and nodded, then said, "I appreciate your commitment and loyalty to me and to the cause, Oliver; more than words can say." Washington paused, then continued. "Before joining Gates, I'd like for you to deliver a message to Clara from me asking her to continue her prayers for the army and for the hope of a free America. We need women like her who fight on their knees as much as we need men who fight in the field."

Oliver could not have smiled a bigger smile. "Yes, General Washington. As you order." He then rose to get some sleep when the planter from Mount Vernon grabbed his right arm and said he was promoting the young man from Derby to the rank of Lieutenant. "If Lafayette can be bestowed the rank of Major General without ever having fought one battle..." Washington wisely paused, "You've earned this, Lieutenant Atkinson."

Saluting, the young soldier said, "Thank you, General. Good night."

Because Oliver was in and out of Philadelphia in a couple of days, he saw Peter once, who proudly announced that he married Maggie. She was already six months pregnant with their first child.

"We gonna call him 'Oliver' if it be a boy, or 'Olive' if a girl."

Her owner permanently "lent" her to Peter's owner, only requiring a small sum of silver each year to help offset his loss of labor.

Oliver could not have been happier for the two but burned deeply over humanity's ability to treat others like cattle. They spent an hour together before Oliver headed back to Yards to get some sleep, then left before the sun rose to go home to Clara.

A Lieutenant's uniform awaited Oliver back in his room. He tried it on, and it fit perfectly as far as he was concerned, though a little big, which was fine because he was still gaining weight lost during his incarceration. He'd make his ride north in civilian clothes until nearing the Cole home. He'd then stop and put it back on before surprising Clara and her parents.

Mrs. Yard, as usual, had a meal ready for him when he sauntered sleepily, but dutifully, downstairs, as he prepared to leave. She also had food for him to take and a canteen full of boiled water she cooled overnight in the ground for him. Her daughter no longer loved Oliver. In fact, she pretended like he was a ghost when around. This was her response to feeling rejected by him. He still didn't notice her.

Speckle seemed not to want to be disturbed at such an hour. She'd better get used to it, he told her as he saddled her and aimed her north through the city, across the Delaware, up the western side of New Jersey as far from British troops as possible, around New York City, through Hartford, Connecticut, and then a few miles east of Cambridge to Cole's Tavern and Inn.

CHAPTER 32

It took six days, riding Speckle as hard as he could, to arrive in Massachusetts. It was her first real test of combined speed and endurance. She did well, but knew he would need to find a horse more suited to his military calling. Speckle was the perfect horse for home use and local travel. He was thankful he never had to flee the Redcoats. It just wasn't in her. She could, however, trot at a modest pace for distance, which he believed bought him half a day's travel, allowing him to return to his love that much sooner. When he arrived at Clara's, he would set out to find and buy the best horse he could.

"Wait a minute," he thought to himself. "Buy? With what?" Oliver then realized that he had been in the service of the Continental Army for over two years and had yet to be paid! He didn't have a penny to his name. Perhaps he could give an IOU from the Congress to a sympathizer or patriot for a horse, not that he was authorized to do so—though had done this once before, but he was on official business from General Washington so "it should be okay," he reasoned. Perhaps he could help sweeten the transaction by making Speckle part of the deal, though he really wanted to give her to Clara.

He arrived without incident and stopped a half mile away near a crop of trees to change. It was dark, so he felt comfortable being able to put on his new uniform without being seen in a state of undress. Oliver was quite anxious. He hadn't seen his love in two years. He had written to her a few times while recovering to explain why he hadn't corresponded with her for so long, but he didn't get any replies. This worried him, wondering if something tragic had befallen her, or worse, she had fallen out of love with him.

It was around 9 p.m. when he opened the tavern door and stood there with his hat under his arm. The main room was empty. "One minute, please," he heard Mrs. Cole call from the back. Seconds later, she emerged and saw him, nearly collapsing at his feet. "Oliver!" Tears broke from her eyes as he rushed to her and hugged him. "Oliver!" she said while pulling back, her hands on his shoulders.

"Mrs. Cole. I cannot tell you how good it is to see you." He bent in and kissed her cheek.

She stepped back and looked him up and down, seeing how tall he had grown, but also how skinny he was. "You must be hungry." She started towards the kitchen.

"Mrs. Cole?" he asked with a concerned look on his face. She stopped and turned her head on his way. "Where is your husband? Where is Clara?"

Looking down as she hesitated toward the table and asked him to sit. She sat across from him and told him that her husband had died six months earlier after his horse got spooked and threw him, breaking his back.

"Oh, no. I am so sorry. So tragic. What a great man." He reached across and grabbed her hands and held them. She was silent for a moment and seemed unable to look him in the eyes. "Mrs. Cole?" She finally looked up. "And Clara?"

Just then, the door swung open and in walked a jubilant Clara on a young man of twenty-four's arm. "Whose horse is that?" Seeing Oliver, she froze, and ran to him. He shot off the bench, and they hugged as one would expect long lost lovers to do.

The young man cleared his throat so hard, that his unusually large Adams Apple nearly got tuck in his mouth. Yet Clara ignored it. Her arms remained wrapped around the love of her life. After a minute of squeezing and tears, they released each other. Stepping back for a look at him in his uniform she said, "We were told that you were killed at Brooklyn, Oliver."

"Yet, here I am in the flesh!" He said less than sarcastically. Looking at the young man on whose arm Clara entered, he asked, "And who are you?"

"Reginald Webb. I assume you are the hero, Oliver Atkinson?" he asked, sniggering.

"Respect this man!" Clara shot back at Webb.

"Yes, I am Lieutenant Oliver Atkinson. Where are you serving? You look of age."

"What is the obsession people from Massachusetts have with this war? I am from Vermont. We aren't one of your colonies."

"So, what are you doing here in the land of brave patriots?"

"Business. And," he said hesitatingly with a smirk, "finding a wife, or rather, found a wife" he said smugly as he stepped up to Clara and put his arm around her.

Oliver drew his sword to strike him, but Clara screamed out, "Stop it! No!"

A raging Oliver lowered the long blade to his side and gave this faux consort to his queen a steely look of controlled fury. Webb smiled scornfully back, unwilling to back down.

Mrs. Cole stood and demanded they all sit down, pointing to an end seat away from the men for Clara to fill. The force in her command moved the three to obey, but Oliver's eyes never left Webb's.

"Oliver," Mrs. Cole said gently, "it was reported that you had died in Brooklyn. Clara didn't leave the house for six months afterwards, almost never leaving her bed. Mr. Webb stayed at our tavern one night with his father as they had business in Boston..."

"With the British or after they'd departed?" Oliver demanded, still looking at Webb.

"Our allegiance is to those who can pay us, Atkinson. But, so you can turn down the heat on your boiling temper, we paused our interactions with England once America declared independence."

The lieutenant turned his gaze at Clara. "Are you in love with him?"

Anxiously Clara looked down then at Webb, before returning her eyes to Oliver. "I thought you were dead. In my mourning he entered and took some of the pain away."

"I asked if you were in love with him? I sent you letters from New Jersey while I was recovering, but you never responded."

"Letters?" Clara looked quickly at her mother. "What letters? Mother?"

All eyes turned on Mrs. Cole's fear-filled face. She spoke to Clara. "After mourning Oliver for so many months...well, he," looking at Webb, "brought joy back to your heart again. I didn't..." Turning to Oliver she began to cry and beg for forgiveness, doing the same looking at Clara. "I've been mourning Papa, too! I'm so sorry, Clara!" She shot off the bench and ran into the back. Oliver and Clara looked at each other dumbfounded.

Webb cleared his throat again. "This should have no bearing on our engagement, my lovely Clara." He bent over and kissed her cheek while grabbing her left hand. She didn't reciprocate the affection. "Right, Clara?"

Mrs. Cole rushed back into the room with a handful of unopened letters from Oliver she'd kept from her daughter and tossed them on the table. Clara grabbed one and tore open the envelope and began reading. Webb tried reading over her shoulder, but she turned away so he couldn't. A new stream of tears began flowing down her flushed cheeks.

Oliver, who had been silent and stoic, grabbed her right hand, and she squeezed back.

Webb protested, "Darling, the invitations have been sent out. Our home is half built. My mother has the wedding planned. It's all been quite an expense, you know."

Simultaneously, Clara and Oliver arose and moved to embrace each other with a hug so hard that Mrs. Cole was amazed they didn't pass out for lack of oxygen.

Webb also stood up, ungraciously acknowledging defeat. "Well Mrs. Cole and Clara, I certainly wasn't marrying up socially. Ahh, but her looks are unmatchable." Oliver was in his face in an instant, grabbed him by the collar of his coat, and as Clara opened the front door, was tossed violently to the ground outside.

"We don't expect we'll be seeing you again, Mr. Webb," Oliver said, then shut the door. Seconds later Webb was off into the night.

"I'm so sorry, I'm so sorry, Oliver. Had I known!" she said as they embraced and kissed. Finishing, they looked at Mrs. Cole, who was dabbing her eyes with a cloth. Clara moved to her side and tenderly said, "You were only trying to protect me, mother. Oliver and father dying so close together must've made it harder on you than I thought as I was lost in my own sorrowful state." The women embraced, and Oliver joined in.

Finally separating, Oliver pulled a message he'd been carrying from Philadelphia for Clara. "Here's another letter for you, Clara."

"Who is it from?" she asked excitedly while opening it up. "It's from General Washington!" She read it reverently, then to the other two. "Lieutenant Atkinson, please tell our Commander-in-Chief that I will faithfully continue exercising my duties as an intercessor for the army and nation."

* * *

The family spent two days together catching up on personal events. When it came to Oliver's turn to talk about Brooklyn and his imprisonment, he was careful not to say too much about the horrors he endured on the HMS *Scorpion*, except to generally speak of his capture, his cousin, his length of stay on board, and how he escaped and recovered.

The next day, the hot August sun beat down on the two renewed love birds as they walked to a pond not far from the tavern and sat with a picnic basket underneath a large oak tree. There, they carved each other's names in the tree, ate, and kissed passionately, both recognizing the danger of wanting more before marriage.

"Will you marry me now?" Oliver asked. She nodded her head excitedly and reached over to kiss him again. "Or," he said laughing, "Do you still want to wait until the war is over?" She thrust herself upon him again. "If you aren't sure, just say so!" he said as they went back in for a deep kiss while rolling in the grass.

Rising a moment later, they hurried back to the tavern and told Mrs. Cole what they wanted to do. Mother raced out the door and thirty minutes later brought Parson Brown back with her, as well as a local farmer, Jed Bloomfield, to be a witness. Clara put on her finest dress, and Oliver his new uniform, and before this small gathering and God, the two young folks became Lieutenant and Mrs. Oliver Atkinson. Oliver put on her bride's hand Mrs. Cole's wedding ring.

The newlyweds spent the night in the marital bliss of discovery and intimacy, sleeping well into the morning the next day, until being called into the tavern's main hall by Mrs. Cole. Dressing, the two lovers entered the hall and asked if there was a problem. "Not yet," Mrs. Cole laughed. "But we are supposed to open soon, and I need Clara's help! I'm way behind!" They laughed.

"I'd stay to help but I need to link up with General Gates in New York."

"Mother, I'll be right back. I promise!" Clara grabbed Oliver's hand and dragged him back for one more occasion of intimacy before he left.

An hour later, Oliver, well-stocked with provisions, saddled his new horse that farmer Bloomfield had given him in exchange for Speckle and as a part of a wedding present. Oliver had ridden him the day before for the first time, and the farmer promised him he'd never ride a faster horse. He wasn't kidding. Oliver was quite pleased but now was going to test his stamina while hoping he would remain calm in battle, something no cavalry man knew until the muskets and cannon were fired. He decided to name his new horse "Freedom."

After kissing his wife goodbye with promises that lovers make when departing, and hugging Mrs. Cole, warm tears streaming down their faces, he mounted Freedom and was off, heading west over the mountains to find Gates somewhere between Albany and Saratoga.

CHAPTER 33

SARATOGA

Freedom held his own the first few days of hard travel. Oliver felt they connected quickly, and joked to himself that the horse was glad to be off the farm and outside the fences. Farmer Bloomfield admitted he rarely rode the horse because it had two speeds: way too fast, and not at all. Oliver found the horse to be quite responsive and discovered he was more than speedy.

As with his first trips to Virginia and the Carolinas, the lieutenant didn't know this part of the country at all. Plus, he had to cross over a mountain, something he wasn't crazy about, but was relieved it wasn't cold, icy, and snowy.

He was guided by a map from one of Washington's best mapmakers, Robert Erskine, who had never been to the area, but had consolidated a few old maps and took directions from two soldiers who were from up that way, to hastily put something together for the lieutenant. He guessed he had another three days' ride at the pace he was on, believing, at least for now, that Freedom was up to the task.

Oliver decided to stay west and not veer north into the Vermont region to eliminate the possibility of running into enemy scouts. He had not yet heard that Ticonderoga had fallen back into British hands but felt wisdom directed him to enter New York just south of Albany and then ride northward.

He came to the foothills of the Taconic Mountains that

bordered New York and Massachusetts and decided to camp there that night after performing a short reconnaissance of the area to make sure there were no unfriendlies around.

Frankly, he didn't want to be bothered by friendlies either.

He was still recovering from his time on the *Scorpion*, at least, emotionally, with difficulty sleeping, a major element of the enduring wounds. The night terrors would come and go, but he was free of them on his wedding night. Not wanting to alarm any kind patriots who put him up for the night, he thought it best to suffer alone until he was able to exorcize these nightly afflictions.

He did notice that it helped immensely to think about Clara until he couldn't stay awake any longer. He didn't want to force exhaustion on himself, but if the terrors came, his chances for sleep that night would be small. He was perpetually exhausted. At least this way, he could control the exhaustion and ruminate on the delicacies of his wife's words, touch, and devotion until he couldn't keep his eyes open.

He began praying again, asking God to relieve him of these attacks. His prayers were short. He was still angry and confused over the necessity of his imprisonment. But with each succeeding night on the road, due to the combined thoughts of Clara and what he presumed to be the grace of God, they seemed to be less frequent and less horrifying. Demon characters in British military uniforms disappeared one by one with each passing sleep.

The next morning, Oliver and Freedom ascended Taconic Mountain. As they reached the top, just after noon, Oliver decided to relieve himself, rest Freedom, and use his new spyglass to survey the valley before him for friend or foe. As he buttoned up, he felt a presence. He looked up to see that he was surrounded by the most marvelous looking creatures he'd ever glimpsed.

Six men with light brown skin, shorn hair except for a long braid in the back, deer skin pants and vests that had bright colored patterns of beads descending in rows, slowly closed around him. Each had a musket, cartridge boxes, knives, and hatchets. A few wore glorious robes, while some had plumed hats on. The tallest wore what resembled a turban, and another had a bouquet of what he thought were eagle feathers arranged on the back of his head. Each had various colors and paint on their faces. They were fearsome and glorious.

Adrenaline and fear drove his hands up in surrender. One man spoke a strange language Oliver had never heard before. The warriors lowered their weapons, lowering the tension also. Oliver could see the tension on their faces relax. Puzzled, he risked slowly lowering his hands, eyes darting back to the men in front of him to make sure they didn't re-raise their weapons.

The man with the turban approached Oliver and said in English, "You are safe with us. My name is Tewahangarahken," and he stuck out his hand for a very reluctant Oliver to shake.

The lieutenant struggled to pronounce his name. "Tewgarden?"

"No, lieutenant, Tewahangarahken. It means in the Oneida speech, 'He Who Takes Up the Snowshoe.'"

"He Who Takes Up the Snowshoe, my name is Lieutenant Oliver Atkinson of the Continental Army."

The men shook hands. The Indian leader said, "You can call me Han Yerry. It would be easier for you." He smiled. Oliver reciprocated.

Oliver hadn't yet fully let down his guard, as he needed an answer to an obvious question. "Han Yerry, if I may be so bold as to ask why you haven't yet put a hatchet through my head and a knife in my belly?"

"Yes, of course. We are of the Oneida Tribe of the Iroquois people who have chosen to fight with the Americans against the British. Your fear is understandable as most other tribes have chosen to side with the British. You have nothing to be alarmed about with us. As you said, you'd be dead by now and we would be long gone with your scalp if we weren't your friends."

Oliver did his best to read the man's unspoken language and that of the other five. Satisfied they were friendly, he said, "I have another question, if you will oblige me, Han Yerry."

"My English? I speak Dutch, too. I lived with a man and wife from Germany and the Netherlands for a short time. They educated me on the culture of the white people."

"Fascinating, truly. I am certain you have the most amazing story, but I have orders to go to New York and so must be on my way."

"Lieutenant Atkinson, we are a scout team sent out by General Gage. We've been tracking the British after their retaking of Fort Ticonderoga in July."

"They did?"

Han Yerry nodded. "Some of my men are hunting to bring provisions to Gage's army. My people are meeting just south of Albany and will then move north to where the general is currently camped just south of Saratoga."

"Those are my exact orders from General Washington," Oliver said. "I don't know this land very well. Mind if I travel with you?"

Han Yerry smiled and nodded, then turned to his men and spoke in his native tongue. The men smiled and nodded at Atkinson, who reached out and shook each hand again. He also reached into his bag and brought out some candy Clara had given him and offered some to the men. Their faces lit up as brightly as any child upon receiving the perfect Christmas gift.

What Oliver thought would take three days took only two. Han Yerry and his men taught him more effective ways of traveling, camping, and how to read nature to find resources for his various needs. He also taught Oliver about the Iroquois tribe and more specifically, his people the Oneida, and why four of the six tribes were backing the British. The British promised to keep settlers out of their ancestral land was the biggest reason.

His people opted to support the Americans for several reasons, remarkably, and most importantly, because of a relationship forged between them and an American missionary to their tribe named Samuel Kirkland. They also didn't trust the British, who had trampled on their lands already as they marched through their protected territory on their way to attack Fort Schuyler. Han Yerry told Oliver how his people provided corn and medicine for the hungry and sick soldiers.

"What fantastic people, these Oneida. Certainly, they will be benefactors of liberty as well," Oliver thought to himself. They enjoyed each other's company, and equally marveled at Oliver's story from England to the present, thinking him to be a special man of God having survived the prison ship.

CHAPTER 34

On September 10, 1777, Han Yerry, his men, and Lieutenant Atkinson connected just south of Albany, New York, with reinforcements sent by General Washington to help support General Horatio Gates who was settling into the north side of a village called Saratoga.

Marching in together, they arrived to find that Gates was having his men erect defenses on a series of bluffs and on Bemis Heights. Han Yerry learned that his hunting party had already returned with a few weeks' worth of game for the army, and that some had gone north to scout the British, and another group south to see if British reinforcements were coming from New York.

Entering the general's tent to introduce himself to the round-faced Gates, who seemed cold and rude to him immediately, he was ignored. Perhaps it was because he was in the middle of an argument over battle plans with another general named Benedict Arnold. Oliver recognized Arnold from a Sons of Liberty meeting. His conduct in the tent was an abomination to Oliver. He was quite petulant and perilously close to insubordination as he and Gates shouted back and forth at each other, neither hearing the other. Arnold stormed out of Gates' headquarters tent, while Oliver stood at attention waiting to be recognized.

Finally, Gates looked up from a map at Oliver. Looking him over, he asked, "Who are you?"

Oliver saluted Gates, then presented him with a dispatch and his orders from General Washington. Looking them over, Gage nodded his head then asked without looking up, "And when will they be here? We should be at battle soon."

Oliver didn't know how to respond.

"Please answer me, lieutenant."

"General Gates, sir, my deepest apologies, but I don't know the 'who' of whom you are asking, sir."

"Reinforcements, lieutenant. Didn't you just come from Washington? Did you ride so quickly as to have passed by without seeing continental soldiers marching this way?"

"I had orders elsewhere first, sir, to Massachusetts, sir." Oliver remained calm and at attention but couldn't recall any military officer being so rude and condescending.

"Oh." The general shrugged and said, "The ego-driven man you just saw leave my tent in a huff is General Benedict Arnold. I am assigning you to be under his command for now. And, no, it isn't punishment. He will need some cavalry support for the coming battle. The British have arrived and are a short distance away. Have you ever been in battle, lieutenant?"

"Yes, sir." Oliver paused as the general looked at him as if to say, "Well?" "I fought at Lexington, along the Bay Road, Moore's Creek Bridge in North Carolina, and Brooklyn, sir."

Gates' countenance noticeably eased up as he paused from looking at his map. Placing his spectacles on the table, he walked over to Oliver and respectfully shook his hand. "Forgive my distraction when you announced yourself. I'm not one to usually humble myself, but please accept my apology for my gruff behavior towards you, Lieutenant Atkinson. Your heroic service is well known in the Continental Army. I am honored to have you serve under me." He walked back to his map. "Do you have any idea how many men General Washington has dispatched to support my efforts here?"

"No, sir, not entirely, though I know your cause here is of

utmost importance to him," Oliver dutifully remarked.

Gates flashed a dubious smile, then went back to his map. Pointing with his finger he said, "My Indian scouts have alerted me that General Burgoyne has sent part of his army under General St. Leger west so they can pivot here and attack Albany from the west in a pincer move. Burgoyne will be proceeding down the Hudson River. It is our full expectation that General Clinton will send forces from the south to pigeon-hole us, giving us no escape." Standing up, he pounded the desk and shouted, "We need more men!"

Over the next few days, militia from all over joined Gates and his army at Saratoga, swelling its size close to fifteen-thousand men. Gates still seemed anxious.

Oliver was at his headquarters when the legendary Colonel John Morgan arrived with his four-hundred strong regiment of Virginia sharpshooters. Oliver had never seen guns quite like the ones Morgan's men carried, and at six-two, figured him for a Virginia man, and he was correct. It was called the Pennsylvania long rifle and was made by German immigrants. The barrel was significantly longer than the standard musket, with a kill range of about two hundred to three hundred yards. The range of a musket was a hundred yards. Morgan took him to an area where Oliver could fire the unique rifle, and immediately saw he was a better shot.

"I'd hate to be wearing a red coat with that in your hands. Keep it. Now, what's this I hear about you getting captured by the British?"

The two exchanged stories of being captured by the British. Oliver named his new weapon "Mrs. Belle."

By the morning of September 19, Gates had learned that the British forces coming from Manhattan inexplicably turned back south. Burgoyne was not going to get reinforcements after all. It also became clear that St. Leger wasn't going to make it either. The time was perfect for Gates to engage the British. He believed he could trap them against the Hudson and limit their escape, especially since his forces were now easily double that of Burgoyne's.

Oliver was reassigned as a forward scout for Morgan's infantry, which he was quite grateful for. He couldn't say it out loud, but he found Arnold to be the most vainglorious person he'd ever met.

The Colonial Army met the British on Freeman's Farm. The Virginia riflemen were ordered to flank the British on the left and try to annihilate the Redcoats from a distance. Gates and his forces had mixed results, and by the end of the day, it appeared that despite heavy Redcoat losses, the day belonged to the British.

Then Gate's army dug in, greeted a few more groups of incoming militias, and waited for the British to attack.

In normal life, Oliver might have been offended by the Virginia sharpshooters. They were gruff, brawling, crude characters. But they could fight. And they loved the idea of freedom. Oliver saw in them a physical resolve equal to the intellectual and philosophical resolve of the Sons of Liberty. While most of these men had read Thomas Paine's *Common Sense*, there were few other books they could discuss together. Oliver liked them immediately, and they liked him, especially once they had learned of his ordeal aboard the HMS *Scorpion*, and of the battles he'd been in.

They nicknamed him "Book." Oliver just called them brothers.

Early on October 7, 1777, as the air began to cool with the onset of fall, the well-fed and well-armed men of the Continental force under General Horatio Gates watched as the British army made its move to strike at Saratoga.

Lieutenant Atkinson, who had been on an early morning scouting mission, alerted Morgan to movement toward an open area. He had seen a reconnaissance-in-force of British soldiers approaching. Oliver reminded Morgan, never being one for traditional fighting, of a grove of trees near a bluff adjacent to the Hudson River called Bemis Heights that provided perfect cover for his riflemen. It also created a perfect bottleneck for advancing British forces. The battle was on as Morgan's men fired upon the constricted British forces.

Oliver spied a British officer he thought was Brigadier General Simon Fraser, took aim with his new rifle, and pulled the trigger. In seconds, he saw the man fall to the ground. Panic ensued around the British line as one officer after another was picked off.

The British army was in disarray. Gates pressed the battle with repeated attacks until Burgoyne commanded his men to retreat to the Great Redoubt by the Hudson.

The battle was over, and it appeared to Oliver as he rode across its fields that there were three British casualties for each American casualty. The groaning sounds from wounded and dying men reminded him of some of the sounds he'd heard on the *Scorpion*. Having just killed for freedom, he ignored the cries of the wounded British, while seeking help for his brothers in arms.

While surveying the area, Oliver took out his spyglass and thought he recognized Benedict Arnold's horse with a man underneath it. He raced up to see Arnold trapped underneath the dead beast. Calling two militiamen nearby, they pulled the horse off Arnold, who was seriously wounded in the leg. Oliver turned Freedom, who had performed beautifully under fire, and sprinted for medical help.

Gates sent a runner that night to Burgoyne's camp to see if he would surrender. He was rebuffed. Burgoyne still held out hope that reinforcements would come. Gates knew they weren't going to show. The next day, on October 8, freezing rain fell relentlessly, prohibiting Burgoyne's army from a northern escape. Instead, they hunkered down, but Gates, being impatient seeing that victory was his, surrounded the army and caused the British general to surrender on the 17th. Gates allowed Oliver to accompany him when he accepted Burgoyne's surrender.

During the celebratory night in the Continental camp, Oliver, while eating with Morgan's riflemen, who were enjoying their rum, was called to General Gates' tent. There, Gates ordered him to get word of the capitulation to General Washington and the Congress in Philadelphia as quickly as possible. "Once the French hear of Burgoyne's surrender," Gates told Oliver, "They will give us more than materiel aid. They will give us men, and they will give us ships!"

CHAPTER 35

VALLEY FORGE

Oliver, sober and excited, rode all night. It seemed Freedom was sharing the same exuberance of victory in not only vanquishing the British from the battlefield but having watched the once-boastful and cocksure Burgoyne surrender his army in total humiliation. Oliver thought this win might keep the Americans engaged for some time, inspire more recruits to join militias and the Continental Army, and move congress to get the army more weapons, supplies, and food. And, as Gates said, draw in the French.

The cool air helped keep Oliver awake, but by morning he had ridden at least seventy miles, and knew it was time to rest for a short while. They awoke a few hours later with frost covering them and got back on the road. It was like this for a few days, always seeking to sleep in groves, as he didn't know the lay of the land and who were loyalists and who were patriots.

Hearing testimonies of men all over the northern states, he was confused that there were still so many loyalists comfortably living among the patriots. He was told some were legitimate supporters of King George, while others were hedging their bets, not believing the Continentals could triumph. Some thinking this way believed they'd be rewarded for their loyalty and be given the lands, property, and wealth of the annihilated rebels, and so proved to be thorns in the sides of every patriot. If he went to sleep in the wrong place, he anxiously considered, he might wake up within the pearly gates, having performed his last service for the patriot cause.

Staying on the western side of the Appalachian Mountains, he skirted past New York City and British scouts. Still, he had to keep his eyes wide open for anything and anyone who might be considered an enemy. He had no news of recent movements of either army, so in a sense he was riding blindly. He considered crossing into New Jersey, but instead he rode south toward Allentown, then cut southeast toward Philadelphia, where he thought Washington and his army would be.

Pausing on a bluff near Allentown just after sundown, he saw the city in a vast valley. It was dappled with oil lamps shining through windows, the glow of fireplaces burning strong, and the brilliant light of a full moon washing over homes and buildings making the area look like it was covered with light snow. He thought it beautiful.

It had been a long day, and the post-battle exhaustion was catching up to him. It's impossible, he thought, for anyone to understand the intensity of absolute extremes in battle. He also knew Freedom had given everything he had but needed a day's rest. They were close to their goal, Oliver having ridden his new friend hard for six days but felt that driving his companion as hard for another day might injure him.

Coming back down the bluff, he heard the click of a musket that he'd heard a million times before. Expecting to hear an immediate blast, Oliver went from wincing to eyes wide open as his shoulders lifted his arms in the air.

"Who goes there?" A man in standard colonial clothes walked out of the shadows with a terrible limp into the small clearing at the base of the hill, with a gun pointed directly at Oliver.

He thought he might as well die bravely if the stranger was a loyalist, so gave his name: "Lieutenant Oliver Atkinson of the

Continental Army."

Both men could see each in the waking moon's light. The stranger lowered his musket.

"Oliver Atkinson?" the man curiously asked.

"Yes, and you are?"

"Joseph Brighton. We never met, but I, too, served under General Washington at the Battle of Brooklyn. I was on the last boat evacuated with the general. I crawled back from a mile away, my leg nearly blown off by fragments of a cannon ball."

The men just looked at each other for a moment.

"May I get off my horse, Mr. Brighton?" the Lieutenant asked.

"Of course, of course!" he said as he hobbled as quickly as he could move to Freedom and Oliver. They shook hands. "We waited for you," he said emotionally. "Thank you for keeping the fires going. You saved many lives."

Brighton embraced Oliver and asked him back to his home if he planned on staying in the area that night. Oliver eagerly agreed and was grateful. He'd only slept in a proper bed for two nights in the last few months, and his blankets were already rank from sleeping on them outside in the various weather changes of rain and freezing temperatures. The blankets never dried, and the wool fibers absorbed odors, mud, manure, and his horse. Clean sheets were heaven. A hot meal would be manna.

At dinner, after Oliver took care of Freedom and placed him in a warm barn. Brighton, a single man who'd never married, which he blamed on an internal gas problem that wouldn't go away– Oliver experiencing his confession less than an hour into his stay, told him what he knew about the fall of Philadelphia to the British. The Continental Congress had fled a hundred miles west of Independence Hall to York, Pennsylvania, and Washington and his army were wintering in Valley Forge, Pennsylvania. The army was a protective buffer between the British and the Congress. Oliver was only fifty miles from General Washington, and ninety miles from York.

As he fell asleep, he wondered about the well-being of Peter, the state of the army and the nation, and the love of his life. Concerned but exhausted, he was out quickly.

Oliver decided first to go to Valley Forge on Gates' orders. Brighton advised Oliver on the route he should take. It added an hour to his travel, but he was energized at the thought of seeing General Washington and his men this cold November day.

Arriving at a Valley Forge's disheveled camp, he was surprised to see so many women and children milling about. Everyone seemed to be doing something, but nothing looked like it was getting done. The camp was in bad shape. Oliver soon learned why after being directed to a home that Washington was occupying.

Entering, he was warmly greeted by the General. Oliver detailed the resounding victory and subsequent surrender of Burgoyne. He also boasted about Morgan's Riflemen and let Washington know that Benedict Arnold was severely wounded in the leg, but that his contribution to the victory was enormous. He spoke of the unusually heavy loss of British officers that occurred, including that of Brigadier General Simon Fraser. This seemed to delight Washington as much as the victory and surrender.

"General Gates has sent word through a number of couriers to make sure word gets to Franklin in France as soon as possible, saying they will now be sending men and ships in addition to their general aid." Washington heartily agreed.

The commander-in-chief explained, without Oliver asking, why the camp seemed to be in disarray, saying that the tents weren't permanent, that the men were gearing up to go into the surrounding forests and cut down trees to make more secure, weather-friendly log cabins for what they believed would be a nasty winter. They had time before the war resumed in the spring to do this, and with women and children in the camp— wives and children of soldiers, as well as hangers-on, the tents would not provide adequate protection and comfort.

General Washington asked him to lead foraging and hunting parties, knowing the coming winter would be a difficult one. He was told a log cabin would be built that he would share with other officers while he was running back and forth.

Leaving his office home, Oliver saw Joseph Plumb Martin, the friend he made in New York at the public reading of the Declaration of Independence, struggling with a mule who was not interested in hauling the large pieces of timber harnessed behind it on a sled.

"Joseph!" Oliver called out.

Seeing his friend, he called out "Whoa! Whoa!" while pulling on the reins as the mule wrestled with him before stopping. Oliver warmly approached and stuck out his hand. Martin saluted him first, then returned his smile while taking his hand. "Thought we lost you at Brooklyn, Lieutenant Atkinson."

"Lieutenant?" Oliver cocked his head while asking.

"Oh, yah, General Washington has laid down the law in regard to military decorum, practices, and discipline. He says if we want to be a victorious army then we must act and train like one."

"I understand, corporal," he responded with a wink. "Dinner tonight? I may have another detail you'd be better suited for."

Martin looked at his beast then back at Oliver. "Please. I hate these things!"

Later, they caught each other up over corn stew. Meat was heavily rationed, even at this early point in the winter. Oliver could've been served meat, but he chose to sit with Martin and a few others closer to his age. These were his friends, but he still had to honor Washington's command to maintain a gap between soldier and officer. He agreed with the general.

Martin smoked a pipe as he and Oliver strolled through a fortified camp in the making right as the sun was setting.

"I've never seen so many women in camp before," Oliver noticed.

"Seems every man brought his wife to war. Their kids, too. Plus," he playfully elbowed Oliver, "there are a few other kinds of women in our midst, if you know what I mean!"

"Corporal, please."

Oliver had struggled to pray and read his Bible since escaping captivity. It's not that he didn't believe in God anymore or doubted His existence or goodness. He was still numb from his macabre ordeal on the prison ship. Though less frequent, the night terrors began having the same impact on him. But his moral compass was still operational, and the idea that prostitutes might be dwelling among them wretched him.

The thinking, battle-tested lieutenant was having difficulty processing the enlightened authors who were so influential among the elite, many of whom oversaw building the new nation, and who swore that mankind was good by nature, when in reality, he saw the opposite his entire life. Cultures and countries had no bearing on the human condition. Deep down inside, he realized, "we are all the same."

Resisting the compulsion to judge others beyond the borders of biblical fences, the largest mirror he held was before his own heart that exposed his wickedness. Log after log appeared until there was a forest growing in his eyes. What seemed to get worse by the day was his overwhelming attraction to the opposite sex. Even after getting married, it wouldn't go away. Everything in his life was in the furnace, as if war wasn't enough. Hence, the revolt in his stomach over the presence of painted ladies parading through camp.

His cabin, one of the first built, was ready for him. Washington personally assigned him to that bunkhouse, with three junior officers as his mates.

Awaking rested the next day, he headed out with the agreeable Corporal Martin and two other men to begin foraging for food they could "winterize," and for animals to use for meat. They were also told to look for any items that might be useful in camp. They were given hundreds of Continental dollars and told to make deals using as much pressure as they could. Oliver put the money in a leather satchel. It was the very money he would've printed at Paul Revere's shop had he stayed there. Smiling as he jogged through the very good memories of his early days in America, he wondered how his Boston family was doing.

CHAPTER 36

The foraging began in villages and towns close by that were not heavily populated. A few patriots gave bushels of apples, turnips, and corn, while loyalists refused to help at any price, especially when offered the "worthless" Continental Dollars. They were able to buy a few milk cows, a few beef cattle and hogs, about twenty gallons of vinegar, wooden crates of canned peas, peaches, and pickles. Salt was plenty, and they even brought back some extra pots and pans to cook with. Clothing was hard to come by. Shoes were one of the most sought-after items.

After six weeks of necessary monotony, the perimeter of the search expanded so much that they would be days away from camp. They found themselves crossing into Delaware and Maryland. This gravely concerned the two, who were now alone on their expedition.

Relieved to find the hunting in central Pennsylvania more profitable, they were able to bag deer, turkeys, and other birds and wildlife.

On Oliver's eighteenth birthday, having celebrated New Year's Eve about eighty miles from camp, Oliver aimed his long rifle at the largest buck he'd ever seen. Its antlers made him look ten feet tall. He lined up the glorious creature, and from 200 yards away dropped the deer in its track. It was the last deer they found for the next three days.

"Let's head back to camp," Oliver breathed heavily out.

"We've not room for even a pigeon left on our sleds. I'm ready."

"Crazy thing is, this meat won't last our camp a day, and winter has only just begun."

Using mules to pull sleds they'd made to carry the cleaned animals, extended their trip to three days.

Joseph quipped, "I still hate mules but am glad we have these two beasts along. I would've hated to see you carry all of this back by yourself!"

"These beasts you denigrate were bred by General Washington himself at his Mount Vernon estate."

"I still don't like 'em!"

On their return to Valley Forge, they got the full blast of a southern Pennsylvania winter: freezing rain, snow showers, and blizzards that lasted a full day.

"I'm beginning to hate the army life," Martin said while slogging up a slippery hill on foot as the sheet of ice laid the night before made it dangerous to ride.

"You realize that I came all the way from Derby for this. I don't recall in any Sons of Liberty meeting or in any of the raucous discussions in Philadelphia anything about freezing being tied to freedom. I must've missed something in the recruitment material."

They laughed and froze the entire way back to the camp.

* * *

Valley Forge, the "little city," became the fourth-most-populated area in America, and it looked like it as well with all the log huts spaced one after another in equal measure along rows up to a mile or more.

Oliver was pleased with its diversity, making it appear more homier than it really was. With all the wives running about, he considered sending for Clara but decided against it as Washington told him to be ready for any instant order he might give. Free blacks and slaves worked alongside white folks, men and women,

311

Indians, Protestants of all denominations, a few Catholics, and, of course, the indigenous religions. Had it not been wartime and freezing, Oliver surmised, it would've been a wonderful town to call home.

But as the gray winter days slowed to a crawl, food supplies became scarce. Meat was difficult to find. His foraging was now a ten day round trip. What made their expeditions worse was that Continental currency had less value with each passing day. Hard currency of the British was asked for, but little of it existed in the camp. Things were getting desperate. The pressure on Washington would've ruined most other men.

Worse still, by 1778, uniforms, clothing, and shoes, for many soldiers, were in such disrepair that they did not protect the body against the elements or keep men warm as they worked and trained. This led to illness, loss of toes and feet, and poor morale. Dangerous health conditions developed in the camp when human waste was not properly disposed of, and personal hygiene was not a priority for the men, who were living in close quarters. Dysentery, typhoid, typhus, and influenza spread throughout camp. Disease killed nearly one in six men, totaling three-thousand soldiers.

Atkinson's role changed. When not running dispatches back and forth to York, as Washington sought supplies and food provisions from Congress, Oliver worked diligently with the executive staff to increase morale, keep the soldiers warm, and occupy them with projects to fortify their defensive positions.

Washington knew his army wasn't ready for the spring when generals went to war, so was relieved when forty-eight-year-old Friedrich Wilhelm Baron von Steuben rode into camp on February 23, 1778. Speaking almost no English, von Steuben introduced himself as an accomplished officer in the highly regarded Prussian Army. Oliver thought him an imposing man whose large size and demeanor demanded respect. He felt a call to aid the Americans with his skills as an inspector general, a disciplinarian, a molder of highly trained fighting forces.

Oliver later learned from a letter that Washington received from Ben Franklin that von Steuben wasn't all those things in Prussia. In fact, he was none of them. And by the time General Washington learned the truth he didn't care. Von Steuben was a wonder-worker teaching the troops to be more efficient loading and firing their weapons, how to properly fight with bayonets, and the basics of hand-to-hand combat. He drilled them to the point where Washington knew he had a fighting chance in the spring.

It was during this time that Washington received another letter from Franklin that celebrated France's entrance into an alliance with the rebels, lifting their spirits, buoying their faith they could still win the war. Washington jubilantly remarked to his staff what they already knew: this meant more cash, some credit, weapons, supplies, and troops. Washington was as enthusiastic about the French Navy's possible contributions as anything else since the Continental Navy was barely existent.

Oliver said to the men under his command, "France believes in our cause. We are assured victory now!"

However, Washington was gravely concerned with the poor condition of his men, because, as the weather got warmer, disease spread more quickly. Plus, nearly three-thousand men were not battle-ready because they didn't have adequate clothing.

Lieutenant Atkinson survived the winter, though flu sidelined him for a few weeks. Some of the wives helped take care of him, and the general and his staff would occasionally check in on him. Even Martha Washington stopped by every few days.

By June, the weather had cleared up, and Washington thought it time to be the aggressor, especially when he learned through his Philadelphia spy network that British General Clinton had been ordered to abandon Philadelphia after learning of the French-

American alliance. The commander-in-chief saw this as an opportunity and trailed the British back to New York City, harassing them along the way with light infantry. However, Washington knew he needed a political victory because General Gates was being a nuisance, trying to employ politics to take command of the Continental Army.

Lieutenant Atkinson was sent ahead to scout the British and bring word back. Soon, the English army had reached Sandy Hook, New Jersey, a town across the bay from Manhattan that Oliver wouldn't have imagined visiting once, much less twice, and got word back that the British Navy was going to transport them out of the Continental Army's reach.

Washington commanded Major General Charles Lee to take one-third of the army and attack the British at Monmouth. Oliver led a small detachment of cavalry to strike from the left flank. Meeting at Monmouth Courthouse, Oliver knew immediately that Lee's plan was botched, scattering some soldiers while sending the rest in retreat. Oliver held his line as long as he could, but cannon started raining down on his position, so he ordered his men back to the main force.

Washington arrived shortly thereafter, reconfiguring the battle plan, leading to an inconclusive result, though with great loss to the Continentals of 600 men. What was important for Washington as much as victory was to see that men trained by von Steuben demonstrated great discipline in the field of battle, giving him hope for future victories.

With the general's permission, Oliver went to the home of the Blossoms but was told by a neighbor that they had fled the area when they learned the British were coming. Disappointed, he left a note of thanks with the neighbor to give to them upon their return and rejoined the army.

CHAPTER 37

THE SPY

After establishing new headquarters in Fredericksburg, New York, in September 1778, General Washington called Lieutenant Oliver Atkinson to his large oval field tent made of flax linen with distinctive red edges and asked him about his work with Paul Revere and The Mechanics. Entering, Oliver saw a table with a few books on it next to a cot, three chairs and a small desk, then explained that he had been little more than a courier, delivering notices of when and where meetings would be held, and didn't do any spying. He was still relatively new to Boston and had no contacts other than those in the tight-knit Sons of Liberty.

"Have you heard of Nathan Hale?" the general asked Oliver.

"No, sir, I have not," the young lieutenant replied.

Washington went on to explain that he was an American officer who had briefly penetrated the British perimeter around New York City to gather information on their enemies. He was caught and subsequently hanged by the British in New York City on September 22, 1776. "It is reported that his last words were, 'I only regret that I have just one life to lose for my country.'"

Oliver was moved by Hale's declaration. "He is a hero, General."

"Indeed," Washington said as he moved around his desk. "One area we gravely lack is intelligence from Gage's domain." Placing his hand on Oliver's shoulder he said, "I need your help."

At that moment, a handsome and enormous man, Major Benjamin Tallmadge entered the room and was introduced to Lieutenant Atkinson. Tallmadge looked at Oliver curiously, then said, "You requested me, General Washington?"

"Please sit." All three did, with Washington facing them from behind a small desk. "Lieutenant Atkinson worked with Paul Revere and his Mechanics, a network much like one you're establishing, before and during the British occupation of Boston. I would like you to find a way to use his experience in what we previously discussed."

Uneasy with what he was being directed to do, Tallmadge responded, saying, "Sir, I have no doubt of Lieutenant Atkinson's experience and skills gathering intelligence, but you've promised that I would get to choose my own people, wanting to keep it so clandestine that none will know each other is working for the American cause. His knowledge that we exist makes me terribly uncomfortable, if I may be so honest, general."

Oliver shifted uncomfortably, remaining silent, his eyes looking at his feet and not the tent flap by which he wanted to escape. Pensively, Washington leaned back in his seat. Tension was heavy in the room as Tallmadge squeezed his hat, fighting temptation to speak more plainly to the general. Finally, the commander leaned forward and spoke to Tallmadge.

"Lieutenant Atkinson has proved his loyalty to our cause and to me as much as anyone under my command. Are you aware that he spent nine months on the HMS *Scorpion* and escaped?" Looking now at Atkinson, he continued, "You have those you trust, and I have mine."

Standing back up, Washington resumed, "Lieutenant Atkinson will not be working in New York City or Long Island, but in Fairfield, Connecticut, which we discussed would be the relay point for gathered intelligence. I am moving much of my army to that area. He will be my personal courier. He will never know anything else about your operation, and they will not know about him, except by the name John Derby."

The general winked at Oliver, who was amused by his English hometown's name as his choice.

"Do you understand?"

A controlled Tallmadge said, "Very much so, sir. And I am grateful to Lieutenant Atkinson for his past and future contributions to our critical mission." Turning to Oliver he said, "Would you mind dining with me this evening? I'd like to get to know you as you have some power over whether my neck remains free from a noose."

Oliver nodded, saying, "Gladly, Major."

Dinner was held that night at Major Tallmadge's plain wall tent. It was as spartan as Washington's, but half the size—just barely enough for them both to dine on a wooden crate. The hour together was cordial without being friendly as they dined on chicken pot pie prepared for them by a lady friendly to the major. It was the best part of the night for Oliver. It was also apparent to Oliver that this man didn't like the general pulling rank on him, so the lieutenant sat humbly while listening to the lecture he received regarding the major's demands and expectations. John Derby didn't pry for information regarding the major's plans, how he had set up his network, who was involved, how he recruited turncoats, gathered intelligence, transmitted and communicated intel. All Oliver concerned himself with was what his job was, and no more.

"Major Tallmadge, I'd like to thank you for dinner this evening, which no soul will ever know about."

"Are you being sarcastically insubordinate to me, Lieutenant Atkinson?"

Atkinson stood up, pushed in his chair and grabbed his hat. "General Washington just assigned me to a role of sitting and waiting, hardly what an experienced veteran of this war desires."

"Oh, do tell," the major snarkily prodded.

"From the greens of Lexington, to Moore's Creek Bridge, to Brooklyn, nine months on a prisoner ship and then Saratoga, not to mention surviving Valley Forge," the major's face revealing respect, "I'm going to be parked away from the war by the Long Island Sound waiting for a boat to appear as an occasional runner for General Washington."

Tallmadge stood. "I see your point." He walked up to Oliver, their noses almost touching, "But if you so much as ask to know the name of anyone you meet, I will personally shoot you as a spy!" The major then took a step back and said, "Goodnight, Lieutenant Atkinson."

His role at the back end of this operation was not a good use of his experience and skills, he knew. Still, Washington assigned him to this, leaving Oliver to wonder if he were being silently disciplined.

His mission was simple: he would meet a member of the network, whose real name he would never know, with whom he would never have a personal or professional conversation, after they rowed twelve miles across the Long Island Sound under cover of darkness while avoiding British ships dotted across its many miles. Once the boat arrived, a code would be given so that each party knew they were linked. A handoff of intel would be made before the rowers would immediately return to the other side. Oliver would race, without distraction, to General Washington and hand off the intel and return to his station.

Spying was only modestly interesting to Oliver, though he wasn't really doing any. He was the back end of dangerous work being done by others. Not his preferred type of adventure, though adventure was no longer fantasy to him. This was life and death. It was less about the excitement and more about the accomplishment. It was less about the personal glory that so many others pursued, but about purpose and meaning for a greater good, for the welfare of the many.

Sometimes he'd pause to consider his own internal speech to make sure he really believed it or was he trapped in a self-perpetuating philosophy over true conviction. His consistency with convictions that he expressed and convictions he lived with convinced him that he believed in these ideals. But to be sure in case anything changed over time with each battle and experience, he would perform an inventory of his heart and mind.

As he walked back to his tent, he was pleased with what he saw, so he fell asleep thinking of Clara in his arms, hoping it would turn into a dream that would carry him through the night.

He was no longer having night terrors.

CHAPTER 38

This duty, waiting on dispatches for General Washington, was monotonous. Other than reading, exercising, and training his men, he would wait. Then wait some more. There were times when he fantasized about nearly getting caught but finding a way to heroically escape upon permanently subduing his pursuer. But it never became a reality. He had no one to complain to about his assignment. He lived in a rented room with dark black curtains from a widow near Black Rock by Fairfield, Connecticut, that was so small, he could sit on his bed and bathe, shave, and eat his meals. He read every book he could get his hands on to bide his time. If ever asked, he could probably prepare French cuisine as well as any Parisian chef, he joked to himself. He was bored. There was little else for him to do except train.

He was promoted to captain and given charge of a company. This was to help with his cover story, though, unlike some of the other companies, and despite Oliver's known experience as a fighter, a scout, and long-distance courier, he and his men stayed relatively close to Washington through the winter, spring, and early summer months of 1779.

During their time in Fredericksburg, Washington had been asked on more than a few occasions by some of his officers why Oliver remained close by when he could be an asset on the western front in Indiana and Illinois, or in the South to help train the many patriot militia that existed there, especially since there was a growing consensus that the British, having mostly failed in dividing the Continental Army in the North, would next turn their attention to the South and drive a wedge between the Carolinas and Georgia and the rest of the Colonies. Perhaps, with Spain having just declared war on Britain, Captain Atkinson could support the Spanish in the Louisiana territory as a major battle seemed looming there? Oliver wondered about these as well, just never out loud.

Washington patiently listened to it all, and would always respond, "Few of us have fought as Atkinson has fought or endured as much suffering as he. His days in battle are not over, but for now, I'm giving him rest."

When Oliver was alerted to a mission, he would slip away unnoticed, and within a couple of hours, be back in his quarters after relinquishing what was given to him directly to General Washington. At first, there were momentary sparks of excitement for John Derby as he performed his clandestine duties. But after a while, despite understanding the importance of his role, he became enervated. He was now a year into this duty, which had received high praise from General Washington, but had to be honest with the Commander-in-Chief and express his thoughts.

The only action Oliver saw was on July 7 near his home in the Black Rock area of Fairfield, Connecticut, along the waterfront. It also happened to be one of the few nights Clara had been able to visit him, having been accompanied by Parson Brown for protection. After an early evening dinner with Martha and George Washington at Webb's Tavern in Stamford, Connecticut, on roasted duck and mixed vegetables, Oliver and Clara were driven back to his room in Black Rock to continue getting to know each other. But as they passed by the home of Henry and Anne Cranmer, Oliver noticed a dark pair of men's trousers hanging from a clothing line leg side up.

Oliver stared at the garment as they passed by, trying to hide the anger on his face.

"Is something wrong, darling?"

Turning to her he said, "I'm afraid the rapturous joys of our evening will have to wait."

"Oh?" she responded with disappointment.

Nodding, he continued. "The duty of a Continental soldier beckons."

"But I don't recall General Washington giving you any orders. Why am I finding out about this now? I'm not happy, Oliver! I've come all this way to see you and..."

"Clara, please don't ask me to explain. Trust me. As soon as I complete my task I'll be back in your arms."

She was silent until they returned to their room.

Later that night while strolling the area looking for any unusual activity, as he would do the day of a night drop, he spotted about 250 British soldiers headed towards him. An attack was under way. He sped off to alarm the closest military force near him, the 4th Connecticut militia, and Lieutenant Jarvis' guns stationed at the shoreline.

Oliver was ordered by Washington that he was not to engage, but to retreat to an observer's distance and report to him what he saw.

He burned inside not being able to fight as he watched a short battle occur. The Americans were routed as the British swarmed into the streets, looted the town, and burned churches. Upon seeing their intention, Oliver raced back to the widow's home and grabbed her, Clara, and whatever he could carry and fled the town moments before the house was set ablaze.

He knew he would not have made a huge difference in the outcome, but he felt cowardly, though Clara saw him as her personal hero. He couldn't explain how he felt to her. He was also concerned about his reputation among his men for having such unusual favoritism with Washington. Some rather enjoyed not having to fight, while others felt neglect of duty and commitment to the cause. Oliver knew it was time to have a discussion with the Commander-in-Chief.

Oliver sought and was granted an audience with General Washington in his tent, and as he was about to lay out an apologetic for better use elsewhere, Washington raised his hand as if to say, "One moment," and said, "I can see on your face how weary you are. You've performed your duties well. No one has a clue what you've really been up to. I was going to give you an option for your next appointment, but I have a feeling I know what you will choose when hearing the following."

"I'd be happy with any assignment that involves action, sir," the captain assured him. Washington gave him a "cut-the-crap" smile and proceeded.

"The British are now in control of Savannah, Georgia. They plan on moving up the coast to take Charleston with more than thirteen-thousand men supported by fourteen warships. Obviously, we can't let them do this, but we don't have a navy to defend the port or our soldiers. I need you to head south with your company to support Major General Benjamin Lincoln's force of five-thousand men in Charleston. You won't be alone, although I haven't decided yet which army will follow."

"They plan to choke Lincoln into submission, then into surrender," Oliver added.

"Precisely. We can't let that happen," the general firmly said.

"Yes, General Washington. Thank you, sir. We will leave tomorrow." Oliver saluted General Washington.

"Oliver," Washington said tenderly, "You did exactly what I asked of you working for the Culper Spy Ring. Yes, that's what it's called, between us, of course. It seemed like an insignificant duty, but I can assure you that it was almost as important as anything else you've done in the war for American liberty. You will understand in time."

CHAPTER 39

THE SOUTHERN CAMPAIGN

Oliver mobilized his light company of fifty men and gave them Washington's orders. Some had to say goodbye to wives and children, and he to Clara, who was able to visit a few times, though they agreed she would stay with her mother to help at the inn until the war was over, while others were ready for something different, especially with the blustery winter they were enduring. They knew the South was more temperate, and with freezing temperatures and snow harassing Connecticut, the men were thrilled to be headed south. Oliver was simply thrilled to be on the move again.

He'd become as "bored" as General Washington observed. He needed action and adventure and was now gratefully on the move again.

About an hour before daylight, Oliver and his men headed south for Charleston to support the South Carolina militia and Continental Army under the command of Major General Benjamin Lincoln. It was now late February, and it would take them at least a month to get to their destination. He was going to ride as far and as fast as they could and knew he was going to learn much about his men he couldn't learn from purely drilling them endlessly. They were headed to battle. Only then would he know what he had.

It was now 1780. It seemed like there was no end in sight for the war. The twenty-year-old had learned that many in Parliament were growing weary of the fighting and its exorbitant costs, bleeding dry the Crown's coffers, and that the people of England had tired of losing their sons to what they considered a meaningless piece of real estate a month's voyage away. Many wanted the British to sue for peace and turn America into a trade partner and help secure their hold of Canada. He hoped these were true.

Atkinson joined the many on his side who felt that if they were able to wait out the British long enough and help exhaust their treasury, fight on their terms as best as they could to string out the war, and send home as many dead Regulars and officers as they could, England would eventually give up. Perhaps more easily said than done, he concluded. What they needed was a signature victory over a significant army. If it were to happen, it would be in the South.

The Americans hadn't a chance to retake New York City, regardless of the confidence General Washington had in their ability. Again, Oliver believed the war was going to be won in the South, so he was pleased to be heading there. It was time to end this opposition to liberty immediately. He admitted to himself that he was tired of war. It was no longer glorious. But it was necessary. So many had given so much for the cause of freedom to lay down their arms now.

As he told one of his officers during their drive south, "You don't stop the birth of a nation when the contractions are at their highest."

As they crossed from North Carolina into South Carolina, Oliver concluded within himself that once the war was over, so were his traveling days. He'd move to Wilmington, North Carolina, start his printing business, and look for other opportunities to make a difference in his local community and church. It was going to be the simplest life he could create.

After four weeks of hard riding, Oliver and his company came upon the abandoned house just over the South Carolina line about a hundred miles west of Wilmington that he had stopped at on his first visit to the area. It seemed like two lifetimes ago to him. However, this time he saw a woman on the porch doing something to the door, so he decided to stop. At about the same time, she saw him and his men and grabbed a gun.

"Identify yourselves!" the old woman shouted. As soon as she said that, a woman of about thirty opened the front door and stepped out on the porch.

"They're Continentals, Mama," the younger woman said, as the old lady lowered her gun. "My apologies, sir. She's mostly blind."

From his horse, Captain Oliver tipped his cap and introduced himself and explained why he was there. He then asked, "Is this your home?"

"No," the younger woman answered, "it's my brother's. Was my brother's. We recently learned he died fighting at Stony Brook. His name was Alton Bryant. Did you know him?"

Oliver looked to see the old lady resuming what she'd been doing, which was scrubbing the soap notice of Alton's announcing he'd gone off to fight the Redcoats, as well as his note. A lump formed in his throat. His arm started to reach towards the old woman, but he stopped, and it fell to his side.

Quickly regaining composure, Oliver said, "I did not, ma'am." He turned to his men, "Did any of you know Alton Bryant?" They shook their heads.

Oliver's face couldn't hide the tear that ran down it, nor his nose the sniffles that followed. "This home saved my life." Oliver went on to tell of the twenty-four-hour period he spent there on that brutal winter day. "Do you have food, ma'am?"

She looked at her mama and then the ground.

Oliver turned to one of his men and commanded him to take one of the deer they'd just killed to their kitchen.

"Thank you, sir," she said, clutching her hands at her chest.

"Very happy too, ma'am. Have you any news about Charleston?"

She shook her head, "No," then warned Oliver about the large contingent of loyalists through the middle of the colony, "stretching nearly clear to the coast. They're more savage than the British."

Captain Atkinson rode off as the old woman yelled to them, "Avenge my boy!"

They entered Georgetown, South Carolina, a small coastal town about sixty miles north of Charleston, two days later, having heeded the warning given by the Bryant woman to avoid the middle of the colony.

A scout returned with news that Charleston was under siege. Lincoln's forces were trapped and had missed the window to depart, having been talked out of retreat by the locals. This cost the American cause great harm and loss of men. Oliver knew this near fatal blow might be the end of the war, their cause, and their lives.

He and his men had ridden hard for more than seven-hundred and fifty miles, were tired, and now they had no army to join. Oliver felt like fleeing back to Clara to protect her from the coming British terror, but he extinguished that impulse quickly.

"I need a few minutes to think," he told his officers, before riding just outside of town to a patch of trees. Dismounting, he took out his hatchet and began swinging it ferociously at a palmetto tree. After a minute of furious swings, it dawned on him that the tree was doing more damage to his tool than he was to the tree.

Running and rage. His men needed a leader. He gathered himself and returned to the men, who were being welcomed by the town's folks to stay in homes and taverns for free.

Settling in for the night, he met with his officers to discuss what they should do next. As they talked, word came to them that

General Huger, whom Oliver had met after the battle of Stony Brook in New York the previous June, was in Moncks Corner, some thirty-five miles west of Charleston, and was in command of light infantry and cavalry sent there to protect a supply route to the city. With Charleston now cut off, it was instantly decided that they would leave for Moncks Corner before daylight.

He sent a courier ahead of them to alert Huger that reinforcements were on the way. As Oliver watched the young man bolt out of camp, he allowed himself a moment to recall his days with Paul Revere. He felt a shot of joy race through his body.

Now, as he sat proudly on Freedom, he turned his attention back to his men. "We have about a fifty-mile ride, men. We must get there before the sun sets as General Huger and his force of five hundred are exposed. Let's go help our fellow patriots."

They're cheering was muted as they didn't want to awaken their sleeping hosts. Stoney-faced, Oliver led his men southwest towards a dark sky.

* * *

Late afternoon, April 10, 1780, thirty-five-year-old General Isaac Huger, a wealthy European-educated merchant and planter from South Carolina turned Continental military officer, sent a few men out to greet Atkinson and his contingent and escort them to his camp. Once they arrived, Huger and Lieutenant Colonel William Washington, head of the cavalry, greeted them warmly, but were clearly exasperated.

"Stony Brook seemed like such a long time ago," Oliver said as the two shook hands.

"And it might have been forever for us if Lincoln had been a general and not a party host," Huger barked. "We're stuck out in the middle of nowhere, and they'll come gunning for us next. Now my orders seem ridiculous!"

After introductions, the officers retreated to Huger's tent where they apprised Oliver of the Charleston siege. Oliver now came under Chevalier Pierre-Francois Vernier, who commanded some of the Pulaski Legion who were mustered in Baltimore.

"My last order, captain, was to guard this route as a baggage train meant for General Lincoln and his staff to pass through. Obviously, there's no way to get into Charleston. But I doubt they'll continue with their fancy balls and parties anyway."

All but Oliver chuckled at this comment. Seeing this, the rosy-cheeked Huger cleared his throat, then briefed Oliver that an attack on their position was imminent. "It won't be by the British, or at least by any large contingent of British, but loyalist forces under their command. We're sitting ducks, but my orders are to wait for the baggage. Can you believe that?"

Oliver was shown to his tent. After making sure Freedom was situated, whom he kept next to his tent and not with the other horses, he walked among his men and encouraged them, explaining that they were going to be there at least a few days, to rest, but to stay ready as he believed an attack was imminent.

"Keep your firearms with you at all times," Atkinson ordered.

He fell asleep by 9 p.m. on April 13. A few hours later the familiar sound of muted distress from Freedom woke him. It was less a whinny and more whiney when trouble or concern were near. He made this strange sound repeatedly until Oliver appeared. Groggily he calmed his horse as he listened while scanning the area, his eyes taking a moment to adjust to the dark. In the quiet between night and morning, Oliver heard what he thought was men marching. Not like on Bay Road. This was more of a soft measured step.

He quickly saddled Freedom then bolted to Huger's tent with his rifle, not even in uniform, and tore open Huger's flap, startling him awake. Just above a whisper, he locked eyes with Huger and said with intensity, "General, we're under attack."

Now sitting up on his elbows, Huger cocked his head and looked around then said, "I don't hear anything."

At that, the night exploded with gunfire as fourteen-hundred loyalists and a few British Dragoons under the command of the infamously barbaric British Lieutenant Colonel Banastre Tarleton, blitzed the camp on horseback and foot, shocking the Continental force. It was chaos. Men half-awake were being sliced by sabers and shot.

The soldier who had guard duty in the narrow passage between swamp land and the camp had fallen asleep.

Patriots raced wildly about trying to identify the enemy in the darkness. In the short battle that occurred, fourteen men died, many more were wounded, and sixty-seven men were captured. The rest absconded on foot into the swamps as Tarleton's men captured all the American cavalry's horses. Except Freedom. Most of the officers, including Huger and Washington, fled into the swamp on foot, as did Oliver, but on Freedom.

Vernier asked for quarter from Tarleton, who instead of being noble, had the man slashed with sabers, ending his life.

The next morning, Oliver searched for men from his company and found only two, both on foot. He ordered them to stay under Washington and gave them permission to shoot the guard who had been on duty if they ever had the chance.

Atkinson made his way in and out of the swamps of South Carolina looking for a friendly force, but found none, until he was awakened by the click of a musket one morning while sleeping in the driest patch of land he could find in the clothes he was wearing when he escaped. Opening his eyes, he saw a fierce-looking man dressed in deerskin staring down on him.

"Are you a loyalist or a patriot?" the man demanded.

"I'm Captain Oliver Atkinson of the Continental Army. I hope this allows me to keep my life?"

The bearded man grinned as he lowered his gun. "Humor in the face of death might be the best thing. Come with me."

Oliver rose, and stored his bedding on Freedom, then followed the bearded stranger.

"My name is James Caldwell. I'm part of a company of some of the most colorful men you'll ever meet. Let's just say we enjoy fighting and harassing the loyalists and British in the most unconventional ways. I'd like you to meet someone."

An hour later, the two entered a camp of a few dozen men on the outskirts of the swamp. Breaking forth through a curious crowd was the diminutive Lieutenant Colonel Francis Marion.

"Look what I found, Francis!" Caldwell said laughing.

Oliver introduced himself, then explained what happened at Moncks Corner, briefed him on the war up north, and submitted to his command.

The modest Marion motioned with his hand, "As you can see, we don't have the manpower to fight the British head-on. We know that Cornwallis..."

"Cornwallis? I thought Clinton..."

"No," Marion said, "He's headed back to a life of luxury in New York."

"So, Cornwallis is in command," Oliver confirmed.

Nodding yes, Marion continued. "I'm certain he's going to march into Virginia, gathering loyalist militias making his army undefeatable. He intends to choke off the South from the North. According to you, New York and the North are still at a stalemate. Not if Cornwallis owns the South." He made a motion like taking a knife to his throat. "We use unconventional tactics I learned from the Cherokee Indians. If we meet the British in the open field, we're dead. But if we can attack certain elements of their forces, mostly their supply lines, and random loyalist militia, we can slow down their advance, draw them into the impossible swamps, reduce their weapons, food, and other supplies, attack their rear, sack scouting parties, and generally put a little fear into them," Marion said with a smile.

"And do this until General Washington sends a force down here to hit the British head-on," Oliver added.

Smiling, Marion said, "Exactly. We won't end the war, but we can make the British miserable and miserably slow."

"I'm at your service. Lieutenant Colonel Marion," Captain Atkinson said, saluting.

"No titles or salutes here, Oliver."

Over the next few months, Marion and his men trained Oliver on the tactics of swamp warfare, surprise mobile attacks, and how to survive in the swamp. The men serving under Marion were farmers, business owners, and common South Carolinians who were first loyal to their Colony, but also staunch supporters of the rebellion who believed the best use of their knowledge and skills was to wage uncommon warfare.

CHAPTER 40

By July, they had engaged the loyalist and British forces in all the ways he'd described to Oliver, performing much of their warfare along the Pee Dee and Santee Rivers. Now, Cornwallis, having grown tired of this pest and his swamp men, sent Tarleton after him. Tarleton's reputation grew as a dishonorable warrior by showing no mercy to citizen patriots and soldiers.

Marion and his men led him on a wild chase through the swamp, always staying a few steps ahead of him, engaging his force on their terms. Frustrated, Tarleton called him a fox, leading to Marion's nickname of Swamp Fox, which he and his men loved.

Oliver delighted in serving under Marion. It was the most unusual form of warfare, but it made sense. He agreed that traditional warfare could integrate many of the tactics he learned.

Marion received word that General Gates was on his way to Charlotte, North Carolina, to take over the southern Continental forces. Oliver knew how much General Washington distrusted Gates, especially after Saratoga, for which Gates received most of the praise despite Benedict Arnold's heroics and the impact of Morgan's riflemen on the battle's outcome. Washington had long known that Gates was after his job. He was a glory-seeker. Washington thought him an average field commander.

General Nathanael Greene was the Commander-in-Chief's first choice to head south. "Congress must've voted Greene down," Oliver guessed in conversation with Marion as they marched to an area south of Charlotte to connect with the highly effective

Delaware and Maryland lines, along with twenty-one-hundred North Carolina militia and seven-hundred Virginia militia. This force was more than double the size of Cornwallis' army. The men felt confident they could beat the British under Gates' leadership.

When the Swampers arrived at the American camp, they were commanded to stop just inside. General Horatio Gates, who one subordinate called a "lion in society," came out and inspected Marion and his men, not hiding his disgust over this vagabond group of ragtag fighters. Approaching Oliver he asked, "Captain Atkinson, how did you fall in with these men?"

Oliver gave him a brief history from Washington's orders to support Lincoln at Charleston, Moncks Corner, to the present, and hailed Francis Marion and his men for their imaginative warfare and disruptive tactics.

"You have been promoted, Marion, and so I have an important mission I want you to go on since you know this land so well," Gates said. He gave him orders to go on scouting missions and report back to him. It was obvious he didn't want him around. Dutifully, at that moment sensing the general's contempt for him, he turned around and took his men out from the camp and crossed back into South Carolina.

Oliver was furious. Gates just sent away a most effective leader and weapon. Remaining calm on the outside, he submitted to Gates and was assigned duty to the Virginia militia. He spent a few days drilling them, and saw how green they were, and, frankly, not ready for battle. The heart was there, but they were not prepared. He communicated this to Gates upon being asked for a review, and Gates simply said, "They'll be fine. We'll overwhelm the British. You'll see."

On August 15, after a dinner that immediately had the effect of a purgative on most of the men, Gates marched his army towards Camden, where he planned to overrun the thousand-man garrison there. Oliver requested they wait another day, considering the condition of the soldiers. Most were weak and dehydrated, affecting their readiness on the battlefield. His suggestion was rebuffed, and at 10 p.m., they began their march. Oliver saw that the march was a mess from the start, as most of the militia force had never moved as a unit this large before, and many were collapsing from dysentery.

Cornwallis had learned that Gates was on the move.

By 2 a.m., along the Great Wagon Road just north of Camden, the Continental Army and the British Army almost ran into each other.

By morning, both sides had deployed their men for battle. Captain Atkinson had been ordered to position his soldiers on the American left flank directly opposite Cornwallis' best soldiers. Oliver reminded Gates that the untested militia from Virginia and North Carolina were facing Cornwallis' best men. It could be a bloodbath. He reminded Gates of the honor it was to be placed on the right flank in the British Army because of their proven skill and formidability. Again, Gates spurned his advice and ordered him back to the line. "You will not make a coward out of me!" Gates boomed as Oliver left this side.

Oliver went up and down the line encouraging his men, telling them to expect a frontal attack, to stay calm, fire, reload, and prepare for bayonets. Fear before battle was normal for most. What he saw in their eyes frightened him. Not one of them appeared ready for what was about to happen.

Scanning the battle lines, Cornwallis must've seen the weakness in the American deployment immediately. He may have considered it a ruse at first but discerned that it wasn't and sent his best troops charging at the militia with bayonets drawn.

After a volley, the Virginia and North Carolina lines melted in the morning heat as the best of Britain broke through what remained of the line. The barely trained Americans dropped their weapons and fled the field in panic, retreating while ignoring Oliver's and the other officer's commands to stop and return to battle. It was chaos.

As Oliver attempted to restore part of his line, he felt a thud in his right ear, as if some giant took a huge bite from it. Blood immediately began to flow. He put his hand to the ear and discovered a large chunk of the top of the ear was missing. Blood cascaded down his face and hand.

Ignoring the pain, he went looking for Gates as he saw Tarleton's men on his left creating a wedge between the American forces. It was a route. Gates's arrogance assured the battle was over quickly. What was supposed to have been a relatively easy victory for the Continentals disintegrated within an hour.

Atkinson couldn't believe his eyes when he spotted Gates fleeing the battlefield on his horse. Oliver squeezed Freedom, shouted in his ear, and off he went chasing after the general, who by now was passing his panicked army. Oliver thought at first Gates would outrun them to turn and drive them back to the engagement, but he kept going and going. After one mile of hard riding, he finally caught up to the general. Pulling alongside at top speed Gates shouted, "Don't bother me, Atkinson!"

"Where are you going, sir?" Oliver begged.

"Where you can't," Gates replied through heavy breaths.

"Where's that, General?"

"Home." And with that Oliver slowed down Freedom to a halt as he watched the greatest act of cowardice imaginable occur before him: a general abandoning his army, his nation, and his reputation at the expense of his men to save his own life.

Oliver turned Freedom around to head back to what was left of the battle, but it was clearly over. He now saw men fleeing in different directions away from the British. Knowing Tarleton's sadistic reputation, if he returned, he'd likely die at his cruel hands. Oliver was powerless to engage.

He looked through his spyglass and saw Cornwallis' army scavenging for weapons, food, blankets, and such from their camp.

Where was he to go? Should he try to find Marion? Head back north to find Washington? Gather what remained of the army until another officer arrived to take command? He was disturbed, confused, and afraid: the American Revolution was hanging by the thinnest thread, and he felt a noose tightening around his neck. Freedom moved hesitatingly back and forth as if in the same mind set.

Was this the end?

His thoughts turned to Clara. Memories of her exploded into the light of his mind as a natural defense against the encroaching darkness he was feeling. She'd seen him for only a few days since they married. His death was always a possibility, but not the death of a new nation. He never imagined it would be stillborn. His hope and his promise to Clara was that he would help deliver to her the freedom that the founding fathers promised, even if it was delivered posthumously. She knew this, accepted it, but the idea that he would return a wanted man for crimes against the Crown was not something they had ever discussed, or had privately considered.

Providence.

The boy from Derby had been sent to America for his freedom and that of the Colonies. It all seemed to be collapsing on him now. So, he rode Freedom out of the clearing and away from British eyes and into some woods to pause and gather his thoughts.

He dismounted, got down on one knee, and began to pray with burning tears. He couldn't remember the last time he cried, but whatever had been reserved for so long came pouring out over the next thirty minutes. He barely spoke any words. His tears, mixed with mucous and a still bleeding ear, cried out to the Lord for mercy, wisdom, and strength.

As the salty flow dried up, it occurred to him that the past thirty minutes probably equaled or exceeded the total time he'd spent in prayer since escaping the *Scorpion*. He resolved to pray daily regardless of the outcome of the war, and to return to the relational presence of the Lord.

CHAPTER 41

Oliver retreated to Salisbury, North Carolina, about forty miles north of Charlotte, having gathered about four-hundred men from the Camden debacle. He had hoped to have persuaded more men to join him, but the truth was, there were two-thousand casualties at the Camden battle. Many of the Continental Army that was left were gathered in Charlotte. Many of the militia from both states who survived just went home to salvage their lives, families, and homes, having lost confidence in the cause.

However, this wasn't as troubling as the desertion of five cavalry soldiers under his command.

While Oliver understood the despondency many men were feeling after being routed at Camden, the grumblings within and without his ad hoc camp while they waited for Gates's replacement disturbed him, as they bordered on mutiny, in his opinion. Gates, after all, had abandoned his men on the battlefield. "Why can't we go home also?" they asked.

Though desertion was nothing new in the Continental Army, it became more difficult for many leaders to keep men believing that their battle was divinely ordered. Oliver had witnessed the hanging of one deserter and the flogging of a few more. And now, having learned that five Continental soldiers under him had left in the middle of the night to return home, he anguished at what he would do for their punishment when they caught the men.

The search party returned by late afternoon the next day with four of the five men. Oliver demanded they remain bound and watched over until morning when he would decide their fate.

Throughout the night, Oliver sleeplessly struggled with the idea of having to discipline his own men. This was a first for him. He had ridden into battle with these fellows, ate with them, exchanged stories of their families and of their hopes after victory was gained. And now, the sun that set minutes ago was already peeking over the eastern horizon. He rose up with what he hoped was a solution.

He ordered the guards to walk the men outside of camp to a large dead oak tree. Understandably, the four frightened men thought they were going to be hanged.

Giving away none of his weariness, Oliver's angry eyes burned deeply into each man's soul. "Look at me, soldier," he ordered one who was weeping uncontrollably. When the man wouldn't, he ordered a sergeant standing at his side to prepare the rope for the tree. Quickly, he and another man moved to a broad branch and tossed a readied rope over it.

The weeping man struggled to lift his head, as if refusing to look at his hangman would make him disappear. Finally, he caught his breath between sobs and looked Oliver in the eye. His commanding officer saw fear and regret on his face.

"Ready, sir," the hanging sergeant declared.

Oliver looked at the weeping deserter and noticed that the other three men looked ready to faint.

"I have three questions for you men before I sentence you. One, where is the fifth man?" Oliver demanded.

"Captain Atkinson," said one of the deserters, "he went south when we went west."

Nodding his head as he paced before them, their captain asked, "Why did you desert your fellow countrymen?"

The captives were silent, at first until Oliver drew his sword.

"We'd lost hope. We were hungry. We wanted to salvage what we could of our farms," a second soldier answered.

Oliver put a hand to his chin as he scanned the men before him. "What would you do if you were me?" Oliver asked.

Each of the men were shocked by the question. Looking at each other for an answer, the first man spoke up. "Captain Atkinson, you are a good and righteous man. Speaking for myself, your judgment will be fair whatever you decide." The sudden flashback to similar words he'd professed to Captain Coffin on *The Beaver* unnerved him. Regathering the moment, he saw the other men nod their heads in agreement.

Oliver's entire body exhaled. He wasn't prepared for this answer. He had hoped for a way out without denying his responsibilities or justice and it came to him.

"I have been with three of you since we left Connecticut for Charleston. I've known you each to be excellent soldiers. You," he said to the other man, "You recently joined us after Camden after the army was scattered. Why didn't you just leave for home then?"

With a quivering voice, he responded, saying, "I thought I was a man of duty and honor, sir. I went looking for you. But every night of sleep I'd hear my wife and children calling for me to come home. I've been afraid for them more than for myself, sir."

"We all hear our families in our sleep!!" Oliver shouted. "Sergeant, you?"

The hangman nodded.

Oliver continued. "Where were you looking to find hope? What is its source? Hope without courage at the gates of Hell is simply vain cowardice. These men behind me believe something better awaits us all because we believe in the destiny God has ordered for America!"

He paused to look back at the men. The camp was now fully awake, and many of the men had joined to witness the goings on.

In a conversational tone, their cooled-down commanding officer finished his thoughts. "We all miss our families. The sooner we end this war the sooner we'll be with them. Would you return to your families as cowards, yet still believe in your right to share in the victory and spoils of war?" Turning to the sergeant, Oliver commanded, "Thirty lashes each, sergeant."

At that, he quick-walked to his tent and was unable to eat the entire day.

CHAPTER 42

He expected Nathanael Greene to arrive soon and assume command from the disgraced Gates, and he wanted this mixed group of Virginia and North Carolina militia men to be ready to fight in full capacity by that time.

He had received word that the Over-mountain Men from the western side of the Smokies gained victory at King's Mountain, but Charlotte was a losing battle for the patriots. In fact, many of them retreated to Salisbury and were now training with Oliver. Word also arrived of the successes of Marion, and the "Carolina Gamecock" Brigadier General Thomas Sumter, as well as Daniel Morgan and his famed fighters. Men were still battling. Many hadn't given up. He was proud of the men who remained to train, and soon he felt they were ready to take on any army in the world. Despite these truths, it didn't seem like the Americans were winning.

His wounded ear wasn't healing well. A local doctor used mixtures of egg, oil, and rum to keep the wound clean, and Oliver repeatedly changed the bandage. A fever hit him hard at the beginning of November and lasted several weeks. The doctor moved him into his home where he and his wife cared for him. Lieutenant Charles Causey of Rhode Island took over the daily training of men. After a night of hallucinations and cold sweats, the fever broke, and within two days Oliver felt strong enough to continue his command.

He admitted later that he thought he was going to die and

thought of his mother dying from fever and of Clara's face as it might look upon hearing of his death. Oliver caught himself during these fleeting moments and forced himself to cease such morbidity. But they returned occasionally, sneaking up on him, until he was healed.

On December 1, 1780, Oliver's army connected with Greene and his growing force and went with him to Charlotte the next day. On December 3, Greene, who limped from a childhood accident, suffered from asthma, and bore a smallpox scar on his right eye, formally relieved the absent Gates and gathered the officers to discuss his unorthodox plan to divide his smaller army and force Cornwallis to split his larger one. But would he take the bait?

He did.

The British general sent Tarleton after Morgan while he pursued Greene. Greene sent part of his army to support Daniel Morgan, whom Oliver had served under at Saratoga, as he harassed the British on the western side of South Carolina all the way to Augusta.

Greene took the balance of his force through North Carolina, hoping Cornwallis would chase him and fight on Greene's terms. For this, he needed North Carolina reconnoitered up to Virginia. He also needed a supply route from Virginia and directed the Quartermaster, General Edward Carrington, to fulfill that task.

Turning to Oliver, the Major General asked if he wanted to be a part of the reconnoiter team or remain with his men and march with him. Oliver didn't hesitate. "Stay with my men, sir."

They marched north out of Charlotte five days before Christmas. Oliver and his men were sent to gather supplies, protect the local patriots, and harass the enemy at his rear when Cornwallis appeared. And he would.

Cornwallis and Tarleton chased their targets across North- and South Carolina for months, with only a few engagements occurring, one most notably being the whipping Tarleton took at the Battle of Cowpens.

Oliver returned with news about Cornwallis and joyfully reported to Greene. "General Greene, we have Cornwallis so frustrated from being unable to catch us that he has burned everything that slows them down."

Greene smiled slyly. "Really?"

"Indeed! Quite severely. He's torched tents, wagons, and anything else that was not related to fighting, just to speed up his army."

"Our plan is working. We got to his head. May a musket ball follow!"

Cornwallis wanted his men unhindered, carrying only ammunition, salt, and medical supplies. Greene understood what this meant, and knew they, too, would have to be quicker or would be gravely surprised and, possibly, destroyed. Still, after numerous skirmishes, Greene said to Oliver, "We fight, get beat, rise, and fight again." Oliver shared this with his men, and Greene, having dinner a quarter mile away, heard the shout of men in response and wondered what it was all about.

Another birthday had passed, as had the anniversary of his arrival in America. He was now twenty-one. Oliver had little time to reflect on these typically celebrated days but sneaked a peak at them from time to time. He wanted to avoid sentimentalism, believing it might make him weak in heart and mind and slow his vigorous march towards victory. Later. There'd be plenty of time to look back once the vision of America's revolution had been fulfilled. And to do it with Clara in his arms.

He'd turned out to be a handsome young man, though was still quite thin. He believed the *Scorpion* hindered his physical growth.

Many officers confided in each other over meals and on walks away from the men's concerns about the war. Was it slipping away, or were they winning? Was it going to be an endless mix of wins and losses? Would they ever win one of the bigger battles?

Atkinson wondered what General Washington was thinking. Certainly, he had a plan. Yet, Oliver's attention was squarely on General Greene's risky but ingenious strategy.

Greene's men didn't limp away but accomplished what they wanted: maximum damage to the enemy, and a draining of their resources, while drawing them further away from their supply lines emanating from Charleston.

"I can almost hear Cornwallis say to his staff," Greene offered at the end of a strategy meeting one morning, 'Just one more victory and the South is ours!'" Every eye was on him knowing he hadn't finished. "Fool's gold," he said confidently, causing the men to laugh and shout.

Greene learned that the Continentals were winning in South Carolina and Georgia. This news encouraged the men further as they crossed creeks and rivers while heading north to the Virginia line before pivoting back into North Carolina. It was unique warfare, combining a mix of Indian tactics and traditional European style fighting. Oliver had the highest respect for his commanding officer and understood Washington's preference for him.

Greene raced his army north at a speed that allowed Cornwallis to stay just close enough behind, offering only a few engagements, such as at Guilford Courthouse on March 15, 1781. After a ninety-minute battle, Greene's troops left the battlefield giving the British the win, but not before inflicting great damage to the Redcoats with little injury to his men.

Cornwallis desperately needed to resupply, so he led his men to Wilmington, North Carolina. Oliver thought about the Moore's and was certain they'd get out of harm's way. Greene let the British go. His men needed rest.

CHAPTER 43

YORKTOWN

Benedict Arnold had broken George Washington's heart. He had been conspiring with the British to hand over the fort to them at West Point in exchange for twenty-thousand British pounds and a commission in the British army. Arnold was a greedy glory hound who spent wildly and thought he was underappreciated by everyone he met. Oliver had been in a series of meetings with him and thought him to be disrespectful and borderline insubordinate. But Oliver believed him to be an excellent battlefield leader.

Washington had great fondness for him, but this was not enough for Arnold. He was fuming mad at Gates for discounting his heroic role at Saratoga. Gates had taken almost all the glory for himself, with barely a mention of Arnold in his report to Washington and Congress. It wasn't lost on Oliver that the two biggest egos in the military turned out to be the biggest cowards.

There came a point when Arnold saw an opportunity to get rich, get a commission, and earn a command worthy of his abilities. He needed to give the British a prize that would, above all, get him the money. The command ran a close second. Arnold had married Philadelphia socialite Peggy Shippen, whose tastes for the finer things exceeded Arnold's bank account. What's more, she was a loyalist.

Major John Andre of the British Army began to woo the American officer through Peggy. Andre was a friend of her family, and soon, serious discourses raised a plan to hand over West Point, located on the Hudson River. Whoever owned the fort owned the upper Hudson. It was perfectly situated to make sailing quickly by it nearly impossible. A curved channel demanded that ships slow down and offer an easy target for its cannon. The British had the Hudson to the south. If they had the fort, they would also own everything north to the Hudson Bay and be able to wreak havoc on American supply chains and troop movement. It was a golden prize, and Benedict thought it was worth twenty-thousand pounds.

The traitor learned that he'd been found out and fled West Point just as Washington was arriving. John Andre had been accosted by ruffian thieves who found a letter in his boot that told the tale of Arnold's defection. Andre was hanged, Arnold got away, and Washington was devastated. Nevertheless, the Americans held the fort through the war.

Now a Brigadier General, Benedict Arnold, was on the loose in Virginia with an army under his command. Having sailed up the James River, he attacked the unprotected state capital, Richmond, on January 5, 1781, chasing away Thomas Jefferson, who fled when his call for militia went mostly ignored by men who felt they had done their duty. Arnold razed the town, which infuriated General Washington.

Washington feared Arnold would run uncontested across Virginia and bolster Cornwallis' southern strategy. He commanded Major General Marquis de Lafayette, now twenty-three, to sail to Yorktown and begin a campaign to rid Virginia of the British. He thought Major Oliver Atkinson would be a good addition to his staff and summoned him.

Oliver arrived March 25 and re-introduced himself. He learned that Lafayette was low on provisions, and his army was depleted. Their task was big, but Oliver respected the Major General's confidence and positivity, which he in part must've learned from

General Washington, Oliver thought.

Because of the lack of supplies and men, Lafayette shared his strategy of hitting hard, moving fast, getting away, and preserving his resources. He wanted to be an annoyance and slowly cut away at the British numbers. Washington chose to send Oliver to him because of his experience in this radically new American form of warfare he executed under Marion and Greene.

The Frenchman's primary mission was to capture Benedict Arnold and hang him immediately. Washington even put a five-thousand guinea bounty on Arnold's head. But things went wrong quickly. The French Navy failed in its mission to dislodge the British Navy from the Chesapeake Bay, allowing easy resupply for British forces. Then the French ships scurried back to Rhode Island. Lafayette's French troops were stuck in Baltimore. Next, General Philips reinforced Arnold with an additional two thousand troops.

Lafayette got word that Cornwallis was on the march from Wilmington with his army of over seven-thousand troops and headed right at him. But before he could engage the British and capture Arnold, he was called back to New York.

Washington wanted to retake New York, while his French military advisors suggested trapping Cornwallis at Yorktown and forcing him to surrender. This was his best chance to end the war, they said. Knowing how tired of the war the British were at home, a major loss like this would create a political firestorm in London that would force their foes to sue for peace, they argued. The American general agreed that their recommendation made sense and was their last best chance at victory.

Washington and his army, including French soldiers under Rochambeau, marched south for fourteen weeks, arriving in Williamsburg, Virginia, on September 14. As Washington headed south, Arnold was headed north having been recalled to New York.

Oliver appeared at Washington's headquarters, where the general warmly greeted him.

"Please tell me you at least stopped by Mount Vernon for a day, sir?" Oliver asked Washington, noticing that he was now wearing a powdered white wig that barely masked the whitening of his natural hair. The once shallow pockmarks on his face had deepened. The general appeared ten years older than the last time he saw him. What hadn't changed was his commanding presence and the authoritative resolve in his voice.

Washington shook his head, "No," then said with a smile, "I was there for three days. I had to check on my wheat and roses."

Later at dinner, the general's executive staff, which included the newly-promoted Lieutenant Colonel Oliver Atkinson, was told by the group that French Commander Francois Joseph Paul de Grasse had sent the British fleet running back to New York and now owned Yorktown Harbor and the Chesapeake Bay. However, he refused to stay for long, wanting to get back to the Caribbean after hurricane season ended. Washington and his men would have to act quickly before their foes repopulated the harbor with ships. This victory by de Grasse also meant that Cornwallis was now landlocked and would not be resupplied or reinforced.

It was time to act.

The commander-in-chief explained his plan to gather supplies and as many men as they could, and to immediately begin building siege works. Oliver was directed to take a squadron and ride the perimeter of camp looking for holes in their lines as well as for any British movement. Plus, to help keep an eye on their flank.

With twenty-thousand soldiers, including seven-thousand-eight-hundred Frenchmen, Washington began his siege September 29. The Allied army drove Cornwallis back from his outer position deep into Yorktown. Still, the British kept up their bombing of the American siege lines that kept edging closer to them.

On October 2, Oliver saw movement to his right as he was about to turn back across the left side of the lines. He immediately recognized Banastre Tarleton was trying to flee. Oliver alerted Lauzun's Legion, a French unit, and John Mercer's Militia, who engaged them head on and drove them back to Yorktown.

By October 9, American and French cannon were in place, blasting Yorktown toward submission. Washington watched as building after building fell. The British army was being decimated. The French ships fired cannon balls as well. Oliver thought it was only a matter of time before Cornwallis capitulated and offered Washington his sword. But the proud British general resisted.

On October 11, the siege line was moved four-hundred yards closer, but redoubt No. 9 and No. 10 prevented the American troops from encircling all British positions. They were the last true British fortifications before the city line of Yorktown.

Day after day, Oliver and his men would recon the area and report their findings back to Washington.

A moonless night on October 14, due to thick passing clouds hovering over the little peninsula, gave Washington and his army added cover for the attacks of redoubts No. 9 and No. 10. Vanquishing them would most likely give immediate victory to the allied forces. Cornwallis would be left with no hope.

Washington ordered all batteries within range to begin firing on them to soften them for the night's assault. The French were going to move on British and German forces at redoubt No. 9, while Alexander Hamilton was to lead a strike at No. 10. Intel showed that there were swampy mud moats around these positions, and that they were fortified with abatis, which were sharpened trees pointed outwards towards any attackers as an obstruction, making the climb into these strongholds extremely difficult and hazardous.

Boldly, Oliver requested that he be able to participate in the attack with Hamilton's light infantry. Washington initially thought his service on the periphery that night would be more valuable. It was supposed to evoke either a desperate response from Cornwallis, or, most likely, force him to surrender. "I prefer you watching our flank."

"Sir, permission to speak," Oliver respectfully requested. Washington turned back to him and gazed at the young officer for a minute before speaking.

"Frankly, Lieutenant Colonel Atkinson, I think you've earned the right to choose for yourself. I'll let Hamilton know you'll be joining him for the raid tonight."

Oliver saluted, struggling to contain an ear-to-ear smile, and said, "Thank you, General."

Hamilton's party gathered around 6:30 p.m. just as a diversionary attack was under way. Giving them directions, he ordered his men not to load their guns until right upon the redoubts, and to fix bayonets for "the fight of a lifetime." Explaining the ground conditions around their target, he chose half of his men to prepare to wield their axes on the abatis formations. Hamilton could see in the men's faces that they knew this was their chance to end the war and gain independence, go home to their families, and begin the next stages of building this new nation.

While waiting to move out, someone bumped Oliver on his right side. Oliver turned to see Sergeant Joseph Plumb Martin grinning at him. Martin said, "You keep following me all over America. What do I have to do to lose you once and for all?" They shared a laugh.

"You don't make enough to get rid of me," Oliver playfully said.

"What pay?" the man from Milford asked.

"Exactly," Oliver grinned.

"Move out! Absolute silence!" Hamilton ordered.

At the hour when darkness pushes down the receding sun, Hamilton's men moved forward, crouched to minimize their silhouettes against the deep purplish sky, nearly holding their breath in case their thundering hearts could be heard.

Some of the American force covertly moved to the rear of redoubt No. 10 to prevent the British from escaping. Sergeant Martin moved forward on the soft, damp ground next to his friend Lieutenant Colonel Oliver Atkinson in the main assault force. The cannon had stopped, but they heard the diversion in effect some distance away. Their eyes darted about them, expecting an attack.

Suddenly, the explosive sounds of six successive cannons burst behind them, sending cannon balls screaming overhead at the British stronghold. Bloody screams erupted.

A group of "sappers," whose job it was to remove any impediments in the way of the attack, took out their axes and tore through the abatis to make holes for the Americans to advance through. They next began pulling down the long line of sharply shaved timber abreast at the far incline to the redoubt.

Only British soldiers could stop the men now.

In the remaining moments of light, the Americans crossed through the water-logged slop of the man-made ravine between them and the small fortress. Trudging through the swampy mess, feeling as if he might lose his shoes in the mud, Oliver, with a fixed bayonet, silently began his charge up the slope through a breach the sappers had created.

Oliver wondered why they hadn't been spotted. Before he could finish the thought, a British sentry fired upon them and sounded the alarm.

The battle was on as gunfire rained down upon the Americans.

The common shrieks of the battle-wounded and dying replaced the cannon blasts. The night was mottled with bursts of ignited powder, appearing like a swarm of crazed fireflies, exposing thick sulfur smoke that burned the eyes of the advancing men.

Oliver's pulsing heart drove his legs up the slope where he was met at the top by a Regular who pointed his gun in Atkinson's direction. Without hesitation, the young man from Derby thrust his blade through the man's heart. Instinctively, his head swiveled as he looked for his next target.

Turning to his left he saw a Regular aiming his weapon at him from ten feet. Atkinson rushed him with his bayonet extended, screaming madly before tripping over a body just as the weapon was fired, the lead ball just missing him. Jumping to his feet, he leapt upon the Regular as he was attempting to reload. Knocking his gun away, he pinned the man down on the dirt, and just as he was about to ram his blade into the man's neck, he froze. Looking back at him with terror and rage was a familiar face.

It was his cousin.

All at once, the battle stood still, instantly quiet. Blood rushed to Oliver's head, and he felt as if he might pass out.

His cousin head-butted him, knocking him back to reality and off of him. As the patriot shook his head, he saw his cousin lift up Mrs. Belle with the butt in the air and blade point down over his chest. As he brought it down, Oliver rolled to his side, the blade striking deep into the dirt. As the cousin pulled the blade from the ground, Oliver kicked out his legs, sending him toppling to the ground, allowing Oliver to once again pounce on him, this time without pause. Taking a knife from his belt, he rammed it into the side of his cousin's neck, his dying eyes pleading for mercy, twisting like he was opening a difficult bottle top, until the body went limp.

Using his rifle as a crutch, he quickly lifted himself to his feet. While looking for his next engagement, he felt a thud in his left breast that knocked him back into a cannon-caused crater, dropping his rifle as he fell. The guilty Regular charged him. Oliver saw fury on his face as he raised his bayonet to strike. Oliver tried lifting his hands to defend himself but was unable as the bloody blade came straight for his abdomen.

Lieutenant Colonel Atkinson closed his eyes when he felt the worst pain he could ever fathom flashed like lightning through his left leg. He opened his eyes in response to see the Regular who bayoneted him fall dead with Sergeant Martin standing over him, breathing heavily, the dead man's blood dripping from his blade.

"I'll be back, Oliver," he said, eschewing military protocol by addressing him by his first name. He turned and re-engaged the enemy. Within a few minutes, the battle was over, the redoubt secured.

Oliver was moved to the medical station. It was determined that he had taken two musket balls, not one. The doctor guessed they had arrived at his chest almost simultaneously. The blade had torn up his left thigh. A delirious Oliver was in so much pain he couldn't think.

Sergeant Martin entered the tent with General Washington, who was there to see the wounded. Martin knelt at Oliver's cot and told him he was a hero, that the first soldier he killed was aiming at him.

Washington noticed Oliver, and called for the doctor, who explained the Lieutenant Colonel's condition. The general called for his personal surgeon to operate. Within three minutes, surgeon James Craik was operating on Oliver after dosing him with opium. Opening him up, he took his ball remover and easily extracted the first musket ball. As he did this, another doctor put bandages on the wound to prevent flies and dirt from getting into its opening. This puncture would be addressed once the second ball was removed. But there seemed to be a complication. Dr. Craik rapidly shook his head in small movements, his left hand on his head as if solving a difficult puzzle.

Martin, who was watching, asked what the problem was.

"It appears the second ball is resting on the subclavian artery. If I nick it while trying to remove the ball, he will bleed to death." He held his ball remover up against the light of a whale oil lamp and examined it as if looking for defects, then placed it on a bandage at the bedside table. "I need to make an incision into the muscle around the ball first.

Taking a small scalpel, he asked the assisting doctor to hold open the wound with his fingers and motioned for Martin to give him light from his lantern. He cut a small incision in the muscle around the artery, which gave him access to safely remove the second musket ball. They then cleaned up the wound in Oliver's leg and bandaged it.

"He's going to be fine," Washington's surgeon assured Martin and those in attendance.

The first doctor administered additional doses of opium to Oliver until he finally fell asleep about 3 a.m.

The opium haze lasted three days after surgery, but as one of the attending doctors was about to give him another dose the morning of October 18, he declined its administration. He hated how he felt on opium and convinced the doctor that he would endure the pain naturally if there weren't any other options. The doctor offered some alcohol. Hating the taste of alcohol, he opted for camphor, but it did little to stem the continuous pain. He endured as much as he could, but when it got severe, he would agree to low doses of opium. He'd heard of its addictiveness and wanted to avoid that.

More than the pain, though, he and the doctors were concerned about possible infections, so Oliver submitted to whatever curatives, ointments, or preventions they suggested. So far, his wounds were stable.

Distractions from his pain included ongoing thoughts of Clara and the dreams he had for them. General Washington and Sergeant Martin visited him daily, which provided temporary relief and lifted his spirits.

"How are you feeling, Oliver?" General Washington asked one day.

"Other than the never-ending excruciating pain, I'm ready," he said smiling, "to return a few books I borrowed from the professor in Derby." Washington and Martin looked at each, then back at Oliver. "I won't be long."

Motioning to a doctor as he departed the tent, Washington advised him to better regulate the dosages of opium being given to his prized patient.

Hamilton came once, as did a few of the men under his command.

In lucid moments, he wondered what was to happen to him. Would his wounds prevent him from working and having a normal life? Where would he go, and how long would it take for him to recover?

And he thought about Clara. How would Clara receive the news of his injuries? In all his letters to her, he never spoke of the horrors of war, but mainly he assured her that he was fine, though he had told her after Camden that the top of his ear had been shot off, "though I'll still be able to hear you say just how wildly in love with me you are." How would she take this news of more serious wounds? For now, he would wait to write to her until he was given new orders.

Throughout the preceding few days, Oliver was surprised to hear continued sounds of war. Cannon belched in the distance, guns barking madly, and groans, cries, and screams of wounded men who had been brought to the medical tent for surgery, for care, and to die.

But this morning, after rejecting the doctor's dose of opium, he heard the sharp beats of a distant drum signifying a truce. He knew it came from the British. Minutes later, Sergeant Martin ran into the tent to Oliver's side and let everyone know that a white flag had been raised, and the British officer was blindfolded and being led behind the lines to begin negotiations.

"It's over, Oliver. It's over!" he said excitedly, before pausing and calmly asking if he was well. Oliver nodded. "I'll be back when I hear more, my friend."

Later, Oliver learned that General Washington refused Britain's first request to be allowed to surrender with traditional honors based on Cornwallis' treatment of the surrendering American Army at Charleston. Cornwallis finally agreed to Washington's terms, and on October 19, 1781, the British formally surrendered. However, as Oliver later learned, Cornwallis professed illness and refused to attend the ceremony, sending Brigadier General Charles O'Hare in his place. Washington refused to take Cornwallis' sword, but instead directed it be given to General Lincoln, the offended officer at Charleston.

The Americans captured more than eight-thousand men, thousands of guns, hundreds of pieces of artillery, and twenty-four ships, in addition to wagons, horses, and assorted supplies.

Later that day, General Washington entered the tent where the wounded and dying lay, and spoke individually to each man, kneeling with them, and praying when asked. Finally coming to Oliver, he asked how he was mending.

Smiling, Oliver said, "Well, I assure you I don't have any more books to return!" They laughed quietly. Joseph kept ribbing Oliver about that story, and he didn't mind. "My recovery, I am told, will take some time. But I won't be losing any body parts, which is a good thing."

"Yes, recovery, Lieutenant Colonel Atkinson. I was thinking

how best I could facilitate your recovery seeing that the war is basically over for you. Transferring you to Clara in Massachusetts might not be the greatest idea with your wounds, and I don't think Mrs. Washington would look kindly on me knowing I had the power to get you two back together but did not exercise it." Oliver looked confused. Pausing, the general looked around and continued, "Mount Vernon is a short sail away from here. You and Clara will be our guests until such a time as you are able to resume a normal life." He paused again, looking for a reaction.

His eyes wide, he smiled through his haze, and asked, "Am I hallucinating again?" The general shook his head. "How will Clara be notified?"

"When I left New York for Yorktown, Martha sent for Clara and asked if she'd join her at Mount Vernon. I can't imagine she'd turn down that opportunity, can you?" he smiled.

"Yet another reason why you are the Commander-in-Chief, sir," Oliver beamed.

CHAPTER 44

THE MOUNT VERNON REUNION

The doctor gave Oliver permission to leave the battlefield hospital and head for Mount Vernon. The general arranged for a sloop to carry Oliver and some of the general's things to his home in Northern Virginia. The passage would be much quicker than rough overland travel, minimizing the discomfort of his healing wounds.

A cart was sent for Oliver to take him down to the dock early the next morning, but he asked for some crutches so he could walk nobly to the boat. After about ten steps, he felt his pride in the form of great pain in his leg and beckoned for the cart to return.

With help from the two sailors assigned to guide the boat north, and an attending physician, Oliver boarded and was then directed to a comfortable cot-like bed in the stern. Because the fall weather was unusually cool, Oliver covered himself with thick wool blankets. Once they got underway and entered Chesapeake Bay, his chattering teeth prompted one of the sailors to get him a third blanket.

The water was somewhat choppy for most of the trip, winds dueling back and forth across the boat. The sailors were kind to Oliver, and made sure he remained comfortable, watered, and fed. The doctor changed his bandages. After all, he was a guest of General Washington.

At Mount Vernon's landing, the sailors easily moored the vessel and helped Oliver disembark after one of Washington's slaves brought a cart for the guest. Moments later, Diggs joined them and gruffly greeted Oliver, much like he did the first time.

The slave, whose name was Ezekiel, rolled Oliver's cart as gently as he could across the manicured lawns towards a quaint little cottage used for guests of the Washington's.

"How's da general, sir?" Ezekiel asked.

"Quite well. We beat the British at Yorktown. The war is nearing its end."

"Oh, good, that's so good. We not see him much these years. Good man, he is," the slave joyfully projected.

Arriving at the door, Ezekiel stopped pushing the cart, put it down on its two legs, and said to Oliver, "Just a second, Mr. Oliver." He knocked on the door, and it swung wide open, as if being pulled off its hinges. Clara excitedly emerged, bursting into joyful tears as she hugged a shocked Oliver, who tried rising from the wagon until pain ricocheted throughout his body.

Slumping back down, he held her and whispered, "Gently, my love. My chest stopped two musket balls recently."

Ezekiel and Diggs helped him into the cottage. Once what little property came with him was unloaded, the two men left, leaving the two newlyweds alone. "I could use a warm sponge bath, my love," he said with a wink.

"Anything for you. Oh, honey, I've prayed non-stop for you that God would have mercy on you and spare me from such grievous pain. And he did." She leaned into him, and they kissed with a slow passion they'd not done before. As Oliver healed, they would learn more about each other in this honored, sanctified way.

An hour later, Martha Washington arrived to say hello and to see if they needed anything. With her was a young female slave with biscuits and jam. They were appreciative but declined her generosity for the time being. "As soon as you are able, Oliver, I expect you at my dinner table. I promise you it will be just a step above battlefield chow," she said laughing before exiting.

The next day, a doctor from Alexandria, Virginia, eight miles north of Washington's estate, arrived to tend to Oliver's wounds. He was happy with his progress and saw no signs of infection. "I'll be back every few days to look in on you. If you need me beforehand, send someone to get me. In the meantime, rest and use your leg as little as possible for the next few weeks."

The doctor estimated that Oliver's downtime would be about three months. This gave him time to write to his friends the Reveres, the Adamses, Hancock, Peter—hoping someone would read it to him, and Clara's mother to see how she was doing with the new help, and a few others he had met along the way. Oliver hoped his letters would be answered before he left Mount Vernon for who knows where, which is what led him and Clara to the second thing.

"You mentioned Wilmington, North Carolina, to me in a few letters, saying it was the loveliest place you'd ever been, and that the Lord was calling us there," Clara said. "My heart is in Massachusetts, though, probably because that's all I've known. And who wouldn't love to live here in Virginia!"

"When I'm able to travel, I want to take you to Wilmington. If you absolutely can't stand it, we will move to wherever you want to go," he offered.

"Meaning you'd have to change the Lord's mind," she said, laughing. "I wasn't aware your persuasive powers were so great, my dear husband."

"I got you, didn't I?" They both laughed.

"You were easy," Clara teased. "I knew I had your heart from that first time I saw you as I passed by in that carriage." She approached him and softly stroked his hair.

Gently taking her hand, he brought her in for a kiss. "Now, about Wilmington."

EPILOGUE

While the war continued until September 1783, it was over for Oliver and Clara. Though fully recovered, Oliver would spend the rest of his life with a slight limp, which he called his "final gift" from the British.

The Atkinsons remained guests of the Washingtons until the spring of 1781. With the help of Diggs and Ezekiel, they loaded up a carriage gifted to them by the general and his wife and headed south to Wilmington to a plot of land on the Cape Fear River gifted to them by the Moore's, who both had passed away in 1777, but had a lawyer hold the land in trust in case Oliver came to claim it.

Before leaving Mount Vernon, Oliver petitioned the Continental Congress for back pay—he had not received any compensation during the entire war. John Adams was horrified at this and gave him his entire wage at the rate of a Lieutenant Colonel. He figured he'd earned it, and it would've been too complicated to go back and figure out how much he was owed at each rank and for how long. Plus, the Congress was about to dissolve anyway.

The Atkinsons used this money to build their home and start a printing business, exactly like the shop he helped run for Paul Revere. Stationery, wedding invitations, poetry books, and finally a newspaper, *The Wilmington Examiner*. At first it was a monthly but quickly grew to a weekly. News from Hanover to Brunswick, and Pender to Onslow counties fed him stories, while businesses bought ads, and readers enjoyed the local gossip and occasional "news from afar."

Over the next decade, Clara miscarried three times. She thought she had offended God in some way, until Rev. Thomas Blanchard of St. James Episcopal Church, along with his wife, Grace, ministered to her with scripture, prayer, and provided general comfort. Shortly thereafter, she became pregnant again.

Returning home from the print shop one afternoon in 1791, Oliver received a message from President Washington. He was to pass through Wilmington as he toured the south and was hoping to stay with him for a night. Of course! It was the biggest celebration the town had ever thrown. Citizens, dignitaries, and elected officials lined the street that led to Oliver's and Clara's home. Children ran alongside his horse, Prescott, and men and women stood in awe. After dinner, the president and Oliver went for a walk where he was asked to join Washington's administration. Later, Adams and Jefferson did as well. Madison finally got the message.

"I hate politics. I have since Philadelphia."

Washington roared with laughter and agreed it was a necessary evil meant only for a few.

Saying goodbye for what they knew was the last time, the two men embraced and wished each other Godspeed.

After Washington left the next morning, Oliver saddled up a horse and rode out to the ocean, something he told himself he didn't do enough of. Same with horseback riding. It just wasn't the same for him after the thousands of miles he logged with the Sons of Liberty and Continental Army.

He returned from his ride to find a healthy baby boy in the arms of their house manager, Mama Megs, but the mood was not celebratory. Clara had died while giving birth. He wept uncontrollably while holding his boy, who he named, George

Revere Cole Atkinson, grieving deeply that he hadn't had the opportunity to be there with his wife. Some ladies came from church to feed and clean the boy. This they did until George was five.

Oliver never saw another woman romantically again. He had no interest. He poured himself into his work, which had now expanded to an import-export operation extending from Savannah to Boston with contacts he'd made in the army. It wasn't about greed, but it was about money. He began secretly buying slaves and emancipating them, giving them a choice to work for him or leave. Most went north.

In 1807, after seeing George off to the University of North Carolina's law school, it suddenly struck him that he had the power to emancipate Peter also. He didn't know whether he was alive or not, but he kicked himself for having been so forgetful. He blamed it on his premature white hair–what was left of it and immediately made plans to go to Philadelphia.

Two months later he was standing before Peter's new owner, a man he immediately despised, and negotiated both his and Maggie's freedom, along with their two children. He paid twice the market rate and would've paid more. It was a glorious reunion that didn't stop. They moved into a cottage on his property about one hundred yards away that had a glorious view of the river, and they began working as paid employees taking care of his home and property.

Joy had been fleeting once Clara passed. Reuniting with Peter changed that.

His son George opened a law practice and served one term in Congress before deciding he also hated politics. He and his wife would bring over their five grandchildren to see grandpa regularly.

By 1812, things intentionally slowed down for Oliver. His businesses ran themselves and were quite successful. His presence was only needed for occasional matters that popped up. He didn't have any earthly needs. Occasionally, he'd visit the Thalian Association to see a theater production, go to church socials, or take rides into the country. He had his books but decided one day that he would build Wilmington a library and donate every book he had to it, plus order more to make sure the variety was robust.

But he was bored.

As he sat on his porch waving at neighbors on their evening stroll, he thought about embarking on one more adventure before he expired. He recalled the stories of his youth that inspired adventure in his young heart, and suddenly that child was begging for another go.

That opportunity came in March 1815.

President James Madison summoned Oliver to Alexandria, Virginia, where he and his wife Dolly were living while the White House was being restored after getting torched by the British during the War of 1812. The invitation promised he would not be asked to take a job requiring him to move to Washington. His son George should come as well.

A month later, he and George sat before the fourth president of the United States.

Leaning over, he extended a sealed envelope to Oliver, who took it. "This letter is to King George. It will be an introduction to some ideas that I have that I believe both nations should explore. It is like an amendment to the Treaty of Ghent. We have not had a diplomatic presence in England since Jonathan Russell suspended his functions as Chargé d'Affaires there in 1812."

"Are you asking me to move back to England, Mr. President?"

"No. But have you ever thought about returning?"

"There's nothing there for me," Oliver responded coolly.

"Truthfully, I think there is. Your adventure is to find out what it is."

"Adventure! How did he know?" Oliver rose and paced for a minute, his face revealing his anxiety. He looked at his son and said, "Well?"

"This is quite an honor father. I think the President is right. I'll manage things until you return."

Madison spoke up, "I was thinking you should accompany him."

Three months later the grand Port of London was in sight. He had to remind himself to keep breathing. They were met by a delegation from the King's Court, including his personal secretary, a Mr. John Barrymore, and toured London in the most elegant and comfortable carriage either had been in.

The next morning, they were taken to Buckingham Palace, being sternly warned that they had five minutes and no more with King George. When they arrived at his door, they heard a man scolding a child for not eating all their peas. A firm knock on the door quieted the voice down.

Receiving them, King George asked about their lives, and Oliver shared his story, frequently pausing being mindful of the time limit he was given—the King would keep commanding him to "Carry on! Continue." Starting from his days in Derby to the present, in as few words as possible, skirting past the Revolution, for the most part, he apparently entertained King George with his narrative.

"You knew Effringham? Legendary parties!"

After thirty minutes, a frustrated secretary finally shut things down, reminding the King he had two lords waiting for him. "Mad" King George directed him to take Oliver and his son to Derby to see his old home. Once they left the room, the scolding of the imaginary child continued.

He learned the home he had with his parents was gutted in a fire, so they went to his uncle's home. From the outside, the dwelling looked like it hadn't been lived in for years. When knocking on the front door, it seemingly opened of its own volition. Oliver and George entered. It was eerily uncomfortable. No one responded to his calls. There was an inch of dust on everything.

Oliver slowly walked up the creaky stairs to his bedroom. The bed was in the same place. It suddenly dawned on him to see if the laths in the wall he'd hidden books in still had something. A longshot, for certain, but when he gingerly pulled back the frail wood it shredded in his hand. Perched before him was the Bible the vicar had given him the day of his mother's burial. Pulling it from the wall he saw it was quite aged but in readable condition. Clutching it, he fell to the bed and wept until it hurt. Kneeling at his side, George stroked his back.

Finally, Oliver held the Bible up and said, "Providence."

He read that Bible in the morning and evening right before supper every day for the next ten years. He loved catching the last day's light on its pages that helped his fading sight.

One morning after the grandkids left, Maggie fixed him some warm apple cider as fall had subsumed summer. He mentioned that he was feeling especially tired that morning and went to lie down. Putting on his spectacles, he began reading Revelation twenty-one in his old Bible, and before he finished, a glorious light of warm love enveloped him, sending him on to his greatest adventure.

POSTSCRIPT

EFFRINGHAM

Shortly after General Greene arrived to take command from Horatio Gates, a messenger from General Washington arrived. The dispatches included orders for Oliver to leave at once for Virginia to support Lafayette, Washington's protégé.

Oliver had met Lafayette earlier in the war. He was not liked by most of the other officers due to his privileged upbringing. They believed he bought his way into the army, and most definitely bought his rank as a general. It mattered none to Oliver. He was pleased with any help they could get. Funds were low for supplies and ammunition and he had money.

One day in 1780, Oliver received a parcel from Lafayette containing twenty pounds sterling in a leather pouch. The Frenchman knew American money was worthless, and that the colonials wouldn't trade for francs, so he smuggled in thousands of British pounds to purchase what the army needed. The funds at first surprised Oliver until he remembered that Lafayette was paying off a debt he owed him.

Two years earlier at Valley Forge as Oliver was trying to nap, someone was running through the camp yelling in French, "Normandie! Normandie!" Oliver knew this was the name of Lafayette's horse. Exiting his quarters, he heard the Frenchman offer twenty pounds to the person who found his horse.

Still having not received a penny from Congress, Oliver

mounted his horse before the rest and raced through camp. Acting on a hunch, he galloped two miles away to a private horse farm. It was peak breeding season. He was there in minutes, and he saw Normandy had leapt a fence and was chasing down a mare. Oliver waited a few minutes until Normandy found a willing mare, and he then was able to get a bridle on him and lead a frustrated horse back to the grateful Lafayette.

"My horse is quite French," Lafayette quipped.

Bobbing the sack of money in his hands, Oliver knew immediately what he was going to do with the twenty pounds. He sealed the coins with a note in what he hoped was in an indestructible package and mailed it to Baron Effringham in England.

Effringham. Perhaps he would see him again one day and they would laugh over their shared experience? Probably not. Frankly, he didn't want to see the Baron, and he was certain it was mutual. He'd embarrassed his former master by ruining a business deal, to the extent Oliver could not have guessed as it set off a chain-reaction of poor decisions that would ultimately leave him penniless within five years.

With his estate gone, his London home acquired by another for one-tenth of its worth, and his business empire insolvent, Baron Effringham would finish his years in modest comfort with the help of some aristocratic friends who felt compassion for him. Invitations to London's parties, balls, and public spectacles had stopped.

He ended up retired to an estate in the north of England about thirty miles west of Newcastle near a town called Carlisle, just south of Hadrian's Wall. He hated the weather, but he hated poverty more. It was his only option.

Over the years he would occasionally wonder what happened to Young Atkinson. Consumed with bitterness towards those who had bested him in any way, he oddly found himself reminiscing warmly about this unique young man that helped bring about his ruin.

Apparently, he didn't lead a rebellion in England like he feared. He didn't affect England's political climate. However, he learned from a friend of a source that the boy had made it to America and was a minor figure in the American War for Independence. Perhaps he had an effect on England after all.

The disgraced Baron's mind became so forgetful that by 1780 he was barely able to recognize the friends supporting him. One day, a package arrived at the Carlisle property addressed to him. It was from the Americas and did not have a return address.

A servant brought him tea on the front porch where he enjoyed watching the sun set in the evening. Struggling to open the box, the patient servant stood by and asked if he wanted assistance? Then without waiting for an answer, grabbed the package and easily untied the hemp string that secured it, broke open the top flap that was folded over one underneath, secured by a strong adhesive.

"Well, what is it? Come on now!" Effringham said excitedly.

The servant pulled out a yellow flag with a coiled snake rising with its mouth open and tongue out as if ready to strike. There were words underneath the snake.

"Don't tread on me," said the dutiful helper.

"Don't tread on me?" Baron sat back wondering what it meant.

The servant pulled a leather pouch out of the box that had a note attached to it. Holding it up, he asked the Baron if he wanted him to read the note.

"Yes, yes, of course, Go ahead!" said the decrepit noble pauper.

Clearing his voice, the servant held up the note to catch the last rays of sun beaming from the west on the parchment, and read,

"Dear Baron Effringham, I sincerely hope this letter finds you prospering and in good health. My name is Oliver Atkinson…"

The Baron's eyes lit up with slight recognition. "Oliver

Atkinson," he wondered aloud. His eyes then drifted back to the reader.

The helper continued.

"You may recall that I fled from your estate seven years ago. My uncle from Derby gave me to you in payment for a debt he owed you but could not pay. You would allow me into your library..."

"Young Atkinson!" the Baron blurted out with glee as he shot up out of his chair with the first vigor he'd shown in a year. "Yes, yes, I know you! Yes! Go on. Is that it?"

The surprised servant cleared his throat and continued reading.

"Thank you for exposing me to many great books."

"Young Atkinson!" Effringham said gleefully.

"I was forced to pay a debt I did not owe, allowable only in a corrupt legal and social system that has been England for as long as I understand. I escaped to America, the new nation your King is at war with, and have joined them in their fight for liberty. Still, I have decided to send you ten pounds to pay back the debt my uncle owed you, and an additional ten pounds for interest at the loss of my service. I hope this settles the matter between us."

The servant opened the pouch and took out twenty pounds and handed them to the Baron, whose eyes grew wide at seeing more money than he had since he went broke. The aging man thumped down in his chair just looking at the money in disbelief.

"Should I finish reading to you the letter, Baron?" asked the servant.

A moment passed before he answered, "Yes."

"May God bless you for the rest of your days. Sincerely, Oliver Atkinson. American."

Looking up, the Baron asked him to hold the flag up again.

"Don't tread on me."

"Indeed," Effringham said as he eyed the rising coiled snake,

"Yes, yes, I do remember you, Oliver Atkinson." A slight smile curled his outer lips. "The matter between us is now settled."

AUTHOR'S NOTE

Our nation is celebrating America 250 in 2026. We made it! 250 years, and the great experiment continues. What a history it's been! And this glorious anniversary inspired me to tell the story of our founding through the eyes of an indentured orphan from England who became a stowaway on a ship bound for America in 1773. He, too, was looking for freedom, to have an opportunity to break free from social, economic, and political constraints that told him he was little more than a servant of the powerful without hope in becoming everything God had created him to be. His story is America's story, and it's still being authored today.

My family's North American roots began with the Mayflower's arrival in Provincetown Harbor, Cape Cod, Massachusetts, in 1620. I am a direct descendant of William Bradford. The risk these Pilgrims took in the pursuit of freedom is indelible in the spirit of all Americans, whether they came before or after these brave souls. Oliver has a similar story. My grandfather Berton Robbins was president of the Mayflower Society. My mother was active in both the Mount Vernon Women's Club and the Daughters of the American Revolution.

Additionally, my father's ancestors took up arms for the Revolution in North Carolina. I am proud of our service to our founding.

There is something ingrained in the soul of every living person that cries out for freedom, whether it be financial, political, or spiritual. The nation that has manifested this like no other is the

United States of America. We are not a perfect union, but a more perfect union, one that was born with language in its most sacred political and social contracts that has the ability to self-correct, heal, and thrive.

There are times when I wonder if I have appreciated this freedom as much as I should, as much as this nation deserves. There are times when I have been angered, even disgusted, with what has occurred at the hands of this nation. Overall, I am proud of this country, which has shown respect for our Creator and, in return, received remarkable mercy and blessings throughout its history. And we've not kept this blessing to ourselves, but have been the most generous nation on earth, providing financial aid to poor nations, spending our blood on battlefields to assure world peace, or in the sending of missionaries to bring the only gospel that provides eternal freedom.

In this book, you'll be introduced to a couple of my direct descendants, such as Ethan Allen and Charles Carroll of Carrollton, who signed the Declaration of Independence. The name Carroll is still in our family today. My mother carried it as does a niece. Actually, its origins trace back centuries before Charles, and I expect it will persist for many more centuries to come. At least, I hope so.

My family history includes railroad barons, copper, gold, and silver mine owners, a senator, movers and shakers in film and television, Navy admirals, captains, commanders and enlistees, a couple of marines, an assistant to two presidents, professors, historians, real estate agents, sportswriters, authors, a groundbreaking woman photographer, members of all classes, proudly including southern sharecroppers and public bathroom attendants. We've all been volunteers in our communities, churches, and schools. We've loved America, and America has loved us back.

By the time I was thirteen, I had read nearly every book in my parents' expansive library, yet I was not a resolute scholastic student. Their histories, biographies, and cold war novels allowed me to live in worlds that excited me and stirred my imagination. For some reason, I was more drawn to the past than the present and future, and I found a home in the lives and histories of yesterday. It also helped that my father, Wilbur D. Jones, Jr., shared his love of history with me from an early age. He earned a B.A. in History from the University of North Carolina, and I the same from Indiana University. My father has authored or co-authored over twenty books. This is my first.

My mother's father was the XO on the ship *The Shaw* when it was bombed at Pearl Harbor–my mother, her brother and mom had just arrived two weeks earlier and witnessed the entire attack. My grandfather was later wounded at Iwo Jima and was awarded the Navy Cross. My family seems to have been on scene during key moments of our nation's history.

I wrote "Oliver" for numerous reasons, but primarily for two: history is exciting when written properly (and I hope I've accomplished this to your liking), and I wanted all ages to be drawn into the amazing story of our founding; and, to remind us all of how and why this nation was born, and to recapture the American spirit during our 250th anniversary and beyond that we may fulfill the destiny God has for us, to remain a beacon of freedom to the world.

To learn more please visit my website and YouTube Channel:
    www.davidjones3.com
    Oliver's History Project @ Oliver's History Project

CAST OF CHARACTERS

John Adams (October 30, 1735-July 4, 1826)
A fierce advocate for independence, Adams played a central role in diplomacy and the Continental Congress. He later secured crucial alliances and helped define American republican government.

Abigail Adams (November 22, 1744-October 28, 1818)
An influential correspondent and advocate for women's rights, Abigail shaped political thought behind the scenes. Her letters provide critical insight into revolutionary ideals. Wife of John Adams.

Samuel Adams (September 27, 1722-October 2, 1803)
A master organizer and propagandist, Adams mobilized popular resistance to British rule. His activism helped turn political dissent into a mass revolutionary movement. Cousin of John Adams.

Benedict Arnold (January 14, 1741-June 14, 1801)
Once a brilliant and courageous American general, Arnold was instrumental in early victories such as Saratoga. His later betrayal became a lasting symbol of treason and the moral stakes of the Revolution.

Crispus Attucks (c. 1723-March 5, 1770)
Killed in the Boston Massacre, Attucks became the Revolution's first martyr. His death symbolized British oppression and fueled colonial outrage; he was of Black and Wampanoag heritage.

Daniel Boone (November 2, 1734-September 26, 1820)
A legendary explorer, Boone helped open western lands during and after the Revolution. His life embodied American expansion and frontier independence.

Charles Carroll (September 19, 1737-November 14, 1832)
The only Catholic signer of the Declaration, Carroll represented religious liberty in the founding. His wealth and influence strengthened revolutionary legitimacy.

Thomas Clinton (March 9, 1730-July 23, 1795)
British commander-in-chief after Howe, Clinton struggled to control the colonies. His divided strategy weakened British efforts.

Charles Cornwallis (December 31, 1738-October 5, 1805)
Britain's leading field commander in the later war, Cornwallis surrendered at Yorktown. His defeat effectively ended British hopes of victory.

Thomas Cushing (March 24, 1725-February 28, 1788)
A leading Massachusetts politician, Cushing opposed British taxation while maintaining legislative legitimacy. He helped bridge radical resistance and formal governance.

William Franklin (c. 1731-November 17, 1813)
Son of Benjamin Franklin, William remained loyal to Britain. His choice illustrates the Revolution's deep personal and political divisions.

Benjamin Franklin (January 17, 1706-April 17, 1790)
A renowned scientist and statesman, Franklin secured the vital French alliance. His diplomacy turned the Revolution into an international war Britain could not win.

George III (June 4, 1738-January 29, 1820)
King of Great Britain during the Revolution, George III represented imperial authority. His refusal to address colonial grievances hardened the push for independence.

Francis Marion (c. 1732-February 27, 1795)
Known as the "Swamp Fox," Marion pioneered guerrilla warfare in the South. His tactics disrupted British supply lines and control.

Thomas Gage (1718-April 2, 1787)
As military governor of Massachusetts, Gage attempted to suppress rebellion. His failures helped ignite open war.

Horatio Gates (July 26, 1727-April 10, 1806)
Commander at Saratoga, Gates oversaw the pivotal American victory that convinced France to intervene. Though controversial, his success altered the war's trajectory.

Nathanael Greene (August 7, 1742-June 19, 1786)
Washington's most gifted strategist, Greene broke British control of the South through maneuver warfare rather than decisive battles. His campaigns exhausted British forces and made ultimate victory possible.

John Hancock (January 23, 1737-October 8, 1793)
A wealthy merchant and president of the Continental Congress, Hancock became the Revolution's most visible civilian leader. His bold signature symbolized defiance of British authority.

Patrick Henry (May 29, 1736-June 6, 1799)
A powerful orator, Henry galvanized resistance with uncompromising rhetoric. He framed liberty as worth any cost.

William Howe (August 10, 1729-July 12, 1814)

British commander early in the war, Howe failed to decisively crush the rebellion. His caution allowed the Revolution to survive.

Isaac Huger (March 19, 1743-October 17, 1797)

A South Carolina general, Huger defended key Southern positions. His service strengthened resistance in the Carolinas.

Thomas Hutchinson (September 9, 1711-June 3, 1780)

A loyalist governor, Hutchinson enforced British policies in Massachusetts. His actions deepened colonial resentment.

Thomas Jefferson (April 13, 1743-July 4, 1826)

Primary author of the Declaration of Independence, Jefferson articulated the philosophical case for revolution. His words defined American ideals.

Marquis de Lafayette (September 6, 1757-May 20, 1834)

A young French nobleman, Lafayette became a trusted American general. He symbolized international support for liberty.

Benjamin Lincoln (January 24, 1733-May 9, 1810)

Lincoln commanded American forces in the South and later accepted Cornwallis' surrender.

Joseph Plumb Martin (November 21, 1760-May 2, 1850)

An enlisted soldier whose memoir provides a rare common-man view of the war.

Daniel Morgan (July 6, 1736-July 6, 1802)

A rugged frontiersman and tactician, Morgan led riflemen to decisive victories, including Cowpens.

James Moore (c. 1729-January 15, 1781)
A North Carolina patriot commander, Moore helped defeat Loyalist forces in the South.

John Parker (July 13, 1729-September 17, 1775)
Captain of the Lexington militia, Parker ordered his men to stand their ground.

Paul Revere (December 21, 1734-May 10, 1818)
A skilled artisan and patriot courier, Revere warned colonial militias of British movements.

Paul Revere, Junior (January 13, 1760-April 4, 1813)
Son of Paul Revere, he served as an officer and continued the family's civic legacy.

Rochambeau (July 1, 1725-May 10, 1807)
Commander of French land forces in America, Rochambeau coordinated with Washington.

Lord Stirling (October 17, 1726-January 15, 1783)
A Continental general known for bravery and sacrifice in major battles.

Banastre Tarleton(August 21, 1754-January 25, 1833)
A feared British cavalry officer infamous for brutality in the South.

Benjamin Tallmadge (February 25, 1754-March 7, 1835)
George Washington's intelligence chief and spymaster.

Friedrich Wilhelm von Steuben (September 17, 1730-November 28, 1794)
He professionalized the Continental Army through discipline and training.

Joseph Warren (June 11, 1741-June 17, 1775)
A leading patriot who died at Bunker Hill.

George Washington (February 22, 1732-December 14, 1799)
Commander-in-Chief of the Continental Army and foundational leader of the republic.

Martha Washington (June 2, 1731-May 22, 1802)
She sustained morale and unity throughout the war. George's wife.

ACKNOWLEDGMENTS

To the entire team at Simply Francis Publishing, thank you for your immediate excitement and acceptance of Oliver and his story, and for your encouragement and assistance in helping me bring key aspects of the story of America's birth to life. I owe a huge debt of gratitude to Rhonda and Frank Amoroso for believing in this project, and specifically to Frank for offering editorial guidance: show don't tell!

I'd also like to recognize the editorial ability of Clayton Boyce, who proved that sometimes the sword is mightier than the pen as he dashed and diced my 160,000-word first draft with thoughtful care and patience. A sidebar: It turns out that Clayton bought my boyhood home from my parents–we learned this after the fact! It is indeed a small world. I'd also like to thank Tom Beattle for introducing us and believing in this project.

To Jay Atkinson, who took the second draft and offered substantial insight and encouragement that led to further improvements of the novel. You may have noticed that Oliver and Jay share the same last name. I had my character's first name set and was looking for a rhythmic last name, and ended up choosing "Atkinson" after Jay and his wife Laurie became major supporters of another friend's global ministry that helps Indigenous churches provide comfort for their communities after natural disasters. It's called Hope Over Crisis. Thank you, Jay and Laurie.

A special shout out to my friend Bill Anagnos, who from day one has encouraged me daily and told me how proud he was of me for pursuing this dream. I cannot thank Teddy Perez enough for his collaboration in creating two trailers for this book. His cinematic sensibilities polished my rough material, making them impactful and entertaining.

Finally, to my father, Wilbur D. Jones, Jr., who not only bequeathed to me his love and passion for American history, but has lived it as a Navy Captain, an assistant to two presidents, and a military historian, having authored or co-authored over twenty books. My father is also responsible for President Trump signing a bill that would designate at least one city annually as a World War II Heritage City. Wilmington became the first city because of their massive contribution to the war effort. What's more, he introduced me to my publisher Simply Francis. Dad, you continue to inspire me to pursue and preserve American history.

www.ingramcontent.com/pod-product-compliance
Lightning Source LLC
Chambersburg PA
CBHW071547030726
47593CB00001BA/67